"Puts a unique twist on the paranormal world, leaving the reader begging for more. Yasmine Galenorn's imagination is a beautiful thing."
—*Fresh Fiction*

"A great start to a new series."
—*Smexy Books*

"This is the first in a new urban fantasy series and I am definitely looking forward to the next one . . . There is great worldbuilding here and that is one thing that I love about Ms. Galenorn's books."
—*Book Binge*

Praise for the Otherworld series

SHADED VISION

"Chilling, thrilling, and deliciously dark—Galenorn's magical fantasy is spectacularly hot and supernaturally breathtaking."
—Alyssa Day, *New York Times* bestselling author

COURTING DARKNESS

"The work is, as are all of Yasmine Galenorn's, magical and detailed and fantastic."
—*Fresh Fiction*

BLOOD WYNE

"A tapestry of excellent writing."
—*Fresh Fiction*

"This is a great series and I cannot wait for the next book!"
—*Book Binge*

HARVEST HUNTING

"Heartbreaking and enlightening . . . A five-star read!"
—*Fresh Fiction*

"A fantastic adventure that leaves the reader satisfied and yet wanting more."
—*Night Owl Reviews*

BONE MAGIC

DEMON MISTRESS

NIGHT SEEKER

An Indigo Court Novel

YASMINE GALENORN

BERKLEY BOOKS, NEW YORK

THE BERKLEY PUBLISHING GROUP
Published by the Penguin Group
Penguin Group (USA) Inc.
375 Hudson Street, New York, New York 10014, USA

Penguin Group (Canada), 90 Eglinton Avenue East, Suite 700, Toronto, Ontario M4P 2Y3, Canada
(a division of Pearson Penguin Canada Inc.) • Penguin Books Ltd., 80 Strand, London WC2R 0RL,
England • Penguin Group Ireland, 25 St. Stephen's Green, Dublin 2, Ireland (a division of Penguin
Books Ltd.) • Penguin Group (Australia), 250 Camberwell Road, Camberwell, Victoria 3124, Australia
(a division of Pearson Australia Group Pty. Ltd.) • Penguin Books India Pvt. Ltd., 11 Community
Centre, Panchsheel Park, New Delhi—110 017, India • Penguin Group (NZ), 67 Apollo Drive,
Rosedale, Auckland 0632, New Zealand (a division of Pearson New Zealand Ltd.) • Penguin Books
(South Africa) (Pty.) Ltd., 24 Sturdee Avenue, Rosebank, Johannesburg 2196, South Africa

Penguin Books Ltd., Registered Offices: 80 Strand, London WC2R 0RL, England

This is a work of fiction. Names, characters, places, and incidents either are the product of the author's
imagination or are used fictitiously, and any resemblance to actual persons, living or dead, business
establishments, events, or locales is entirely coincidental. The publisher does not have any control over
and does not assume any responsibility for author or third-party websites or their content.

NIGHT SEEKER

A Berkley Book / published by arrangement with the author

PUBLISHING HISTORY
Berkley mass-market edition / July 2012

Copyright © 2012 by Yasmine Galenorn.
Excerpt from *Shadow Rising* by Yasmine Galenorn copyright © 2012 by Yasmine Galenorn.
Cover art by Tony Mauro. Cover design by Rita Frangie.
Interior text design by Laura K. Corless.

ISBN: 978-0-425-25032-7

BERKLEY®
Berkley Books are published by The Berkley Publishing Group,
a division of Penguin Group (USA) Inc.,
375 Hudson Street, New York, New York 10014.
BERKLEY® is a registered trademark of Penguin Group (USA) Inc.
The "B" design is a trademark of Penguin Group (USA) Inc.

PRINTED IN THE UNITED STATES OF AMERICA

10   9   8   7   6   5   4   3   2   1

ALWAYS LEARNING   **PEARSON**

ACKNOWLEDGMENTS

Thank you to my beloved Samwise. You are my joy, my love, and you hold my heart in your hands. To my agent, Meredith Bernstein, and to my editor, Kate Seaver: Your belief in me means so much. To Tony Mauro, an incredible cover artist. To my assistant, Andria Holley, and my volunteers, who help me keep track of everything. To my "Galenorn Gurlz," those still with me, those who have come into my life, and those who crossed over the Bridge—I will always love you, even through the veil.

Most reverent devotion to Ukko, who rules over the wind and sky; Rauni, queen of the harvest; Tapio, lord of the woodlands; and Mielikki, goddess of the Woodlands and Fae Queen in her own right. All my spiritual guardians. And to the Fae—both dark and light—who walk this world beside us, may we see you in the shadows and in the shimmer of ice.

And the biggest thank you of all: *To my readers:* Your support helps me continue to write the books you love to read! You can find me on the Net at Galenorn En/Visions: www.galenorn.com. If you write to me snail mail (see website for address or write via publisher), please enclose a stamped, self-addressed envelope if you would like a reply. Promo goodies are available—see website.

The Painted Panther
Yasmine Galenorn

All war is deception.

—SUN TZU

When it is obvious that the goals cannot be reached,
don't adjust the goals, adjust the action steps.

—CONFUCIUS

The Beginning

The code of the Akazzani: To observe. To record. To embrace silence.

The role of the Akazzani: The Akazzani are the preservers of knowledge. They are the guardians of the past. The Society neither interferes with, nor directs, events. Born nine to a generation, from the hidden fortress of Mazastan, the Keepers go about their work, in secrecy and privacy. Only the researchers whom they employ walk among the nations of the world, searching for information. The oracles of Mazastan are culled from both yummanii and magic-born, and they train in both the darker magical arts and martial arts, for they have—over the centuries—been forced to protect their sanctuary from invaders. No one has ever successfully breached their defenses.

—From *Secret Societies of the World*

Chapter 1

The night was still. Snow drifted slowly to the ground, where it compacted into a glazed sheet covering the roads. Favonis—my 1966 sparkling blue Pontiac GTO—glided through the empty streets as I navigated the icy pavement. We had to be cautious. The Shadow Hunters were out in the suburbs tonight, searching for those who braved the cold. They were running amok, and New Forest, Washington, had become their hunting grounds.

Equally dangerous, Geoffrey and the vampires were also out in full force, patrolling the streets. Clusters of dark figures in long black dusters wandered the shopping areas, their collars turned up, hands in pockets, searching the crowds for Myst's hunters, trying to prevent any more massacres from happening.

At least we could bargain with the vamps and have a chance of winning through reason. They weren't like the Vampiric Fae; they weren't out to destroy everyone they met. But still, it all boiled down to the fact that two bloodthirsty predatory groups now divided the town. And they were aching to shake it up.

As for us? We were on a reconnaissance mission.

Kaylin was riding shotgun. My father, Wrath—King of the Court of Rivers and Rushes—and Lannan Altos, the vampire I loved to hate who had become an unexpected ally, sprawled in the backseat.

We were on our way to see what was left of the Veil House, if anything. We'd been holed up for two days, planning out our next moves. Finally, tired of being cooped up, I suggested an expedition. If we could sneak back onto Vyne Street, we might be able to scavenge something useful from out of the ashes.

I dreaded seeing the pile of rubble. I expected to find a burned-out shell filled with soot and charcoal, soggy from the snow. So when Rhiannon had suggested coming, I stopped her. Better that I go rather than my cousin. She'd grown up at the Veil House. She'd lost her mother there. Asking her to go on a raiding expedition would have been cruel. Besides, the four of us were the least likely to be killed. I'd wanted to bring Grieve, my lover, but it was dangerous to have him so close to the Golden Wood at this point.

A glance over my shoulder told me that my father was doing his best to avoid touching the metal framework of the car. The iron in the car hurt him, but he swallowed the pain, saying nothing. I admired his strength and reserve, and thought that finally I had a role model—someone I could be proud of in my family. But as he lurched against the side, a nasty thought struck me.

"You don't think I'll develop a weakness to iron, do you? Favonis has never bothered me before." I'd only recently discovered that I was half–Cambyra Fae—one of the Uwilahsidhe, the owl shifters—and that Wrath was my father. And the Fae did not get along with iron.

"You are worried about this?" Wrath leaned forward, still looking ill at ease. "Have you noticed a problem?"

"No. It's just that . . . I wonder, as more of my Fae lineage comes to the surface, will I be more vulnerable to the things you are?"

"Eyes back on the road, please. I don't fancy dying in this contraption." He gave me a slight shake of the head. "If you were to develop our intolerance to iron, it would have happened by now. The only reason you didn't discover your owl-shifter capabilities earlier was because of the spell I laid on the pendant. I hid it for you, charming it so that you would not remember until you were ready. And I also placed a spell on you, when you were a baby, that you remain unaware of your heritage until you found the necklace and I could teach you how to fly."

"Good, because I love my car." I longed to flip on the radio, to listen to some sound other than the quiet hush of our breathing, but it wasn't a good idea. We were doing our best to avoid drawing attention. I'd wanted to make this trip during the day, but Lannan couldn't travel then. And during the day, we would have been far more visible to Myst and Geoffrey's spies. So here we were, in the dark of the night, creeping through the streets, hoping to find something at journey's end that would help us.

"What are we looking for?" Lannan asked. "I don't understand why you want to go back to that husk of a house. I have money. If you need something, I can buy it for you."

I shook my head, glancing toward the rearview mirror, even though I knew I wouldn't see his reflection. "Not everything we need can be purchased. Especially with Myst and Geoffrey hunting for us. I want to see if we can find any of our magical supplies. Last week, I finished making a lot of charms for Wind Charms. If any survived the fire, they might come in handy. And I just need to see . . ." I paused.

"You need to see the Veil House and what happened to it." Kaylin said. "A reality check."

I kept my eyes on the road, even as my voice was shaking. "Exactly." I nodded. "But don't even use the word 'closure' to me. There can never be closure, not until Myst is dead and routed out of the wood."

I pressed my lips together, still bitter over the way things had fallen out. Two of our most powerful allies had turned their backs on us because I refused to go along with a plan that would have changed me forever. I'd refused to let them turn me into a monster, so they walked away and left us dead in the water.

As if sensing my thoughts, Wrath leaned forward and put his hand on my shoulder. The weight and strength in his fingers reassured me. "You chose the correct path. It may be more difficult than the one Geoffrey offered you, but you must trust in your instincts, Cicely."

I nodded, trying to rest the feelings of betrayal that ran through my heart. What was past was past, and we'd have to do without either Lannan's people or the Summer Queen's help. And that brought up another sticky matter. My father, Wrath, was married to Lainule, and he had chosen to help me rather than side with her. A sick little fear niggled inside of me—would she come after me, too, for claiming his allegiance?

As I turned onto a side street, I flicked off the headlights. We'd wing it in the dark from here. Favonis fishtailed and I eased the wheels into the skid, slowly pulling out before we bounced off the curb. The silent fall of snow continued, as the long winter held us hostage in her embrace.

*

Fifteen slow minutes later, we approached the turnoff onto Vyne Street, a cul-de-sac. This town—and the Veil House—had been the only home I'd ever truly known. For years, I'd longed to get myself off the streets, to run away from my mother, who was a strung-out junkie and bloodwhore, and return to New Forest. Now that I'd gotten my wish, all hell had broken loose.

As we approached the end of the road, where the Veil House had stood until two nights ago, I realized I was holding my breath. What would we find? And would we have to fight off a host of Myst's Shadow Hunters to get through to the ruins?

I pulled into the drive, finally daring to look over at the house. A blackened silhouette stood there—and my heart began to race. It wasn't burned to the ground, there was still something left. I reached for the door handle.

"It's not all rubble!!"

I started to jump out of the car, but Lannan snaked over the backseat and looped his arm around my neck, yanking me back. "Be cautious, my beautiful Cicely. The night is filled with predators. Don't go running over there without us in tow." His voice was seductive but oddly protective.

I glanced over my shoulder at him. Lannan Altos, with his jet black vampire eyes that gleamed in the dark, set off by the golden hair that fell past his shoulders. He was gorgeous, and a freak, and his fingers lingered on my skin. I tried to ignore the lurch in my stomach at his touch.

"Point taken." I'd been so eager I'd almost lost my head. And losing my head could lead to losing my life. I was learning, but over the years I'd had plenty of occasions on which I'd had to leap without looking, and I'd gotten used to hitting the ground running. But here we had to bide our time. The hunters who dogged our heels were far more deadly than any perv or junkie or cop on the street.

I leaned back in my seat, staring at the house. Beyond the three-story Victorian stood the Golden Wood, which spread out, buttressed against the foothills of the Cascades on its far edge. But the golden glow of the Summer Queen was only a memory, and now the forest belonged to Myst, with her spiders and her snow. The aura of the trees burned with a sickly greenish blue light, and I began to tremble. Evil lurked within the woodland, and a ruthless darkness.

I closed my eyes, calling for Ulean. We were bonded, she and I—she was the essence of the wind, an Elemental linked to my soul, and we worked as a team.

Do you sense anything out there?

Her words came in a rush through my mind. *Yes. Two of the Vampiric Fae are around back of the house, hunting. If you creep up on them, I'll be able to keep your scent from traveling ahead of you.*

Anything else I should know?

She is out there, far in the forest, weaving her magic. And she is hungry, and angry. You stole Grieve back from her—she wants your blood and your soul. Myst is growing stronger even as the winter strengthens.

I nodded, then turned to the others. "Two of the Shadow Hunters are on the far side of the house. Ulean will run interference for our scent, but be prepared to take them down. No prisoners, no survivors."

No prisoners. That had become our creed. I was still getting used to the feeling of being a killer. "Murderer" wasn't a label that weighed easily on my mind, but it was what it was, and Myst was who she was, and in the deadly game of *us or them*, I wasn't willing to sacrifice myself or my friends.

We quietly climbed out of the car and I craned my neck, listening. My father did the same. Lannan and Kaylin stood guard, poised for trouble.

A gust of wind howled past and I projected myself onto the slipstream. A whisper rushed by. I listened, focusing to catch the faint words. It wasn't Ulean. *What did you find? Does anything live within the house?*

And then an answer: *No flesh. No life. Nothing of importance. Only trinkets. She will not want them.*

The Shadow Hunters. And they were probably searching for the cats, looking for food. No worries there, though. We'd managed to save all of the felines from the flames and falling timbers, and they were tucked away, safe and sound, back at the warehouse with Luna.

I turned to the others. "We go in. Take them down. Wrath, can you change into your owl form? They won't be expecting you."

My father nodded, stepping away from us. He shimmered and then, in a blur, lifted his arms. They became feathered wings, an almost six-foot span. His body transformed, shrinking, and then there he stood—a great horned owl, majestic and beautiful, a study in grace and danger.

I sucked in a deep breath, my blood stirring as it recognized his. Beside me, Kaylin let out a little sound. Lannan stiffened, watching my father with almost too much interest. His obsidian eyes glittered, taking in every nuance of the metamorphosis.

When Wrath was ready, he launched himself off the ground and took to the air, circling us as I jerked my head at the others. Crouching, I moved forward slowly and cautiously. Wrath disappeared around the house, his wings silently propelling him through the night.

Are you ready? We're about to go in.

Ulean's hushed reply echoed through me. *I will slip ahead and disrupt your scent. They will not know you are coming.*

And so we moved. I took the lead, with Kaylin behind me and Lannan silent as the night behind him. For some reason, Lannan's stealth surprised me, though I don't know why—vampires made no sound when they chose not to. Perhaps it was because he was so flamboyant. Perhaps because he always had to have the last word. Whatever the case, we proceeded in unison, stooping through the shadows, keeping to the sides of the ruined Veil House.

My fan was looped around my wrist. With it I could summon up gale force winds against our enemies, even a tornado, but Lainule had warned me to use it with caution. Magical objects had a way of possessing their owners if they weren't careful. In my other hand, I held a silver dagger my father had given me. Kaylin was armed with shurikens, and Lannan carried no weapons. He *was* a weapon.

We circled the house, the scent of sodden ash and charcoal filling my nose. I caught my breath, once again struck by the loss we'd endured. But worse yet was the loss of my aunt Heather. She had been the heart and soul of the Veil House. Thinking about her, living under Myst's rule as a vampire, made me cringe. I forced my attention back to what we were doing. One thing at a time. As for Heather . . . she was long lost to us. There was nothing we could do but attempt to release her spirit, and that meant finding her— and staking her.

As we rounded the corner, there they were. *The Shadow Hunters. Vampiric Fae.* They lurched up as we rushed in, and one of them let out a low hiss. The cerulean cast to their skin glowed in the light of the falling snow, but instead of the pure black of vampires' eyes, the black voids glittered with a swirl of white stars.

I rushed forward, trying to reach them before they

transformed. As I moved toward one, Wrath came winging down with a shriek and grappled the other by the shoulder.

The Shadow Hunter screamed and twisted as my father raked his skin. As Wrath flew out of reach, Kaylin sent a flurry of shurikens into the man. I launched myself at my opponent, with Lannan right on my heels.

The Shadow Hunter saw me coming and pulled out an obsidian dagger. Crap. Their blades were usually poisoned, so sharp that they could rip through skin like a hot knife through butter. And I had a particularly hard time with obsidian. The stone unleashed my predatory nature and I didn't have control over the effects yet.

I darted to the side as he brought the blade to bear. Lunging past his outstretched arm, I drove my own dagger deep into the muscle above his waist. He let out a scream and began to transform as Lannan came in from the other side.

The Shadow Hunter shifted, his mouth unhinging as his jaw lengthened and he went down on all fours, into a monstrous dog-beast with razor-sharp teeth. He rushed toward me, even as Lannan landed on his back and brought his fangs down onto the back of the creature's neck, distracting it.

I grabbed the chance, plunging my blade between its eyes. As the Shadow Hunter screeched, Lannan reared back, driving his fangs deep in the flesh as he ripped open the veins. A fountain of blood bubbled up, spurting into the air, foaming over the side of the beast. With a throaty laugh, Lannan began to suckle from the wound.

I stumbled back, yanking my dagger out of the creature's skull, unable to look away. There was something primal, something feral and wild and passionate about watching the vampire feed. I wanted to reach out, to run my hand through his hair, to brush his lips with my own . . .

Ulean howled around me. *Cicely! Watch your step— you are too close to the flame.*

Shaking my head, I forced myself to turn away and brushed my hands across my eyes. *Damn it.* Ever since I'd drunk Lannan's blood, there'd been a bond between us that I did not want. Like it or not, it existed, no matter how hard I tried to deny it. I'd noticed, over the past few days, that I felt him when he was nearby, like a shadow creeping behind me, waiting. As much as I tried to hide the sensations from Grieve, I was afraid my lover had noticed.

Shaky, my knees weak, I turned to see that my father was back in his Fae form. He and Kaylin were finishing off their opponent. Wrath carried a curved dagger and he slit the man's throat quickly and quietly, stepping away as the Shadow Hunter clutched at his neck and went tumbling to the ground.

They lay there, silent bodies in the snow, as a pale stain of blood spread around them, dyeing the brilliant white with dark crimson. Lannan pulled away from the creature, which had reverted to its Fae form. He wiped his mouth on his hand, his eyes glittering. His shirt was stained with blood, and he fastened his gaze on me.

Stepping forward, he reached for my hand, and unable to look away, I let him take it. With a slow, sinuous smile, he lifted my fingers to his mouth, kissing them one by one with his bloody lips.

A shiver raced through me, a live wire that set me aflame. There was something about the blood splattered on him, about the savage way he'd torn into the Shadow Hunter, that set me off. As if he could sense my thoughts, Lannan's smile turned into a smirk, and he squeezed my hand so tightly I grimaced, then he slowly let go, dragging his index finger against my palm.

My wolf growled. I pressed my hand to the tattoo on my stomach. Grieve could sense my feelings, and he wasn't happy. I quieted him, even as Lannan leaned close to my ear.

"I can smell your arousal," Lannan whispered. "I'll fuck you right here if you want me to, baby." But then Wrath called to us, and he backed away.

I turned to find Kaylin staring at me, but he said nothing. Instead, he motioned to the house. "We should get in there and see what we can find before any of their kinfolk arrive."

Not trusting my voice, I nodded. The back of the house had been the most damaged, and I wasn't sure how much I trusted the roof over the kitchen. Most of it had burned away, but there were still patches held up by support beams that had survived the inferno, albeit heavily damaged. The front of the house looked much more stable.

"We go in through the front door," I finally said. The others followed me, Kaylin first pocketing the obsidian knives from our enemies. We hurried back around the house and up the front steps.

The house is clear?

Ulean shivered against me. *Yes, the house is empty, but do not tarry. The woods are alert tonight. The hunters are awake and active. They are searching for you and Grieve. And all who helped him escape.*

"We have to hurry, Myst's people are out in full force and we don't have a lot of time." I jogged up the stairs and pushed open the door. We hadn't even had a chance to lock it when we were rushing to escape.

As I entered the living room, it hit me just how much had happened in the past few weeks—and how much we'd all lost.

⚜

My name is Cicely Waters and I'm one of the magic-born, a witch who can control the wind. I'm also part Cambyra Fae—the shifting Fae. Uwilahsidhe to be precise, which means I can shift into an owl. On that front, I only recently learned about my heritage and in no way have honed my abilities. But in a few short weeks I've learned to love being in my owl form, and I've found a freedom I'd never before experienced. Flying, soaring over the ground, has offered me an escape I've never before felt. I always felt like a part of me was missing. Now, I feel whole.

When I was very young, Grieve—the Fae Prince of the Court of Rivers and Rushes, and his friend Chatter—came to my cousin Rhiannon and me and taught us how to use our magical abilities. It was Grieve who bound me to

Ulean, my Wind Elemental, telling me I would need her help. In a sense, he was foreshadowing my life to come.

When I turned six, my mother, Krystal, dragged me down the stairs of the Veil House, and we headed out on the road. My aunt Heather and the only stability I'd ever known vanished in the blink of one afternoon.

I learned early on how to survive on the streets. I'd longed to return to the Veil House, but Krystal—a meth head who used booze and drugs to dim her own gifts—wasn't capable of surviving on her own and so I stayed with her until she died in the gutter, a bloodwhore who'd serviced one bad trick too many. Until that day, I'd kept us going, using my ability to hear messages on the wind to stay one step ahead of the cops and the drug runners.

And now my mother was dead, and I'd finally returned to New Forest, Washington. But too little, too late. My aunt had been captured by Myst, and my cousin Rhiannon was terrified for her life. Myst holds the town in her icy grip, and she's out to spread her people throughout the land, to conquer the vampires and use the magic-born and yummanii—the humans—as cattle.

In a past life long, long ago, I was Myst's daughter. And Grieve had been my lover then, too. We'd defied our families to be together, rampaging through the bounty hunters and soldiers who sought for us. We'd hidden behind rock and tree, snared them in traps, and I'd torn them to shreds, reveling in the blood.

Grieve and I had fought for our love, killed for our love, and—at the end—when we were cornered and couldn't escape—died for our love. We had bound ourselves together forever with a potion designed to bring us back together again in another life.

Now, we're back, and we've found one another again. Once again, we're caught between the Cambyra Fae and the Vampiric Fae. Only this time, Grieve is the one bound to the Indigo Court. Myst turned him into one of her own. And now, the vampires are playing into the equation. I'm tied to Lannan's shirttail by a contract that he insists on enforcing.

Some of our allies have chosen to betray us, so we're in hiding, on the run, fighting against overwhelming odds. Only this time, it will be different. Neither Myst nor the vampires will win. Grieve and I will weather the storm. We have no other option.

✤

Once we were inside, I flipped on a pale flashlight. The living room had survived the fire, with soot and smoke damage, but the weather was creeping in through the caved-in roof in the kitchen, and I shivered at the ravaged state of the room. Myst's people had been through here, that much was apparent. The upholstered sofas were shredded as if by wild dogs. Holes marred the walls, the beautiful old antiques had been scratched and broken.

I slowly walked over to my aunt Heather's desk. She'd never sit here again, writing in her journal. The sight of the injured wood made me glad that I'd come, and not Rhiannon. It was bad enough to lose her mother to the enemy, but to see how many of the memories of her childhood had been destroyed? I wasn't about to put her through that. As I ran my hand over the hand-carved oak, now dented and scratched along the polished surface, my heart ached.

"I'm sorry." Kaylin's voice echoed softly behind me. "Can I do anything to help?"

I turned, gazing into his smooth, unlined face. Kaylin's soul had been wedded to a night-veil demon while he was still in his mother's womb and he hadn't ever been fully human. Gorgeous, he was Chinese by descent, with a long ponytail trailing down his back. Lithe and wiry-strong, Kaylin Chen was over one hundred years old and had seen more than his share of sorrow. So when he lightly touched my elbow, I knew he understood.

I sought for something to say, but there were no words. I was in a dark spot, and I didn't know the way out. Finally, I looked around the room. Everything seemed hopeless. But a picture on the wall of Heather and Rhiannon spurred my tongue.

"Family memories. If you see any pictures . . . for
Rhiannon . . . like that one . . ."

He nodded, taking the picture off the wall, and then
began to hunt through the sideboard on the opposite side of
the room. After a while, he moved out into the next room.

I turned back to the desk and yanked open one of the
drawers that had remained untouched. And there, I saw my
first sign of hope. Aunt Heather's journal, containing her
magical notes, intact with the map that showed the Veil
House as a major power juncture on several crisscrossing
ley lines.

I pulled out the journal. It was cold in my hand, slightly
damp, but unharmed. Shoving it in my bag, I shuffled
through the rest of the drawer. The bank book, an envelope
of cash—of course, the Shadow Hunters would have left
these things. Myst's people had no use for money, but we
could use it.

After a quick look-see, I just swept everything into the
bag and then glanced at the piles on the floor surrounding
the other upended drawers. Not much had been left intact,
but there—a ring of keys. Not sure what they went to, I
added them to the bag.

Lannan had vanished, but after a moment he reappeared,
carrying a large bag stuffed full of plastic bags and jars. "I
found your herb stash. Thought these might be useful."

I nodded, fishing through them. Some of these I could
use. Some had been healing herbs that Leo had used to
make healing salves. *Leo.* "Crap."

"What's wrong?" Lannan was on instant alert, darting a
look over his shoulder at the door. "Do you sense something?"

"No. I was just thinking about Leo and how he fucked
us over." I pressed my lips together and glanced up into
Lannan's eyes. A mistake—you should never stare at a
vampire directly—but I didn't care.

Lannan's eyes were the center of the abyss, cold and
unfeeling. "Leo made his choice. I told you that Geoffrey
was not to be trusted." He hefted the bag over one shoulder.

"Don't blame the boy. He chooses what many would choose—to align himself with immortals over frailty."

"Don't *blame* him? Leo trashed Rhiannon's world. They were *engaged* and he turned his back on her. He fucking knocked me across the floor. And Geoffrey . . ." I shuddered. "Geoffrey wanted to *turn* me—the same way he'd turned Myst. He wanted to use me as a weapon to bait her."

Eons ago, Geoffrey, the Regent of the Northwest Vampire Nation and one of the Elder Vein Lords, had attempted to turn the Unseelie Fae. It was then that Myst had been born, turned from his lover into a creature neither vampire nor Fae. A terrifying half-breed, she was more powerful than both Unseelie and vampire. And she was able to bear children. She had become the mother of her race and Queen of the Indigo Court.

Lannan brushed away my fear. "Forget about Geoffrey." His voice coiled seductively around me as he leaned against my back, one hand around my waist. "*I* want to turn you but not in order to use you against Myst. I want you for a playmate. But you, Cicely Waters, you would be no fun if I made it too easy. I like a little fight in my playthings."

I caught my breath, steeling myself as his lips tickled my ear, his fangs dangerously close to my neck. "Better find another toy." I pushed his hand away from my waist. He let go, only to grab my wrist, his fingers holding me in an iron grip as he delicately rubbed against my skin, setting off yet another unwelcome spark in my stomach.

"Remember your manners, Cicely. Or I'll have to give you another lesson in etiquette." His words were soft but threatening.

The glimmer of the flashlight on his hair made him sparkle as if a golden nimbus surrounded him. A memory flared, with me caught in the blood fever, crying out, "*My angel of darkness . . .*" My words echoed through my thoughts and I let out a little moan. I was walking on thin ice—I'd felt the sting of Lannan's perverted lessons too many times now.

Lannan watched me closely, a look of delight spreading

across his face. "You're thinking about me. Inside you. If only we hadn't been interrupted, I could have finished and you would have been mine. Can you *really* think that I don't revel in your reluctance? But you have to admit, I've become a valuable ally."

I let out a long, slow breath and nodded. "Perhaps, but I don't trust you."

"Good. You shouldn't trust *anyone*. I don't understand why you trusted Leo to begin with. He stuck his nose so far up Geoffrey's ass that I'm amazed you didn't suspect him earlier. He's just doing what his nature begs."

"Stop, please. And don't defend Leo."

Lannan snorted. "Girl, if Geoffrey gives him what he wants, your cousin better lock her doors at night, because he'll be coming for her. I know his type."

"If he hurts her, I'll never forgive him." If Leo came after Rhiannon, I'd stake him myself.

Tipping my chin up with his index finger, Lannan shook his head. "My sweet Cicely . . . if Geoffrey turns him, Leo won't *bother* asking for forgiveness. Vampires have neither need nor desire for atonement. I am what I am. I'm a predator. I'm your master. And I have no remorse for any of the things I've done in my life. Save, perhaps, for leaving Regina behind. The thought of my beautiful sister in that house with Geoffrey . . . I fear for her safety, even though she's the Emissary to the Crimson Court."

I pulled away and kicked at the rubble. There was nothing else of value here. "You had to. You didn't have a choice."

"Now you come to my defense? You're a confusing one, Cicely. Perhaps you're right, perhaps not. But we should go, if you are done. Here come your father and Kaylin." And once again, he was all business.

We carried what bags and boxes we'd found out to the car and eased out of the driveway to head back to the warehouse that had become our temporary home. All the way there, Lannan leaned over the backseat, resting a hand on my shoulder.

I knew Wrath and Kaylin were watching, but there was

nothing I could do to stop him. Lannan was an ally we needed, and if I protested, he'd only find another way to screw with my head. And another mind-fuck was the last thing I needed right now.

Chapter 2

By the time we got back to the warehouse, I'd managed to regain some of my composure. We made sure we hadn't been followed as we pulled into the parking lot and drove around the back, parking behind an old school bus that had long ago seen better days.

I cut the engine and leaned back, breathing a sigh of relief. As much as I longed for the Veil House, this was more familiar to me—living on the run, hiding in abandoned buildings, keeping one eye open as I slept. Maybe I wasn't cut out for a normal life. Maybe I was destined for life on the wing.

As we carried our loot to the back entrance that Kaylin had cleverly hidden with a tangle of loose boards, a stack of old tires, and several abandoned vehicles, Peyton opened the door. She'd been on the watch for us and she took one of the bags from me, carrying it into the living quarters we'd quickly pulled together for ourselves.

The building had been a warehouse in better days, and the stark industrial walls were gunmetal gray, with beams and poles and odd little cubbyholes lining the inner chambers. Kaylin had been living here for a while before he'd invited us in, so we had jury-rigged electricity. He hadn't wanted to draw attention by using too much, though, so for heat we were using a burn barrel. The warehouse was big enough, the ceilings high enough, and several windows were cracked and broken, so the smoke wasn't much of a bother and it dissipated by the time it reached the outdoors. But it was cold and chilly and grim.

While we were gone, the rest of our little band—Peyton, Rhiannon, Luna, Chatter, and Grieve—had lined up several tables and now, we spread out the contents of our goods on them. Grieve moved over to my side and slid his arm around me. I caught my breath, this time in a good way.

"I was worried about you. I sensed . . ." He let his words drift off, but his gaze flickered to Lannan. "Are you all right?"

Nodding, I ducked my head. "I'm fine. There were a few tense moments, but everything's okay." I leaned in, feeling Lannan watching every move I made, and rested my mouth against Grieve's soft lips. He pulled me to him and I lost myself in his touch, in his kiss. Grieve was my love, and no matter how my body responded to Lannan, my heart would forever belong to the Fae Prince with the shining stars in his eyes.

A slow warmth rose in my belly, his body felt right against my own, and I inhaled deeply, filling myself full with his scent. He smelled like autumn leaves and rain showers and danger and safety all rolled into one. His heart beat fast against my touch as I laid my hand on his chest. Grieve was alive, and he loved me.

"I want you," I whispered, hungering to sneak off, to drive away the cold and the snow with his touch. But we couldn't—not just yet. "I feel safe with you."

"Later. I promise." His words were so low that I was the only one who could hear him, but his touch pledged so much more than those words could express.

I nodded, not trusting myself to say more, and gently moved away. Everyone was looking at us, especially Lannan with his cold, dark stare, but I didn't care. I cleared my throat and searched for what to say. Rhiannon gave me a pleading look and I nodded, knowing what she desperately wanted to hear. Time to get down to business.

"First—some good news. The Veil House isn't nearly as far gone as we feared."

Rhiannon let out a little cry and her fingers flew to her mouth. Chatter—Grieve's friend and another of the Cambyra Fae—moved to rest his arm gently around her waist. I noticed the quick smile she flashed him. As I had thought. Leo had been her way of settling. She'd loved Chatter all along.

"Does it really still stand?" She leaned forward, breathless. "You aren't joking?"

"I'd never joke about something like that. Oh, it's definitely taken some heavy damage. The kitchen and basement will have to be rebuilt, but with work, we can restore it. However, that idea is on hold until we destroy Myst. We killed two of her Shadow Hunters while we were there."

"I have another surprise." Grieve held up his hand and dashed into a side room, returning after a few seconds with his arms full. "While you were gone, I scouted around this rambling monster of a building and found two space heaters. They're good-sized."

"Heat! Glorious heat!" Luna rubbed her hands together as Kaylin took them from him and plugged them in.

Grieve frowned. "I hope they still work. The burn barrel helps, but it doesn't do much good over here by the table."

Kaylin flipped the switch and bingo, a draft of air began to blow toward the table. The space heaters must have been used during power outages, because they were big enough to heat a small room. As the elements heated up, warm air began to take the edge off the biting chill. I smiled, and so did the others. There was nothing like heat to lift the spirits when the wind was howling at the door.

"Good job, man." Kaylin clapped Grieve on the back. "I've lived here for quite a while and didn't know about them."

"I've a knack for finding things." Grieve smiled then, and laughed. "I wish I could have gone with you today."

"Yes, but the Veil House is so close to the Golden Wood, it would be too easy for Myst to latch onto you again. And this helps us so much more—we needed the heat." I leaned in and kissed him soundly. My stomach rumbled. "First heat and now, I hope . . . food?" I looked at Luna. "Is there anything to eat?"

She nodded, and while Kaylin and Wrath sorted through what we'd brought back with us, Rhiannon and Luna set out a loaf of bread, some peanut butter, and a large packet of beef jerky. Rhiannon added a two-liter bottle of Coke, while Luna carried a large pot of chicken noodle soup over to the table. Peyton brought the mugs and plates.

I stared at the meal. Good. I could eat everything. I knew the soup was safe, and that was the only thing potentially a danger. I was deathly allergic to fish and carried an EpiPen wherever I went.

Luna shrugged, looking embarrassed. "I'm sorry it's not anything fancy, but . . ."

"Hey, it's food. I ate out of Dumpsters when I was a kid, so this is a feast in comparison to some of the meals I've had. I'm not turning up my nose at anything on this table."

The soda was cold and I chugged down two glasses before moving on to the bread and peanut butter. Grieve stared at the food, finally accepting a hank of the beef jerky and a plain piece of bread. My father sniffed the peanut butter and opted for the jerky and bread, too. Chatter decided to be adventurous and bit into a p.b. sandwich, his face taking on the look of a confused cat with peanut butter stuck to the roof of his mouth.

The soup was like those Lipton soups—mainly just noodles and broth—but it was hot and salty and filled that need for something warm in my belly.

After the gnaw of hunger faded, we began to sort through the bags, able to take off our jackets thanks to Grieve's space heaters. I held up Heather's journal. "I found this. We might be able to use it."

Kaylin handed me a small bag and I stared at it, knowing exactly what was in there. "You found my magical tools."

"I checked upstairs. It wasn't all that dangerous. The steps were in no hurry to collapse under me. I think they're still structurally sound. Anyway, yes—I found your magical tools. I also packed a bag with clothes for all four of you girls. I brought whatever seemed appropriate for our situation." His dark eyes flashed with a glimmer of a smile and I found myself grateful he was on our side.

Peyton let out a delighted cry. "My cards—you found my tarot deck!"

Lannan chuckled. "I've seen gamblers less thrilled to see a deck of cards. Yes, I found your deck and thought you might be able to use it." For a brief second, he sounded almost pleasant.

"We also have a bag full of herbs, along with some of the charms I made. I managed to grab a big bag of cat food, too, by the way. So somebody should go feed the cats. They'll be glad for something other than the tuna we've been giving them." Kaylin had laid in a large store of tuna, and out of deference to me, he'd moved it into the room we set up for the cats. I was willing to scoop the litter boxes, but I wasn't about to take over feeding duties with fish on hand.

"Don't bet on it," Luna said. She rolled her eyes. "But that means . . . well . . . there's tuna for those of us who can eat it. But we'll save it for a last resort and I'll warn you well in advance," she added, turning to me. "I'll make certain we keep your food away from anything that might have fish in it."

That wasn't terribly reassuring, given our circumstances, but I knew that if push came to shove, they'd need to eat whatever they could find.

"Let's hope it doesn't come to that." I glanced through the rest of the bags. "Good, somebody brought *The Rise of the Indigo Court* and *The History of the Vampire Nation*." The words popped out before I realized that Lannan was standing right there. I jerked up my head. He was standing, arms crossed, head cocked to the side, one booted foot propped up on a chair. His leather pants shimmered in the dim light hanging over the table.

"So . . . you have a copy of our history. You know, not a terribly wise idea of you to advertise so in front of me." He slowly lowered his foot to the ground and slid his hands in his pockets and sauntered toward me.

"I wouldn't have, if I'd thought about it first." My mouth had gotten me in trouble more than once.

Lannan backed me up to the wall, lifting the book out of my hands. He flipped through it, occasionally glancing at me. I had no idea how vampires read, considering their eyes were jet with no white, no gleam other than the spar-kle that made them look like obsidian orbs. But read they did. And Lannan Altos was actually a professor at the New Forest Conservatory. I had the feeling he'd abused his authority far more than once.

Grieve let out a low growl and shifted into a wolf, shov-ing himself between the vampire and me. Peyton and Luna gasped. Wrath stiffened as Kaylin stepped forward. Lan-nan just stared at the beast with unblinking eyes.

I caught my breath. Grieve was really pissed. Anger wasn't the only reason he took wolf form, but Lannan had pushed his buttons—his territorial instincts had been invaded. He stood his ground, forcing Lannan away from me, his gaze never leaving the vampire. I poised, ready to throw myself between the two. But then Wrath came to my rescue.

"Altos, put down the book. Leave it for now. Grieve—back away. The vampire will not hurt our Cicely tonight." It was a command, not a question.

Lannan turned to my father, locking his gaze. After a moment, he shrugged and deliberately dropped the book on the floor at my feet. "No matter if you have it. We are not terribly vulnerable to your kind, so feel free to read it. If nothing else, perhaps you'll learn why you should pay proper respect."

He sauntered past Grieve, refusing to acknowledge him. Grieve shifted back, but I could feel my wolf tattoo still snuffling. Chatter reached out, touched Grieve on the arm and gave him a warning shake of the head. Grieve glow-ered and shook him off but did nothing.

Cambyra Fae were known as the shifting Fae. My father—Wrath—was an owl shifter, as was I, even though I was only a half-breed. Grieve could shift into wolf form, and Chatter could turn into a pillar of flame, I'd found out.

From the very beginning, when Krystal had dragged me away from the Veil House, I'd dreamed of a wolf following me, watching over me. When I was fourteen, I began to see him in the shadows, watching me, and I thought he might be a guardian of some sort. I still hadn't known at that time that Grieve could take wolf form. A year later, Dane—my mother's boyfriend of the month—and I got high one night while she was out turning tricks, and he tattooed my vision onto my stomach.

Dane had already given me three other tattoos. On my left breast, a feral Fae girl peeked through the leaves of a deadly nightshade plant. Both upper arms were banded with identical blackwork tats—a pair of owls flying over a silver moon, with a dagger piercing through it. And then he tattooed my wolf for me.

An ivy vine wove its way across my left thigh. Dappled with silver roses, it crossed my lower abs, extending to my ribs under my left arm. Interspersed among the roses was a trail of violet skulls, and right at my naval, a grayish silver wolf stared out at the world, his eyes emerald and glowing.

After that, I would feel the wolf shift and growl when danger was present. At times, when I was lonely, I talked to the tattoo, and it felt like the wolf was actually listening. And then, when I returned home for a brief visit a few months after getting my wolf tattoo, Grieve had met me out in the woods, and I realized that instead of trusting him like I had when I was a child, my heart had shifted, and at seventeen, I had grown up and was falling in love with the Fae Prince.

✦

The Golden Wood was in full glory, trees thick with leaves, and the brambles were growing full with hard little berries that would burst with their rich black juice in August. The woodland smelled of sunlight and dust and lazy afternoons, and my feet were silent against the path leading through the clustered undergrowth that lined both sides of the trail.

Rhiannon opted to stay back at the house—she'd become reclusive, and I knew something had happened but she wouldn't talk about it. All Heather would tell me was that there'd been an accident a couple of years back and Rhiannon wasn't the same girl she had been. I wanted to ask my cousin about it—we'd always told each other everything—but whatever had happened this time seemed sacrosanct.

So one afternoon, late into the week Krystal had allowed me to visit, I wandered out to the wood where Rhiannon and I'd played as children. As I set foot on the path, the glimmer of sunlight swept me into a world far from the dirty streets of San Francisco, of L.A., of whatever city through which Krystal and I were currently prowling. They were all just names by now—one blurred into the next, and the one we'd just left was as indistinct as the one we were heading toward.

I stretched my arms wide, inhaling deeply. I'd been home the year before—my first time since Krystal dragged me off—and I'd cried when I'd had to leave. Rhiannon had been silent then, too, but I'd thought that she was just sulking over some argument with her mother.

It was during *that* visit that Grieve stepped out from behind a tree and I remembered all those long days of childhood, when he and Chatter had taught us magic, never straying out of decorum, never being anything but a safety net for us as I learned to speak with the wind and Rhiannon learned to harness the flames.

Letting my mind step onto the slipstream, I blew a low whistle, and whispered, *Grieve, are you here? I'm home again. Come to me!*

And a few moments later, the Fae Prince stepped out from behind a tall cedar. He was dressed in camouflage cargo pants, with no shirt, but I knew that his clothes were illusion. His platinum hair streamed down his shoulders, and his eyes glittered blue against the olive skin of his body. He was built, lean and muscled, and so alien he was exotic. Yet . . . alien as he was, Grieve was familiar to me.

"Cicely . . . I've been waiting for you." His voice was strained. He wouldn't stop staring at me and I began to feel exposed, raw. And then I noticed a box in his hand, wrapped with a ribbon.

"What's that?" I pointed to the box.

Grieve stared at it for another moment, then silently handed me the box.

I stared at it. "A present?"

He leaned against a nearby tree, sliding his hands into his pockets. "I found this . . . I would have given it to you last time, but I misplaced it. You left it when . . ."

I opened it, pulling on the silk ribbon. The box was shaped like a wooden heart and my pulse began to race as I flipped open the hinged lid. Inside was a sparkling pendant. It was small—child-sized. A crystal butterfly that my aunt had given me on my fifth birthday. It was the only pretty thing I'd ever owned as a child, and when I realized I'd lost it, I'd been heartbroken.

I caught my breath. "I lost this—the day that my mother took me away from here. I thought it had disappeared forever."

"I found it after you left and kept it safe. I knew you'd come home someday. Last year, it was hidden among my things and I couldn't find it in time before you left again. But when it surfaced, I put it where I could grab it any time you called to me. I know how much you loved that necklace when you were little. I just wanted you to have it again. To have something to hold on to from your childhood."

As I cradled the pendant next to my heart, I realized that I was also holding my breath. And in the next moment, I heard myself thinking, *I love him. I'm in love with Grieve.*

My wolf stirred, and it felt as if it were stretching, luxuriously, enjoying the sun as much as I was.

Grieve glanced at my stomach—I was wearing a crop-top—and a slow smile stole across his face. "You're wearing my symbol. Cicely, you're all grown up now. Since last year, you've become a woman." His voice played across my heart as surely as if his fingers had stolen across my skin.

I shivered. "I had to grow up. I *wanted* to grow up."

"Are you still with your mother?" His eyes flashed. I knew how he felt about Krystal, but he seldom said more about her than to ask if I was still in her care.

I nodded.

"No matter, then. Come, let us walk in the wood and you can tell me what you've been doing the past year."

As he reached for my hand, I knew that if I gave it to him, I'd be lost. His voice set me spinning, and his scent was that of oat straw and apples and long grass after a cool rain. He watched me carefully and right then, I knew that he knew. He knew how I felt, and he was offering me more than his hand. He was offering me a chance at love, a chance for a life, a chance to belong to someone. He was offering me his heart.

I bit my lip, staring at his hand. The long thin fingers were delicate, and yet they could probably twist the head off an enemy. I knew that Grieve was volatile, but he'd always been just. And he played no games.

Do I dare? Do I dare take a chance on loving him? On letting him into my life? Can I ever have a life free of Krystal, free of the constant running? Do I dare choose love?

Ulean, who was sweeping along beside us, laughed, her voice tinkling on the slipstream. *Dare you not?*

And with that, I made my choice. As my fingers touched his, he enclosed them in his hand, then drew me to him.

"My Cicely. I will never hurt you."

He tipped my chin up to look him in the face, and I lingered over his beauty. And then, slowly, my world came tumbling in on me as he leaned down and his lips pressed against mine. The fire built as I slid into his arms, reveling in the feel of someone who wanted to hold me, someone who wanted to love me, someone who would never let me go.

"I love you, Grieve. I've always loved you—first as a child and now . . ."

"I am a Prince. Someday, when you're ready, you will become my Princess and rule by my side. Now that I have you back . . ." His voice trailed off and an odd look flashed through his eyes. "It's been so long, so very long . . . I've waited for you to return to me for so long."

"What do you mean? It's only been a year."

"No, so much longer than that." But when I asked what he meant, he only shook his head as his mouth covered mine, pressing his hard, lean body against me as he drew me into the kiss. The world began to spin. The pact was made as I handed over my heart to Grieve that day. And I knew that I'd never be free—no matter whether I was three thousand miles away or in the next room, I belonged to Grieve. And he belonged to me.

⚜

As Lannan left the room, I glanced at Grieve.

He motioned to me. "I have something to show you. It won't take long." He held out his hand and I took it, as he led me through the room. The others went on cataloguing our finds.

"Lannan is an ass. Don't let him goad you."

"I'd like to run him through, but you won't let me. But someday, I won't be so congenial and the vampire will find himself subject to a stake in the heart. For now, however, I will accede to your wishes." He led me to one of the doors near the back of the large room. "Close your eyes or I'll have to blindfold them."

Curious and cold, I obediently closed my eyes. I heard the door squeak open, and then Grieve led me through and the door squeaked again and closed. "We're almost there," he said. "Just a little bit farther."

And then I smelled something—it smelled like vanilla. Grieve took both of my hands in his, holding them by the wrists. He leaned close and whispered, "Open your eyes."

I blinked. We were standing in a small room and in its center was a claw-foot bathtub—it didn't look hooked up to plumbing, but there it was, filled with steaming water, piled high with fragrant bubbles. The room was lit by a good twenty candles, all white, as the scent of vanilla and gardenia wafted through the air.

"How—where . . . ?"

"While you were gone, I decided that you needed a hot bath to relax. I know you hate being stuck here, and I know how much the Veil House meant to you. And you do love your baths." He pressed against my back, wrapping his arms around my waist as he nuzzled my neck. "The others know—we won't be disturbed for a while."

I sucked in a deep breath. As the fragrance of vanilla and gardenia washed over me, I couldn't resist. I shed my clothes, shivering in the chill of the room. "You are the sweetest, most loving man I've ever known, Fae Prince or not."

He smiled, looking satisfied. "I was hoping you'd let yourself enjoy this."

"Are you kidding? Miss out on a bubble bath? With you, I hope?" And then I turned, pulling him to me by his collar. "Grieve, I love you. I hope you know just how much I love you."

He took my hands in his and grazed them with his lips. "Trust me. I do, Cicely."

"Join me?" I crawled into the big clawfoot tub, sinking into the water with a long sigh. Luxury—pure, simple luxury.

"In a moment. I have another surprise for you."

He moved over out of the reach of the candlelight and I heard him tinkering with something as I leaned back in the tub, reveling in the delicious touch of the water on my skin. It felt like I was being cradled, rocked gently by the waves.

After a moment, Grieve returned, carrying a TV tray that he set next to the tub. It held a plate of Swirl-Delight Cupcakes, and a thermos of what smelled like peppermint tea.

"I'm sorry it's nothing more than some junk food but . . ."

Grinning like a crazy woman, I wiped my hands on the towel next to the tub and grabbed a cupcake. "Are you nuts? These are golden! Now get in here."

Grieve laughed, and just like that, he was naked. He crawled in the tub with me and sank back, a wicked smile on his face. "This is what I like. You and me in hot water together." He shook his head. "How can you eat that? It's nothing but sugar and fluff."

"I like sugar and fluff." I bit into the cupcake and closed my eyes. The next moment, I felt a hand under the water, rubbing my leg. "That feels so good. I just want to float here in the warm bubbles forever and forget the world outside."

"I'm afraid we cannot do that, but for the moment, we can ignore the world." And then he leaned forward between my legs, kissing me, pressing me back against the tub. The kiss went on and on, dizzying and deep and filled with his hunger.

Before I realized what we were doing, he slid inside me, moving slowly, the water rippling at our sides, splashing over the sides in little drips and drops. I closed my eyes, thrilling to our slow rhythm and the comforting scents and the candlelight.

"This night was not meant to be for sex," he whispered. "This was meant to give you a rest. But I need you now. I need to be inside you."

"Sex is okay." I kissed his nose. "Sex is good, and sometimes sex in the tub is the best." I popped another bite of the cupcake into my mouth. Feeling almost giddy, I laughed. "And sex and chocolate are really good."

"Give me a bite." Grieve's starlit eyes flashed and his teeth shimmered in the dim light. He was dangerous and fierce yet . . . yet . . . he was my Grieve.

"I thought you didn't like sugar and fluff," I teased him, holding the cupcake just out of his reach.

"The sweeter the bite, the more delicate the blood." And then he snapped at my fingers, playfully nibbling on them, drawing the cake into his mouth. A crumb stuck to the corner of his mouth and I moved forward, my gaze never leaving his, and licked it off. As I leaned back, with him still filling me full, he moaned and shifted, moving inside me, thrusting deeply.

I gasped, pushing against him, my clit rubbing against the base of his cock. "Don't stop. Just keep going forever."

"Sugar and fluff have their place, but Cicely, for you, I would give you black raspberries and honey, and rich, warm roast beef cooked rare and juicy. I would serve you beet soup, and rich cream puddings . . ." He nuzzled my neck. "And dress you in a silken gown, to wear under the moon, with a circlet of silver for your hair."

I began to cry, so aware of him, so aware of *us*. "Will we ever get out of this mess? Will we ever make it out of the dark and the snow?"

Grieve paused, gently kissing away my tears. "I believe we will. I *have* to believe it. But Cicely, wherever we are, as long as we're together, we live in the heart of Summer, where I am the prince and you are my princess."

"I don't need to be a princess. I just want to be your wife." I rested my head on his shoulder, and he slowly began to move inside me again. We moved leisurely, without hurry, our breaths rising and falling with the ripples in the bath. Without warning, our passion flared and Grieve stared deep into my eyes as I came, crying out as my world expanded. Then, a moment later, Grieve moaned, his jaw clenched as he rode the wave. After he finished, he rested his head on my breast, and we stayed locked together, in our own private world, until the water cooled.

As Grieve helped me out of the tub and wrapped me in a thick towel, he slipped a box in my hand. "I have another gift for you, love."

"More? The bath and cupcakes were wonderful." I paused to look at the box. It was plain but held shut by a sparkling blue ribbon. "What is it?"

"Chatter hid it for me, and while you were out at the Veil House, he surprised me. When we escaped from Myst he managed to smuggle it out. Please, open it."

I pulled on the ribbon and lifted the lid. There, on a velvet cushion, sat a necklace. A butterfly. Like *my* butterfly, only this one was sapphire and emerald and garnet—real stones, on a silver chain, gleaming lustrous in the candlelight.

"My butterfly—this is a copy of the butterfly necklace I had when I was little." I looked up at him. "I still have it. You found it for me, and I've kept it hidden in Favonis since I bought the car. Safely tucked out of sight, where it can't get lost."

"That one was for your childhood, from your aunt. This is for your life as a woman. As my woman." He gently lifted the necklace off of the pillow and draped it around my neck. "I still remember how much you loved that necklace."

"How did you know I'd come back this time?" I gazed up at him, my eyes brimming with unshed tears.

"Lainule promised me that you would. And in my heart, I knew we couldn't be forever separated. I felt you decide—through the wolf tattoo on your stomach." He fastened the clasp around my neck and the pendant fell between my breasts. I tucked it under my shirt.

"Hey in there! We need to plan! Hurry it up!" A pounding on the door startled us.

"Coming." I quickly dressed, then stopped Grieve before he opened the door. "I want you to know something. I love the necklace and love what it represents. But most of all, I love the gift you handed me in the Golden Wood. You gave me your heart—and that means more than anything ever will. I'll never stomp on it, I'll never abuse it." I held the necklace close to my breasts, feeling it warm my soul.

"I can take almost any torture. But I can't take the thought of life without you." He kissed me lightly on the forehead, then touched the necklace beneath my shirt. "Wear this charm, and I'll always be near you."

Someone knocked on the door again.

Grieve gave me a wry smile. "I suppose we should get out there, but before we do, do you want the last cupcake?"

I stared at the snack cake. "Leave it. A charm that our future will be filled with cupcakes and fluff and the lightness of summer."

As the last of the candles died down, leaving us in darkness, I opened the door. Clean, ready to plunge back into the battle, we returned to the main room.

❧

Lannan was still there but about ready to leave to do whatever it was he intended to do. He watched every move we made as we reentered the room but said nothing and vanished around the corner.

Grieve glared after him, whispering, "I hate that he can make your body respond to him."

"But my heart doesn't. Bodies are . . . physical. I can't help my reaction—he's a vampire and I've drunk his blood. But my love for you is never tainted by his touch."

"I *hate* that he can make you enjoy his attentions. I know that you can't stand him and I would do anything to put an end to his attentions. But there's nothing I can do to stop it except to kill him and you won't allow me."

"You *can't*. Not yet. We need him, as much as I hate to admit it." Lannan was a necessary evil at this point, and we all knew it—especially Lannan. Which meant he could be as cocky as he wanted and get away with it.

"As you wish. But if he hurts you, I will stake him, brutally and with as much pain as I can bring to bear. You belong to me. And no one can sever our bond." Grieve pulled away, shoving his hands in his pockets. He began to pace. "I feel cooped up, trapped here. But if I go out, Myst will hunt me down."

Luna, who had been standing back, watching but saying nothing, stepped forward. "You know that my sister is one of the Akazzani. Maybe she can help us? I told you, they have a lot of ancient texts. *The Rise of the Indigo Court* can't be the only treatise written on the Vampiric Fae. There *has* to be more information hidden away in the vaults of the Society. Maybe . . . maybe there's something about reversing the process, if you aren't born into the Indigo Court?"

We turned to her. She was a pretty woman, shorter even than I was, and plump, with long dark hair gathered back in a sleek ponytail. Her eyes were the color of her hair, ringed with silver sparkles. Luna was a bard, one of the yummanii—human, but her magical powers were stronger than the average person, and her voice was like a melody scaling a mountain, crystal clear and ringing one moment, throaty and rich the next. Kaylin had been instantly drawn to her—I could see it in his demeanor, but I had no clue whether she felt the same way. Or if she even sensed his interest.

"Do you think there's a possibility of finding something to change Grieve back?" It had not occurred to me that we might be able to reverse the process.

She shrugged. "I haven't a clue, to be honest. But we can find out."

"How would we go about doing that? I thought the Akazzani is supposed to be a closed society." The thought of diving into those books, of perhaps gleaning far more than a cure for Grieve, lured me in. And what if we could find other vulnerabilities that we could exploit against the Indigo Court?

"Zoey is loyal to me. I know her oaths bind her, but if I tell her what's at stake . . ." Luna pulled out her cell phone. "I should call her."

"They allow cell phones in their midst?" Kaylin cocked his head, giving her an odd look. "Last I heard, secret societies at least tried to stay . . . well . . . secret."

Luna snickered and blinked a flirty look at him. I didn't even think she realized she was doing it. "This is the twenty-first century, not the 1900s. They not only allow cell phones, but they sanction occasional visits home, as long as the society member observes the rules. Zoey could sneak out the books and return them when we're done. Books are to be used—information should flow rather than be locked up away from the world. Though Zoey's the only member of my family I'd trust with the information about where we are and why."

She paused, waiting for me to give her the go-ahead. I looked around. Kaylin nodded. Peyton and Rhiannon added their approval. My father remained silent. Lannan was out of the room.

Grieve slowly inclined his head. "I'm willing to chance it if she can find anything. I have to shake these bonds. I'm tired of feeling like my hands are tied."

Majority ruled.

I turned back to Luna. "Go for it. Call her after we finish our meeting." She nodded, sliding her phone into her pocket. I glanced around. "I guess we'd better haul Lannan's ass back in here. We need everybody present because I want all the input that I can get. I have an idea, too."

Lannan reluctantly joined us, looking bored. He stared at me, ignoring Grieve's dirty glances. My father just shook his head and rubbed his brow. He gave me a look as if to say, *You caused it, you fix it.*

As we sat around the table, I looked at each one in turn. We all had our strengths, we all had our weaknesses. I wasn't going to lie: The fact that Lainule was no longer on our team stung. The same with Anadey and Leo. They weren't exactly enemies, but they had all betrayed us, in one way or another. So much had gone wrong, so fast.

"I think I know a way we can regain Lainule's help. It's dangerous, but in my opinion, it's the only thing we can do. We need Summer's help, and I don't want to be the one dividing my father from the Queen of Rivers and Rushes." I looked up at him. That little piece of guilt wasn't going to go away.

"You are not the dividing line, my daughter. Lainule has her own mind and we've argued over many things throughout the years. This is simply one more squabble." His eyes lit up. "The Queen of Summer has a temper as volatile as fire pouring from the sun. She embodies the flame. It is her nature."

"Yeah, but I don't like being on the wrong end of her torch. And we *need* her. We need her to give up on Geoffrey."

Luna cocked her head to the side. "Why is she so desperate that she would be part of his plans?"

"Cicely knows why." Wrath gave me a warning look.

I nodded. "If Myst finds Alissanya—Lainule's heartstone—she can destroy the Queen of Rivers and Rushes. And with Myst controlling the woodland, she *will* find it. It's only a matter of time. Lainule is a desperate woman, Summer Queen or not. She was hoping that Geoffrey would help her destroy Myst before that plays out."

"What do you need from us?"

I sucked in a deep breath. "I want your opinion on this. I think, if we can recover Lainule's heartstone, she will help us. She's afraid now—if Myst finds it, she will die. If we find it, she will regain her strength."

"You have no idea of the ramifications of what you're proposing." Wrath stared at me, slowly standing. "And you should not talk of this in public." He grimaced. I'd never seen him look so irritated.

I glanced around. "What public? We're about as far from *public* as we can get in this town."

"You know what I mean—you speak in front of yummanii, magic-born, and worst of all—vampire." He leaned forward and for a moment, I thought he was going to strike me, his expression was stern and terrible and piercing like the eyes of an owl. But all he did was take my chin in hand. "Daughter, even now, you trust too easily."

I bit my lip. I hated making him upset. But we had to start trusting somewhere, and as bad as we'd been burned already, we only had our little ragtag group we'd managed to pull together.

"I know it's dangerous, but we haven't got a choice. Either Lainule fades and dies through lack of her heartstone, or we recover it and she lives. She can't go after it. Her people can't go after it. *Your* people."

"What exactly is a heartstone?" Luna asked, glancing from Wrath to me.

I plunged ahead. My father was right to be wary, but we were running out of time. "It's a part of Lainule's essence, from her heart, encapsulated in a gem, deep within the Golden Wood. If Myst finds it, she can immediately destroy Lainule. The Queen of Rivers and Rushes is too far away from it and she's fading. Unless we find it and take it to her, Lainule will die."

Lannan let out a sharp bark. "You cannot let Summer die."

Wrath turned to him. "What do you care, Altos?"

"If Lainule dies, then Myst has no checks. Geoffrey's not going to be able to stop her, as much as he'd like to think he can. She will flow through, set up the long winter, destroy my people, and all others with us. I do not wish for that any more than you do, Owl King." Lannan leaned forward. "I will help you, and I will keep your secret because it is for the good of my people to do so."

Grieve reached for my hand and I gave it to him. He lifted it to his lips and kissed it gently, then lightly nipped the skin. "You are my chosen for a reason. But how do you plan to find where she's hiding the gem?"

Chatter and I glanced at each other. I cleared my throat. "When Chatter and I journeyed to the Bat People, to help wake Kaylin's demon, we went through a secret passageway. I'm pretty sure we were close. Instinct tells me Lainule may have hidden it down there. It looked like it hadn't been used for a long, long time and . . . I sensed something in the area."

Grieve nodded. "You could be right. The heartstones are sacrosanct, but we live in desperate times. I say we do it. Lainule was always aloof, but she was never a fool, and for her to link herself to Geoffrey in his mad scheme does not bode as normal for our Lady of Summer."

Chatter cleared his throat. "I agree. We know where the passage is, we know how to get there. We must go in and search there carefully. If we journey by creeping through the forest, they shouldn't see us and we'll have the time to hunt for the gem."

I turned to Wrath. "We have no choice. If we want Lainule on our side again, we have to bring her the strength to stand with us. Until then, she's in Geoffrey's pocket. And suppose he decides that since I won't let him turn me, that he might try with Summer? Can you imagine what might happen if he turned Lainule? Surely she wouldn't be as bestial as Myst, but there's no guarantee she'd be sane."

My father blanched. "I had not thought of that. Surely Geoffrey isn't mad enough to try." He paused, then sucked in a deep breath. "He is, isn't he? He's just crazed enough to attempt it."

"I think he might be." I bit my lip. I didn't want to hurt my father or scare him but the thought had crossed my mind more than once and I was learning to pay attention to my instinct.

"Very well. We go in search of my Lady's heartstone. I just hope Myst doesn't catch us." Wrath deflated, dropping to the chair next to me. "But then Myst is coming and will take us all unless we do whatever we can to stop her."

Outside, the wind howled around the factory and I had the uneasy feeling we were being watched. The Shadow Hunters were on the prowl, and their Queen was driving the snows behind them.

Chapter 3

But we couldn't go after the heartstone that night. It was too late and too dangerous. We'd need to go during the day, when it was less risky. And there were other things we had to attend to first. I sprawled on the makeshift sofa, closing my eyes, wanting nothing more than a long, warm, comfortable night's sleep.

Peyton dropped to the seat beside me. She let out a huff, then said, "Rex is coming. I finally got hold of him. At least he's still alive."

Rex was her long-lost father who had shown up on her doorstep a few days back, after abandoning her mother and her when she was a little girl. Peyton hadn't been home to meet him. Making a deal with the vampires, Anadey had sold me out in an attempt to prevent the meeting from ever taking place, but her betrayal was in vain. Rex was still alive, and now Anadey was an outcast to us. Peyton had taken it hard, but she was soldiering on.

"You made certain to warn him to make sure he's not followed, right?" The last thing we needed was for the vampires or the Shadow Hunters to track us down by following him.

"He's not stupid." Peyton gave me a sharp look, then grimaced. "I'm sorry. Yeah, we talked about it. He's being careful. He'll be here tomorrow morning. This is the first time I'll have seen my father in . . . over twenty years." She looked like she was going to cry but then grabbed the dishes from the table, carrying them off to the utility sink in order to wash them.

"There's another thing we need to discuss before we track down the heartstone. We did a hasty ritual to band the Moon Spinners together, but if we're going to ask for help from the Consortium, we'll have to do things by the book. They don't cotton to people trying to buck the trends."

Rhiannon tapped her fingers on the table. "Aren't you forgetting something?"

I frowned. "I don't think so."

"What about the fact that you told Ysandra Petros that you and Kaylin are married? It was Kaylin's dumb idea at the time—and though I see what he was getting at, things didn't work out the way we thought they would. She's going to expect to see a marriage license. She pretty much said so before we left."

We didn't know a lot about them, but the Consortium served as an international organization to which a good share of the magic-born—at least those in high places and with any public notoriety—belonged. They laid down rules of conduct and enforced them. Heavily. They also backed up members who ran afoul of the law—as long as it was a blatant frame-up—or afoul of enemies. They were an impressive association, and their membership was daunting. The real *Who's Who* of the magical set.

And since Peyton and I had started magical businesses together without realizing that all such enterprises needed to be registered with the Consortium, we were on the hook for becoming members. Ysandra Petros, a high-ranking member of the organization, had dropped in for a visit when we opened the doors of the Veil House to customers for Wind Charms and Peyton's endeavor—Magical Eye Investigations.

When Marta, the town witch for New Forest, left me her

business and her position as the official leader of the now-defunct Thirteen Moons Society, I'd apparently earned a place in the ranks of the Consortium. Marta had been Peyton's grandmother and Anadey's mother—but Anadey and her mother were at odds. Because of a vision, Marta had named me as her heir before Myst killed her. But now, I had to come up with a magical society to replace hers—and so the Moon Spinners were born.

I'd been leery at first, but now with Geoffrey taking a trip into La-La land and Lainule ignoring us—we needed the Consortium's help. When in danger, any help is usually better than no help at all.

"Oh. That." I turned to see Kaylin laughing. "And just what do we do about this? I'm not about to marry you just to back up your lie, especially now, with the situation so out of hand. I don't know what possessed you to encourage me to tell her that or why I even listened to you."

"We were trying to keep the whole matter with Myst quiet, and with Heather in Myst's grasp . . . well . . . we needed a ruse as to why we were all living there, and we needed it quick. Rhiannon—and you—yeah, she would have bought that. But I didn't think she'd believe that Leo and I were just dropping by. Chalk it up to stupidity, but then we've all done some stupid things, haven't we? You were just as flustered as the rest of us." He gave me a *whatever* shrug and went back to sorting out the stuff we'd purloined from the house.

"Oh, for Pete's sake. I'm just going to tell her everything. At this point, they're bound to find out at some point, and if I admit I lied, she might be more apt to forgive me rather than if she discovers it later on." Ysandra had seemed a reasonable person. At least, I hoped she was.

You run a risk once she discovers you were deceiving her, but that may be the least of your worries. Ulean's voice was gentle in my ear.

"We could go through with it." Kaylin grinned at me.

I let out a sigh. "Oh, Kaylin, I like you, dude, but you have to be kidding."

Kaylin set down the sack of herbs he'd been sorting and dropped to one knee. "Oh, Cicely, marry me!"

"You can't marry Cicely." Grieve didn't sound at all happy.

"I'm not *Lannan*. I'm not trying to *fuck* her. But seriously, I'm joking. Don't have a fit." Kaylin stood, dusting his hands on his jeans, and then started to laugh. "Yes, my idea was stupid. Of course we'll tell her the truth. I'm really not trying to co-opt your lover."

Grieve let out a snort. "I know. I know. I just feel so damned helpless right now. I'm caught between being who I was and being a monster. I feel the urge to hunt rise in me and I push it down. I feel Myst's call, but I fight it off because I hate her. I cannot let myself become one of her creatures. Yet . . . how much longer can I go on living like this? None of you trust me." He reached down to stroke my cheek, smiling sadly at me. "And I understand why. I don't even trust myself. But at least I recognize the potential within . . . the potential to become a ruthless killer."

Grieve's conflict made my heart ache. How were we going to resolve this? Luna's suggestion that there might be a cure locked away within the Akazzani's archives gave me a glimmer of hope. I just prayed it wouldn't be dashed away.

Kaylin sat down next to Grieve, folding his elbows on the table, his expression sober. "I understand. Really, I do. When my night-veil demon entered my soul while I was in my mother's womb, it forever changed the potential of who I could become. A fact I learned all too well when Cicely helped to wake my demon. There was a horrendous struggle between us—the night-veil and me. And I'm still not sure exactly who won. I don't know if I'm Kaylin with the waking demon in his soul, or the demon with the memory of Kaylin in his soul."

Restless, he crossed to the nearest window and stared out into the snow. "We're all changing. Cicely, your memories are waking . . . You are beginning to remember the time when you were Myst's daughter. The obsidian knife would have bent your nature if you'd kept using it."

"It already did that." I stared at my hands. I'd used one of the Shadow Hunters' knives, only to find it strengthening the part of me that had once been Myst's daughter. I would have gone into a killing frenzy if my father hadn't stopped me. The taste of the enemy's blood was thick in my mouth, and I still remembered the intense joy of stabbing the knife through his body. "We're all twisted. We've all lost part of our souls because of our battle with Myst."

Rhiannon came quietly over to sit by my side. "You are experiencing what happened to me when I was thirteen. When I . . . when I called the flame and burned up the little girl in the car, it took away a part of me forever. I know what it's like to be ridden by a power. Perhaps this transformation, it's something that links us all?"

"Perhaps." I wondered if Luna had her story to tell as well. Peyton was consumed by her werepuma side at times. And Chatter . . . well . . . Chatter seemed the solid one. The one untouched by the madness. He alone stood as a bright shining beacon to me, a symbol of friendship and loyalty, but looks could be deceiving.

"So, what *are* you going to do about the Consortium?" Rhiannon forced a smile and took my hands. "Marta wouldn't let me be part of the community after my . . . accident. But Ysandra invited me in with you. So I consider that one a victory."

I squeezed her hands, bringing them to my lips to kiss them lightly. "Yes, it is most definitely a victory. I'm going to tell Ysandra the truth. I have her card with her phone number. I'll call her tomorrow and talk to her."

Wrath stood. "I can take word to them. They are not always grateful to see the Fae, but they have never turned on us. I can fly there in my owl form."

"No—we need you here." I was worried. I'd just found my father, I didn't want to lose him.

"You forget, my dear. I am King of Summer. King of the Court of Rivers and Rushes. I have many tricks up my sleeve." He took my hand and pulled me to my feet. I leaned against him and he hugged me. *Warm, paternal, caring.* He would never be the suburban father I'd imagined, but he was *my* father and he cared about me, and that's all that mattered.

"I know. But don't go. Please stay with us."

"Very well. If you wish it."

I turned to the others. "I want you all to know that whatever happens with the Consortium, happens. I'm not going to let our panic create a tangle of lies. There are a few things I'd rather not tell them, but I'm done with lying."

"I think you're making the right choice." Luna gave me a sheepish smile. "They have so many ways to pick up on liars . . ."

Kaylin flashed her a quiet look, then shrugged. "As you will. But I still think we could pull it off." Another sly grin, but I knew he was teasing.

"Truth is our best approach. Hopefully, we won't look like total idiots." I was regretting ever following Kaylin's advice, but it had seemed the best way to hide the fact that Heather had been kidnapped. And at the time we didn't dare tell them about Myst—we weren't clear on who we could trust with the knowledge. Now that we knew we couldn't deal with the Mistress of Mayhem by ourselves, we might as well admit it.

Kaylin finished spreading out the herbs and began sorting them into piles. Luna joined him.

"We need more supplies." He held up a bag of dried leaves, squinting at it. "Is this mugwort or vervain?"

"Vervain, I think." Luna joined him at the table, helping to separate the herbs.

"Thanks, Luna. You know, I think that tomorrow, we should sneak out of town, over to Monroe, and see what we can find. We'll have to take my car. Your GTO is too recognizable, Cicely. I don't want to be run off the road."

"You don't believe the Shadow Hunters would try that, do you? They don't work with technology. I doubt if they can even get into a car, let alone drive one." I picked up a couple of the bags containing woven garlic charms. "Maybe I should wear a strand of this while I sleep to keep Lannan out of my bed."

"Not such a good idea." Lannan interrupted, entering the room again.

I whirled around, blushing. I'd been joking, at least partially, but Lannan might not see it that way.

But he simply shook his head, and added, "While the Shadow Hunters may not try to run you off the road, Geoffrey might. If he even suspects you're going to the Consortium for help, chances are he'll try to stop you. He wants this war all to himself."

"I had him pegged all wrong, didn't I?" I'd thought Geoffrey the most reasonable of the vampires. But that theory had been shot to hell.

"What about me? Do you think you pegged me wrong?" Lannan cocked his head, flirting.

I glanced over at Grieve. "No, I think I've got your number down pat. Here, have a necklace." I tossed the garlic charm his way but Kaylin caught it midair and pocketed it.

"What was that?" Lannan stepped forward.

"Nothing, just a stupid impulse," Kaylin said. "Ignore her. She's tired."

"I see." Lannan continued to stare at me.

I decided that retreat was my best ally. "I'm going to sleep. We'll talk more in the morning. Grieve, join me, my love?" I'd been an idiot. Sassing Lannan was one thing. If he was in a good mood, he'd overlook it. But actively throwing a garlic charm at him? Stupid beyond the max. I could only chalk it up to exhaustion. I turned to Grieve. "Come with me?"

But he glanced at my father, who shook his head no, and reluctantly, Grieve leaned over to kiss me. "Not this evening. I suggest you and the other girls retire to your bedroom. We spruced it up today so it's a little more comfortable. You'll be safe there. Chatter and I will watch over you during the night."

I wanted to protest that we didn't need watching over, but that was stupid. We needed all the help we could get. We were all strong, but none of us was invincible, and even with Ulean at my side, I was as vulnerable as Myst's next victim. Perhaps even more so.

I yawned, stretching as I avoided looking at Lannan. "Yeah, we'll sleep. We need to rest. My body is weary and my mind—wearier." I motioned to Luna, Peyton, and Rhiannon. "Come on, girls. Let's get some downtime."

"Here, take these." Chatter handed us cherry-stone warmers—cherry stones my aunt had sewn into bags that were heated in either a microwave or—in this case—in the range oven. We'd tuck them under the covers near our feet and they'd keep us toasty into the cold, chill night.

"Thank you. What about the space heaters?"

"Not a good idea to have around so many flammable items," Kaylin said. "But the blankets are piled high like they were last night and the stone warmers should help take the edge off."

And with that, we entered the shrouded room.

I made sure the door was closed before we tucked the warmers under the covers and changed for the night. We were relieved to have nightclothes again. The past couple of nights, we'd slept in our jeans and sweatshirts. While upstairs at the Veil House, Kaylin had managed to scavenge enough clothing to provide each of us with several changes of jeans, shirts, along with underwear, nightgowns, and robes. He'd also scrounged up a few more personal items that we might need and for that, I blessed his heart. I was PMSing like crazy and cracked open the ibuprofen after I slid into the comfy flannel gown.

The room was set up with a bunch of old cushions serving as one big bed. The four of us women could easily fit on the makeshift mattress. A half bath to the left offered a working toilet and sink. I longed for a toothbrush, but for now the tube of toothpaste Kaylin had found, and our fingers, would have to do. If we did make a supply run, we were laying in a supply of toothbrushes.

After we changed and washed up as best as we could, lingering under the hot water as it splashed across our hands, we slid beneath the covers, our heads together in the center.

"Do you think we can win? Do you really think we can take down Myst?" Rhiannon said after a moment.

"Dark thoughts aren't the best thing to discuss before

bedtime." I must have sounded a little too harsh because Rhia looked hurt. Relenting, I burrowed under the covers as far as I could and added, "I don't know, but we'll try. If we can get hold of Lainule's heartstone, we'll stand a better chance."

Peyton sounded strained. "I wonder what my father will be like. You know what it's like, Cicely—never to know your father. How do you feel now that you've met him?"

I thought about her question before answering. "Honestly? Relieved that he wasn't some freak. That he wasn't a junkie. Given Krystal's addictions, there was no way to tell. It's odd, because my birth was planned by Lainule and Wrath. Krystal was a tool. A pawn to bring me back into this world. I can't help but wonder if Wrath cared about her. He . . . he's so far beyond what my mother could ever have hoped to be. Or anyone she could hope to be with."

Ever since finding out he was my father I'd played out a dozen scenarios in my head about how they met. Maybe she was out in the woods, walking, and he showed up out of nowhere and stole her breath away. Maybe he snuck into her room in bird form and then, like a prince out of a Faerie tale, turned into the handsome king, promising to take away her worries. Maybe . . . maybe I'd never know, and maybe that was best.

Peyton sniffled. "I used to imagine that Rex had to be dead. Otherwise, surely he would have come back to find me, to find out if we were okay. I couldn't let myself believe that he was alive and happy, knowing that he'd left behind a daughter who never got to know him."

Rhiannon murmured in soft agreement. "I'm still in the dark about my father. I have no clue who he was, or what I am. I'm just . . . a woman who once killed a little girl with my fire, and my mother is a vampire, working for an evil queen." She sounded lost and frightened.

"Are you thinking about Leo?" I sat up, gathering the covers around me to wrap them tight against the cold.

Rhia let out a forced laugh as she scooted over next to me and leaned her head on my shoulder. "Leo? I don't know if I ever really knew him. I thought I did, but now I think . . . I was in love with the idea of being in love. Or maybe I loved the man I thought he was, but in reality it was a sham. He let me believe he was who I wanted him to be. Not once did he ever tell me he was interested in being a vampire."

I hated sticking up for the scum, but there was a part of Leo that I understood. The all-too human side. "He probably knew how you felt. He wanted you to love him and said the right things, made the right moves . . . Don't we all do that at times?" I paused, wondering whether I should ask the next question. But since we were having an impromptu girls' night, I decided to go ahead. "And what about Chatter? Did you ever talk to Leo about him?"

She shook her head. "No, never."

"But you thought about him."

Rhiannon let out a soft sigh. "I met Chatter in the woods a few times when I was a teenager—I don't think Grieve knew, we kept it secret. But I couldn't believe we had a chance." She looked up at me. "I don't think I've ever loved anybody else. And I always remembered him. How caring he was, how gentle, how I trusted him and he never let me down. He gave me my first kiss, out there in the woods, when I was fifteen. But I couldn't tell him about the little girl. I was too ashamed. I thought he'd hate me, so I never went back again."

Luna had been listening to us, watching us in the dim light of the twenty-five-watt exposed bulb that lit our chamber. She pushed herself to sitting, too, huddling under the covers. "I listen to all of you and I think how lucky I had it. My family loves me, even if they don't understand me. I've never had a great love, but I've never had great loss, either. I've only sung about it. I guess I've lived vicariously through my music."

I reached over and took her hand. "You are holding up remarkably well. And we're grateful—and glad—you're here."

She crossed her legs. "It's nearly midnight. I should call Zoey. It's morning where she's at."

"Where are the Akazzani located?" Peyton asked.

Luna shook her head. "I can't tell you that. I don't even know myself. But I do know the time zone difference. It's midmorning where she is."

"Go ahead. I don't think we should keep this secret any longer. Myst is determined to spread her contagion. If we don't survive, someone outside of New Forest should know what's going on. That's why we're going to the Consortium, too." It was time to spread the word. If Lainule was right, Myst had other cells of the Vampiric Fae scattered around the world.

Luna moved to a quieter spot in the room and flipped open her cell phone. Not wanting to make her any more uncomfortable than she might already be about asking for her sister's help, I turned to Peyton.

"Did your father say when he was going to be here?"

"Around eight or nine." She rested her chin on her knees. "I really don't know what to expect, so I'm trying to expect nothing."

I stared at my feet, poking up under the covers, and wiggled my toes against the cherry stone warmer. It was toasty, and I tried to relax into the warmth and coax it up my body.

"This is just too bizarre. It feels like a million miles and a thousand years since I left La La land to return home, but in less than two weeks . . . everything I ever thought was true has been turned upside down. To say I feel lost is an understatement."

Rhiannon nodded. "I've been getting used to the weirdness over the years, I guess. My mother . . . she kept track of the odd events going on. But now . . ." She pushed back a long strand of the coppery red hair that hung down her back.

My cousin and I were fire and ice. I had hair as black as the night, sleek and hanging straight just past my shoulders. My eyes were emerald, and I now realized their color came from my father. At five feet, four inches, and 140 stocky, athletic, curvy pounds, I was a fireball of muscle. Rhiannon was taller and willowy, lithe like a dancer, with long curling red hair and hazel eyes. She was the spitting image of Heather.

Aunt Heather used to call us amber and jet when we were little. But we called ourselves twins. We were born on the same day, on the summer solstice—Rhiannon under the sun, during the waxing half of the year, and me under the moonlight, after the year switched over to waning. We were twenty-six now, and I wondered if we'd make it to our next birthday.

"I promise you, we will put her to rest." It felt horrible to say, but I knew the fact that Heather was now a vampire weighed heavily on her mind.

She nodded to me, her face a frozen mask. I wondered what she was thinking, but she chose to remain silent, scooting over to me. I lifted up my covers and let her slide beneath them. We pulled her blanket over the top of mine and the added warmth felt good. I wrapped my arm around her and she rested her head on my shoulder.

Luna returned then. "Zoey will be here as soon as she can. She's breaking a lot of rules to help us, but she thinks there are some more texts hidden away and she'll sneak out what she can. She said she can get away in a couple of days. I didn't ask how. I got the feeling it's another one of those things I'm not supposed to know about."

As she crawled back under her covers, shivering in the chill night air, I glanced at the clock on the wall. "We're well past the witching hour. We should get some sleep. And pray that tomorrow we start sorting out this mess. At least Lannan will be all beddy-bye then and I won't have to deal with him. Honestly, if he were human, I'd slap him with a lawsuit for stalking."

Peyton barked out a sharp laugh as Rhiannon and I snuggled down under our blankets, holding hands like we had when we were children. I hoped there were no spiders or rats around, but the long weariness of the day, the fear of returning to the Veil House—it all compounded to summon me into sleep.

As the soft sounds of Luna's and Peyton's breath came whistling by on the slipstream, Ulean swept around my cousin and me, a gentle shroud of protective energy.

Thank you. I'm afraid.

Ulean whispered gently next to my ear. *There is much to fear in the dark. There are monsters under the bed and in the closet, and now they walk abroad at will. But there is life here, and hope. I sense change on the wind. Others will offer help. As with Lannan, do not write them off simply because you dislike them.*

Her voice—I say *her* loosely because Elementals truly have no gender—trilled lightly in my ears, blowing around me like a soft billowing cloud. I sank into her cadence, letting her words lull my mind.

"Cicely, sleep deep. Dream of the paths that are ruled by the Summer. Follow the sparkling lights, for they have much to teach you."

Unable to tell whether it was my father's voice or Ulean's, or perhaps both in harmony, I finally let go of consciousness and slid into a slumber so hard and deep that it felt like I was melting into the earth.

Chapter 4

The path stretched out before me like a golden dream. Summer had come again, and I breathed in the warmth of the day as the drifting light rippled through the air. Reaching out, I caught a sunbeam, holding the yellow prism in the palm of my hand, close to my heart like a precious treasure. The drowsy sounds of bees lighting from flower to flower and the shriek of the Stellar's jays echoed around me. As I closed my eyes for a moment, the safety of summer washed over me like a cleansing wave.

The prism radiated heat through my hand. As I gazed into the brilliant gem, I saw Rhiannon, standing brilliant and tall and terrifying. Older than now, but still unmarred by time, she looked far stronger than I'd ever seen her and her expression was set, determined and fierce. She was cloaked in a velvet green dress, and she held out her hand toward me—and from the palm sprang sparks, flaring into flames dancing on her skin.

"Cousin," she whispered. "My moon-born twin. I need to wake up. You need to wake me up from my dark night's dream."

As I watched, transfixed by her image, Chatter stepped

up behind her, wearing the green of summer, and he placed his hands on her shoulders. He leaned down to kiss her, and as I watched, the flames in her hand danced with joy, and the light around them grew so bright I had to look away.

The next moment, I was back on the path, heading into the woods. As I came to a huge, spreading cedar tree, I thought I recognized it but couldn't place where I'd seen it before. And then Ulean rushed around me, dancing, and I could feel her joy in the whirl of leaves that went sailing around me.

Summer is rising again. Summer will not be lost . . .

I looked around for Lainule, but couldn't see her. As I closed my eyes, letting the warmth rush around me like a welcoming shroud, something tapped me on the shoulder. I opened my eyes and saw a green light, floating in front of my eyes. A pale ball of energy, it bounced at eye level, then floated over to the roots of the tree. I followed, Ulean guarding my back.

I knelt and parted the fronds of the maidenhair ferns that surrounded the trunk, and a deep reverberation chimed from the base of the tree. It began with a faint thunder, echoing the beating of my heart, but then slowly began to rise. I cleared the ground directly in front of the cedar's trunk. A trapdoor emerged. It reminded me of the one hiding the tunnel through which we'd journeyed to visit the Bat People.

A bronze handle glimmered, and the bubble of light gently rested on it.

"You want me to open this?"

The light bounced once . . . twice.

I reached out and the light moved to the side. As I grasped the handle, a shiver raced through my fingers, up my wrist and arm. I looked in, and there was a vortex of color, a whirlwind of green and gold and brilliant red. The spinning colors caught me up and sucked me in, and I began to fall, the ground disappearing beneath me. As I careened downward, I knew that I was on the right path . . . I was heading toward salvation and hope, and for the first time since I'd arrived home, the shadow of Myst could not follow me.

※

Cicely, wake—time to wake up. Ulean's breath hit my face and I woke to the gentle touch of her breezes gliding across me.

Squinting in the dim light, I pushed myself to a sitting position and shivered. Disoriented, I looked around, confused. It had been a dream—only a dream, yet I looked at my hand in which I'd been holding the imprisoned fire, and it was warm, almost glowing. As I yawned and glanced at the clock—it was six A.M.—Rhiannon stirred and rolled up, leaning on one arm. She rubbed her eyes with her free hand and shook her head.

In my dream, she'd been so much more powerful, so much stronger.

She squinted at me, quirking her lips into a smile. "Morning. Do we have to get up now?"

"I think we'd better. Peyton's father will be here in a couple of hours, and I want to contact Ysandra as soon as possible." Pausing, I stared at her. "Did you dream—anything odd, by chance?"

She frowned as she huddled under the blanket. "I don't know . . . maybe." After a moment, she cocked her head. "I seem to remember dreaming about somewhere . . . somewhere I felt safe. And . . . Chatter was with me. But that's all that I can recall."

I debated telling her what I'd seen, but it might just have been wishful thinking, and until I had time to think more about it, I decided to keep my dreams to myself. I slowly stood and stretched, wincing. The cushions we'd slept on may have been soft, but they weren't the same as a cushy bed, that was for sure. Rhiannon grumbled as she pushed herself to her feet.

As the bracing air hit me, I rubbed my hands on my arms. "Damn, it's cold." My teeth were chattering and I craved a cup of steaming coffee.

Peyton and Luna opened their eyes at my words. They

yawned and then followed suit, dragging themselves reluctantly from beneath the covers. I sorted through the clothes till I found a fresh pair of jeans, along with a clean turtleneck and—best of all—clean underwear. At least we would have a few days' worth of clean undies before having to do laundry in the sink.

Rhiannon wrapped a light throw around her shoulders. "I need to wash up." She headed for the bathroom.

Peyton and Luna sorted through the clothes until they found their own things. Kaylin had no real sense of color or style coordination, but that didn't matter right now. I shivered again and followed Rhia's example, hugging one of the blankets around my shoulders.

"Are you ready to meet your father?" I glanced over at Peyton.

She shrugged. "Yes, though I'm so afraid things will go badly and then I'll wish I'd never heard from him. I know everybody thinks it's better to know than not know . . . but sometimes I wonder about that. Living in a fantasy land can be a lot easier than facing reality."

"Especially with the reality we're up against." I gave her a soft smile. "I'm sure he'll be wonderful. After all, look at Wrath. He's not what I ever expected, but somehow . . . it fits my life that he's my father."

The werepuma/magic-born woman nodded. Peyton was tall and sturdy, muscled and with dark long hair and dark eyes. Her native heritage showed through her Caucasian side and she was a combination of the exotic and down-to-earth practicality.

"Should we plan out the trip to rescue Lainule's heartstone?" Luna frowned as she held up a long skirt and a button up shirt. "This should do." She began singing a faint chant over the clothes and—as she sang—the wrinkles vanished from the material.

"How did you do that?" I sat up, intrigued.

"Simple enough. Some of my magic is kitchen-witch-oriented. I can sing the wrinkles out of clothes, make sure a boiling pot never overflows or burns, charm seeds to germinate faster and grow stronger."

I'd never known much about yummanii magic. The magic-born primarily worked with the elements, but I knew there were other types of spells, other types of magic. "What else can you do? Are your spells linked to an element?"

She shrugged. "My magic is all linked to song. If I get laryngitis, my powers are disrupted. I first discovered my abilities when I was young. I sang to my toys and one day they started dancing. Freaked my mother out. But my grandma was a spell singer—which is what they call it in my family, and one cousin also has the power. We're not sure where it came from but Grandma used to talk about her grandmother being able to conjure with song."

"You have perfect pitch, don't you?" I couldn't keep on key to save my life, but I could recognize talent when I heard it.

With a slight blush, she ducked her head. "Yes, and I have the ability to sing any song I've heard even one time. I seem to have an audiographic memory—like photographic, only for music."

Peyton nodded. "What does the music do to you?"

Luna bit her lip, looking distant as she searched for the words. "It's hard to explain. Something about music resonates in my soul. That sounds melodramatic but really— the notes *vibrate* in my inner core. I can feel them spread throughout my body and I can grab hold of them, use them to manipulate the world around me. My parents don't have the ability, but they are talented in other ways. They've always just called their talent 'lucky chance' because they seem to luck out a lot."

Just then, Rhiannon came back from the bathroom and I took her place. I cleaned up with a quick sponge bath, sprucing up as best as I could. I'd give anything for another bath like yesterday, but I had a feeling that had taken all evening for Grieve to arrange and I wasn't about to ask him to do it again. I'd file it away under memories, and make do with washcloth and soap.

My nose felt slightly runny—the cold was getting to me—and I slathered some cream on the chapped skin.

After brushing my hair, and dressing, I stared at myself in the mirror. I felt like I'd aged a decade in the past couple of weeks . . . it showed in my eyes, and I held tight to the sink.

Whispering to my reflection, I said, "I wonder . . . what it would have been like to have a normal childhood, to have some memory I could hold on to where I wasn't running or hiding or trying to protect my mother?"

Grieve and Chatter gave you a taste of that. Ulean whistled around me.

They did, but even then, they were preparing me for the life I would face. But yes, those golden days before I was six and Krystal dragged me away . . . I cherish them.

A wash of memory swept me back to rare sunny days spent in the woods, crouching in puddles of sunlight, listening to Grieve and Chatter explain how the magic of wind and fire worked. I lingered in the memory for a moment, closed my eyes and drifted in the images, but there was no time for self-indulgence.

With a last glance in the mirror, I straightened my shoulders. Time to get moving for the day. Every hour we let go by was another hour Myst stole away a little more of our town. We needed to put a stop to her, regardless of the cost to our own lives.

Peyton and Luna took their turns in the bathroom as Rhiannon and I headed out to the main chamber where the others were waiting, with the exception of Lannan. Relieved we'd have the day free of the vampire, it briefly crossed my mind that I could track him down and stake him while he slept. But as I gazed around the giant warehouse, I realized I could spend all day hunting for him and never find a clue. Lannan wasn't stupid, and he knew how I felt.

Rhiannon put some soup on to heat for breakfast. Kaylin had managed to outfit the warehouse with a range, and there was a sink against one wall that had obviously been used by workers who needed to clean up. It was rusted, but wide and deep, and the water was still running and it was clear—apparently the pipes weren't a total loss. He was helping Chatter feed the burn barrels and I crowded near, huddling against the heat.

"Morning. Want some toast? I have an old toaster over there. It chars the bread on the corners but still works." Kaylin pointed to the counter near the sink. I saw a loaf of bread, a tub of margarine, and a toaster that had seen better days.

"Thanks." My teeth chattering in the chill air of the main warehouse, I popped two slices of bread into the toaster. "Did you guys eat yet?"

Kaylin nodded. "We had sandwiches for breakfast. Chatter is in the other room, working on more charms. He shooed us away, saying he needed silence so he could concentrate. Wrath is outside, patrolling the perimeter of the warehouse. We don't know if the Shadow Hunters are still affected by the light, but I don't think Geoffrey and Lainule have given them the antidote for the plague yet."

"I'm not even sure if they're still planning on doing so. Think about it—while they definitely took the Indigo Court down the wrong track, the light-rage *does* incapacitate them during the daylight."

All of them except Grieve, who'd been given the antidote when we rescued him. Though still part of the Indigo Court, at least now the light didn't send him into the raging madness that it did the other Vampiric Fae.

"Yeah, but it also makes them far more vicious. The vampires might not care, but Lainule . . . I think she would." Rhiannon brought over mugs of chicken soup and set them on the table as I carried a plate of toast over. Charred edges or not, the bread smelled all buttery and good.

"Lainule will be much more apt to help us once we find her heartstone." I dove into the food, my stomach rumbling. It felt like everything I ate just vanished the minute it went through my lips. The cold was burning up energy, the worry was eating away at us, and I never seemed to feel full anymore.

"Do you really believe that?" Kaylin asked, turning to look at me.

Rhiannon, Luna, and Peyton joined me at the t...

"I *have* to believe that. We have to have som... And then, as I looked up, my sight fell on Rhi...

once again the image of her strong, tall, incredibly powerful flashed before my eyes. We locked gazes.

"Rhiannon . . . you need to work with Chatter. Anadey was helping you master your control over the fire and she's lost to us now. Chatter can take over."

She nodded. "I've been thinking about that, too. I'll find him after breakfast."

As we dug into breakfast, several of the cats rubbing against our legs in an attempt to cajole an extra treat or two, an alarm beeped, echoing across the incredibly high ceilings.

Kaylin jerked his head up. "That's the pager I gave your father." He motioned for us to stay put as he vanished toward the front of the warehouse.

We pushed back from the table, positioning ourselves for a fight, if need be. I glanced at Rhiannon and she gave me a smoky look, then leaned back and I could feel the lick of the flames surrounding the edges of her aura. Worry crossed Luna's face, but then she closed her eyes and I could feel the swirl of magic surround her. I pulled out my fan, getting it ready.

Peyton drew a nasty-looking blade. She hoisted it—a long dagger with a serrated blade. "Kaylin gave this to me last night. I've done some knife training." As she tossed the blade back and forth between her hands, a feral look stole over her face, her puma just below the surface, waiting to be released.

But it wasn't an enemy who followed Kaylin back into the room. A tall man, as sturdy and dark as Peyton with hair that reached his lower back and was tied in a braid, walked into the room. Wearing dark indigo wash jeans, a cable-knit sweater, and scuffed cowboy boots, it was obvious in a glance that this was Rex—Peyton's father. The resemblance was remarkable. He had something woven into his braid—it looked like some sort of herb or dried flower or something.

Peyton stood, staring at him. As he paused, she began to tremble. "Rex?"

He nodded. "Peyton." And then he held out his arms and

she dropped her dagger on the floor and ran to him, weeping. He swept her into his embrace, hugging her tightly, kissing the top of her head. "My daughter. My baby. Baby girl."

She pressed her face against his chest, then pushed back, hitting him with her open hands. "You left me. You left us."

Rex didn't flinch from her blows. He just held her, letting her smack him until she ran out of energy.

."Oh, baby girl, I didn't want to. Your mother wouldn't let me stay. And she wouldn't let me come back." Taking a deep breath, he held Peyton's shoulders, forcing her to look at him. "Anadey threatened to run off with you, so that I'd never be able to find you. She said she'd give you my letters if I agreed to never come back to the house. So I relented and left. But she didn't keep her promise. I sent letter after letter. Now I know she destroyed them."

Peyton's jaw dropped. "I never saw one of them. Not one."

"I finally realized you weren't getting them when Old Joe One Shoe, a friend of mine here in town, overheard Anadey telling one of her friends that she tore up all my letters. When he told me that, I took off, spent several years on the road."

"Why did you come back?"

He smiled softly. "I decided it had been long enough—the cougars were speaking to me, they sang to me in the night and told me it was time to return home. That my baby girl was in trouble and needed me. So I hit the road and here I am." Rex let her go then, and Peyton didn't step away.

"Mother told me you were an alcoholic. Are you still drinking?"

"I was when I left. But I'd promised her I'd quit. She didn't trust me. Shortly after I left, I joined AA. Never slid off the wagon—not once. I've been sober since you were knee-high. I tried to get her to let me come home again, but she wouldn't hear of it. I think Anadey wanted you all to herself. I think she was jealous when you used to run up to me instead of her." He said it slowly, like a man not wanting to spill secrets, but it rang true.

Peyton nodded. "You're probably right. Anadey has always guarded me. She wants me to have friends, but then . . ." She glanced over at me. "She almost killed Cicely as a payment to keep you from getting to me."

Rex gave me a stout nod. "Miss." He touched his forehead in a two-fingered salute. "Baby girl, why don't you introduce me to your friends."

Peyton blushed. "I'm sorry—I was just so excited. And nervous." As she went round, giving our names and what we did, Rex shook our hands. His skin was warm and his handshake firm, rock-solid. I liked the man.

I think you can trust this man. His energy reads clear. Ulean flurried around me, her breath tickling my neck.

"You should know, we have one of the vampires in our midst, but I doubt if he was among those seeking to kill you. He does, however, have his own agenda." I pointed to a chair. "Sit down?"

Rex swung it around, straddling it. "Why do you let him stay?"

"Believe it or not, he's an ally, though a hedonist and all-around pervert as well." I went back to the last of my breakfast.

Luna slipped over to the counter and returned with a plate of donuts. "Would you like some coffee, Mr. Moon Runner?"

Rex grinned at her. "That would be Rex, my dear, and I'd love some. Black, with one sugar if you have it."

"Lannan Altos doesn't just have *an* agenda," Peyton said. "His agenda is *Cicely*." She glanced at me. "Should I tell him everything?"

"We probably should. While you're filling him in, I'm going to go call Ysandra and see if she is willing to meet with us." I walked to the other side of the room, away from the conversation. Pulling out my phone, I hunted through my purse and found the card Ysandra had left with me. After a moment's hesitation, I punched in her number.

Ysandra answered on the second ring.

"Hi, this is Cicely Waters. Remember me?" I wasn't sure what to say—should I just spill out all the information at once and chance sounding like a raving idiot? Or play the mysterious card and hope she wouldn't hang up on me?

"Cicely—of course I remember you! I'm so glad you called. Have you filled out the paperwork yet? We're looking forward to meeting you and your new Society." She sounded pleasant enough, almost like she really was looking forward to seeing us again.

I closed my eyes and plunged in. "Ysandra, we really need to talk to you. It's an emergency. Is there any way you could meet us in Monroe today? There's a diner there—Penny's Pit Stop. Please, will you meet us there this afternoon? There's so much I need to tell you and I can't do it over the phone."

She paused, I could almost hear the thoughts running through her head. Then, "Yes, I'll meet you there at three P.M."

"Please, be very careful on your way. And tell someone where you're going. New Forest is a dangerous town now. Marta and Heather found out the hard way. We're in trouble. And we need the help of the Consortium." My voice cracked and I realized just how scared I was. The fact that Ysandra agreeing to meet us made the tears well up was proof of the stress.

She paused again, and then simply said, "Three P.M. I will be there." And then silence.

I flipped my phone shut, a sense of relief flooding over me. There were so many things that could go wrong, but she *was* coming. I had a sudden flashback to childhood, to so many nights when I prayed for the cavalry to come riding in to rescue Krystal and me. But no one ever came.

As I returned to the others, Chatter entered the room. He was watching Rex intently. The look on his face was thoughtful and for once, I thought maybe, just maybe, our luck was turning. I let out my breath, forced a smile to my lips, and rejoined my friends.

Chapter 5

"I was high on the mountain when she found me," Rex was saying. "Stretched out, almost dead, but I knew my name, and I knew my place in life. I'd walked through the fire, and so earned my place as one of the elders of the Northwest Puma Pride. Even though I left for a long time, they kept my place open for me. They told me, 'We knew you would be coming home. It was meant to be.' And it's time for you, Peyton. Your time to undergo the vision quest is overdue."

Curious, I glanced over at Peyton. Listening rapt to her father, her eyes glistened with tears.

"I can't go now—I'm needed here. But afterward, *if* we get through this, I'll be ready. Will the pride accept me, though? I'm half-magic-born." Her lower lip trembled and I thought of the Lupa clan and how much the werewolves hated the magic-born.

"There is a big difference between wolves and cats," Rex said, glancing over at me as if he could read my mind. "We are magical in nature, the wolves not as much. They fear magic, where the puma clans revel in it. As do all the big-cat-shifters. That's one of the things that attracted me to your mother to begin with. I've told my people about you, and the Elders have offered you a place in the pride. But first, you must go through your vision quest. Pass through the fire and you will forever be one with my people. *Your* people." He leaned back in his chair, his arms crossed across his chest. "But you need to know there's a chance of dying. There's always a dance with death when you go in search of the fire."

Peyton nodded, staring at the floor. "I will try. I want to know more about your people—my people."

I happened to glance up at the clock on the wall. It was barely nine thirty. "Today, I'm meeting Ysandra at three P.M. Kaylin and Rhiannon—you come with me. Chatter, would you and Peyton and Rex help Luna do whatever you need to in order to make us more secure in this place?"

"What do you want me to do, my love?" Grieve stood at the doorway. As he joined us, sitting on the table next to me, I reached for his hand but he shook his head.

"Before you continue, I'd like to have things out in the open." He looked at the others. "I touched on this before but let's talk about it. None of you really trust me. Not even you, my loyal Chatter. And you have every right to feel that way. After all, I belong to Myst—she turned me. But please know, I'm doing everything I can to keep control of my darker nature. I was not born this way . . ." He hung his head, wincing. "I was not born to this. I love Cicely. She is my all. I'll do anything to keep her safe."

Rex tilted his head, frowning. "I'm still kind of fuzzy on the facts surrounding the Indigo Court. Fill me in?"

I sighed. "Long story short: Geoffrey—you know who he is?"

Rex nodded, a somber cast across his face. "I've had several run-ins with him long time back before I left New Forest. He's dangerous. I believe he was a warlord before he was turned?"

"Yes, and he is still a warlord at heart. A thousand or so years ago, Geoffrey got it into his head to turn Myst—who was one of the Unseelie. They were lovers, and they hatched a mad scheme to turn her into a vampire and then the two of them would conquer the land. Typical delusions-of-grandeur crap, except for one little problem. When he drank her down and then gave her his blood, she didn't die."

"Let me guess—something to do with her Fae nature?"

I rolled my eyes. "Oh yeah. Myst recovered insanely fast, able to use both her Unseelie powers *and* the vampire powers she gained from Geoffrey. And as an added bonus, she was able to breed children with her dual nature. When she realized how strong she was, she turned on Geoffrey and tried to destroy him. The vampires managed to drive the Vampiric Fae into obscurity, but the Indigo Court spent the following centuries breeding and waiting. A great war between the two factions was prophesized by their freak-show Blood Oracle—Crawl—and apparently Grieve and I were to be the catalysts in it. And it seems we were."

I paused, glancing at Grieve. His eyes were the black of the void, shining with stars. He cleared his throat. "In another life, Cicely was Myst's daughter—her name was Cherish. I was one of the Cambyra Fae, named Shy. I wasn't a wolf-shifter then, but instead I belonged to the Ursiasidhe, the bear-shifters."

"I didn't know that you were a bear-shifter then." I stared at him.

"It's never come up. Anyway, against all odds, we fell in love and, betraying both our peoples, ran away together."

"I bet that went over really well." Rex gave me a sad smile.

Frowning, I narrowed my eyes. "They chased us down. We ravaged a swath through the countryside in our attempts to escape. Or . . . *I* ravaged. Somehow I have a feeling I caused most of the damage."

Grieve took my hand. "We both did, love." He lifted my palm to his lips and kissed it gently. "In the end, we were cornered. I had a potion I'd bought from a sorceress. The drink was deadly, but fashioned to bind our souls together into the afterlife. We drank it knowing that although we would die, we'd find each other again in a new life. And so we have."

"Romeo and Juliet." Peyton said, her voice sad.

"Yes . . . only this time around, I'm also part Cambyra Fae. And Grieve . . . though he was born a Prince of the Summer Court, is now one of the Vampiric Fae. And once again, we're on the run." My words drifted away and I turned to my love. "This time, I want to end the cycle. I want to live my life with you . . . for you."

My lip trembled as Grieve pulled me into his arms. My heart pounded, a drum in the night, echoing my love for him as we stood there. I rested my head on his shoulder, his lips pressed against the top of my head. The warmth of his body made me want to cry.

After a few moments, Rex broke the silence. "So, does Geoffrey know you are Myst's daughter?"

"Yes. And he wanted to use me to get back at her—to turn me like he turned her." I pulled away from Grieve, but as I did so Ulean came sweeping up beside me. *Trouble. There is trouble brewing outside. Hurry. Enemies. Wrath says they are whispering about Rhiannon.*

Instantly, I jumped aside. "Ulean says there's trouble outside. Wrath warned her. Rhia—you stay in here. Grieve and Luna, guard her with your life. Don't ask questions, either of you."

I pulled on my jacket—my blade and fan still in the pockets—and headed for the door. Kaylin, Chatter, Peyton, and Rex followed me into the blinding snows.

⚜

Ulean guided us out one of the side exits, where we found my father, leaning against the building, waiting.

I ran up to him. "What's going on? Who is it?"

"Day-runners. And no, I didn't see Leo among them, but they look well armed and out for trouble." He brushed a swath of snowflakes off his hair. "They're around front, looking for a way in."

"Split up, then. Peyton, you take Chatter and Rex and head that way. Kaylin, come with me and my father." I pulled out my fan, getting it ready. I preferred working with the wind rather than with a blade. It felt more comfortable.

"What do we do when we find them?" Peyton began to shimmer, and I knew she was about to transform.

"Catch them if you can—we need to know what the fuck they want. If they put up a fight and we can't take them down without harming them . . . kill them." I shivered at the cold streak in my voice, but we were at war.

They nodded and headed off to the left. We swiftly crept along the building to the right, crouching as we went. My father pulled out a wicked-looking dagger—brilliant silver flashing in the eternal whiteness that shrouded us. Kaylin held his shurikens, and I readied my fan.

The warehouse was a long, gray metal skeleton stretching out under the silvery sky. With the snow on the ground, it blended, a blur that reminded me of staring out over the ocean on one of those days when the sky was the same color as the water. The snow mimicked cresting waves on the surface.

As we came to the end, I called Ulean. *Is there anything directly around the corner?*

No, but they are close around the other side. Be cautious when you reach the next turn. They are waiting and they know you are coming. There are four. Two waiting on your end, two on the other.

How did they find out? And can you possibly get word to the others? Chatter can hear you if you want him to.

I do not know how they were warned, but I can tell by their stance, they are waiting to ambush you. She swirled around me, a shroud of caution. *I will take word to Chatter now.*

I sucked in a deep breath and turned to Kaylin and Wrath. "Ulean says they know we're coming. They're not around this corner but around the next. Ulean's taking word to Chatter now. There are two on the other end, waiting down there, and two on our end."

"I suppose since they know we're here, we might as well . . . Hold on." Kaylin stood back, looking up. "We can still get the drop on them."

I followed his gaze. There was enough junk nearby to create a pile that would allow us to reach the roof. We could go up and over. Wrath caught our plan and shimmered into owl form, smoothly gliding up to land on the roof and transform back. He leaned over, his hand out, to help us scramble up from the junk to the roof.

As silently as we could, we crawled up the A-line roof. The snow was cold under our bellies as we forged a silent path. The gentle flaking of fresh snow landed on our shoulders, our hair, our backs. My hands were freezing, but I didn't want to put on gloves. They interfered with using my fan, and I couldn't afford the time spent yanking off a pair of gloves in order to unfurl the weapon.

As we reached the top of the roof, I cautiously slithered over the apex and edged my way down to just before the edge, peeking over. There they were. Day-runners. They wore the same style of clothing Leo had worn, and I could feel *vampire* written all over them. Wrath and Kaylin joined me.

The drop to the ground was daunting—we'd crawled up a fifteen-foot pile of crap in order to get on the roof in back. But the snow was knee-deep, so maybe the landing wouldn't be so hard. The men were still waiting and I was surprised to see that the others hadn't already engaged their pair, but as I looked down to their end, I saw that they'd had the same idea. They were on the roof, in approximately the same place we were.

I can make others hear me when I choose to, and it seemed a good idea to tell them what you were doing. They chose to approach in the same manner. Ulean sounded almost giddy. The wind was picking up and I could feel her responding to it, even as my own body did. It coaxed us to come, to play, to dive in. My owl self beckoned me to shift and fly out on the gusting currents, but I pushed the urge away.

With a glance at Kaylin, who gave me a thumbs-up, I swung my feet over the edge and dropped directly on top of one of the men. Kaylin followed, landing to take down the other, and within the blink of an eye, Wrath joined us.

I heard a loud shout from the other end—the others must have attacked at the same time we did—but I'd learned by now to keep my eyes on my own opponent. I quickly rolled up off the ground. When I'd landed on the man, I'd gone down on my knees, but the snow had cushioned the worst of the shock. As I rose to my feet, I was surprised to see that he was already standing.

"Who are you? What do you want?" I circled him warily, as Kaylin mirrored my movements with his opponent.

"Stand back. Or you'll regret it." With one quick sweep, the man I was facing pulled out something fist-sized and opened his palm for us to see.

"Fuck, a *grenade*? What the hell are you doing with a grenade?" My first thought was that Geoffrey had sent them here to blow us all up, a suicide bombing mission. Bloodwhores would do whatever their masters asked. But something in his demeanor told me he was no bloodwhore. No, day-runners were more valuable than bloodwhores.

"You—and the redhead—come with us and we'll let the rest of them go." He flicked his finger toward the pin.

I glanced at the grenade, then back at him. "How bad do you want us?"

"My orders are to bring the two of you back with me." As he spoke, the two men from the opposite end of the building herded Rex, Peyton, and Chatter back toward us. They, too, had a grenade.

"No. You want us *that* bad, you're not going to blow us up." I shook my head. "This is so not going to happen."

"You think so?" The man stared at me, his duster dark against the snow, and then he nodded to his buddy, who marched over and grabbed Peyton, dragging her in front of me. He tied her hands behind her back, and then pulled out a roll of duct tape and quickly strapped the grenade to her, while his partner kept us at bay with the other grenade. As he looped a string around the pin of the grenade and stepped away from Peyton, unwinding the string as he went, I suddenly realized what he was doing.

"Stop—don't. Don't do this."

"You and your cousin come with us and we'll let this one go without blowing her into a thousand bloody pieces."

As I began to panic, Wrath suddenly turned into an owl

and headed directly toward Peyton. Kaylin sent a shuriken into the man's hand. He screamed, dropping the line leading to the grenade's pin. At the same moment, Chatter turned into a pillar of fire and began spinning toward the man still holding the grenade.

"Get back! Get back!" I screamed to Rex, as I dove for a nearby snowbank. I shaded my eyes, tried to see what was happening without raising my head too far, but a large explosion lit up the area. Sharp screams filled the air, one after another. I staggered out from behind the snowbank, glancing around wildly. As Wrath lobbed something the other direction, yet another explosion rocked the ground.

Trying to catch my breath, I tried to ascertain who was still standing and who wasn't. Rex was over by Peyton's side—apparently he'd run toward her instead of diving for cover. He was stripping the ropes off of her hands. Chatter was standing there, looking slightly crazed. I ran over to him and he opened his arm to me.

I grabbed him around the waist, holding tight. "Oh, Chatter, I thought you blew yourself up."

"My fires are far greater in power than his weapon. But we'd better take care of the one who is left." He nodded over to where our opponents had been standing. "Best to assess who he is and what they were after."

The first man with the grenade was nowhere to be seen, but shredded material and body parts told me that he'd gone up in the explosion when Chatter engulfed him. The man who had tied up Peyton was on the ground, bloody and dead—Kaylin was leaning over him with a dripping blade. Wrath had taken out the third man, who was now sprawled dead near his feet. And the fourth was cowering on the ground, his hands in full sight above his head.

I hustled over to him. "Take your coat off. Slowly. Drop it on the ground."

He obeyed, and then I made him strip down all the way. When he was standing shivering and naked, I nodded.

"No hidden explosives. You can put on your boxers and undershirt again." He did, as I motioned for Kaylin to pick up the guy's clothing.

"Let's get him inside and see what we can find out about him. Blindfold him first, though." We couldn't let him go, but on the off chance he escaped, I didn't want him casing the joint for info on us.

We dragged him inside. Rhiannon gave me an odd look.

"We heard explosions. Are you all okay?" Luna hurried forward. When she saw we'd tied the man up, she pulled out a chair and pushed him into it, firmly knotting the ends of the cord around his wrists to the back of the chair.

"We're okay. We survived to fight another day." I frowned, feeling useless.

Peyton clapped me on the shoulder. "At least you weren't tied up with a grenade strapped to your chest." She tried to force a laugh, but her eyes told me just how drained she was from the experience. Rex came up behind her and led her to a chair, stroking her hair with an unexpectedly gentle hand. I glanced at him and he gave me a soft smile. Right then, I knew that he would love Peyton more than her mother had ever professed to.

"Yeah . . . that was . . . unexpected." I cleared a space on the table and pulled up a chair, looking at our prisoner.

Rhiannon turned then, and her eyes lit up when saw him. "Erik!"

I stared at her, openmouthed. "You *know* him?"

"Know him? Leo and I double-dated with him and his girlfriend several times." She suddenly dropped to a chair. "What the hell was going on out there?"

There was no way to avoid telling her. "This guy and three others came to kidnap the two of us. I'm not sure who the hell sent them—"

Rhiannon paled. "Erik is a day-runner for Geoffrey, just like Leo."

Erik snorted. "Leo ain't no day-runner anymore."

A knot in the pit of my stomach churned. "What do you mean?"

"Geoffrey turned Leo. He's one of the vamps now."

"Vampire?" Rhiannon deflated, a look of horror on her face. "You mean . . ."

"I mean, Geoffrey gave him what he wanted." Erik spit on the floor, then shivered. "It's cold, can you give me a blanket or something?"

"You tried to kill us, and you want a blanket because you're cold?" He had balls, that much I'd say for him.

He shrugged. "Believe what you want. I wasn't sent here to kill you. I was sent here to take you and Rio back to the boss men."

"Rio?" Now I was confused.

Rhiannon bit her lip, tears forming in her eyes. But she left them unshed. "That's what my nickname was among Leo's friends." She examined him, shaking her head. "I can't believe it. Leo's really a vampire now?"

Erik let out a little sigh. He sounded almost disappointed. "Yeah. Geoffrey turned him yesterday. And that means, no more hanging out together. Leo already thinks he's better than us. Geoffrey promised him that if he served him faithfully, he'd turn him, and now that it's happened Leo's already flying high on the pig."

I smelled sour grapes. Maybe we could turn this to our advantage. "What happens to you if you go back without us? Geoffrey was smart enough to outfit you with grenades. Obviously he knew we wouldn't go without a fight."

Erik shivered. "The Master's not going to be pleased."

I motioned to Kaylin. "Get a blanket, would you?" Then, casually, I turned back to Erik. "Maybe he won't do a thing. Or maybe . . . he'll give you to Leo to play with. How is Leo handling the whole vampire thing, so far? He thirsty? I hear newborn vamps have an incredible thirst and they don't care who they suckle from."

Erik nodded, paling. "Yeah, he's been working Geoffrey's stable, all right." He turned to where he must have guessed Rhiannon stood. "Honestly, I didn't want to bring you in. Leo's pissed at you right now, but he said he's willing to take you back if you apologize. And you"—he looked in the direction of my voice—"he hates. He told me . . . Never mind."

I could just imagine what Leo had said about me. I'd

rather be locked in a room with Lannan any day now that I knew Leo had gone over to the Crimson Court. He wouldn't last long, though, if he kept up his snotty attitude.

"Yeah, I know what he thinks of me. What does Geoffrey want with me?" As if I didn't know. I had the feeling that our prestigious Regent was looking to turn me as per his original plan.

"He doesn't tell his day-runners all his plans." He squirmed a little as Kaylin dropped the blanket over him, but then his teeth stopped chattering. "What are you going to do with me? You going to kill me, too?"

"See, we have a problem here, Erik. We can't really let you go back to Geoffrey now, can we? Or maybe . . . maybe we can." I circled him, longing to give him a punch or to twist his hair or pinch him—anything to pay back what he'd threatened to do to Peyton.

"Send him back as a messenger?" Kaylin wasn't as hesitant as I was. He reached out and gave Erik a sharp slap on the cheek. "Buck up, old boy. Maybe you won't die after all. At least not until Leo gets his fangs in you."

"Yeah, maybe he won't die right away." I nodded. "Erik, listen to me." I leaned down and spoke gently into his left ear. "Does Lainule know that Geoffrey sent you here?" I watched him squirm as he tried to avoid my breath hovering around his neck. I reached out and played with the jugular vein. "My lover Grieve could easily take a nip out of you. Or Lannan, perhaps. You know we have Lannan Altos on our side?"

"Please, not *that* freak. Though I don't know if Leo's going to be much better." Erik fidgeted and then his head lolled forward and his voice was soft but clear. "No, the Summer Queen doesn't know about this. Geoffrey told me to keep it all on the down-low. That we weren't to let anybody know what we were doing. She—they—had a big argument the other night. I heard them. She threatened to stake him and he ordered her out of his mansion."

So there was trouble in paradise.

"Do you know why they were fighting?"

"Not really, but it was about you. She was saying they'd

made a huge mistake. Geoffrey was yelling at her, saying that if she had let him take you by force, the plan would have gone off without a hitch." He stopped, then breathed very slowly. "Are you going to kill me? You might as well. Geoffrey will know I talked, and he'll punish me. Or he'll give me to Leo, who's going to be pissed out of his mind that I'm coming back without Rio."

"You're quite the loyalist." Rhiannon walked over and gave his leg a sharp nudge with her toe. "I'm disappointed in you, Erik. I thought we were friends."

Erik shrugged. "Day-runners have no friends. You should have figured that out by now. We're bound to our masters and there's no getting away. The only way out is either to become a vampire, if they'll agree to it, or a bloodwhore, or die."

Rhia knelt by his side and lightly put her hand on his knee. "Leo always planned on this, didn't he? He wasn't doing it just for the money." Her voice sounded strained, and I realized that all her illusions about Leo were crashing to the floor. Even if he wasn't her true love, she *had* loved him. And betrayal hurt.

Erik hung his head again and when he spoke, I had the feeling he genuinely regretted what he was saying. "Yeah . . . he told me when he first started that he wanted to be a vamp. He told me he wanted the power and money and respect that came with it. When he met you, he started talking about how he planned on first becoming a vampire and then bringing you over to be with him." He coughed, adding, "Rio, he really does love you . . . in his own way."

"You mean he's wants to *possess* me. He doesn't give a damn about what I think. He wants me under his control. I'll bet . . . you said he's going through Geoffrey's stable. You don't just mean he's drinking from the bloodwhores, do you? He's fucking every woman he can, isn't he? Am I wrong?"

After a pause, Erik shook his head. "No. You've got him pegged."

I motioned to the others and we moved away where he couldn't hear us. Being a yummanii, he wouldn't have exceptional hearing. As we gathered in the far end of the room, I glanced back at our bound, blindfolded prisoner.

"What do we do with him? We have two choices. Kill him or send him back. Ten to one, if we set him free he's going to bolt, try to run. Geoffrey and Leo will kill him." For the first time, I actually wished Lannan was awake. We could use a vampire's input on this. "We could keep him till Lannan wakes and ask him, but Geoffrey will know something's wrong."

"No, he won't." Kaylin shook his head. "He won't know anything is amiss until tonight because Geoffrey—and Leo—have to sleep during the daytime. They'll be aware of something going on when they wake to discover Erik and his cronies aren't back, but there's not a damned thing they can do through today. I say we keep him here. Tonight we'll ask Lannan for his opinion."

We headed back to the bound day-runner. "So, you know Lannan Altos? If we ask him what to do with you, what's he going to tell us?"

Erik paled even further and struggled a little. "Lannan Altos is a freak. You're going to hand me over to him? Why don't you just kill me now and get it over with?"

Curious and about out of patience, I tapped him on the shoulder. "Tell me something, Erik. Haven't you ever wanted to be a vampire? Why did you become a day-runner in the first place?"

His answer took me by surprise. "My mother was sick, and we couldn't afford her medicine. I couldn't work three jobs to pay the rent, keep her in the drugs that made her last year bearable, and be there for her in the evenings. So I asked Geoffrey if he'd take me on as a day-runner. I worked damned hard and soon he was paying me really well. By the time my mother died, I realized there was no getting out, so I stayed."

"Do you have a girlfriend, Erik?"

Rhiannon shook her head. "I don't think I've ever seen him with the same girl twice, have I?"

"Nah. I knew better than to get involved. You get entangled, fall in love, and Geoffrey and his cronies have something to hold over your head. I decided it was better to stay single. Live for the day and enjoy what I could. That way, if he got pissed at me, I would be the only one to pay for it."

Angry, because I was beginning to like him despite what had happened, I motioned to Kaylin. "Take him in a different room and make sure he's covered up from the cold. Get him something to eat."

As Kaylin and Chatter lifted the chair and carried Erik out of the room, I glanced at the clock. It was nearly one thirty. "Kaylin and Rhiannon and I had better get a move on if we expect to drive up to Monroe to meet Ysandra. Rhia, get your coat. We'll take Kaylin's car." I'd rather take Favonis but it was too recognizable. And after our little tiff with the day-runners, I had no desire to be a speeding target.

While waiting for Kaylin to return, Grieve and I slipped off in one of the side rooms. He took me in his arms and I slid my hands along his skin. We'd had very little privacy since coming here and I wanted him—here, now, inside me.

He pressed his lips to my forehead as I listened to the beating of his heart. "Cicely—be cautious. Please. I can't lose you."

"You won't. No matter what, you'll never lose me." My emotions threatening to break through, a tear slid down my face as I gazed into his eyes. His long platinum hair coiled down to his shoulders and for a moment, I could almost see the cornflower blue his eyes had been before Myst sunk her teeth into him.

"You're my world." His lips sought mine and I lost myself in their soft touch as his tongue gently explored my mouth. And then the passion rose and we were clutching one another, his hands slipping beneath my shirt as my breath came in ragged pants.

"I want you. *Now* . . . I *need* you." My heart was beating a million miles a second as his hands stoked the fire that raged between my legs, in my breasts, throughout my body.

He slid one knee between my thighs and I rubbed against it, my clit aching for his touch, my pussy wet and hungry for his girth.

"How long do we have?"

"Five minutes, if that." But even as I spoke, I unzipped my jeans and shoved them down, turning to lean against the wall. Grieve slid one hand around to stroke my clit and the ache rumbled through my belly as he drove his cock inside of me, from behind, plunging between the slick folds of my cunt. I tried to keep quiet but couldn't help let out a soft moan as he began to thrust—at first slow but then driving himself into me again and again, as he pounded deeper and deeper into my depths.

"You are mine, Cicely Waters. You're mine, and no one will ever take you away from me. I'll kill any man who touches you. And I'll rip out Altos's heart if he dares to hurt you."

And right then, I knew he would. Grieve would let the dark side of the Indigo Court out to wreak havoc if Lannan tried to fuck me again.

But thoughts of Lannan and retribution vanished as Grieve stroked me into a frenzy. I bit down on the strap of my purse, longing to scream, longing to let loose and echo my hunger from the ceilings. But before I found my voice, before it became impossible to keep silent, I suddenly felt myself at the precipice, and as Grieve let out a long, slow groan—coming deep within me—I tumbled over the edge, my body jolting with the force of our orgasm.

Chapter 6

Rhiannon and Kaylin just grinned when we came out from the broom closet, and I realized everyone had heard us. There was no way to prevent our voices from echoing in such a large space. My father diplomatically avoided me, while the others immediately scrounged for something with which to busy themselves.

Kaylin motioned to the door. "We'd better get a move on."

I nodded. "Yeah, let's go."

Grabbing my coat and my weapons, I followed him and Rhia outside, where Rex and Chatter were burying the bodies of the other day-runners under the snow and ice. There wasn't much else they could do with them for now. Rex was holding an arm from the guy who'd managed to go boom, and Chatter was staring at the scattered remains, a quiet, pensive look on his face. He'd told me that he didn't like to use his natural form—a pillar of fire—because of the fury that possessed him. Now I understood his reluctance. He'd been terrifying in his destruction.

"We're taking my car, right?" Kaylin headed for the black Mercedes that he'd tricked out. I nodded, following, with Rhiannon behind me. I called shotgun while Rhiannon slid into the back behind me. As we edged out of the warehouse's parking lot, I realized that even though we'd just been here a few days, this place had become a safe haven. I dreaded leaving it, because I had no clue what might be out there waiting for us.

As we turned onto the highway—the warehouse was right on the outskirts of New Forest—a fear flickered in my heart. What if we didn't make it back? What if, when we returned, we found the town had vanished, like some magical Brigadoon, along with Grieve and my father and Luna and Peyton? They were my family, my clan, my tribe.

I turned around in my seat. Rhiannon stared at me with haunted eyes. Without a word, she reached forward and we clasped hands.

"I love you, Rhia."

She bit her lip. "I love you, too, Cicely. In all of this . . . the one good thing is that you've come home. I missed you so much."

I squeezed my eyes tightly shut, wishing away the darkness and the eternal winter we'd been plunged into. *What if we don't make it back . . .*

You will drive yourself mad if you think too much. Do not worry—you will return to New Forest, and the town will be here, Cicely. And so will Myst. She's waiting. This is a pivotal time in the history of the vampires and the Fae. And you are right at the helm in this uneasy little war. Ulean brushed my cheek, her slight breeze comforting.

Highway 2 wound through wooded land, a valley that acted as a vast ravine between the jagged foothills of the Cascade Mountains and, to the west, beyond a series of rolling hills and a swath of land, the I-5 freeway with the bustle of big-city life. Seattle was a vastly different city than Los Angeles had been . . . or San Francisco or any other number of cities my mother and I'd drifted through. I could live in Seattle and be happy.

The snow grew heavier the farther we got from New Forest. We were headed east, toward the mountains, but

Myst's reach was extending. The entire western half of the state was feeling her chill.

Trying to push thoughts of the Winter Queen out of my mind, I turned my attention to the upcoming meeting with Ysandra. Would she be pissed that we had lied to her? Or would she understand once I told her what had really happened to Heather and explained why we'd scrambled for a cover story? Would she be able to help us? Would she be willing?

No sense borrowing trouble before it lands on your doorstep, Cicely.

Once again, Ulean soothed my ruffled feathers. We didn't even know if the Consortium's help would be worth anything. They might turn out to be so much hot air. Or a bureaucratic nightmare. But we had to try.

Kaylin cleared his throat. "Rhiannon, are you okay? Now that you know about Leo?"

Rhia rested her elbows on the back of my seat, her chin on her hands. After a moment, she let out a long breath. "Honestly? I don't know. My heart is breaking. It's hard to accept that I've been living a lie without knowing it. But I wonder, if all along, I sensed it would never work out. If I really search my heart, maybe I knew we'd never get married. That could be why I kept putting off choosing a wedding date. Leo was always pissed by my hesitation but something held me back. Some aspect of self-preservation . . . some inner light within me . . . saw through his illusions."

"I am so glad you found out before it was too late." I turned again, struggling against my seat belt, to try to kiss her forehead, then returned to solemnly watching the road ahead.

Rhiannon wasn't done, though. Apparently Kaylin's question had offered her permission to talk about the situation. "But did I *really* find out in time? From what Erik said, Leo is out to kidnap me. I have to stake him if I'm ever to be free. Once he gets an idea in his head, he won't let go. Frankly, the thought of him out there, wanting me, scares me to death now that I know he's a vampire."

She said it so casually I almost missed the gist of her meaning. When her words registered, I sucked in a deep breath.

"You really plan on staking Leo?"

Solemnly, she nodded. "Yes. I don't think there's any other way to be free from him. It's almost as bad as my mother, except my mother didn't ask for it—she did it to save Peyton. Leo—he *wanted* to become one of those monsters. He *chose* the path. And he did it for glory and money and power. He's going to be far more dangerous than Lannan, mark my words. Lannan likes to humiliate, but he's behaving himself around your father and Grieve. Leo doesn't have that much restraint."

"Lannan's been alive for thousands of years. He has more control over his actions, though he's far more powerful than Leo can possibly be at this point."

"True, but Geoffrey is Leo's sire and mentor. That makes him dangerous. Geoffrey is as powerful as Lannan, isn't he?" Rhiannon frowned. "When you get past one or two thousand years . . . can another thousand make any difference?"

"I don't know, to be honest. Lannan's older than Geoffrey, and chances are he could be the Regent if he wanted to be. But Lannan doesn't want the responsibility."

Kaylin flipped the windshield wipers to high speed as the snow began to fall thicker and faster. "Not to change the subject, but I don't like this. This storm is setting in to be a bad one. We can't spend a lot of time talking to the Petros woman—I want to get home before too late, and the roads are going to be bad. They're already icing up even though it looks like they were plowed this morning."

Even as he spoke, the car swerved and he eased into the skid, avoiding a fishtail as he lowered the speed and leaned forward to look out the window, keeping his eyes firmly on the road. The windshield wipers were going full speed but could barely keep up with the snowfall.

"As I said, it's going to get worse before it gets better."

"That seems to be the general theme of our life lately, doesn't it?" I glanced at the map on my phone. "Penny's Pit Stop is near the entrance to the town. Take the exit leading to North Kelsey Street, then turn onto West Elizabeth. The restaurant should be a block or two down from there."

Kaylin glanced over his shoulder briefly at Rhiannon. "Fasten your seat belt again, please. We're in dangerous territory. Ice and sleet on the road, snow coming down. I really don't want to worry that if we have an accident, you'll go sailing through the back window or something."

Rhiannon settled back in her seat and fastened the belt. Another two slip-and-slide moments, and another fifteen minutes put us on the streets of Monroe. It felt odd to enter a town that wasn't under siege, at least not yet. But if Myst wasn't stopped, she would spread the cancer of the Indigo Court in this direction, and eventually, everywhere. Thanks to Myst's long winter, it seemed like we were headed toward another "Little Ice Age."

But as we entered Monroe, the constriction in my chest loosened and for the first time in days, I felt like I could breathe as I looked out the windows. No vampires were out and about yet—but vampires weren't the danger here. No, the holiday shoppers went about their lives, blissfully unaware of the war going on just a stretch down the highway.

A glowing neon sign in the parking lot of Penny's Pit Stop cut through the gloom. The brilliant blue and yellow lights led us into the lot, which had been plowed earlier, but the empty parking spaces were beginning to cover over again. Kaylin gingerly parked in a spot that seemed the least likely to keep us prisoner.

Breathing a deep sigh of relief—we'd actually made it here in one piece—I slipped out of the car. Almost immediately, I was hit by the cold, my breath sucked out of me in one quick rush. I snuggled my jacket tighter around me, and covered my nose with my hand, trying to warm the air before it hit my lungs. Rhiannon and Kaylin joined me, and we hurried across the compacted snow toward the entrance and pushed through the door.

The blast of heat was like honey on warm bread. It oozed over me and I let out a long sigh, breathing deeply. The ache in my side eased as I was able to take a full breath without the slashing cold driving deep into my side.

"Welcome to Penny's Pit Stop. I'm Rae-Ann. May I help you?" The hostess hurried over, though one glance around the place told me that Penny was going to be taking it easy tonight. Only three tables held patrons, and one booth had a woman sitting in it—Ysandra.

I pointed to the booth. "We're here to meet her."

As Rae-Ann led us through the carpeted dining room, quiet music played in the background. It wasn't wet-dream elevator music but classical, and it soothed my thoughts as I tried to relax.

Ysandra looked as prim and proper as I remembered—with a high-button, ruffled yoke shirt in a rich plum that contrasted with her black skirt. Her blond hair was pulled back in a chignon, with lacquered chopsticks holding it in place. A pair of leather driving gloves were neatly folded across her handbag. And it *was* a proper handbag, double strap, designer by the looks, in classic ecru.

She wore half-glasses, and if I tried to put an age on her, I'd place her somewhere between thirty and seventy, which pretty much meant I had no clue—she didn't look old but she didn't feel young. Ysandra was one of the magic-born and a very powerful witch. We slid into the booth as she gestured for us to join her. As she closed her menu, she smiled.

"Kaylin, Cicely, Rhiannon—I'm pleased to see you again."

The waitress waited until we were seated before handing us menus.

"Please, my treat. Have a bite to eat." Ysandra glanced at the three of us. "Peyton isn't joining us?"

I shook my head. "Family business. Her father returned. He's been gone since she was young." Not sure how to approach what we were about to tell her, I glanced through the menu.

The waitress waited, pencil poised over her pad. "Do you need a few minutes, or do you know what I can get for you folks?"

Ysandra nodded at me. "Please, go ahead."

I folded the menu. "Cheeseburger, please, with a salad

instead of fries. And hot chocolate. I'm allergic—anaphylactic—to fish and shellfish. Please tell the chef."

"You got it, honey. And I'll make sure the chef knows about your allergy." She jotted down a note on the pad.

Rhiannon handed her the menu. "Chicken soup and grilled cheese. Hot chocolate sounds good."

"And for you, hon?" She turned to Ysandra and I stifled a giggle. Anybody who called Ysandra "hon" was a brave, brave woman.

Ysandra apparently thought so, too, by the look on her face, but she was polite enough to avoid commenting. "A bowl of your creamy potato soup and turkey on rye, please. No mayonnaise. Butter instead."

The waitress nodded, jotting it down. She looked over at Kaylin and a slow smile spread across her lips as she drank him in. I glanced at him. He'd been handsome when I met him, but ever since the night-veil demon awaked in his soul, his charm had increased.

"Burger and fries. A large glass of milk." He gave her a half wink and she hurried off, giggling.

"You have a way with the ladies, young man." Ysandra gave him a measured smile. "How does your wife feel about your flirting?"

I sucked in a deep breath. Time for the truth. "Yeah, about that. We have a lot to tell you, and I'm not quite sure how to start. It's complicated."

"Perhaps at the beginning? That's generally the easiest, most direct route." She folded her hands, patiently waiting. I could feel a slight hum of energy surrounding her.

Magic . . . she's using some sort of magic. Ulean swept by.

Can she sense you?

I don't know. She is a powerful witch, but I cannot fathom where her powers lie.

I glanced at the others, then steeled my courage and dove in, telling her—as briefly as I could—how I'd been called back here to find Marta dead at the hands of the Indigo Court, the Thirteen Moons Society defunct, my aunt turned into a vampire, the Summer Court rousted from their woodlands, Myst taking over the Golden Wood, myself embroiled in a lopsided deal with Geoffrey and the vampires, Lannan's hold on me, and the burning of the Veil House. She remained silent as I continued to lay out the fallout from the whole mess.

"When you showed up the other day, we were afraid— we didn't know what to tell you and I'd been ordered to keep my mouth shut by Geoffrey. We panicked and Kaylin thought we'd appear more stable if we told you we were married. The truth is, we're not and we have no plans to be."

I sat back, shutting my mouth as abruptly as I'd opened it. I'd kept a few things from her. I did not tell her about the heartstones. I wasn't ready to, not until we found Lainule's gem and returned it to her.

Ysandra's expression remained calm as the waitress set out our drinks, but I could feel the wheels turning at a furious pace. After a moment, she withdrew a sheaf of papers from a briefcase sitting by her side. Pushing them across the table, to me, she handed me a pen.

"Fill these out. *Now.* I'm authorized to offer a special dispensation and induct you directly into the Consortium in case of an emergency. And I think we've long passed that state. We've known about some of this for a long time but haven't had the chance to investigate it. Had we realized how bad it's gotten, we'd have already been into New Forest. With the town under siege, and since you are Marta's heir, that makes you the magical authority for New Forest. We need to seal this officially and bring you and your Society into the Consortium. Have you picked a name for yourselves?"

I nodded. "The Moon Spinners. We've held a couple of brief rituals to bind ourselves, but that's all we've had time for."

"Then the Moon Spinners it will be. And all you need is the consent of all members. Their names, please? List them on that field there. And also, you need to list the person whom you would choose to lead the group should something happen to you. Do not select your cousin. Do not ask why." She pointed to several blank lines on the form.

As I stared at the form, my mind reeling, Kaylin cleared his throat.

"It does not bother you that we aren't all of the magic-born? Peyton's half-werepuma. Grieve is . . . well . . . Cambyra Fae and Indigo Court. Chatter is Cambyra Fae. Even Cicely here . . ."

"Yummanii, magic-born, Were, contrary to rumor, we do not care about heritage as long as the applicant wields magic in some form and is willing to abide by the Consortium's rules." She let out a long sigh. "This will also protect your lover from being targeted by our members. Because the moment you sign that form, the Indigo Court becomes the enemy of the Consortium."

"You don't need to check out our story?"

"Oh, *trust me*, I know you are telling the truth." A sly smile fluttered across her face.

Deciding not to press the matter—I wasn't sure I wanted to know the answer anyway—I paused, my pen hovering over the form. "The vampires already own me. Can I legally sign this contract as well as the one with them?"

"Unfortunately, Geoffrey's contract will not be nullified by the tricks he attempted to pull. However, your contract with the Consortium does not conflict with your connection to the vampires, and we are not claiming you as an employee. We are requiring you to swear an oath not to betray us, but that should not conflict with your servitude to the Vampire Nation." She grimaced even as she said the words.

I hung my head. "I did what I had to."

"I never said you made the wrong choice. We all do what we have to when duty calls. That is one of the hardest lessons in life. Sometimes we are required to do what we do not wish to do. Sometimes we sacrifice our own happiness for the good of the whole."

We fell silent as the waitress brought our food. The smell was tantalizing—it had been a while since we'd had a decent meal, but I still felt awkward, as if I'd confessed dirty secrets to Ysandra. As the waitress spread out our food, I toyed with my burger.

"Eat. You need the strength. I am not judging you,

Cicely." Ysandra's voice was gentle and the look on her face, concerned.

She speaks the truth. Give her a chance. This one's energy is helpful and powerful. She speaks only when she's thought through her words. She says what she means. As Ulean gusted around me, Ysandra shivered.

"Cicely, would you tell your Elemental to hold off on the breeze? It's cold enough outside without bringing the storm in here." Ysandra winked at me.

I jumped. "You know I have a Wind Elemental? How did you find out?"

"I think the question is more how can I not know?" She spooned her soup, properly and with a sense of authority. "Eat. Then finish the paperwork and we'll be off. The sooner I get back to the Consortium, the quicker we can discuss how we can help you."

I bit into my sandwich, holding it with my right hand as I finished filling out the forms with my left. I had a feeling some of the horror stories I'd heard of the Consortium had been exacerbated by those who had been rejected by the organization.

Rhiannon swigged down her drink, then opened the pamphlet that Ysandra handed her. "Rules and bylaws?"

Ysandra nodded. "There is an expected level of decorum. Once a member, during any time when you officially represent the Consortium, you must abide by certain regulations. This means that any function the Moon Spinners attend as a group, you are attending as members of the Consortium. It also plays into your magical business, Cicely, and that of Peyton's. There are ethical standards you will be expected to abide by."

"Somehow I doubt we'll be needing those rules, since both our businesses went up in smoke when the Veil House burned." I smiled ruefully. "We can rebuild, but it's going to take money, which we don't have. And we have to eliminate Myst first. If we went back now, she'd just send her Shadow Hunters after us again."

Ysandra dabbed the side of her lips with her napkin. "Money is not necessarily an issue. The Consortium has its own worldwide financial institutions for our members. We issue our own credit cards, make loans, offer complete banking services—everything you could possibly need. Open only to members, of course, and their immediate families."

Startled, I laughed. The sudden turn in the discussion seemed so alien from what we'd been discussing. "Do you offer a free toaster with every new account?"

Ysandra chuckled as she tucked the papers into her briefcase and handed me a certificate, already prepared, with the Moon Spinners name, and my own, on it. "No, but we offer a free prosperity charm or a dozen green enchanted candles. Will that suffice?" And with that the tension seemed to break and we all relaxed and finished our meals.

Kaylin glanced at his watch. "We'd better get moving. It's growing dark, the roads are treacherous, and the danger increases after dark."

As Ysandra began to stand, I stopped her. "You had the certificate already prepared. And you seem . . . I don't know . . . when we told you about Myst you were quiet, but you didn't seem terribly surprised."

Her gaze flickered from my face to Rhiannon's, then to Kaylin's. "The Consortium makes it our business to know everything we need to know. I knew that I'd be giving you that certificate today. One of our seers told the Council that it would be necessary. And . . . as to Myst . . . as I said, we've always known about the Indigo Fae."

I must have looked startled because she laughed lightly and touched my arm. A tingle raced through my body like a jolt of lightning—not painful but not exactly pleasant. But it was strong enough to leave me jarred.

"The vampires think they have an exclusive hold on that knowledge, but they are mistaken. The Vein Lords have long considered themselves to be the top of the food chain, but they have never crossed the Consortium. They have no real clue about the power our Society wields. And we intend to keep it that way until the day they choose to waken the sleeping dragon."

Her lips stopped moving, but I could still hear her inside

my head. *Cicely, know this: If push comes to shove, the vampires could never win against us. And we should prove a sturdy force against Myst. We have an elite task force with whom I will discuss this situation. That is all I can tell you for now. Keep the knowledge to yourselves, and do not tell Lannan Altos or any of the vampires. But look for us to send help shortly.*

I glanced at Kaylin and Rhiannon. They, too, wore surprised looks and I had the feeling they'd heard everything I had. We all nodded.

As we headed for the door, I asked, "What magic do you work with? You are one of the magic-born, correct?"

She nodded. "I am. I work with pure energy. The energy of thought, of communication, and of lightning."

I pushed open the door and we headed out into the snow. As we were about to separate, her to her car and us to ours, a growl—low and threatening—alerted me.

Incoming. Werewolves. At least five.

Shit! I hadn't been prepared for a fight. My belly was full and I was already tired from the altercation with the day-runners earlier. I whirled around to see the pack headed for us.

"Werewolves!" They didn't look like they were from the Lupa Clan. In fact, they looked even surlier and nastier.

"I smell the stench of magic-born." The tallest one stepped forward and—before I could say or do anything—he threw a punch my way, hitting me in the stomach and knocking me back into a snowbank.

Kaylin had his shurikens out within seconds, and Rhiannon jumped back, squinting as she whispered some chant. I struggled to my feet.

Ysandra, on the other hand, simply placed her briefcase and bag down behind her in the snow and held up one hand, palm toward the lycanthropes. They jostled for position, but within a moment a shockwave raced through the air, knocking all of us on our butts. The werewolves looked startled, nervous.

Kaylin grabbed Rhiannon and helped her up, then me. Ysandra simply stood where she was.

"You have a choice." Her voice was even and so scary cold that it frightened even me. "You can turn tail and leave us be, or you can lose your hearing forever, along with your equilibrium. If you don't think I can do it, you'd be sadly mistaken. I am no youthful witch, new to her magic."

One of the werewolves started forward, but the leader shook his head, grabbing the man by the arm. "She's *Consortium*," was all he said, and the five began to back away, hands in the air.

"Get in your car and drive out of here now." Ysandra gave a little nod to us. "Do as I say."

"But will you be safe if we go?" We couldn't just leave her standing there.

She let out a cold, harsh laugh that seemed incongruous with her looks. "Do not let appearances deceive you, Cicely. Trust on instinct rather than what you see."

Kaylin motioned to the car. "Get in. Do as she says."

I started to protest, but Ulean swept around me in a spinning vortex.

Do as Kaylin says. Do as the witch says. She is far more than you perceive—I can see her energy now and it is frightening in its power. She could destroy the werewolves' hearing with a whistle, she could rupture their eardrums with one clap of the hands. She does not need our help.

The intensity of Ulean's thoughts hit me like a brick. She wasn't joking. I nodded, backing up to the car, keeping one eye on the werewolves who stood near their trucks, staring at us. Rhiannon and I climbed in as Kaylin turned the ignition.

Ysandra called out something—I couldn't quite catch what because I was too busy gawking rather than listening to the slipstream—and the werewolves turned, jumped in their trucks, and peeled out of the parking lot.

As we headed in the opposite direction, I glanced in the rearview mirror. Ysandra picked up her briefcase and bag like nothing had happened, daintily stepped into her sedan, and within seconds, she'd driven off into the night.

Chapter 7

On the drive home we didn't talk much. Watching Ysandra bring a pack of werewolves to their knees had been sobering. If that's the kind of power the Consortium had, I wanted in on it. I didn't know how much I *trusted* them, but I'd rather align myself *with* them than against them.

"We have to tell Lannan we talked to her, but let's wait till he's asleep to discuss the werewolves, the task force, and the fact that the Consortium knows all about the war between the vampires and the Indigo Court."

"Spot on." Kaylin flicked the turn signal as we eased off the highway, onto the street leading to the warehouse. "Somehow I think even Lannan would go running back to the Crimson Court with that information, as much of a rogue as he is."

We pulled into the parking lot and he turned off the ignition. We'd made it back to the warehouse without anything worse than a few swerves.

As we swept into the central room, everybody was eating. Everyone except Lannan, who was sitting off to the side, a smirk on his face as he flipped through an issue of *Vamp*. A slut magazine catering to the bite-me set, the monthly rag featured gaudy pictures of women—and men—dressed in little to no clothing, advertising their services for hire as bloodwhores.

He glanced up at me, his long lashes fluttering against the obsidian gleam of his eyes. Very slowly, he closed the magazine and set it to the side. "So, our illustrious trio returns." Slipping off the arm of the chair on which he'd been sitting, Lannan sauntered over to me, circling me as I shrugged out of my jacket.

"Cicely, my sweet Cicely. Where have you been?"

I tried to ignore his proximity, but the feel of him behind me set me on edge. Shivering, I tried to ignore the magnetic pull he had on my body.

"We talked to Ysandra. The Consortium has accepted us in on an emergency basis. I signed a contract with her." I turned to Lannan—I knew he was going to raise a stink about it. And I wasn't mistaken.

"You seriously believe that will release you from your obligation to the vampires? Geoffrey's actions do not negate the contract between you and the Crimson Veil. Don't fancy yourself footloose, my dear Cicely." He leaned in, his face inches from my own. My wolf ruffled its fur— Grieve wasn't happy, that was for sure. "And didn't Geoffrey tell you *not* to talk to the Consortium?"

I stood my ground. "He warned me about them, yes. But given that I now trust Geoffrey just about as much as I trust Myst, I'm not necessarily concerning myself with what Geoffrey told me." I flashed him a snarly leer. I wanted to bait him. *Just a little.* "So, are you going to run back to him and tell him what I've done?"

Lannan froze, his gaze narrowing. He looked two seconds short of baring his fangs, but after a moment, he pulled back. "Don't tempt me, girl. Don't ever fancy yourself the winner in our little game of wit and will."

"You're edging onto shaky ground, Altos." My father stood, motioning for Grieve to remain silent. "Remember, you stand in the presence of Summer whether Lainule is here or not—I am the King of Rivers and Rushes and I wield no small power. And Cicely is my daughter."

Lannan paused, his gaze flickering from me to my father. Slowly, still swaggering, he disengaged me and headed toward the door. "I must drink and drink deep, and if no one here is offering their services—" He paused, glancing back at me. I looked away. "I shall return soon. And I'll see if I can dig up some information on our newly minted vampire, little Leo."

With that, he was out the door, a blur of motion. I let out a long breath and sank into a chair.

"I still don't like having him here." I waved away offers of soup and a sandwich. "We ate." While they finished dinner, Kaylin, Rhiannon, and I told them what had gone down, including the parts we couldn't talk about in front of Lannan.

"So the Moon Spinners officially belong to the Consortium, then?" Peyton asked.

"That we do, which means we have to keep records of our ceremonies and meetings." Rhiannon held up the pamphlet that Ysandra had given us. "Though, considering we've been inducted on an emergency basis, I think they'll understand if we're a little haphazard to begin with." She paused. "Do you hear that? A tapping?"

Kaylin squinted, heading toward the door. Chatter and Grieve moved to back him up. The rest of us prepared for the worst. It might just be Lannan—though he was fully capable of opening the heavy door himself—or it might be something far worse.

But when they returned, the men were followed by a couple of the Fae I recognized as Lainule's personal bodyguards.

"Is there a problem?" Wrath slowly stood, a look of concern crinkling his face.

The guards knelt before him. "Lord of Summer, we entreat you. The Queen has taken ill and needs you. Come quickly, please." They turned to me. "She asked for you as well."

Without a word, I shrugged into my jacket and, following my father, headed out into the snow.

❧

The moment we were outside, my father took my hand and, letting the guards lead the way, stepped through a shimmer that appeared in the courtyard. I caught my breath as the world shifted. Ulean was with me, and she laid a calming kiss of warm breeze on my shoulder.

This is no trick. This is how the Fae often travel. Your body should respond quickly, with your parentage.

And she was correct—within seconds, the vertigo vanished and the movement as we walked through the swirling mists felt almost familiar—like something I'd once known about but had forgotten.

And then we were in the realm of Summer, and the chill of the snow fell away, though something felt amiss. As we passed silently through the trees, along a rich path toward a glade up ahead, I noticed that the leaves were beginning to turn color—a rich shade of bronze. And that should not be. The trees were always a vibrant green here.

Wrath stiffened beside me, and he tugged on my hand, moving us faster as we neither walked nor glided but somehow moved forward through the sparkling vapors that rose around us.

The birds were silent, and in my heart, I knew something was horribly wrong. The birds never stopped singing in Summer's realm. I closed my eyes, praying we weren't too late to prevent whatever it was that was happening.

Up ahead, a barrow stood. It was not the true barrow of Summer, locked in Myst's grasp in the Golden Wood, but a makeshift refuge for a queen and her people who had been ousted from their home. We came to the edge, and the mist vanished and we stood there, in the silent gloom of evening. The chill hit me then—just a slight tang, a presage of autumn—and I knew that Lainule was dying.

Wrath still remained silent, leading me into the barrow. The guards guided us to a chamber toward the back of the spacious hall. The smell of pungent earth held sway in the air, slightly sour and biting. There were Cambyra Fae everywhere, the people of Summer—my father's people, and my own. They stood as one upon our appearance and, as Wrath and I passed, knelt into deep curtsies and bows.

My blood stirred as I looked into their faces, and for once I felt welcome. Praying they did not know I'd been Myst's daughter previously, I smiled gently, trying not to envision the horror they'd been through when Winter had reached out for their land.

The guards stopped outside a chamber. Wrath motioned for me to attend him and entered through the oak-hewn door. The room was large, though not grand, and a bed—high and only reachable by a two-step footstool—stood against one wall. Silk curtains were draped from each corner of the ceiling above the bed, wrapping around the posts that rose a good eight feet from the floor.

The rest of the room was simple, yet elegant. A large armoire. A dressing table. A bath—looking to be made out of smooth tile—sat cordoned off by its own curtain. I wondered what Lainule's chamber had looked like back in the Golden Wood—it must have been grand, and beautiful. Heartsick, I bit my lip.

As we approached the bed, there was a slight movement and a tall, graceful woman stepped from behind one of the curtains. She knelt before Wrath, but before he could greet her, she stood and her eyes were filled with sorrow.

"She is unwell. You know what makes her ill." She sounded resigned, without hope.

Wrath nodded. "She is too far from her heartstone."
The woman glanced at me, but Wrath shook his head. "It is all right. This is my daughter, Cicely Waters. She is half-magic-born, and an owl-shifter like me. She is one of the Cambyra and will be treated as my heir."

I caught my breath. This was the first time that I'd been introduced to anyone—at least more than a nodding glance—and I hadn't expected him to announce he was my father.

"Lady Cicely, welcome." The woman knelt briefly to me, then returned her attention to Wrath. "Your Highness, she must have her heartstone or the Summer will fade."

"The Queen is the heart of Summer, yes, I know." Wrath

fell silent, then walked over to the bed. Two handmaidens drew back the curtains to show the silent form of Lainule stretched beneath a purple and green comforter, her golden hair spread out on the pillows. Her eyes were open, and she turned to look at us, but I could tell she was weak. I knew she had been fading, but for it to have come on so swiftly must mean that Myst was getting closer to finding her heartstone.

Wrath swiftly climbed the steps leading to the high mattress. He sat carefully on the side, the quilted comforter beneath him shifting ever so slightly. He took Lainule's left hand in his own, interlacing her fingers with his, and lifted it gently to his lips, pressing a soft kiss against the pale skin.

Tears caught in my throat. As I watched the tableau, I knew they were speaking but without words. And argument or not, their love broke through their recent spat and Wrath leaned down and gathered her in his arms, pressing his lips to hers.

"You cannot die. The Heart of Summer cannot die." He kissed her again, and she murmured something that I chose not to hear—it was for his ears only. After a moment, my father turned. "Lainule wishes to speak to you, daughter."

I hesitantly crossed the room, holding my breath, trying not to cry. Lainule looked so delicate and fragile in her bed, so unlike the vivacity of summer. The Queen of Rivers and Rushes let out a long sigh, slow, like a breeze through hollow husks, as I approached.

Wrath stood back as I climbed the three wooden steps, hewn in oak, to the side of her bed, and took my place sitting next to her.

"Lainule, can you ever forgive me?" I wasn't sure what I was asking forgiveness for—perhaps for bucking her will, for choosing my own life over the hope that I might be a weapon against Myst.

But her eyelashes fluttered and she looked up at me, motioning me close. I leaned in, my ear next to her lips.

"The only forgiveness necessary is yours. I should never have agreed to Geoffrey's plan. It was madness to work with the Crimson Court. I know that now. Child, I am dying."

And there it was, plain and simple.

"No, you can't die. We need you. Myst cannot be allowed to rule the land. And . . . *I need you.* I don't know how to be one of your people." The words flowed out of my mouth, and I wasn't even sure what I was saying.

She shook her head, just one simple shake. "Your father will teach you. But without my heartstone, I cannot hope to regain my strength. I do not have long before the Summer fades and Winter claims my soul. She is growing dangerously close to my heartstone. I can feel her reaching out her spindly fingers, searching for it."

"She will not have it." I sat back, biting my lip. "Tell me where it is and I will get it. But you have to tell me where to find it."

"The danger is too great—"

"The danger without you is far greater." I leaned close and looked into her eyes. "I am afraid, but I am more afraid of what will happen should Myst be allowed free rein. You must tell me where to find the heartstone." I thought I knew where it was, but it was simpler to just ask and make certain.

Lainule looked past me, at Wrath, who gave her a simple nod.

"Do you understand what you are offering? No, you do not."

"I'm offering to try to save your life."

"No, Cicely. You offer so much more than that—you make a sacrifice if you choose to do this and I cannot tell you just what that is. Not yet."

Stubbornly, I shook my head. "Tell me where to find it."

Her eyes shimmered, and she paused, then finally nodded. "Very well. You must go deep in the woods, to Grandfather Cedar. Grieve and Chatter know where to find it. Once there, seek the portal that lies beneath the tree. You must enter the portal, then follow the path. Beware, it is guarded by creatures of wild and feral nature. You may be forced to kill them unless you can convince them to let you pass. They are there to protect my heartstone from all invaders." Her breath was raspy, and she paused again, fighting for strength.

"I dreamed this! I dreamed I was doing this." A spark of hope caught flame in my heart and I took her hand, forgetting that she was a queen and I the half-breed daughter of her husband.

"Then perhaps it is meant to be."

"Did you and Geoffrey give the Shadow Hunters the antidote to their light-rage?" I prayed for a no. If they hadn't, we could travel with relative safety during the daylight hours.

"No," she said—the first piece of good news I'd had in a long time. "We disagreed and I destroyed the antidote and all the notes in my temper. And I staked the vampire who knew how to prepare it."

Somehow, imagining the Queen of Summer staking a vampire brought horrible images to mind. But I was grateful to whatever had stirred her wrath.

She opened her lips—now chapped and bleeding—and whispered, "Then go, my child. Seek my heartstone and bring it back to me, if you can. But Cicely—I don't think you realize what this will set into motion. Are you prepared to take the burden of saving my life on your shoulders? It will foreshadow so many changes that might not come to be otherwise. When you save a life, you bear its burdens for the remainder of your days."

My breath caught in my throat. I could feel the immensity of her words looming around us, a curse, a blessing, a prediction. "Yes, I will accept whatever consequences come from this."

"Then go, and the gods speed you. If you can recover my heartstone, I might be able to rise against Myst and push back the snows for a time. My people will go to war for me, if I rouse them. I hoped to avoid this—we've lost so many, but the choices dwindle, and hope now rides at the tip of a sword." With that, she closed her eyes and for a moment, I feared she was already dead. But then she coughed and murmured in her sleep.

Wrath kissed her on the forehead and led me away, his face impervious and unreadable. As we exited her chamber, he turned to me.

"I cannot go with you—the Consort of the Queen may never lay hands upon her heartstone. But Chatter and Grieve will make the journey, and Kaylin."

I didn't want to say it aloud, but I knew that I also needed Rhiannon. She had to go with us. Wrath would try to nix the idea, but in my heart, it was clear that she had to be there. So I kept my mouth shut, nodded, and followed him back into the snowy night.

We were back at the warehouse within the hour. I blinked—it felt like we'd been gone all night, but then time had little meaning within the barrows and realms of the Fae. We gathered around the table and filled everyone in on what was happening. Lannan was still out hunting, which might be a good thing, considering his mood and what we were discussing.

Grieve looked shaken. "I will go, of course. If the Queen of Rivers and Rushes needs me, I will do whatever she requires. But is it wise to have me revisit Myst's domain? She might sense me."

"Then so be it. You must be there. Chatter, too. Kaylin . . . and Rhiannon." I turned to my cousin. "I would not ask you to go, but I had a dream and in it we were searching for the heartstone. And you were with us."

Wrath started to protest, but I shook my head.

"No, she needs to go. This much I know. And we must leave at daybreak. The Vampiric Fae weren't given the antidote Grieve took—Lainule grew furious at Geoffrey over something—I don't know what—and she destroyed what was left of it. So we'll be able to journey during the light without too much worry."

"What about the Consortium? Can't we wait for them?" Rex asked.

I tipped my head to one side, considering. "Lainule is on her deathbed. We must regain the heartstone in order for her to survive. And if she dies . . ." I paused, not really knowing what to say after that. I turned to my father. "What *does* happen when a Fae Queen dies?"

He let out a shuddering breath and I realized how hard the question must be on him. "Then the heirs are run through a gauntlet of tests to determine who will take her place. If there is only one heir, she will inherit the throne without contest."

"Do you and Lainule have any children? I know Grieve is a prince—"

Grieve cleared his throat. "Yes, I am a prince, but I would not inherit the throne, even though I am a relative of Lainule and Wrath. There must be a queen before there can be a king, and he may come from outside the bloodline of nobility. But a princess must bear the blood of the Queen in her veins or her soul. And there *must* be a queen. The King cannot rule alone. If Lainule dies—"

Wrath interrupted. "What Grieve is dancing around is that if my Lady passes over the veil, then I will abdicate to a new queen and her choice of consort." He smiled, his face crinkling with the bare beginnings of crow's feet. "It is all right, Grieve. You may tell the truth without worry I will take offense. This is the way of the law, this is the way of our people."

I stood, staring at my father. "If Lainule dies, then you—"

"Will relinquish my crown and fade through the veil to be with my Lady." He smiled at me. "But take heart, my daughter. You will go tomorrow and do what you can to save your stepmother. And we will cross other bridges when we come to them, should they arise."

I hung my head, wanting to cry. Both my father and Grieve moved forward, but Grieve was at my side first and I leaned into his embrace, tears streaming down my cheeks. I couldn't hold it in any longer—the stress and the fear and the loss hit me as my walls crumbled. I held tight to him, weeping as he pulled me to his chest.

"I love you, Cicely. I love you and I'm here with you. Hold on to me. I am your love. I am your anchor and rock. I will keep you steady." His voice was low, purring in my ear like soothing music, and as I buried myself in his embrace, the smell of apples and pumpkins, of cinnamon and dust, and the rains of autumn swept over me. My love was caught between the summer and the winter—in the limbo of autumn, unable to return to his own world and unwilling to embrace the realm that had claimed him.

"I love you. I love you and I can't imagine being without you ever again." I found his lips, fire building in my stomach as I sought comfort in his kiss. "You will never belong to Myst again—I will never allow it. You are mine. You are my heart, my soul, my passion, my mate."

Grieve swept me up in his arms. I looked up through streaming eyes as he challenged my father to stop him. Wrath stepped aside without a word as Grieve carried me into the bedroom and shut the door behind us.

All thoughts of who might be listening flew to the window as he laid me down on the mattresses, unbuttoning my shirt as I reached for the zipper on my jeans. Grieve gently removed my hand and slowly unzipped them himself, all the while staring into my eyes with his starry gaze. The depths of his onyx gaze swirled with stardust, and I felt myself falling deep into his core.

"Cicely, my Cicely." He leaned down and was free of clothes, his bare chest pressing against my breasts. I shifted and he unhooked my bra, and then hooked his fingers through the sides of my panties and slid them off.

I sat up, still crying, staring at him. He was gorgeous, my love was, his platinum hair streaming down his back, his olive skin glimmering in the low light of the candle. With one hand, I reached out and slid my fingers along his arm, slowly tracing his muscles up to rest my hand on his shoulder.

He lightly brushed one hand against my breasts, caressing the nipples, his fingers tripping over my skin, setting off a series of explosions deep within me that grew like a chain of firecrackers. I gasped as he wrapped his arm around my waist and bent me back, leaning between my knees, his lips covering mine, tongue probing deep, searching for solace.

I closed my eyes, drifting in his kiss, soaking in his love

and warmth as he reached down with his other hand to stroke me. The feel of his erection against my thigh made me spread my legs wider, the hunger within me growing. Everything paled compared to the need to feel him moving inside me, possessing me.

"Love me. Take me, my Prince." I opened my eyes. "Myst will never possess your heart, even if she rips us to shreds."

"She never did possess it, though she tried to claim me. It's always been you, Cicely—when I met you, so many eons ago, I knew that you would be mine. Everyone told me you were the enemy, but in my heart, I knew that if I could not be with you, I'd rather be dead." He bit his lip, moaning as he plunged deep within me, his strokes long and hard. "I will not share you."

The feel of him thrusting within me, of his body sliding against mine as he rode me, spiraled me higher. The soft cries of his passion mingled with mine, and then *a flash* . . . and the world and its cares fell away . . .

❧

I was standing on a hill, under the night sky, feeling the wind brush my cheek. The storm had been fierce and all I could think about was the scent of the rain-soaked cedars and mossy dell, and the fire in my belly as the hunger raced through me and the urge to hunt grew. The moon broke through the clouds, and I dropped my head back. I was Cherish, daughter of Myst, and the world was my banquet, a feast of blood and flesh and desire.

A noise to my left, coming through the woods, alerted me, and I quickly hid behind the nearest tree. With luck, it would be an unwary hunter coming through. The natives of the land were in tune with the woodland, but they had never encountered us before. My mother had recently moved us to the new land, leaving pockets of our people behind. Gone were the peasants and castles and soldiers and cities. Instead, here, the people were few but game plentiful, and there was room for us to spread and begin to expand our colony.

We bred slowly—my mother had had only two daughters, and I was the only one who survived. But we were gaining in numbers, and Myst explained to me that our natures were evolving as the mingling of the vampire blood took hold with the Unseelie lineage. We'd been driven from our home by the untainted dark ones and so had sought a new land in which to live according to our nature.

The sound caught my attention again—someone was walking along the path. I waited, biding my time, until he was near enough to catch. I could smell him—definitely male, although he smelled like sweetgrass and apples, hay and summer days, not like buckskin and hides.

I leaped out, triumphant, my fangs gleaming in the moonlight. And then—there was a moment when the world fell away, and I found myself staring instead of feasting. He was tall, with olive skin, and long gleaming hair. His eyes were shimmering topaz, and he cocked his head, looking at me.

Feast, you fool. Feast. You can take him down. The voice in my head urged me on, but still I stood there, unsure what possessed me.

"Well, are you going to kill me or not?" His voice was smooth, coiling over the words like a snake.

"I . . . I . . ." Unprepared for his easy manner, for the lack of care, I stepped back, tilting my head to squint at him. He was no native, that was apparent. And then I knew: He was of Summer's descent. Unlike the Seelie from back home, he belonged fully to this land. But the scent of summer's breath wafted off him like a beckoning finger, both enticing and irritating.

I knew who he was then. My mother had done her research. "You are the Summer Prince. Your name is Shy, and you belong to Lainule's realm. Run now, while you can, Summer's child, or I will devour you."

He laughed, and his voice beckoned me forward. Suspicious, angry, I lowered my head, staring at him through the fringe of my lashes.

"I am indeed Shy of the Summer's realm. I am Summer's bear-child."

"You should not laugh—do not laugh at me! Do you

know what danger you're in?" I should just have at him, get it over with, destroy the prince of our enemy and be done with it. But something stayed my hand.

Shy's lips crinkled as he smiled. "Oh, I've heard tales of you. Cherish, the gem of the Winter Court. You are of the Indigo Fae—the Tainted Ones. We know well of you, beautiful enemy. We know of your charms and powers. Tell me again, why should I run? Do you really think you can destroy me?" And his voice was honey on the night breeze.

A wash of roses glided by on the wind and I caught myself falling under their spell. Mingled with a faint taste of apricots and the sound of the rushing river, they made me want to tear off my gown and go running through the field, naked, letting the moonbeams bathe me under the wild night.

I tried to tear myself out of the trance, but something held me firm, and then I realized that it was Shy—he had hold of me and I couldn't free myself. I bared my teeth, but the feel of his skin against mine set me aflame in a way I'd never before felt. I gasped, shivering as the fire raced through my belly, Summer's touch sparking feelings I'd only heard of.

"No," I gasped out, but my hands were no longer pounding against his chest but racing over his skin. "No . . ." He pressed against me, hard and demanding, and my body—so long used only as a weapon—became pliant, responding. "No . . ." My breath came in ragged pants as he fisted my hair and laughed low.

"Cherish, the gem of Winter, what say you to the scepter of Summer? Will you bend? Will you fight? Will you yield? Will you . . ." He stopped then as our gazes locked, and within that moment, a lifetime of knowledge passed between us, and my will to fight—my will to destroy—faded like cloth left out in the sun too long.

"Cherish . . ." The triumph was gone. He stood back, letting me go, staring at me, fear and bewilderment crowding his expression.

I could have destroyed him then. I knew it, I could have

ripped out his throat and taken him down, devoured him. But I was as trapped in the spell as he. I searched my memory, trying to decipher what emotions were playing on my senses. I'd never felt like this before, never wanted someone this way. Never wanted to . . . spare anyone. I'd killed hundreds of people over the years, and never once had I questioned what I was doing.

"Shy . . ." My voice was shaking, and I began to tremble and then cry. "What's happening to me? What's this feeling? I don't want this!"

But he stepped forward again, slowly this time, and held out his arms. "Cherish?" It was a question, no longer a demand, and try as I might, I could not resist answering. I stepped into his embrace and he pressed his lips against mine, his tongue seeking mine, his arms holding me tightly.

As our lips met, the world shifted, and we were bound, and I knew then I was forever lost. The gem of Winter had fallen into Summer's hands, and the only thing I knew was that we had both sealed our doom with a kiss. A kiss that I would willingly die for.

Chapter 8

As Grieve and I fell back, his fingers stroking my hair, his razor-sharp teeth and fangs shimmering in the dim light, I came out of my flashback. A noise startled me into realizing that someone was knocking on the door. I wanted to talk to Grieve, to see if he remembered our first meeting as Shy and Cherish the same way I did, but there was no time. I pulled a robe around me as he shifted into clothing again and answered the knock. It was Rhiannon.

She peeked in, blushing lightly, but she merely said, "Lannan's back and boy does he have news. You'd better come out now."

If Lannan said he had news, it was probably important. I scrambled into my clothing. Grieve pulled me into his arms.

"I know, Cicely."

"Know what?"

"I know what happened during the blood fever. Chatter told me."

Damn it! Grieve had known I'd had to drink from Lannan, but I'd kept from him that I'd almost fucked the vampire. The blood fever had held me in thrall and I'd opened myself to him. He'd been barely inside me when the others found us. Ever since then, my body had responded to Lannan in a magnetic way and I knew that it had something to do with drinking his blood, but there had been no choice. Crawl, the Oracle of the Crimson Court, had almost drained me, dragging me into the shadow realm, and only Lannan's blood had saved me.

"Chatter *told* you?" I was going to throttle him.

Grieve smiled, faintly. "He felt it better I know than find out from Lannan. I understand why it happened. I hate the thought, but I understand that if you're ever in that predicament again, it may well have to happen again. But if he hurts you—I will destroy him." The smile left his face.

I paused, not knowing what to say. "I cannot help that my body responds to him, but my heart resists. I can't stand his touch, yet when he puts his hands on me . . . But know this, my love, I will never willingly walk into his embrace. I will never jump into his bed—not by choice. The blood fever—there was no choice. It's like . . ."

"It's like the hunger I feel since Myst turned me," he whispered softly. "This is why I say what I do. I truly do understand. I resist my nature, but if Myst were to appear here, in front of me, the will to disobey would be hard-pressed. So yes, my love, we both are ruled by compulsions stronger than us, yet we fight against them." His lips sought mine and I sank into his kiss, again, floating on the waves that rippled between us.

After a moment, he let me go. "We'd better join the others."

I stood back, letting him lead the way, loving him more than ever.

⚜

Lannan was sitting at the table, leaning back in his chair, looking vaguely amused as we appeared from the doorway. I steeled myself for some snarky comment, but he just nodded for us to sit down.

Without preamble, he said, "Regina has removed Geoffrey as Regent."

We all stared at him; the announcement was out of the blue. Totally unexpected. Regina, Lannan's twin sister and lover, and the Emissary to the Crimson Court, was a scary-ass vampire who gave new meaning to the concept of Type-A personality. She was ruthless and controlled more by her head than her lusts, which was the exact opposite of Lannan. But this was going to extremes, even for her.

"You don't believe in small talk, do you?" I wasn't sure what to say, although a slew of questions flooded my brain. Was Geoffrey dead? Well, of course he was dead, but for good? What the fuck had happened?

Lannan let out a low chuckle. "Small talk is for small minds. Yes, it's true. Poor Geoffrey is no longer Regent, effective immediately. I will serve in his place on a temporary basis." He stood up, a feral grin spreading across his face. "I am now Regent. All of Geoffrey's contracts revert to me. *Including yours.* You now serve me directly." He caught my gaze, challenging me.

Oh fuck. I stared at him, a wave of panic starting to crest through my chest. According to Ysandra, my contract with the vampires held sway. No court in the land would deny its validity. Meaning I was walking a very slippery slope now that Lannan Altos was my master. And it was obvious, he was enjoying my discomfort. This was not the time to mouth off to him.

"Nothing to say, my lovely Cicely?" He was baiting me. I could feel it in his tone. Trying to goad me into something stupid.

Everyone waited for me to respond. I could feel all eyes on me, waiting. Shaking my head, I fumbled for something to say. Finally, I found my tongue. "Congratulations, Lannan. Please, tell us what happened. Where did Geoffrey go to? Obviously, he took Leo with him. And did he try to hurt Regina like he threatened?"

"Such *concern* for my sister. She'll be touched you inquired." Said with a hint of sarcasm. Then, "Geoffrey would be tortured by the Queen if he touched one hair of my sister's head and he *should* know that, but I could not chance that he'd gone insane and would carry through the threat. Which is why I left when he ordered me to do so."

He leaned forward then, pushing up the sleeves of his casual jacket. His arms were scarred, ancient scars that told me Lannan had seen many battles before his mother turned him into a vampire. He noticed my gaze and slowly winked at me. Flustered, I turned my head.

"My sister found out when Geoffrey ordered that my stable be integrated into his. Regina shares my blood-whores and did not take kindly to the thought. She confronted him. He told her that I'd chosen to leave, that I had—perish the thought—fallen for you and that I stormed out when you did. My sister is no fool. She went to Lainule, found out the truth of why I left, and went to the Crimson Queen. And if there's one thing our Queen does not look kindly upon, it's traitorous activity."

The thought of being on the wrong side of the Vampire Queen's wrath was almost enough to make me feel sorry for Geoffrey. *Almost.* Again, a wave of anger swept over me. I'd actually come close to liking the vampire. He'd seemed the most levelheaded of them all, but in this town, in the world I lived in, nothing was as it seemed. Betrayal hid under the guise of friendship, and aid manifested through the hands of the enemy.

"What did the Queen do?" Peyton asked, before I could get to the question.

"It seems the Crimson Court immediately revoked Geoffrey's status as Regent and told my sister to take a contingent of guards and remove him from office. If he resisted, they were to crucify him under the open sky, where, at daybreak, he would fry like a fish, impaled on a harpoon." Lannan snorted and the cold joy in his voice left me chilled through.

You'd do well to remember that Lannan is not your friend, nor anyone else's friend. He may be an ally, but never forget what he is: a vampire, a predator who is older than the castles of Europe and who feels no remorse for anything he does.

Ulean's words rang through me like a silver bell—clear

and alarming. Lannan was no simple hedonist. And I'd better play my cards right, now that he actually did hold the title of master over me.

"I suppose some of his loyal followers found out, because by the time Regina and the guards reached Geoffrey's mansion, he was gone, along with Leo and a number of guards." Lannan shrugged. "This all happened in the past two days."

"Then the day-runners we killed this morning—"

"Were loyal to both Geoffrey and Leo. They must have sent them from their hiding place." Lannan cocked his head, a knowing smile on his lips. "Which means . . . come now, Cicely, you can figure it out."

I knew what he was hinting around at. "Which means that the one we have tied up in the other room can lead us to where they are."

"That's my girl." Lannan stood, crossing his arms. "Our plan is simple: We get to them before they get to us. Geoffrey is no longer welcome in the Court. No one will blink if a certain warlord disappears off the face of the planet. And mark you—we'd best destroy him because he *will* seek to destroy us. Now his only hope is to harness Myst's people for his own, and he can't do so with her at the helm. If he captures you and turns you as was his original plan, you will take the place of your long-distant mother. But this time he intends to keep control."

I shuddered. "I'll slit my own wrists before I let him do that to me."

"Make no mistake, Geoffrey is cunning and wise. You are no match against his wits. And should you believe otherwise . . . Cicely, you think I'd make a vicious and deadly lover, but be advised that Geoffrey's attentions are not without their own perversions. I lent several of my stable to him before I realized they were coming back traumatized and maimed."

I blinked. For Lannan to call someone perverted was a terrifying thought, considering his own nature. "We have to talk to Erik again, before they figure out we killed their posse."

"Being that it's past nightfall, I guarantee you, they've already figured that out." But Lannan motioned for us to bring the man in.

Grieve and Chatter rose and, without a word, retrieved our prisoner, holding his bound arms between them. They thrust him into a chair, none too gently. Chatter looked at Grieve. Grieve nodded, and stood back, his form blurring as he shifted into his wolf form. Baring his teeth, with a low growl, he posed, ready to leap at Erik. Chatter released the gag from the day-runner's mouth.

I sucked in a low breath. They weren't kidding around. But then, with Geoffrey and Leo on our asses, we couldn't afford to play nice.

"We know what happened with Geoffrey. We know that he and Leo are off on their own, and we know why you're trying to kidnap me as well as Rhiannon. You have a chance to make this right. You have a chance to live." I wasn't sure I could promise that, but we had to get him to talk.

He shook his head. "I'm not stupid. I know I'm not getting out of here alive. I'd switch sides, but you'd never trust me. Would you, Rio?" He glanced over at Rhiannon, who paled.

"I don't know. You were Leo's friend. He's a vampire. and if you asked him, he could help you far more now than he could before. But then again . . . you never expressed an interest in being a vamp, did you?"

Lannan waved his hand at her. "Move. I can take care of this."

Rhia backed away without a word. Lannan knelt down, staring into Erik's face for a long moment. Erik tried to look away, but Chatter reached out and held his head steady. I could feel Lannan's glamour weaving around the man. He could force his will on Erik and he had no compunction against doing so.

"Talk to me, Erik. You will tell me the truth. You cannot lie to me, and if you try, I will drain you down and bleed you out slowly and painfully so that you beg for death." Lannan's voice wove sinuously through the room and my hand fluttered to my throat. "Do you understand?"

My wolf shivered. I looked at Grieve, who was watching me, still in wolf form. His eyes were glittering, fastened on me, and I knew he could feel the response that Lannan's command stirred in me.

Erik's eyes fluttered, and I could tell he was resisting. I knew that look, I'd been there before.

With a shudder, Erik croaked out, "Yes, I understand."

Lannan laughed, then glanced at me, and licked his lips. In that instant, I could feel his energy wrap around me like a snake, sliding up my body. I struggled for control. I couldn't let Grieve see what Lannan could do to me. He knew, but knowing was not the same thing as having your nose rubbed in it.

"Very good, my little pecker." Lannan returned his attention to Erik. "So tell me, Erik, and remember—no lying. Where are Leo and Geoffrey hiding?" His fingers stroked Erik's chin.

With a shudder and a look of revulsion on his face, Erik stammered out his reply. "They are hiding in the basement of Inley."

Lannan startled. He frowned. "Did Icarus give them permission?"

Erik nodded. "Yes, for a price. Geoffrey has to bring him fresh bloodwhores. Ten of them over the next year."

Nodding, the vampire stood up. He gave Erik a considered look and then, without warning, jerked his head to the side. We could hear the cracking of bones as Erik slumped in his chair. Rhiannon gave out a choked cry, turning away. I stared in horror as Grieve transformed back.

But Rex nodded. "You did what was necessary."

"I do not need your approval, werepuma, but yes, I did." Lannan looked over at me, his eyes no longer filled with sensual fire but instead aloof and determined. "He betrayed Geoffrey. He would have betrayed us."

Unfortunately, he was right. We could never have trusted Erik not to give us away. Instead of letting the horror of the situation paralyze me, I chose to focus on what we'd learned.

"What's Inley? And who is Icarus?"

Lannan wiped his hands on a handkerchief and turned, Erik forgotten. "Inley is an underground club for vampires and fang hags. Icarus is the vampire who runs it. It is not a place to enter without an escort if you are still breathing." He cocked his head to one side. "I am not surprised Icarus is hiding Geoffrey. He always did have a streak of rebellion in him."

"As Regent, can't you demand he hand over Geoffrey?" Peyton startled us all. She seldom spoke to Lannan, and it was obvious she disdained the vampire.

Lannan swung to look at her. "Astute but not well versed in the ways of vampire politics. Trust me, if I were to walk in there demanding he give me Geoffrey, it would be as if the former Regent never existed. There would be no evidence that he had ever set foot in the place. No, we'll have to plan this very carefully, especially since Icarus technically isn't doing anything against the Crimson Court's edict. Pity I can't go in disguise with you as my bloodwhore."

My stomach lurched. "Me?"

"Yes, *you*. I think I'd rather enjoy that little scenario. You all decked out in skin-tight PVC, looking oh so afraid." Lannan flashed me a nasty look. Damn him, he was doing his best to pay me back for . . . for whatever slight he thought I'd given him this time.

I shuddered. "I'd rather think of another idea, thanks."

"If I chose to do this, you would be obligated to join me. Your contract belongs to me." His eyes gleamed and he leaned back. Cat and mouse. And I was the mouse. "But are you a good enough actress to play the part? Unless I put you under a compulsion . . ." His voice snaked over the words and I stumbled back.

"No!" I could feel Grieve stir, turning on Lannan. I had to diffuse the situation. Having both of them under the same roof meant we were living in a powder keg.

I stopped as he slapped his thigh and started to laugh. I wasn't sure whether that was more disconcerting than when he was being all slinky-feely. "No? More's the pity. But I thought that would be your answer. It was amusing enough to watch your face. No, I believe we will deal with

Geoffrey in a different way. However, tomorrow you will all move into Geoffrey's mansion—mine now—with me. And that *is* an order."

"Are you insane?" Kaylin leaped to his feet. "We're safe here."

"Really? You were almost taken out by day-runners this morning who had very nasty weapons that go *boom*. How much safer can you be than in a mansion filled with vampires?"

I wanted to protest, but he had a point. A valid one. Arguing was useless. I turned to the others. "I don't like it, but he's probably right. But it will have to be in a couple of days. We go into the woods tomorrow." I drew my shoulders back. After tomorrow maybe we wouldn't be relying on Lannan as much. If we could find the heartstone, then Lainule would be restored and we'd have her back on our side.

Lannan held my gaze, then inclined his head. "As you wish. But yes, you will move in with me. Even your cur of a boyfriend."

Grieve folded his arms. "Altos, I warn you: Cicely is mine. I am fighting against my nature, but if you push me, I'll let the Shadow Hunter inside me loose. And I could wipe the floor with you and swallow the shreds. I've been biding my time, but now I will speak. I cannot prevent you from tormenting her. *Not yet.* But touch her unwilling and I will have your heart on a plate for lunch."

Lannan's nostrils flared and at first I expected him to laugh, but his expression grew hard and he tensed. "Wounded, broken, and yet you challenge me. How very noble. How very dangerous."

"Broken, I may be, but I am quite able to fight, able to kill, and more than willing to do either if the circumstances arise. You know my nature—if I unleash it, you would stand *no chance*. Trust me, Altos, it is *you* who are in danger. I have remained in the background, too aware of how easily I can be goaded into the violence that lurks inside of me. But one touch—if you touch any of these women when they say no—I will rip your heart out and revel in doing so."

I stared at Grieve, my heart racing. He seemed taller,

stronger, and I had the feeling something was changing with him. He turned to me, holding out his arm, and I slid into his embrace.

"My love, we must coexist." I turned to Lannan. "It's bad enough that we're battling Myst, but this infighting is going to kill us faster than she will. You know I'm in love with Grieve. You know you won't ever willingly have me. Yet you persist in baiting us." I was exhausted, too tired to think straight anymore.

Grieve reached for me, but I motioned him back. "Enough. Lannan, please, I'm swallowing my pride here. Please just let it be. You'll have your blood tithe every month—I stand by my word and my promise on the contract. But for the sake of sanity, give us a break." I glanced back at Grieve. "And you, my love, I ask the same . . . I love that you want to protect me, but right now all our lives are up for grabs."

Lannan's expression was cold, but after a moment, he said, "I offer the safety of my mansion. I will not require it of the rest of you, but truly, Cicely, you should take refuge with me. You'll be safer there. Geoffrey is not likely to let this affront go without looking for a scapegoat and no doubt, you—as well as I—will be the main targets of his animosity."

He glanced at the others, turned, and headed toward the door. "I must return to the mansion to sort out the mess Geoffrey left in his flight." He paused, looking back, and for a moment, a look of regret swept over his face. "I do not wish to be Regent, but what the Crimson Queen decrees, I shall obey. My sister will send for your things tomorrow night, Cicely. If the rest of you choose not to accept my offer, so be it. But for Cicely, it is an order—as per your contract. You will check in by nine tomorrow night." And with that, he vanished out the door.

I stared at the others. "So, Lannan is now Regent, Geoffrey and Leo are in cahoots and out to get us. As much as I hate to admit it, Lannan is right. We'd be safer in the mansion. At least from Myst."

Grieve cleared his throat and I expected him to argue

but he merely said, "The vampires can protect us better than we can protect ourselves in this place. It's been a good hideout, but we need a true headquarters."

I crooked my elbow around his. "We'll go. But first . . . I have to see if we can find Lainule's heartstone. If we can, that may change everything. This is not a stable game, built on foundations and rules. The stakes are ever-changing and we have to be as flexible as a reed in the wind."

My father, who had insisted on staying with me, even though I told him to go to Lainule's side, nodded. "If you stay in the mansion, I will return to Lainule's side. Truthfully, that is where I belong. But I cannot leave you unattended here."

It hurt to think he was taking himself away from Lainule just in order to protect me. "I'll go. You belong by her side."

Rhiannon stood. "It's late. We've all had a long, hard day. Let's get some sleep. If we're headed out to find the heartstone tomorrow, we'll need all the rest we can get."

"So you will come?" I gazed up at her, marveling at the quiet strength she'd been showing through all of this.

"Of course. Remember? We're fire and ice, amber and jet. We're cousin-twins. Where you go, so will I." And with that, she headed toward the bedroom. Chatter watched her, wearing his heart on his sleeve.

Peyton, Luna, and I stood, and after murmuring quiet "good nights," we followed her. The night winds howled outside the warehouse, and I closed my eyes, wondering just what the hell we were heading into tomorrow.

Whatever lay ahead of us couldn't be much worse than what we'd already been through. And maybe, just maybe, we'd be back on the offensive again instead of playing with a wounded defense.

Chapter 9

At first light, when we were sure the light-rage had hit and driven all but the most resilient of the Vampiric Fae into a comatose stupor, it was time to head out. Everyone volunteered to go, but we couldn't all go traipsing through the woods. Too many bodies attracted too much attention.

"Rhiannon, Chatter, Grieve. You come with me. Also . . . Kaylin. Peyton, you and Rex and Luna gather our things so we can move into Lannan's mansion." Before there could be any protests, I held up my hand. "I know, but we're going. I have to and I'm not going alone."

I so did not want to live under Lannan's roof, but it was for the best. And I had my orders. Lannan would not brook outright disobedience. I'd better do as he said.

Another thought occurred to me. "With both the Shadow Hunters and the vampires down for the day, you might take a drive by the Veil House and see what's going on over there. Maybe look around for anything else we can salvage. Especially since Ysandra said we can probably get a loan to fix the damage."

Luna's phone rang and she answered. After a moment, she hung up and clapped her hands. "My sister will be here this afternoon at two P.M. Zoey thinks she's found something that may help us."

"Where do you have to pick her up?"

She shook her head. "She will find me. She always does. I have no clue how the Akazzani travel, but it's not like we do."

Kaylin looked concerned and motioned me to the side. "I don't like leaving them alone."

"You think they're in danger? The vampires are sleeping and Myst's people are down with the light-rage."

"True, but remember—Leo and Geoffrey sent day-runners to kidnap you and Rhiannon yesterday. Don't you think they might have been more than a little upset when the men didn't return last night? My guess is that they've already assigned somebody else to find out what happened to their little assassination brigade." He leaned against the table, his jeans tight and form-fitting.

I glanced over at Luna. She was watching him out of the corner of her eye. She looked nervous, and vulnerable. And chances are, her sister wasn't geared to fight—Akazzani or not.

Turning to my father, I said, "Kaylin makes a good point. If the day-runners found us yesterday, we should assume that more may be coming to look for us today. And most of us will be off after the heartstone. Can you take them with you? Will it be an affront if you take them into the realm of Summer?"

I wasn't sure how the Fae would take to Rex, especially, because Weres weren't always buddy-buddy with the Fae, but that was the only thing I could think of. They could go to Lannan's mansion but I wasn't comfortable with that until Lannan and Regina woke.

Wrath stared at the three of them. "We don't often welcome strangers into our realm, but in this case I think we might make an exception." He motioned to Luna. "The three of you will accompany me and obey my directives while we are there. Certain rules of etiquette for non-Cambyra apply and you must obey them."

"What about my sister? She won't be able to find me if

I'm in the realm of Summer." Luna began gathering up spell components and stashing them in a bag.

"If she can find you without directions, as you say she can, then we'll wait outside the entrance to the portal this afternoon. Text her to tell her our plans. That way she'll be able to home in on you when it's time, and then we can take her back into Summer with us." He turned to me. "You are sure you wish to risk this? Remember what my Lady said: You do this, and it forever will change your life, and the lives of those around you."

I closed my eyes, searching the slipstream for any hint of what was to come. But it was silent and offered no answers. The only sounds I could hear were the the the gentle movements of Ulean swishing around me. Slowly, I nodded.

"It's Lainule's only hope. I made a promise. I intend to keep it." I turned to look over our supplies. We were taking backpacks with food, water, weapons, and a velvet box in which to put the heartstone, should we find it. "Let's get dressed and head out."

We dressed in layers and then slipped the packs on our backs. I strapped my fan around my wrist, and my moonstone pendant that helped me turn into an owl was hanging around my neck. I was almost to the point where I didn't need it, but it still gave me comfort and a little boost. Lastly, I slipped the dagger my father had given me into my belt sheath, and a shorter blade into a sheath on my boot.

"We really need obsidian weapons—they affect the Shadow Hunters far more than silver or steel." It had occurred to me that if we were all equipped with obsidian blades, it would make fighting Myst's army much easier.

"Obsidian?" Rex looked up from where he was packing a bag. "If we can find a chunk of raw obsidian, I can make us all blades. I'm good at flint knapping. It takes some time, though."

Wrath cleared his throat. "Cicely, we agreed that you would leave the blade alone."

I let out a long sigh. "I know, but I'm rethinking that plan. The Vampiric Fae are especially susceptible to wounds made with obsidian, even though they use the blades. It seems that obsidian is entwined with their nature. I know what it does to me, Wrath, and I'm willing to chance it. I have to learn how to master the power so that it can't possess me, so I can use it."

Holding his gaze, I didn't want to defy him. "I won't take it with me this time, but when I come back . . ."

"You choose a dangerous path. You are no longer one of Myst's people. You are part Cambyra and part magic-born this lifetime. But the blade responds to the memories in your soul. Who knows what long-term use will do to you?" My father crossed his arms. "You will act as you choose, of course, but I have a feeling this can only lead to tragedy."

"I have to take that chance. But we can discuss this after we return. We'd better get moving. It's almost eight, and we have a long journey. Considering what happened last time we went down the rabbit hole, we may be home in a few hours or a few days. If I don't return tonight, go to Lannan's and tell him that we're on a mission for Lainule."

I slowly approached my father. "We'll do our best," I whispered as I wrapped my arms around his neck, hugging him. He squeezed me tight and kissed the top of my head, and as I looked up into his face, I saw the worry carved in the faint lines under his eyes.

"Be safe, my daughter. Come back to me. I rather enjoy being a father." And his eyes crinkled with a smile, even as he frowned.

Stepping back, I turned to Peyton. "Are you ready?"

She nodded. She was driving us to the woods, and we'd call her when we returned. Without another word, we headed out the door. Lainule's life . . . or her death . . . rested in our hands. I intended to return with her salvation, even if everything in my world had to change because of it.

⚹

Once again, we stood at the edge of the woods, though it was an area we had not yet been to. It was a good three miles up the road from where we'd begun our journey to the Bat People. Now, on another mission of life and death, we were facing even higher snowbanks than before. Myst's infernal winter was raising havoc with its blinding storms and ever-chilling temperatures.

Last time, it had been Peyton, Chatter, and me. This time we were five going in, and Peyton reluctantly drove away, leaving us on the side of the road. I waved, wishing she could come with us. She had a good head on her shoulders and a strong back, and the puma inside her was a formidable foe.

"Are we ready?" Grieve looked ill at ease.

"Are you sure you're up for this?" I gauged his energy, trying to read what he was feeling. *Ulean, how is he? Are we too close to Myst for him to accompany us? Will he be all right?*

I cannot say for sure, but he seems stable and willing. You dreamed him there, with you. I think he should go, but keep alert should Myst's pull draw his vampiric nature to the surface.

I sucked in a deep breath and scanned the woodland in front of us. Thick with conifers heavy with snow and large rounded mounds that had to be the undergrowth, the forest was unnaturally silent and eerie. I listened for any sign or sound from bird or animal, but all was quiet save for the hushed fall of the snow as it whirled down around us.

The eternal winter . . . *Fimbulvetr, the winter of winters.* Some believed it would presage the beginning of Ragnarök, the destruction of the gods. Looking around us, I could well believe that.

Turning to the others, I motioned for them to follow me, and began to break a trail through the snow. It was rough going at first, but then we came to a place where the snow had reached three to four feet high, and the crust had iced over. It was hard enough to walk on if we were careful. I dragged myself up onto the sparkling surface and set off, following the map that Wrath had sketched out for us after we'd returned from Lainule's side.

We made good time, walking on the surface of the snow for over an hour without a single sign of a Shadow Hunter, until we came to the edge of a ravine, leading down into a gully where a creek had iced over. According to the directions, we were to head down the side of the hill, then follow the stream for a little over two miles until we came to a wide open glade. There we'd turn right.

The ravine was steep and though it was covered in snow, I knew all too well how many brambles hid beneath the blanket of white, and they had very sharp, very long and hardened thorns. There were also plenty of potholes in which to turn an ankle, and rocks on which to slip.

Glancing at the others, I stepped aside, and Grieve and Chatter quietly took the forefront. This was their wood—they knew it like they knew the back of their hands. Rhiannon and I would follow, and Kaylin would bring up the rear.

Grieve dropped his head back and sucked in a lungful of the icy air. A look of sorrow crossed his face, but he said nothing, simply danced over the edge of the ravine. For him, the snow was no hindrance. He had Myst's blood in his veins—even though he hadn't been born to the Indigo Court, drinking from her had given him enough powers to endure the winter she wore like a cloak.

Chatter followed as gracefully as Grieve but a little slower.

My turn. I plunged over the side, immediately wishing I'd stopped to pick up a walking stick. I cast around, looking for anything that would help me balance. Chatter glanced over his shoulder, saw that I'd already stalled out, and quietly whispered to Grieve, who motioned for me to stay put. I waited as they hunted through the tangle of brush and eventually returned with sturdy branches for Rhiannon, Kaylin, and myself. Then, with the added balance from my handy-dandy walking stick, I took another stab at hiking over the edge.

The slope was steep, and the going rough. I stumbled more than once, plowing through the vegetation covered with snow, tripping on hidden roots and rocks, but I was managing the traverse.

Once I went down hard onto hands and knees, my chin bruising as I slammed it against a fist-sized rock. Wincing from the pain, I let Chatter help me up. Grieve watched, a worried expression on his face, but I just wiped away the dribble of blood from the cut and shook my head.

We moved in silence, a chain of figures silhouetted against the hush of the winter landscape. Rhiannon slipped twice, but she landed on her butt, managing not to sprain or break anything. Kaylin was by far the lightest on his feet of the three of us, almost matching Grieve's and Chatter's graceful descents.

Ulean swept around me, keeping watch as we made our way down the ravine. She distracted me with her continual gusts, but soon it became comforting to know she was there, and her light flutterings blended in with the surreal march we were on.

Through cedar and fir we passed—their boughs heavy with snow, bending down toward the ground. The only sounds that of our breath as it came in steady white puffs, and the steady slide of boots against the snow as we crunched along the surface.

We'd almost reached the bottom when my foot gave way and I found myself knee-deep in a snowbank. The snow here was looser, not quite so compact, and by the time we reached the stream, even Grieve and Chatter were slogging through the powder. The stream was frozen over, though beneath the icy surface, I could see bubbles. It wouldn't be safe to walk in the streambed—the ice wasn't thick enough.

We paused, looking back up the ravine. It seemed more like a mountain than a slope, and I dreaded the return journey. I pulled a protein bar out of my pocket and broke off half, handing the rest to Rhiannon. Chatter and Grieve seemed fine, but Kaylin found a similar bar in his own pocket and devoured it. I chewed the chocolate-flavored crunch and swallowed, then took a drink from my water bottle. After wiping my mouth, I pulled out the map.

"To the right, follow the creek upstream."

Grieve nodded, leaning in to plant a light kiss on my lips. His razor-sharp fangs glistened in the light of day. He sniffed my neck. "I'm so thirsty for you," he whispered, the light in his eyes flickering a dangerous shade of desire.

Stepping back, I put my hand on his chest and he caught it, bringing it to his lips. He turned it palm up, and exposed my wrist free from the glove and jacket. Slowly, his dark, starry gaze never leaving mine, he leaned down and lightly nipped the skin. As a thin line of blood welled up, my body responded and I wanted to strip, to pull him to me, to fuck in the snow and ice. But I forced myself to stand still as he slowly began to lick the droplets off my skin.

"We are in Myst's realm. The feral side of your nature is coming out to play." I wasn't trying to stop him—I knew by now that wasn't a safe thing to do, but I was trying to bring him back to himself.

He paused, his long lashes flickering. After a moment, he drew back with a shudder. "I am not safe here. But there is no turning back. Watch me, Cicely. Chatter—I am relying on your common sense. If you see me slipping too far, get them out of here, away from me."

Grieve looked so stricken I wanted to go to him, to kiss him, to reassure him that I would never leave him again, no matter what, but I knew now that promises were like burning paper in this world of snow and ice: quick to make but easy to vanish into smoke and ashes. Instead, I pressed my fingers to my lips and held them out toward him. He nodded, understanding.

"We'd best be off again. Let's move." He turned and took the lead once more. Chatter gave me a sad smile, then swung in behind him. I followed, Rhiannon and Kaylin again bringing up the rear.

After a while, Grieve held up his hand and we paused. He turned. "We're coming to the glade your father mentioned."

I nodded, so cold I could barely think. The snow kept falling, the flakes thin and small, but they were adding up, and they crusted my eyelashes and chilled my nose and melted against my lips when they hit.

The streambed swerved to the left, as the trail continued right and we were now walking between stands of the stalwart conifers. The next moment we entered a wide glade, ringed by a circle of tall trees. We were still getting our bearings when Grieve shouted as a sudden force knocked him back. I raced forward, looking for what had hit him, and then I saw it. Skidding to a halt, I almost fell face-first into the snow.

A tall bipedal being, glistening and translucent, stood there, towering over me. The face was smooth, no sign of eyes or nose or mouth, and its limbs were angular and ribbed like icicles. An Ice Elemental.

"What the hell? The Ice Elementals usually don't even notice us!" Chatter warily circled the creature, who stood silent, like a robot, waiting.

"I was thinking the same thing. I have no clue." I stared at the Elemental and took another step forward. It moved, ever so slightly, raising one arm. I put my foot down, and it paused, waiting.

"They seem to be intent on keeping us out of this meadow." Kaylin slowly walked forward, stopping at my side.

"They?"

"Look."

I followed his nod, squinting through the ever-falling snow. Several other Elementals were in the meadow, and they were all looking our way. Cripes. What were we going to do? We couldn't fight them—they were too strong.

Ulean? What do we do? Why are they even noticing us?

Ulean whirled past me. She swirled, the skirts of her breeze whipping up the snow to cloud my vision. After a moment, she whispered in my ear. *They are under Myst's bewitchment. I think they are guarding this area for the very reason we are headed through it. Myst knows Lainule's heartstone is somewhere nearby and she is searching. We either fight them or go around.*

Then they must be programmed to fight if we cross a certain boundary. I wonder if we stick to the borders of the meadow, if we skirt the trees . . . will we be safe? I scanned the boundaries of the lea, but none of the Elementals seemed to be next to the treeline.

That I cannot tell you. You must find out for yourself, but I will be here to do what I can, should they move to attack.

I turned to the others, slowly so as not to arouse the Elemental who was standing far too close for comfort. "They're being controlled by Myst. I'm thinking if we skirt the border of the glade, we might be able to get around them. But we have no way of knowing if they're programmed to attack that far out. What do you think?"

Grieve considered the creature. He'd crawled back toward me before standing up and now, a wary, feral look crossed his face. "Myst controls them. I wonder if she can see through their eyes?"

"I don't know, but it's daylight. Did she escape the plague?" I prayed he would say no. The last thing we needed was for Myst to be able to tolerate light.

But Grieve shook his head, resting my fear. "No, she is caught by the light-rage, too. So I truly doubt she's keeping watch. In fact, that may be why she enchanted them—to guard during the time her people cannot walk abroad."

"Ulean thinks it's because we're near the . . . you know." I didn't even want to speak the words aloud just in case there might be someone listening behind a bush or under a snowbank or on the slipstream. Lainule's heartstone was too valuable to put at risk because of an overheard whisper.

Chatter rubbed his chin, then looked at Grieve. "She could be right, but that doesn't mean you aren't also correct. Two birds, one stone."

"Whatever the case, we need to cross this meadow to the other side and enter the copse beyond. It will take longer to circle round, but we'd better give it a try. Stick close to the trees and if the Elementals start after us, dart into the woods. My guess is that they'll stop at the border of the forest." Grieve paused, looking back at me.

Out here he seemed stronger, no longer broken, but in tune with the snow and the winter, and I realized that he could weather this journey more easily than any of us because of his connection with Myst. His biggest weakness was also his greatest strength.

I smiled at him and held out my hand. He took my fingers, slowly raising them to his lips where he kissed them, slowly drawing his tongue over the ends, and then let go. He turned and—once again, as we took up our marching order—led the way toward the edge of the forest, all the while cautiously watching the Elemental nearest us.

Breathing hard, I slogged through the snow, leaning on the branch for support. Rhiannon was puffing away behind me. She might be taller and thinner than I, but she wasn't used to as much physical exertion and I knew this was rough on her. But after a moment, she seemed to catch a second wind.

As we neared the trees, I saw the Elemental turn its head, watching us through whatever magical vision it possessed. I held my breath as it took a step in our direction, then another. But as we approached the edge of the meadow, it stopped, hesitating as if unsure.

Another moment and it turned away from us and took up its stance again, unwavering, unmoving, silent as the pillar of ice it was.

I caught my breath, exhaling with relief. "Score one," I whispered. "Let's hope they all stay away."

Chatter, in front of me, nodded his agreement as we continued trudging along, sweeping the snow with our feet. Grieve and Chatter were essentially breaking the path for the rest of us, so Kaylin, Rhia, and I didn't have it as rough, but it still wasn't easy and more than once, I found myself teetering in the narrow walkway, grateful for the support the fir branch was providing.

We edged a quarter way around the meadow. Another quarter arc and we'd be on the other side, able to take the path leading through the trees. So far, so good. No Elementals moved, no attacks came our way, no Shadow Hunters were near, insofar as I—or Ulean—could detect.

Another five yards, ten yards, fifty, and again we stopped to catch our breath and take a gander at the Elementals. All were standing still, as if listening for a distant call. From this distance, they were almost invisible in the ever-falling snow, and it almost hurt to see their beauty. They were magical, works of art caught in freeze-frame, glistening like gemstones.

We moved on again, slowly, cautiously, and were almost to the fork where we could disappear into the woods again, when a noise to my right startled me.

"And so, old friends, might we meet again. Riddle me this: Who has news that might interest young, intrepid explorers who dare to enter the realm of the Queen Myst?"

I jerked around. There, wizened, old, and haggard, was one of the Wilding Fae—the snow hag who had helped us once before in return for her freedom. Chatter and I froze as she laughed, her voice peeling out softly on the slip-stream.

The Elementals cocked their heads in unison and turned our way. I rushed off the path, into the woods where she stood and they stopped again.

"Hush, hush . . . be silent. They hear you."

"Riddle me this, then, young girl. A bargain must be struck, or certain explorers will be sorely pressed. It is sad to face an old friend who now has become an old enemy. And one who knows of this unwilling traitor, one who was once ensnared in Myst's grasp, has a hankering for fresh meat, but rabbits are scarce this season and the squirrels have fled the forest."

I stared at the crone. The Wilding Fae were frightful creatures of the forest who could help you for good or for ill but always at a bargain. Myst had snared the snow hag once before, seeking to utilize her powers, but Chatter, Peyton, and I had freed her and she had shown us where to find the entrance to the tunnel that had led us to the land of the Bat People.

Now she was back. And apparently hungry. But she had news that we needed to hear. The Wilding Fae were good to their words with bargains, as long as the wording was clear. I glanced at Chatter and he nodded. I let him take the lead. He had more experience with these creatures than did I.

"One we have bargained with before says she has news. I wonder, should this be news the mighty explorers do not yet know?" He leaned against a tree, feigning disinterest. Grieve slipped over and wrapped his arm protectively around my waist.

The snow hag cocked her head, a gleam in her eye. "A young Fae man may guess an old woman thinks to trick him, but he might be wrong. There are dangers afoot in the forest and when the belly is empty, it helps to make bargains."

Chatter pursed his lips. "Hmm . . . then perhaps such a bargain might be struck. But a young Fae man may wonder if such news be worth the trade. And there might be a time lapse in meeting the payment for the bargain. Fresh meat is not easy to come by when a mission awaits."

It was the snow hag's turn to pause. She tipped her head to the sky, letting the snow flutter into her face. One breath, two breaths, three breaths later she gave a sharp nod. "The snow is deep and grows deeper. Fresh meat may make it on the table today or tomorrow or the next day. Whichever day, it will still taste as good as long as it reaches the belly."

"Then if tomorrow or the next day is as good as today for supping, perhaps a deal can be made. Fresh meat of a brace of rabbits or two fat chickens or perhaps a thick steak to feed several mouths in exchange for news new to the ear?"

She cackled and held out her hand. "Bargains must be blood-sealed. One such as a Cambyra Fae should know the rules."

Chatter turned to Grieve, who held out a knife, and—without blinking—sliced his thumb. Blood dripping down the side of his hand, Chatter turned back to the snow hag, who had cut her own hand, and they clasped, shaking tightly, the droplets splattering onto the fresh snow, spreading pink stains.

"Then a bargain is sealed." Her eyes narrowed and she pointed ahead to the path where we were headed. "On yonder path, sitting on a downed tree, waits a beautiful witch. One of the magic-born but turned by Myst for her own use. With flowing locks of red, the same red as one of our explorers. She waits, knowing her daughter approaches, but not realizing that one of the Wilding Fae has struck a bargain for meat. She means to destroy the expedition."

Heather! Heather was up ahead, waiting for us.

"But how can that be? The redheaded witch is a *vampire*. And light shines on the forest, be it dimmed by clouds or not."

"One might ask what kind of vampire she is—one might ask when Myst turns the magic-born, do they become *true* vampires or vampires of the Indigo Court, who may walk abroad in the daylight when the need arises?"

I thought quickly as Rhiannon stifled a cry and turned to me. I looked wildly to Grieve and Chatter for guidance.

"She's right," Chatter said. "If I remember right, the magic-born turned by Myst become vampires much like the Vampiric Fae, able to walk abroad in the daylight, though not nearly as powerful. But that would mean the light-rage did not affect her. I wonder why."

I frowned. "The light-rage affected Grieve, but he is Cambyra Fae, not magic-born."

Before I could say more, Chatter raised one hand and turned back to the snow hag. "Tomorrow or the next day, one who has struck a bargain for meat should stand at the edge of the road near the turnoff to the wishing well, and there the meat shall be delivered at midday. I wonder, does the bargain maker know where this is?"

"Wonder well, you should, but perchance your question might be answered with an affirmation that yes, indeed, the location is known. And now, it is time for one of the Wilding Fae to retreat far away for the day. Too much danger exists in this wood. Too much fear." Without a word, the snow hag vanished into the thicket.

Rhia turned to me, a mute plea on her face.

I held out my arms and she fell against my shoulder, sobbing. Whispering low, so low that the slipstream could not carry my words, I said, "We will find your mother and put her to rest. Myst will claim her no longer."

And then, knowing that we were about to face one of the hardest tasks of our lives, I pushed her back by the shoulders and stared into her face. "Can you do this? Can you even *watch* us do this? We must stake her—destroy her."

Heather, Rhiannon's mother, had been captured by Myst along with Peyton. She'd given her life so that Peyton could live. Myst had drunk her down and turned her into a vampire. Weaker than the true vampires but still possessing her magical powers, Heather had fallen under Myst's spell and now worked for her. And she was waiting for us.

Rhiannon steeled herself, her red hair vivid against her pale skin. "I am ready. We'll do what we must. I don't want her to live like this anymore. She would beg me to release her if she weren't bewitched."

Chatter stepped forward then, and he took Rhiannon's hands. As we watched, he brushed her hair back from her face, and then slowly as their gazes locked, he leaned forward and gently pressed his lips to hers. She wrapped her arms around his shoulders as he encircled her waist, kissing her deeply. I caught my breath and sought for Grieve's hand. We turned away from the silent tableau, giving them what privacy we could, until Rhiannon cleared her throat.

Chatter stepped back, his gaze never leaving Rhiannon's. "You know how I feel, Miss Rhiannon. You have to know how I feel."

She nodded, blushing, whispering, "Please, Chatter . . . call me Rhiannon. I am not your better. I would never think of myself as such."

He smiled, then said, "I like to think you feel the same as I."

Again, she nodded, grinning through her tears. Again, whispering, "I do. I have since . . . I can remember."

"Then I promise you this: Whatever needs to be done, I will do my best to help you do. And I—and your cousin— will be here for you afterward. You need never be alone again, Rhiannon."

And with that, we fell back into marching order and snuck through the woods the rest of the way. Heather was out there, and because we loved her, we were going to kill her.

Chapter 10

As we plowed through the snow, visions of Aunt Heather rushed through my mind. She'd always been the one to comfort me when my own mother had grown impatient with my tears. Until I was six, Heather and Rhiannon and the Veil House had been the stabilizing force in my world. And then Krystal dragged me away. I remember standing on the steps as she pulled me toward the car, screaming because I knew—absolutely knew—that once we climbed in that car and drove away, my life would dive into a pit of fear and uncertainty.

And I'd been right.

Phone calls and the occasional visit home had given me hope. But Myst had stripped all of that away when she captured Heather. We would not be facing my aunt but a monster assuming her form. We had to keep that in the forefront of our thoughts.

We crept past rock and trunk, through the snow, keeping low in the overgrowth, the crisp scent of ozone from the storm filling our lungs. I was cold and wet and my jeans felt glued to my calves and thighs. The only place I felt truly dry was inside my boots and beneath my jacket. I hunkered down as we approached another clearing—the opening to the path we'd been headed toward.

Peering out between the branches I could see Heather standing there, in a gossamer gown the color of twilight, embroidered through with threads of shimmering silver. She was waiting, silent as the grave, her long red hair blowing in the wind. Her lips were red as berries, and her eyes glowed black with the obsidian of the vampires. The handkerchief hem of her gown whipped gently in the breeze, her long sleeves fluttering as if light fingers were moving them.

Rhiannon crept up next to me. She stared at her mother, and her expression said everything her lips could not. Aching loss, loneliness, the pain of watching a loved one who has slipped into the shadows—it was all there, flooding her face. Mutely, she looked at me. I reached out, slowly, to stroke her cheek, and then touched my fingers to my lips and placed them on her own. She hung her head and I waited for her to give the go-ahead. She had to be the one making the decision.

After a moment, Rhia looked up and her expression had changed, a switch had flicked. Her face was a mask of fury, strong and determined. I looked around and found a broken stick on the ground. It would work for a stake.

Rhia did the same, arming herself with a broken twig off of a downed cedar. Grieve, Chatter, and Kaylin mirrored our actions and we were ready.

I have your back. Ulean whipped around me, stirring the air with her frenzy. *Heather must not return to Myst.*

I know, Ulean. I know. This is not easy. She was ... is ... my aunt.

She is your aunt no longer but one of Myst's witches, one of her changelings. Remember—the form is deceiving. Heather will do what she must for Myst. She is owned heart and soul by the Queen of the Indigo Court and owes no other allegiance.

With Ulean playing at my back, I readied my fan in one hand, the stake in the other. At a single nod from Grieve, we charged through the last strip of woodland onto the path, aiming for Heather. Dying time again.

❧

Heather had expected us to come in from the path, not from out of the woods, which gave us an advantage. I whipped my fan forward, whispering, "Strong gust." The resulting wind knocked Heather off balance.

Chatter moved forward, Rhia beside him, but Heather was too quick—the transformation had given her incredible reflexes. She recovered from the breeze and whirled toward me, her hands weaving together a pattern that I knew was some sort of spell. The next moment I went flying back into the snowbank as a nearby piece of wood rose and hit me square in the midriff.

That's right, she works with earth magic. Crap. I rose, shaking from the blow.

Yes, she does, but she's weak when it comes to air, and fire can destroy her, even if the light cannot.

"Please, one last time I beg of you, stop this madness. Let us help you." Rhiannon was screaming at Heather, tears racing down her face. Her heart was breaking and there was nothing we could do to stop it from shattering.

Heather faced Rhia, looking all too ripe and luscious. She licked her lips. "My daughter. My dear, deluded child. I give you a chance. Come with me, come to Myst and let her taste you, drink you deep, bring you into our world. Just think . . . you and I together again. Working side by side, together, forever. You have rediscovered your flame. Think of all we could do, you and I." She held out her hand, the look on her face sure of success.

Rhiannon paused. For a moment she seemed to waver, but then Heather laughed, and her laughter was like an icicle through the heart. Rhia stepped back and held out her hands, dropping the stake on the ground.

She whispered, "Fire, burn through me," and a spray of fire shot forth from her fingertips, surrounding Heather, lighting the gossamer gown aflame.

Heather screamed as the flames roared to life, feeding on the cloth. The next moment, she threw herself into a snowbank, extinguishing the burning material. When she rose, a murderous smile filled her eyes.

"I can play rough, too, my darling daughter." Another whisper, and this time the forest shook, the ground beneath our feet shifting. I lost my balance and fell, as did Rhiannon. Kaylin went sprawling over a tree trunk. Chatter and Grieve caught hold of trees to keep themselves afoot.

Heather was intoning a dark chant, deep and ancient, and terrifyingly old, and the tree next to Rhia began to topple toward her. I screamed as Chatter rushed forward, grabbing her around the waist and rolling clear just as the tree landed where she'd been standing.

I unfurled my fan. "Tornado force." With a wave of my hand, the fan let out a low howl as a funnel cloud appeared, ripping trees from the roots as it headed directly toward Heather. My aunt screamed as the twister bore down on her. She held up her hands.

"Rock and boulder!" The earth shook between the force of the tornado and the thrusting up of some giant behemoth—and then I saw it was no monster, but a huge boulder propelling itself to the surface. Heather ducked behind it as the twister raged over her. Any normal magic-born or yummanii would have died from the force of my attack, but she belonged to the Indigo Court. She held on to the rock, her fingers exerting incredible strength to keep herself from being sucked into the vortex.

As the tornado shrieked off, I felt a tremor from my fan—it raced through my body and I wasn't sure what was happening but I had no time to figure it out now. I grabbed my stake—this could end only one way—and headed over toward Heather.

But Rhiannon was in front of me. She'd broken free of Chatter, and stake raised, she raced to her mother. Her other hand was a ball of flame that coalesced around her fingers, shifting fire that seemed to barely faze her. Heather was just managing to stand again, when Rhiannon reached out and sent the ball of flame singing off her palm, straight into Heather's face.

Heather screamed as the fire caught her hair and sparked

it to life, her red locks becoming a mane of flame. Once again she dropped to the ground, rolling, but as she did so, Rhiannon leaped on her, catching her on her back. She straddled Heather, bringing the stake up above her head with a wild-eyed, glassy look.

"You would kill your own mother?" Heather's voice was soft, so much like it had been before she'd been captured. Her face a mass of burned flesh, she reached up for Rhiannon's neck and grabbed her.

Rhiannon began to choke as she struggled against Heather's grasp. In a raspy voice, she gasped out, "You are not my mother. You are not my mother." Tears raced down her cheeks and fell onto Heather's face, sizzling against the burned flesh.

And then, in a silent moment, Heather paused. Her hands fell away from Rhiannon's neck, and she spread them wide to her sides, waiting. Rhiannon wavered, staring down at Heather.

"You have seconds, only seconds, my love," Heather whispered. "Please, just do it. Release me. I can only keep hold of my sanity for a few seconds at a time. I love you. Don't let me hurt you, don't make me fight to the death or you will surely die. I am too strong, I can bend the earth to swallow us up. Rhiannon, my baby, you must let me go." Heather's voice was tender, like I remembered from childhood.

"Mother . . . I can save you—I can . . ." And then Rhia stopped and shook her head. "I can't save you. There's no coming back for you, is there?"

Heather began to weep through the burned flesh that scarred her face. "Unlike Grieve, I died. I will never live again. And I choose not to live in this state, controlled by a monster, turning into a monster. I have done horrid things since she took me. I cannot live with them on my conscience. Either I become the horror she plans, or I die. Bless me with the gift of death, Rhia. Please, please, don't make me live like this."

Bloody tears poured down her face. Rhia began to sob and so did I. But we had no choice. We had moments, perhaps seconds, before Heather faded back into the freak that Myst had created. I slowly knelt beside them and reached down, kissing Heather on the forehead.

"I'm so sorry I didn't get here in time to save you, I'm so sorry I was too late," I whispered, pressing my hand to her cheek.

Heather's starry darkened eyes glimmered and I could feel the rush of fury coming on her again. I turned to Rhia. "Quickly. It has to be now. Do you want me to do it?"

"Help me. I have to do it, but help me, Cicely. I need you." Rhia gave me a horrified look and I put my hands on hers, holding the stake above Heather's chest.

Heather smiled, then, in one last moment of clarity. "I loved you as my own daughter, Cicely. Know that. And Rhiannon—you will know your father in time. Trust me. You will know." She closed her eyes and a snarl came to her lips. "Now, before I retreat—*now, it must be now!*" Her voice was frantic.

I held tight to Rhia's hands. She was gripping the stake with an uncanny strength, but she was frozen. I came to her rescue and began to drive the stake down toward Heather's chest. Rhia dropped her head back, a silent scream on her face, and she ripped the stake from my hands and plunged it into Heather's chest by herself. A spray of blood fountained up, spattering us both, leaving a dappling of crimson against the snow.

Heather let out a low scream that echoed along the slipstream, and then a rush of wind passed by, and Ulean was there, cloaking us. My aunt lay still, a bloody symbol of what we'd been driven to.

Rhia stared at her, a look of horror on her face. And then Chatter and Grieve were there, lifting us up, away from Heather's body. As they led us away, Kaylin went in and what he did, I could not see, but when we turned, the body was no longer there, just a spreading crimson stain, freezing to the snow as the flurries raged around us. A small pile of dust whipped up and away, into the wind.

I let out a shudder, then a sigh, and pressed my face into Grieve's shoulder. He kissed me softly on the cheek, then on the lips, demanding and fierce, and I lost myself in the feel of his lips against mine, of his skin against mine, of his body entwined around me. We stood, like two silent trees, rooted to the spot, tongues barely touching, softly dancing under the falling snow, until the exquisite pain of losing my aunt, of watching her die at our hands, was forced back into a corner, and blessed numbness swept over me.

Turning, I caught a glimpse of Chatter and Rhiannon. He was doing the same, comforting my cousin, kissing her, holding her, and she had lost herself in his embrace. My heart skipped a beat. This was the way it was supposed to be. Rhiannon and Chatter. Grieve and me. It felt right. It felt true.

Another moment passed, then Kaylin cleared his throat. "We should be off. I know it's hard, but we have to reach Grandfather Cedar. We aren't far. Let's go."

I broke away from Grieve. "You're right. And on we go." As we took up our march again, my heart was both heavy and yet—inexplicably light. We'd just killed the one woman in the world I thought of as my real mother, and yet we'd freed her. Torn her from Myst's grasp. We'd given Heather the final gift, that of release.

I hung back, reaching for Rhiannon's hand. We walked awhile, trudging through the snow, hand in hand. She seemed oddly calm, but I understood what she was feeling. The numbness was a blessing.

And whatever lay ahead of us, we would meet the challenge and do our best, no matter the outcome.

Another twenty minutes and Grieve said something to Chatter. Across a little clearing, we could see the cedar from my dreams—the cedar Lainule had indicated as the entrance to the tunnels leading to her heartstone.

"Grandfather Cedar," Grieve whispered, a reverence in his voice. And indeed, the tree was taller than most any tree in the forest. It towered dark against the sky, a sentinel guarding the forest, with a trunk wide enough to build a home in. "We must find the tunnel."

Chatter parted a swath of ferns. He knelt and blew on the surface of the snow, a faint flame whispering from his lips to melt the snow. After a moment, the glimmering outline of a door with a brass handle atop it came into view. The door in my dreams.

"Can anyone else see this?" I asked, hoping that we'd leave no trace once we climbed into the tunnel.

"Only those of Cambyra blood," Grieve said.

Kaylin nodded. "He's right. I can't see it."

Rhia stood still, staring. "But . . . but . . . *I can.*"

"What?" I whirled, staring at her. "*You* can see it?"

She nodded, her lips pale, as she stared into my eyes. "I can see the door, Cicely."

"Does that mean . . . Grieve, are you sure that only those of Cambyra Fae should be able to see it? Because if so, that means . . ."

"Rhiannon also possesses Fae blood in her veins." Grieve looked at her. "You possess fire magic, like Chatter."

"No," she whispered, pressing her fingers to her throat. "I can't be part Fae. Mother . . . she would have told me."

"My mother never did. And Heather said you will know your father in time." As I stared at her, a suspicion began to form in my thoughts, but I kept it to myself, not even wanting to dwell on the possibility at this point.

"We must hurry. We can speculate on Rhiannon's heritage when we have found Lainule's . . . treasure." Grieve touched the door handle and it sprang open to his fingers, as if it had been waiting for him.

I peered into the darkened opening. A swirl of color began to spin, gold and green and brilliant blood red. *My dream, this was my dream.*

I looked up at the others. "We have to take a leap of faith here. No hesitation, only action."

And with that, I swung my legs over the edge, inhaled deeply, and before they could stop me, I pushed myself over, falling into the swirl of color, leaping into the rabbit hole.

✦

Freeze-frame . . . falling down, deep, there's a swirl of green and gold, and a streak of red, and I'm in the middle of a giant kaleidoscope . . . and I am turning in the air, head over heels, skydiving into a magical well, playing Alice down the rabbit hole . . .

Freeze-frame . . . and the plunge mellowed, the currents catching me up like a parachute. I was able to catch my breath and as I looked up, all I could see were faint glimmers that might have been movement, or just the swirling color of this psychedelic journey I was taking.

Freeze-frame . . . and the sparkling colors vanished as I slid through a low-hanging cloud and landed on my butt, in a deep, dark tunnel, coming down hard on a stone floor. I pushed myself to my feet and moved. If the others were following me, chances were they'd be landing right about where—

Just as I darted to the side, Kaylin landed on his feet in a crouch. He moved to the side next to me. Rhiannon was next, and she nearly took a nasty tumble, but Kaylin managed to catch her before she fell. She flashed me an anxious look as we waited. Within another moment, Chatter and Grieve had joined us.

"How do we get back up again?" Rhia glanced up at the swirling, nebulous, glowing clouds that covered the entrance to the portal. "And what about the trapdoor?"

Chatter shook his head. "Not to worry, I cloaked the entrance. But as for getting back up through that, I have no clue. We'll figure it out when we come to that point."

I moved over to examine the wall. It was glowing with the same shimmer that the other tunnel had had, only this one was brighter, warmer. I leaned my forehead against the smooth wall. Something within the glassy tile connected with me, sparking off images of summer nights, warm and delicious and filled with ice-cream cones and stargazing and dragonflies. I could almost smell the dusky summer evening riding the slipstream as Ulean swept this way and that.

Grieve joined me. "What do you feel, my love?"

I took his hand, slapped it against the wall, palm first. "Tell me what you sense, can you feel it? Can you feel Lainule's heart? This is her private sanctuary. Can you feel the essence of summer, deep within the structure of the tile?"

He closed his eyes, took a long, deep breath. And then, as he started to shake his head, his eyes flew open and he jolted back, panting raggedly as he dropped to his knees and curled over, hiding his face with his hands. "I remember . . . I remember . . ." The pain in his voice tore me to shreds as I ran to him, knelt by him.

"Are you all right? What happened?" I wrapped my arm around his shoulders, but he shook me off.

"I . . . remember what it was like . . . what *I was like* before *she* turned me." He slowly sat up, loss spreading across his face like a blight over the land. "I am tainted. I am tainted. How can I ever be whole again?" A snarl rose to his lips and his eyes narrowed. "How can I live in two worlds at once?"

Chatter rushed forward. "Grieve, can you hear me? You must listen to my voice. Follow my voice. Follow it home. Follow me." His words took on a dark tone, swirling like autumn leaves, and I found myself falling into their cadence as he spoke.

Grieve snarled again, and I could see the Shadow Hunter within him, waiting for release. But he remained in control, his expression set, as he fixated on Chatter's face. I did not speak.

"Follow my voice home, follow it back . . . follow the thread through the snow. Can you see the snow around you?"

As if in trance, Grieve nodded. "All around me. There is only snow, only the everlasting chill and the silver stars in her eyes. She is so cold . . . so terribly cold." He shivered, but Chatter gave me a look that kept me frozen in place.

Chatter whispered to Grieve. "Follow my voice through the snow, follow it through the woodland, through the deep, dark forest. Like a golden thread it unfurls, like a golden arrow, my voice will point the way. Can you see the words on the slipstream? Can you feel them calling you?"

Exhaling slowly, Grieve's eyes began to flutter, and I realized Chatter was hypnotizing him. Rhia and Kaylin stood by my side, frozen, waiting.

"Yes, I can see them." Grieve's answer was quiet, without the snarl, without emotion.

"Follow my words as they guide you through the snow." He paused, then said, "The snow is beginning to melt, turning into a trickle of water. The trickle of water grows, turning into small rivulets, and then into small creeks, into raging streams that follow the path through the woods. See the snow vanish, feel the sun rising higher in the sky as Summer regains the land. Can you see this? Can you feel the warmth on your face as the light returns?"

"Yes, I can see it. I can feel it!" The longing in my beloved's voice cut me to the quick. We had to find a way to break the hold Myst had on him, to clear his blood . . . There had to be a way to turn him back into the noble prince he once was.

"Let the light encompass you, draw you back, bring you back to your heart again, to your core, to your wolf. Let the light into your eyes, let Summer's song fill your heart." Chatter knelt by Grieve, and he reached out and cupped Grieve's chin with his palm. I could see how much it cost him to watch his best friend stagger under the weight of Myst's curse.

After a moment, Grieve took another long breath, and he looked up at Chatter. While no words were said, I clearly heard a whisper of thanks pass between them. Chatter offered Grieve his hand, and as Grieve rose, the two nodded, a private moment between them. I looked away, feeling helpless and hopeless. But then, as I leaned back against the tile, the tingle of Lainule's heartstone echoed through me and I stood, ready to press on.

The tunnel was full of her essence. It was all around us, almost as if she, herself, were here. I turned to the others. Rather than embarrass Grieve by asking how he was, I decided to just continue.

"Ready to go?" I wasn't sure if he'd want to take the lead or not, but Grieve and Chatter moved to the front again.

"We're ready. Let's go." Chatter gave me a quiet nod.

I swept in behind him, Rhia took her place behind me, and then Kaylin at the back. As Grieve led us down the passage, away from the glowing clouds of the portal, the tiles took on a life of their own and whatever spark was within them shone through, as if we were walking through a hallway surrounded by shooting stars.

I wondered how far we'd have to go and how we'd find the heartstone. I wanted to shake the worries out of my head—I'd been too entrapped by my own thoughts lately and the constant questioning of every move I made was beginning to wear on me. Not to mention it had been a couple of days since I'd gone out in my owl form and I was beginning to realize that that was not a good thing. Once I'd unleashed my Uwilahsidhe nature, it needed to stretch its wings and fly on a regular basis.

Speaking of . . . I glanced back at Rhiannon. She'd seen the door. Only those with Cambyra blood could see the door. Which meant . . . I slipped back and took her hand.

"Lost in your thoughts?" I said as she startled, looking up at me as if she hadn't realized I'd been there.

She nodded. "Yes, thinking . . ."

"About your father."

"About my father, yes. If I am like you . . . we are truly twin-cousins. But I can't help but wonder. Do you think Wrath is my father, too?"

I shrugged. "I don't know. He could be. Which would mean we truly are sisters." I found myself hoping that was the case—Rhia was the only sister I'd ever known, and to know that we were not only cousins but sisters would be a blessing. "I hope he is."

She smiled then. "I think I'd like that. I like Wrath."

"I guess we'll have to wait and see." I squeezed her hand. "We'll find out when we return home. If we can retrieve Lainule's heartstone, surely she'll tell us the truth." But the Summer Queen's words suddenly echoed through my mind, rushing through on a cool gust of wind. *When you save a life, you bear its burdens the rest of your days.*

Up ahead, Grieve suddenly stopped. The passage ended, opening into a chamber. Chatter and Grieve slowly entered, standing to the side. I dropped Rhia's hand and walked toward the arch. As I stepped through the arch, my breath spiraled out of my body and I found myself on my knees, facing the most incomparable beauty I'd ever seen in my life. *Any life*.

The chamber was vast. So vast there was no telling how wide or long it was. Filled with giant dark roots of trees and stalagmites and stalactites, it was both cavern and barrow. Pale vines, devoid of pigment, trailed down from the tree roots, like some ghostly mirror of ivy plants gone mad.

They coiled around the rock pillars, around the roots that plunged down through the chamber into the ground below our feet. Like floral snakes hiding in tree boughs, they waited. A sparkle of crystal flowers dappled the albino leaves, violet and rose and brilliant peridot.

I slowly crossed into the chamber, unable to fully take in the beauty that spread before me. A pool shimmered in the center, wide enough that a boat sat on one end. The boat could fit six people and was white, painted with oak and ivy leaves. By the scent, it had been carved from a cedar log.

The pond rippled softly against the shore. At first I thought it was white sand, but when I drew closer, the sand was actually made up of millions of tiny white pebbles.

To my left, the shadows took hold—I could not see what lay between the roots and stone pillars creating a labyrinthine path. And to my right—another path, leading into the distance.

I turned back to Grieve, my breath hushed. "Where are we?" My words sounded lame, breaking the silence, perhaps the first words spoken here in thousands of years.

He shook his head. Chatter did not know either.

I cautiously made my way over to a fallen stalactite, gingerly sitting on it as I tried to figure out where to go from here. Rhiannon joined me. She took my hand as we sat there in silence.

Kaylin crouched near the water, his fingers reaching out to touch it, but he stayed his hand a few inches from the lapping waves, a look of uncertainty on his face. We were at an impasse.

Ulean, I don't know what to do next.

What does your heart tell you?

That I am afraid, and lost.

Then what does your instinct—your gut—tell you?

I closed my eyes, trying to listen past the fear. For a moment there was only a sense of confusion, but then a small voice laughed over the surface of my bewilderment. I listened again, and realized the laughter was coming from me . . . from the Faerie tattooed on my breast.

I caught my breath as a whirl of music raced through me and my feet began to tap in time to the rhythm. Jumping up, I began to dance around the stalactite, laughing aloud, driven on by the mirth and joy in my Faerie's voice.

Rhia was on her feet, joining me, and we clasped hands, leaning back, circling each other as we danced. Her eyes sparkled and she smiled, the years falling away. We were children again, dancing through the Golden Wood, hurrying to meet Grieve and Chatter.

Kaylin moved toward us, but Grieve caught him by the shoulder and shook his head, motioning him back. I could not hear what he said, but Kaylin nodded and stayed his ground.

And then, finally, our circling grew slower and Rhia and I stopped, my hands palm up, her fingers resting lightly atop mine. We gazed into each other's eyes. I began to whisper.

"Wind . . . wind . . . winds arise and come to be my guide."

Rhia opened her lips and her words slid out, flowing over mine. *"Fire rising ever higher, light the way before me."*

"Winds of change, attend me, and never leave my side."

"Flames burst forth from my heart, and light the path clearly."

Our fingers trembled, and a ball of energy—fire and wind—rose between us, emerging from our hands, to hover over our heads. We looked up and watched as it spun around and around, and then—with one quick streak— shot out over the boat, showering it with sparks—and across the pond into the darkness.

Chapter 11

"We cross the water." I turned to the men. "We must go where the boat will lead us—and it will lead us by itself. That much I can tell you." I didn't know how I knew, but I could feel the nature of the vessel in my heart. The boat was alive.

Grieve and Chatter nodded. The boat shifted as we approached, turning sideways in the water to make it easier for us to climb aboard.

I took the front, kneeling and looking out over the water. Grieve sat behind me. On the seats behind him, Kaylin, then Rhia, and lastly, in the aft of the boat, Chatter. The moment we were settled, the boat silently began to glide out onto the water.

The boat cut through the water, a silent creature slicing through the pond, as the ripples spread out along the sides. With need for neither oars nor sails, the magical ride carried us into the mists rising from the surface. As the fog rose up, I wondered where it was taking us. We were obviously in a different realm—we'd crossed through a portal, and should we burrow straight up, we wouldn't find ourselves in Myst's forest. We were traveling in uncharted territory, and dangers, along with our treasure, waited at the end. *Here be dragons*, and all that sort of thing.

As we crossed the pond, the gentle sound of the boat rippling through the water was our only companion. Tensions were high and there was nothing to say until we knew what we were facing. But my thoughts raced in circles. The magic Rhia and I'd done had proven once again to me that we had a bond deeper than just blood. We were fire and ice, the flame and the wind, and together, we made a powerful force.

Grieve reached forward and touched my shoulder, motioning ahead. I squinted through the mists. We were approaching an island, most likely in the center of the pond. My breath leaped to my throat. Was this our destination? Lainule had warned there would be beasts or creatures guarding the way.

The boat swung so that the side was facing the land. I looked back at the others and nodded. Cautiously, one by one, we stood and stepped out of the boat onto the island. As we did, the boat bobbed on the water. I looked around. The surrounding area was lit by a dim glow from the fog and though the air felt chilled, it wasn't with the cold of winter.

I stepped forward, biting my lip, Lainule's warning ringing in my ear. At any moment, I expected some great beast to leap out of the fog and trample us down. But nothing showed itself and so I took the lead, along with Grieve, and we motioned for the others to follow. Rhiannon and Chatter came next, and Kaylin brought up the rear.

The path led into another forest of roots and stalactites, covered with the ghostly ivy vines and sparkling flowers. It was alien and ancient. The path itself was solid, compacted soil and rock, and whispers began to fill the slipstream, voices echoing like distant wind chimes. I paused to listen, holding up my hand. The words began to trill, the soft speech became song, as music began to weave through the chanting and I fell into a light trance, enchanted by the rhythm.

Ulean, who are these singers?

There are many who can enchant with song. Be wary.
Not all foes are foul, and not all beauty is kind.

I closed my eyes, waiting, listening. The voices rose on
the slipstream, coming from behind us. I could barely
make out what they were singing. But after a moment, the
words began to weave around me.

You have journeyed far, 'tis time to rest . . .
Bring yourself here, lay your head on my breast . . .
Close your eyes, drift in waves and foam,
The water's depths are your true home.
Sing tra la fa, Fae, around the cauldron swoon,
'Tis truly time for the Witching Moon . . .

I rocked on the cadence, letting it bolster me against the
swirling mists. Slowly, I felt myself turning, as I headed
back to the shoreline, to meet the water's lapping waves. A
part of me knew this was folly, that magic was being used
against me, but the other part—the part that controlled
limb and will—didn't care. I would walk until the singing
voices bade me to stop.

As I pushed the others out of my way, Grieve reached
for my arm and I tried to shake him off. He held tight. "I
hear them too—I can hear them on the slipstream, Cicely,
but you have to ignore them. They're sirens. They'll lure
you into the water and feast on your blood."

I heard him, from far away, and saw the concern on his
face, but nothing seemed to be able to penetrate the fog in
which I was walking. I shook my head.

"Must go . . . must go to them . . ."

Kaylin came up on my other side and, with a sharp look
at Grieve, grabbed me out of his arms and shook me
soundly. He thrust his thoughts in my mind, his demon
forced its way in and the rough, dark fire burned through
the fog, leaving my thoughts scorched.

I screamed and went down on my knees with what felt
like the mother of all migraines. Clasping my hands to my
head, I screamed again, trying to shake the searing pain
out of my mind. The world was a dark blur of flame and

shadow, and just as I thought I couldn't handle the pressure, it began to dissipate. I blinked. Everything was still blurry, but my vision was beginning to clear.

After a moment, the roaring thunder faded to a dull ache and I moaned and fell back, landing on my butt with a thud. I groaned.

"What the hell did you just do to me, Kaylin?"

"Mind-fucked you. I forced my thoughts into your own in order to break the hold the sirens had on you. No amount of talking would do it." He smiled apologetically. "You're extremely vulnerable to empaths and beasties that work on a psychic level. You need to learn how to shield, but that can come later." He offered me his hand, and with a careful look at Grieve, I accepted his help as he pulled me to my feet.

"You really blasted my thoughts. I feel like I've either got the hangover from hell, or I've been pounded into by a sledgehammer. Mind-fuck is right . . ." But it had worked. And had he not done it, I would be fighting to return to the water. "Tell me, why didn't those things . . . whatever they are . . . attack us as we crossed the pond?"

"Like Myst's Ice Elementals, I have a feeling they won't act until someone sets foot on this island." He shook his head. "We're going to have be very wary. Lainule's protection is magical as well as physical. She has to have wards and spells set up."

"I'm so stupid. I don't know why I didn't think of that." Once again, I felt like a shortsighted idiot.

"We've been fighting on a physical level for days now with Myst—most of her attacks have been via flesh and blood. We're all tired. I dread to think what happens when she decides her Shadow Hunters aren't doing well enough on their own and begins to strike at us magically." Kaylin's face was grim and I realized I had deliberately been avoiding that same thought. We could barely fight back against her warriors, let alone her magic.

"Let's move. The longer we tarry, the more chance we have of setting ourselves up as targets. But keep alert, and if you feel yourself slipping, say something." I shook off the last of Kaylin's shadow and fire, moving back into the lead with Grieve.

Ulean, couldn't you break through the sirens' songs?

You could not hear me. It would seem that something in their magic blocks our communication. I tried to call you back, but you faded out of my reach.

Keep close contact from now on. We can't let that happen again.

As you say. I will, my friend. I have your back, as much as anyone ever can. And you, listen well, and the moment you think you sense something else, tell me—some whispers you will hear better than I. Others, vice versa.

And so we plunged on into the silent forest. The sirens' calls vanished, but I wasn't resting easy. There were darker things ahead, between us and the heartstone, set to protect. And no matter what we told them, they'd fight us because we could be anybody trying to get to the gem that kept the realm of Summer alive.

We pushed through the forest of rock and root, skirting the boulders settled at the base of some of the "trunks." The albino ivy vines tendriled down to coil in our hair and try to hold us back. I brushed them away and they moved like snakes, slithering, rearing back, and I could swear I heard them hiss. But they did not strike, nor did they have thorns or fangs.

They are the eyes and ears of this cavern forest.

Are they sentient?

As sentient as any plant might be in the realm of Summer. Yes, they know we pass, but their thoughts are dark and shadowed, difficult to discern. They do not shout, nor raise a vocal alarm, but they can whisper among one another and let the rest know that invaders are on the way.

And are they doing that?

Yes, they are. I can hear them, though I can scarce give form to their thoughts and words.

I told the others about what Ulean had said, but there was nothing to do. As we passed each vine, Grieve gave it a surreptitious look but did not attack. The less we appeared to be intruders, the less trouble we should have. *Theoretically.*

I began to feel eyes on me from every direction. On us. It was as if the whole freaky forest had suddenly sprung to life, but there was no telling just where that life was hiding. Or whether it even *was* hiding. Perhaps we were seeing the very creatures we were trying to hide from—within the roots of the trees and the giant hanging rocksicles.

We came to a fork in the road. Exhausted, I dropped to the ground.

"We have to rest." I looked up at them. "Is there any chance we can get a little sleep?"

"That might be a good idea. Here, in the realm of Fae, time moves far differently. It's impossible to tell how much time on the outside has passed, but probably far less than in here. Grieve and I are strong here. We can watch over the three of you while you sleep." Chatter motioned to the side of the path. "You'll have to curl up on the ground, but at least it's not cold."

Wearily, Kaylin, Rhiannon, and I settled ourselves on the softest patch of earth we could find. Grieve and Chatter took watch. As we drifted off to sleep, I wondered if I'd dream of this place.

❧

As my eyes fluttered open, I wondered where I was, and then remembered. We were in the realm of Summer, looking for Lainule's heartstone. As I slowly sat up and yawned, achy from sleeping on the ground, my head felt clearer and I didn't feel nearly so out of it.

"Did you sleep well, my love?" Grieve was right where he'd been when I went to sleep, looking no worse for the wear. Chatter was sitting near Rhia, staring off into the distance. As I stood, he woke both my cousin and Kaylin.

"Yes, I think I'm good. How long were we out?"

"Who knows? Time passes differently here. You slept for a while, though." Grieve kissed me gently, and—as Rhiannon and I headed behind some nearby boulders to take care of personal business, he and Chatter began to discuss the path ahead.

When we returned, I realized I felt much better. Rhiannon and Kaylin both looked refreshed, too.

"Which way do we go?" I asked.

"Right, I think." Grieve motioned to the path and we turned and followed him, circling through rock and root, the scent of deep earth and mold thick in my nose. I had no clue where we were going, but instinct told me this was the way. The farther we traveled, the thicker the air became till it was oppressive and heavy on the lungs. The magic was steadily growing. I almost expected to see giant mushrooms and monster crabs like out of some old movie, but neither appeared.

Grieve looked at me and reached out his hand. I took it as we approached a narrowing of the path. The roots here were huge, so big I could only imagine the trees they belonged to. They truly were the rib bones of the world, running through the earth.

As we came to an opening into what looked like a cave within the cavern, where only one person could walk at a time, Grieve pulled me close and wrapped his arm around my waist. He leaned down and gave me a long kiss, then stepped in front of me, shielding me as he stepped into the opening.

"Wait till I call you." He glanced back once, then was gone.

As I stood there, a million thoughts ran through my head. I could barely breathe, waiting to hear his voice.

A scream cut through the air. A woman's scream. I plunged into the opening, followed by the others, and out into a lush inner sanctum. Under a golden green glow that emanated from the walls rippled a small pool, and on the pool, silver water lilies floated. Sparkling lights filled the air, clouding me with a strange perfume. I reeled and went down on my knees as the heady scent overwhelmed me. Rhia and Kaylin were down for the count, too. But Chatter stood tall, his gaze darting around the chamber.

I followed his lead. There, over by the edge of the pond, lay a lithe, nude woman. She looked ethereal, lovely, and yet feral, but she also looked very dead. Her throat had been ripped open, and blood poured down her neck. To her left, stood Grieve, looking distant and aloof. Blood coated his lips.

My stomach twisted. What the fuck had happened? Chatter dragged me to my feet, and slogging through the magical force field, I leaned on his shoulder as he half-carried, half-led me over to Grieve's side.

Grieve looked up as we approached, grimacing as he wiped his mouth and stared at the blood smearing his fingers. Letting out a little snarl, he threw himself down at the water's edge and began splashing water on his face.

"Grieve . . ." Chatter's voice was hesitant. Grieve looked like he was in some form of shock.

My love stared at the water. "Her song was so compelling. I couldn't resist her. And when I drew close, she began to change."

Chatter crouched down beside the dead woman and examined her, brushing her long dark hair to the side. His fingers brushed her skin lightly and examined her fingernails, then stood. "Iron nails. She's one of the Black Annis. One of the Wilding Fae, like the snow hag. Dangerous and deadly, with a taste for flesh. If you hadn't killed her, she would have killed you. Most likely one of the guardians Lainule stationed here. But what was she guarding?"

Grieve winced. "I tore her throat open. She was so beautiful, and her voice so tender, and then she began to shift and I acted on instinct. I ripped her throat out and would have gorged on her blood if I hadn't managed to force myself away from her. But when she died, the spell broke and I was able to stumble away."

The anguish in his voice echoed in the chamber, but there was nothing any of us could do to make him feel better about savaging the Fae. So I decided the best bet was to let it be.

I glanced around, but we were alone. "She had to be guarding something, so what was it? Surely not the heartstone—she couldn't be the only guardian they'd set over it. So what was she protecting?" The magic was still heavy, but the longer she was dead, the lighter the energy was getting. I was almost able to stand on my own.

Chatter nodded thoughtfully. "Makes sense to me." He patted Grieve on the arm. "Come on, let's have a look around and see what we can find."

Grieve slowly stood, his face and fingers wet but clean. He rested his gaze on me, almost as if afraid of what he would see. I gave him a soft smile and blew him a kiss but didn't go near. The Indigo Court side of him was near the surface and I didn't want to set it off again. He seemed to understand.

Rhia and Kaylin struggled to their feet. The weight of the energy was still heavy, but we were all able to stand now. I sucked in a deep breath. The perfume in the air was clearing out. As I began to poke around, Grieve stared into the pool, his gaze fixated on something below the surface.

"Whatever she was protecting is in the pool." He motioned and, following his direction, I could see something glimmering in the center of the shallow water. It appeared to be made of brass, or copper. As I wondered just how we were going to get it out and remain dry, Grieve began to stride into the water.

"No!"

He stopped and turned back to me. "What?"

"There might be something in the water that we can't see." I was getting paranoid of every move we made.

Grieve shrugged. "There might, but there's no other way to find out what she was guarding and I think we will need whatever it is." He turned back to the water and, focusing, steadied himself as he walked farther into the pond. When the level of the pool reached up to his chest, he sucked in a deep breath and dove beneath the water. I stiffened, waiting for something to erupt from below the surface, but nothing happened.

As Grieve broke through the glassy surface again, he held up a small brass box. It was intricately embossed with an oak leaf design, and was about the size of a box of checks, with a hinged lid. While there was no lock, it seemed tightly closed.

Grieve stared at it for a moment, then handed it to me. "Open it. I cannot."

I cocked my head, looking at him, but he didn't explain. As I slowly touched the lid, a tremor ran through my fingers and I caught my breath. A cool wind gusted by and Ulean was at my side, whisking this way and that.

I'm not opening Pandora's box, am I?

No, but you open the door to a dangerous path and an even darker journey. But go on it you must. Lainule has given her consent, and therefore, wherever it leads, I will surely go with you. Open this box and there is no turning back. Open this box and you have sealed your fate.

Do you know what lies within?

Yes, I do. I was here when it was first placed in the waters, a thousand past a thousand years ago and beyond. I was here when the Black Annis was charged to watch the pool. Very few could have killed her, but she was not a match for one from the Indigo Court.

Was she the reason Grieve had to come with us? It suddenly occurred to me that Grieve was here for more reasons than the fact that he'd been part of Lainule's realm. If we were to battle Summer's guardians, we needed someone from the outside. Because even Chatter was no match for the Wilding Fae.

There are many reasons Grieve is here. This is the ascent to a culmination of events set in motion far in the past, the day you first met Grieve.

When I was Cherish, right?

No, long before that. In times neither of you yet remember, destiny had a hand in the machinations of the realm of Summer, and the Indigo Court through you. You can walk through the fire, Cicely. Or you can put the box back in the water, turn, and go. But your choice—regardless of what it is—will alter the destiny of both realms. Ulean swept around me, a driving force.

I stared at the box, my hand on the lid. I could feel it. This had been waiting for me. For a thousand years and more, it had waited for me to come.

I had to make a choice. I glanced up at Grieve. We could run away together. The thought struck me as quickly as a lightning bolt and disappeared just as quickly. There was no place *to* run. If we let Myst win, she would spread out, her Shadow Hunters growing, breeding, feeding, and eventually a good share of the world would be once again encased in ice—only this time it would be ice formed of the frozen blood of her victims.

I shook my head. *I will not run or turn away. I will meet the challenge, regardless of what it means for my future.*

Then you were truly well chosen. Open the lid, Cicely.

Ulean's gusts blew steadily around me, rippling across the waters. I sucked in my breath and opened the lid.

Within the flat, narrow box rested a pair of keys—one golden, one silver. They glimmered, and as I slowly reached in and took the silver one in my hands, a slow, cool rush began to rise through my body. I caught my breath and, not knowing what pushed me, turned to Rhiannon and held out the box. She held my gaze for a moment, then lifted the golden key.

We clasped hands and turned to the water. Something within was compelling me and apparently Rhia as well. As we faced the pond, the keys tightly in hand, the pool of water began to bubble. It fumed and frothed and rippled out in concentric circles as if something had jarred it from below. And then the water began to surge out, a ringed tidal wave splashing toward us out of the shallow crater in which it lay. I panicked—that much water could drown us, but as we stood there, facing the oncoming surge, something inside whispered to be calm, to wait.

"Get behind us!" I barked the order to the others, and Chatter, Grieve, and Kaylin crowded in without argument.

As the surge foamed out of the bowl and toward us, racing white steeds leading the wall of water, I sucked in a deep breath. Rhia did the same. We steeled ourselves, closing our eyes, but the expected impact didn't come. Instead, it was as if we were standing on boulders in the center of a rushing river.

I opened my eyes, cautiously, to see the waves swirling around us, splashing us as they rolled by. But Rhiannon and I—and the men behind us—stayed dry as the waters parted around us.

It felt like we were in some surreal revenge-of-nature movie. The surge seemed to continue for hours, but it must have only been a few minutes, and then the path cleared.

I glanced behind us to see the water rolling through the opening through which we'd come. The Black Annis's body was gone, swept up in the flow.

"Look." Rhiannon's hushed voice focused my attention again and I turned back to the crater that had been the pool of water. There, in the center, a pillar had thrust itself up from the ground. Formed of what looked like skulls, the bones were interlaced with amethyst and quartz, peridot and garnets. A grisly tower, with a door in the center that was gold on top, silver on the bottom, with two keyholes.

A tremor started in my legs and worked its way up to my heart. *This was it.* This was the beginning of the last leg of our journey. We were nearing Lainule's heartstone. I glanced over at Rhia and she nodded. We stepped forward, into the crater, and crossed the sloping bottom toward the tower.

Grieve, Chatter, and Kaylin silently followed behind us. They did not question or try to interfere. Once we reached the tower, we could measure its true height. It was thrusting out of the ground like some gigantic stalagmite, a good twenty feet high. And from here we could see that the skulls were intermingled with leg and arm bones, woven together in a tapestry.

The bones were purest white, shimmering with both their own light and the light of the gems. I wanted to reach out, to caress one of the skulls near me, but when my hand neared it, a low hiss made me withdraw. A golden green snake wove its way out of the eye socket, staring at me as it coiled, waiting. I nodded to it. There were guardians still, and we'd have to walk softly from here on out.

I turned to Rhia. "Are you ready?"

She nodded. "Yes. I think . . . we have to do this at the same time."

And so we stepped up to the door, inserted our keys, and on the count of three, we turned them, and the tumblers clicked into place.

Chapter 12

The door slowly swung open, the keys staying within the locks. The archway was rounded, and the floor within was tiled just like the passage through which we'd first come—the stones shimmering from some dark and brilliant internal light.

I looked at the others, then stepped through. As I passed the entryway, a hush descended, and once again the pressure of ancient magic fell on our shoulders.

Grieve slipped up to my side and motioned for me to stop. "Let Kaylin take the lead. I sense he is needed here."

I nodded, pressing back against the wall to allow Kaylin to slip by. We were working as a single entity now, trusting each other's instincts. Kaylin stopped beside me, touching my cheek.

"You and Rhiannon . . . life will never be the same," he said, then faced front. We fell in behind him, single file—me, then Rhia, Grieve, and lastly, Chatter brought up the rear.

The passage was short, opening into a room. But in front of the room, a lone maiden sat. I would have called her a girl, but she was dressed in a flowing gown and her hair rippled with gold, spilling down her shoulders. She looked as fragile as a butterfly caught in a strong wind. At first I thought she was a spirit—and maybe I was right, but there was no way in hell any of us were going to touch her to find out. The power surrounding her was so strong it shoved us back, like a giant hand separating her from us.

She was playing a stringed instrument that looked like a miniature harp. I listened, trying to catch the music, but the moment she strummed the strings, the wind caught up the sounds and tore them from earshot.

Who is she?

Ulean danced by, whispering as she passed. *She is the Maiden of Knowledge. The Daughter of the Air.*

Is she one of the Wilding Fae?

No, she is far more than that. She is . . . she simply is. This is but one of her avatars. Ulean softly rested on my shoulders, her susurration tickling my ears. *You must answer her questions to pass. If not, she will rip you to shreds.*

Answer her questions? What kind of questions?

I do not know. Whatever she chooses to ask.

I bit my lip. What the hell was I going to do now? I knew—as sure as I knew my own name—that there was no way to defeat this being. The Maiden of Knowledge was beyond fighting. I had the feeling that if I reached out to touch her, my fingers would slide through. But if she chose to go on the offense, her attacks would be all too physical.

How do I—

Do not ask me more. You must figure this one out by yourself, Cicely. It is forbidden for me to help you in this.

I sighed. Ulean would never deny me if it was possible for her to help, so I knew she was speaking the truth. I looked at the others and shook my head, then stepped forward. The Maiden of Knowledge looked up at me, her luminous eyes glittering in the dim light of the passage. I wondered how long she'd been sitting here. How long had she been keeping watch? Did she ever speak to anyone? Did anyone ever come to visit her? And would she ever be free?

Feeling unaccountably sad—her existence seemed so lonely—I moved forward to the point where the energy field stopped me. I cleared my throat. She watched me, unblinking, a soft light washing over her face.

What should I say? What should I do? And then a thought crept into my mind. She was waiting for me to speak. Perhaps, being the Maiden of Knowledge, she was here to give aid and advice.

"We come seeking passage. Will you help us?" My voice seemed out of place, and even though I was speaking softly, it echoed through the chamber as if I were shouting. I winced at its coarseness. Normally I didn't notice my voice, but here, in this place, it sounded rough and harsh.

The Maiden of Knowledge paused, then she strummed her harp, and this time her voice came crashing through the air, so beautiful it made me want to weep and fall to my knees.

"What is it that you seek? Why do you wish me to grant you free passage?" Her words thundered through the air, and I realized that if the wind hadn't caught up her singing, it might have deafened us with its force.

I stammered, taken back by the power of her presence. Suddenly frightened, and feeling like a bull in a china shop, I struggled for an answer that would suit her. "I am looking to help Lainule—the Queen of Rivers and Rushes. She is in danger. I come with her permission."

"Why should I believe you?" Her gaze was now fastened on mine and I felt like she was probing my mind, turning me inside out, shaking out my innermost thoughts to examine them. She rifled through me, stripping away layers of an onion, searching. The feeling was heady and terrifying and intrusive.

I shook my head. "Because I am telling the truth. Because . . . I promised Lainule I would help her if at all possible." That was the best I could think of—it was simple and it was the truth.

"What will you do if I refuse you?"

I stared at her, wanting to say we'd strike her down, but

I knew that was a pipe dream. Or that we'd find another way in, but I knew that wasn't going to happen and would be mere bluster. Finally I shrugged, feeling helpless.

"We will return home and fight Myst without the aid of Summer. We'll fight until she takes us down. And most likely, we will die. Because we need Summer's help to win against the Queen of the Indigo Court."

The Maiden of Knowledge rose from her seat, and her gown fell in waves, a gossamer creation of spiderwebs and silk, of feathers and birds' nests and the cotton of clouds. She approached the other side of her force field. I looked up at her—she was oh so tall, and oh so regal, and I began to realize that Ulean had been right. This was no Wilding Fae but a spirit caught in form, an energy that had never been human but only wore a beautiful face like a mask.

The Maiden of Knowledge slowly reached through the crackle of energy and held out her hand. I sucked in a deep breath.

Faith, I thought. This is where faith came in. I slowly reached out and rested my hand in hers. The feel was less that of skin and more of solidified air.

She wrapped her fingers around mine and then, with one smooth motion, drew me through the force field. I gasped as a thousand pins and needles stabbed me through. The Maiden of Knowledge laughed, but it was neither friendly nor comforting. Her gaze never left my face, and I found myself transfixed as she turned and led me behind the chair. There, against the wall, was the outline of a door.

"May I and my friends go through? Is this the path we need to take?" I was confused. It couldn't be this easy, could it?

Again, she struck her harp. Again, her voice rang out and from this close, it reverberated through my head like a gong. "You were telling me the truth. This is the way. As to your friends . . . they put their lives in your hands. They may accompany you, if they so dare." She stepped back and the field opened. The others filed in slowly. They looked drained, and I wondered what had happened.

The Maiden of Knowledge pointed to Kaylin. "First in line. Do you accept the responsibility? You are the scout, the tracker."

He winced, rubbing his head, and stepped in front of me. "I do."

She pointed to me next. "You are his second. You are the helmswoman, the conquerer. The results of this journey lie squarely on your shoulders and the choices you make. And you," she said, motioning to Rhiannon, "are third. The lady-in-waiting. Do not ask what it is you wait for, you will find out soon enough." Turning to Chatter, she said, "And you, guardian, are fourth." And then she turned to Grieve. "The Wounded King. You follow last."

Wounded King? What did that mean? Wondering at the labels she'd assigned to us, I kept my tongue. I was rapidly learning over the past few weeks that sometimes silence was the better part of wisdom. Grieve nodded and took his place.

The Maiden of Knowledge began to play her instrument and a swirl of sound echoed and vibrated through the walls. And then, slowly, the outline of a door turned to a sparkling veil. I couldn't see what lay beyond, but a strange hum began to emanate from the passage. Kaylin looked back at me and without another word stepped forward into the shadows.

⚜

How long we were in the passage, it's hard to tell. When we emerged, it was into a chamber as golden as the sunlight rippling through the trees at midday. The light was almost blinding. I shielded my eyes—the brilliance hurt and I winced, turning away. Grieve was doing the same, but the others just shaded their eyes. The chamber was so large it felt like we were truly outside rather than far under the ground.

"I feel like I've slept again." I yawned, but my body felt revitalized, as if I'd been through both nap and shower.

"Me too. Look." Rhiannon's voice was hushed.

I turned and, squinting, followed her gaze. There in the

center of the room was a plinth made of gnarled oak and ivy—real ivy. The ivy of the open woodland, not this alien forest of the deep caverns. The plinth rose about twenty feet into the air, and a spiral stair led up to a landing in back of it. Around the base, except at the start of the steps, a deep pit drove into the ground, so deep I could not see the bottom when I gazed into it. But it was wide enough to fall in, and I backed away, not wanting to lose my balance.

I stared at the staircase. "I have to go up there." The pull was so strong that I couldn't ignore it.

"Is that . . ." Rhia looked at me, wary.

"I think so." The pulse of a beating heart drummed from within the column of oak and ivy, running straight down through the tree stump, into the earth below. This was the heart of Summer, the wellspring from whence she sprang. This was Lainule's core, her essence.

The others waited, silent, as I began to ascend the stairs. Formed of green and gold glass, they were slick and spiraled around the trunk. There was no railing, and so I kept to the inside, leaning against the oak as I tried to avoid slipping. One misstep and I'd go over the side, and when I looked down, I realized I'd fall directly into the moat. To where that led, I chose not to speculate.

About a third of the way up, my foot slipped, and I scrambled, going down on my hands and knees with a jarring thud. Shaking, I struggled to stand and, after taking a deep breath, started again. The sound of my boots on the glass echoed through the chamber—the others remained silent, watching below. They couldn't help me. I'd been entrusted with this task by Lainule. I was the only one who would be able to retrieve her heartstone.

As I approached the top, the ivy began to wave, and Ulean swept by.

Beware. Be cautious. You are not through the tangle yet.
What is it?

But I didn't have time to wait for her answer. One of the tendrils reached out and wrapped around my wrist. I struggled against it, but the ivy came thick and fast and began to wrap me up like a spider wraps its prey. I was having trouble breathing and couldn't move fast enough to stop it. Below, I heard Grieve shout. The next moment, the tower quaked and the ivy sucked away from me, leaving me to tumble down the steps until I caught myself. The tower quaked again and I looked down.

The oak was caught in a frost that was spreading up its trunk. Grieve was standing on the steps, slack-jawed, staring as a layer of frost spread from his feet to the steps, and huge cracks began to form in the staircase.

Kaylin vanished as I glanced anxiously up at the top of the tower. I wasn't far from it—but the cracks were spidering up the glass, and soon the stairs I was standing on would break and send me tumbling to the abyss below. I made a run for it, staggering up the slick surface to the landing at the top.

Grieve jumped off the bottom step back to Rhia's side just as the foundation of the staircase shattered and vanished into the crevasse. I didn't have much time. I glanced around the top of the tower and there it was—a crystal box, and within the box I could see the brilliant emerald stone, pulsing with life and with light. I grabbed up the case, trying to decide what to do. Just then, Kaylin materialized on the landing next to me.

"Can you take the case while you're dreamwalking?"

He shook his head. "Yes, I can. As well as your clothing, since you'll have to change into your owl-shape and fly down from here. There's no returning down those stairs. Hurry—strip!"

I caught my breath, staring at him, reluctant to hand him the case. But there was no choice. I pushed the crystal box into his hands and pulled off my clothes, stripping as fast as I could.

The stairs were half gone, shattering like tempered glass into a thousand pieces. I kept my moonstone pendant, but everything else I gave to Kaylin, and he vanished back into the shadows. I glanced down at the stairs. Only a few more and the landing would go. I sucked in a deep breath and stepped to the edge of the landing. As the glass began to break beneath my bare feet, I gathered my courage and spread my arms, toppling over the edge in a freefall.

✦

Arms into wings, body into bird, nails into talons. As I headed toward the ground, Ulean caught me in her updraft and I was aloft, flying around the room. It felt so good— this freedom to soar, to fly, to . . . *what the* . . . from here, I could see handholds carved into the walls. I followed them up, and when I got to the ceiling, found a trapdoor right next to a thin ledge. *This was our way out.* I turned to fly down to the others when the door shattered open and a wave of snow and ice came swirling through.

Holy fuck. Three Shadow Hunters leaned through, their expressions triumphant. And behind them—Myst!

I spiraled down quickly, shifting as I hit the ground. Turning to Kaylin, I whispered, "You have to dreamwalk. You must escape with the heartstone, now."

He tossed me my clothes, the look on his face pained, and I knew he didn't want to leave us. "All right, but take this." He pressed something in my hand as I gave him a sharp nod and he was once again a puff of shadow and smoke, vanishing from sight.

I glanced at what Kaylin had given me. *The obsidian knife.* Gritting my teeth, knowing what was in store for us, I yanked on my clothes, as the Shadow Hunters began their creep down the ledge, using the handholds. Myst leaned in through the trap door, her laughter echoing through the room.

"Too late, too late, Cicely. And my Consort, what a naughty boy you've been. It's time for summer to end. It's time to bring the long night of the world." Her voice was chill, the winds of winter rushing through it. At least she only had three of her Shadow Hunters with her. But three of the Vampiric Fae against four of us? Not even the beginning to a fair match.

Rhia backed up, her expression grim. "We do whatever we have to in order to get out of here."

"Yes. And my first act is this." I swept out my fan and aimed it at them.

Cicely, do not overuse—

There's no choice. I cut off Ulean with an abrupt whisper. *"Hurricane force."* And as I swept the fan, all hell broke loose.

⚜

The winds rose, but this time so did I. I felt myself rise half out of my body, yet I was still attached to my form. I loomed, overshadowing the chamber. I was both my shadow and myself, rising up with the winds, no longer feeling their backlash, but this time they were coming from within me. I tried to catch my breath but my shadow-self did not need to breathe, the winds were breathing for me as they raged forth from my body.

Ulean shrieked, and I turned in her direction. I could see her—the celestial sparkling form that I had only before seen when I was dreamwalking with Kaylin. Now she was clear and huge, and she spun around me.

Draw the wind back! You do not know what you are doing!

But I had to move forward. I couldn't pull the raging winds back to me—they were sustaining me, lifting me up, making me a giant in my own world. The plinth shuddered as the hundred-mile-an-hour winds hit it square on. It shrieked, splintering as bone and branch broke apart, falling to the floor.

I took another step forward, shaking the room as I moved. Behind me, I heard Rhia, Grieve, and Chatter shouting, but I could no longer hear their voices, and right now I had work to do. I turned toward the Shadow Hunters and let out a long breath, and the winds struck the walls, shaking the chamber, howling as they echoed through the room.

The Vampiric Fae shrieked as I headed in their direction. They clung to the walls with a preternatural strength, pressing themselves against the tiles. I threw back my head, my hair whipping in the wind. As I laughed, my laughter rumbled through the room. The obsidian knife was still in my hand and now its energy began to ripple through me, a fierce hunger overtaking me.

I reached the wall and—shadow watching over my body—began to climb, like Myst's people, clinging to the walls as the hurricane-force winds thundered from within me. My heart was buoyed by their strength. I scuttled up the wall like a spider, like an insect, and as I reached the first Shadow Hunter, he cringed as I brought up the obsidian knife.

Kill, bleed, feed, drain him dry, suck marrow from bone, feast on his heart, bathe in his blood and brains . . .

The impetus drove me forward, drove my hand up, brought the knife plunging down into his body, as I ripped, tearing him apart. Laughter came burbling up, and I licked the blade, not caring when it sliced my own tongue. The salty taste of his blood only whetted my appetite and I reached out, intent on drawing him to me, but the winds that buffeted the walls sent him careening to the floor.

Even as he fell, I reached out to catch him and Ulean swept by, catching up the fan in her wake, yanking it off my wrist. I screamed, furious, but she sent it spinning down to the floor.

No! No! You do not dare!

Cicely, come back to me. Cicely, let go of the knife. Let go.

I cannot—we cannot withstand them without it—

Look, Cicely. Look above you.

I glanced up at the walls. The other two Shadow Hunters had scurried up, retreating to Myst's side. She was staring at me, her mouth in a rounded "O" and, for the first time, a look of hesitation filled her eyes. I ignored Ulean and began to climb higher, my gaze fixated on her. She would know what it was like to feel the kiss of her own weapons. The winds howled, raging up toward her and her warriors.

But before I could reach the top, she withdrew, and they were gone. We were alone. I growled, wanting to take her on. But the gusting winds began to recede, and Ulean took that moment to slam against me, making me reach for the wall to hold on, dropping the knife as I did so.

I gasped, shaking my head as my thoughts slowly began

to clear. I looked down, not sure how to get back down. I was exhausted and no longer seemed to have the same knack for climbing that I'd had a few minutes before. Grieve quickly began to scale the wall.

He reached me before I fell, and, using one hand to keep hold of the handholds, he managed to help me up to the top of the room. He looked down and motioned to Chatter, who said something to Rhiannon. She picked up my fan. Chatter gingerly picked up the knife, and they began to climb, with him helping guide her.

Within a few minutes, we were sitting outside the trapdoor, in the snow, staring at the path that Myst and her hunters had forged. It was somewhere near dawn, and they were nowhere in sight. I was almost sorry. If need be, I'd take up the fan and knife again, out here in the open, and get it over with. But inside, a voice of sanity whispered, *Even with the knife and the fan, you could not defeat her. You must have Summer's help.*

I swallowed my regret. *I'm sorry, Ulean. I did not mean to say those things.*

Yes you did, Cicely. At the time, you meant them. As Lainule warned you, overusing the fan can put you at its mercy. It changes you, makes you more a part of its element. Use it too often, with too much force, and it will suck you fully into the realm of air and turn you into a hybrid— a Wind Elemental not endemic to the realm. And most of those who have that happen go mad.

I pondered this for a moment, then told the others what had happened. "The combination of the wind controlling me, and the knife . . . I could have taken her on. I wouldn't have won, but I would have hurt her."

"But then you wouldn't have come back as you." Rhia shook her head. "Your father is right—the knife is too dangerous for you to use until you learn how to master the power of obsidian."

"We had to do something. Myst would have killed us." I shook my head. "I do believe I need to learn how to use the power of the stone, but we were in a tight spot. I now understand what Lainule and Ulean were warning me of about the fan. The power is immense. It will—and has—changed me. I came very close to being carted off by the winds."

"We'd better get back to the warehouse." Chatter glanced at the sky. "We are near morning, thank heavens. I'd say another ten minutes until dawn, which means Myst and her hunters should be hiding from the light."

"We'd better get moving." Grieve stood, holding out his hand to me. "Are you tired?"

"No, I'm strangely exhilarated. And the rest we had in the realm of Summer helped me a lot. What about you?"

"Same here. A little weary but with the adrenaline of the fight, and the sleep we got . . . I'm good to go." Chatter glanced at Rhia and she nodded the same.

I gratefully accepted it, allowing Grieve to pull me up out of the snowbank in which we'd been sitting. "Do you know what day this is? We went in on Monday."

Chatter squinted, closing his eyes. After a moment, he shook his head. "I don't know. But you have your phone. Better call Peyton."

"I'll have to leave a message—they're probably in the realm of Summer with Wrath and they won't get the message till they pop out." I pulled out my phone. "I hope Kaylin got away."

"Yeah, so do I." Rhiannon looked around. "Where the hell are we? Do we even have a clue? The forest looks the same to me here as it does anywhere. We could be twenty miles in, or we could be ten minutes from the road."

I punched in Peyton's number and left a message. Then I tried Kaylin. No answer. Sighing, I left my phone on and shoved it into my pocket. "Which way?"

Grieve glanced up at the growing light. "There—that's east. We head to the west."

As we started slogging through the snow, I began to notice that I felt odd. Odd in a way that didn't feel sick, so much as . . . *changed*. Something *had* happened to me. I pulled the fan out of my pocket. More than once, both Lainule and Ulean had warned me against using it too much, and I hadn't known why. Now I stared at it, wondering if I'd have the courage to ever use it again.

Chatter hadn't given me back my knife, and right now I didn't ask for it. Truthfully, the ferocity of my feelings scared the fuck out of me. It reminded me all too clearly that in another life I had been Myst's daughter. I didn't *want* to remember that, but every day it was becoming clearer that I was going to have to accept that fact and learn to use it rather than run from it.

Myst had been scared of me, when the wind and blood-lust from the obsidian were controlling me. And we needed her to feel fear. We needed her to hesitate, to falter while she thought things through. Every time we could put her on her guard, throw her off kilter, was one more inroad we had to destroying her.

As we plowed through the snow, my phone jangled. By now, it was obvious that morning had arrived, even though all signs of the sun were obscured by clouds. So Myst and her cronies were in hiding.

I pulled out my phone and answered.

"Cicely here. What's up?"

Peyton sounded relieved. "I'm so glad you're okay. You *are* okay, aren't you? It's been two days and we were beginning to worry."

So we'd been in the realm of Faerie for two days this time. This losing time thing was a little intimidating. "Lainule—is she still alive?"

"Yes, she is hanging on—barely. Kaylin arrived back here with the heartstone a few hours ago. But Wrath says you must be the one to present it to her. Where are you? Are you near a road?"

"I don't know . . . we're walking west, in the woods. I have no clue how far we are from a road. Can Wrath fly over the Golden Wood to see if he can find us? He knows where the cedar is, though we don't seem to be anywhere near that at this time. We came out a different way than we went in."

Peyton's voice echoed as she spoke to someone else. After a moment, she came back on the phone. "Yes, in fact, he's headed out the door now. Stay put, out from under the trees so he can see you. The moment he sees you, he'll land, and then you call me back."

"Where are you? Did Luna's sister make it in?"

"Yes, and we have some wonderful news. Well, potentially wonderful. But that will keep. Hurry and position yourself at a point where Wrath will be able to see you. As for us . . . well . . . we're in Lannan's mansion. Several things happened while you were gone and they weren't all good. And Cicely—be careful. Leo and Geoffrey are on the move, and they aren't going to stop hunting down you and Rhiannon. Be cautious."

As she hung up, I glanced around. "Let's get to open ground and then we wait for Wrath. And be careful. Watch out for any day-runners that might be Geoffrey's or Leo's men." I didn't have to warn them that Rhia and I were being hunted. They already knew that.

As we struggled through the deep snow, looking for a clearing, it occurred to me that Geoffrey and Leo were almost as dangerous as Myst. More so, because they knew we could kill them. I may have jangled Myst's nerves, but for now she still claimed most of the game board for her side. Geoffrey and Leo, on the other hand, were playing from the place of "nothing much to lose." And men—or vampires—who had nothing to lose were far more deadly than someone who had a reason to use common sense and caution.

Chapter 13

We'd been walking for about ten minutes when we found a meadow, with a large boulder in the center. We huddled near the granite slab, waiting, and within twenty minutes, I looked overhead and saw the great horned owl. *Wrath.* He'd found us. He circled high, getting his bearings, then slowly settled to the ground, turning back into the King of Summer as he landed. I ran over to him.

"We found the heartstone. But Myst almost caught us. Kaylin took the gem and dreamwalked out of there."

"I know. He was there when I left." My father stared at me. "He told us about the end fight. How did you escape Myst?" His gaze pierced into me and I knew I'd have to tell him what had happened. *Everything*, without censoring myself.

"The fan . . . it took hold of me and I became the hurricane. And then I used the obsidian blade to slaughter one of the Shadow Hunters. Myst and her other two guardians ran. She was scared of me." My words came out in a rush as I realized what I was saying. But it was true. I'd seen her face, felt the shock in her. Myst had retreated.

Wrath pressed his lips together. He let out a long breath

and then wrapped his arm around my shoulders. "Come, we need to get home. Lainule must have her heartstone and you must be the one to present it to her. I cannot touch it. We will speak of these other things later." But under the steady tones of his voice, I could hear the thunder in the distance.

We were a mere ten minutes from the road, though the distance was some nine or ten miles from where we'd begun our journey two days back. I called Peyton and gave her my father's coordinates and as we trudged through the snow, none of us said much. At least Kaylin had made it back. And it was daylight, so I wouldn't have to deal with Lannan—whatever his state—until tonight.

We broke through the undergrowth, out onto the road without any interference and there was Peyton, waiting. She looked grim, as we climbed into the car, but gave me a weary smile.

"I'm so glad you're back. Lannan's been pissed out of his mind and he's been raging around the mansion."

"Why did you go there instead of stay in the realm of Summer?" I glanced at her, then Wrath. Both of them looked uncomfortable.

Peyton bit her lip. "The energy within Summer's realm is like alcohol to my father. He was giddy on it, and one of the guards tried to goad him into drinking wine. Rex is a recovering alcoholic. He felt cornered, and when a werepuma feels cornered, the resulting tiff isn't pretty."

Wrath sighed. "Rex turned into his puma self and went after the guard. He didn't hurt him—" He held up his hand when I shot up, worried that Peyton's father might have been hurt. "Neither man was harmed. But it wasn't an auspicious start and it seemed better to have them join Lannan in his mansion. Luna and Zoey went with them. I checked on them yesterday and they were fine, and Lannan—for all his foibles—kept them safe. The realm of Summer is an uneasy place for any but those of Fae blood, either half or full."

I grumbled, leaning back, but kept my mouth shut. I had the feeling the guard had been deliberately baiting Rex, but there was no way to prove it, and really, what good would it do except to cause even more animosity? So I decided to leave it alone. We had enough problems as it was.

"Is Lannan angry at me for not showing up for two nights?" Better to hear what I was in for now, rather than be surprised when we got back to the mansion.

"Lannan is . . . shall we say . . . livid. He swore that if you didn't come back in one piece, he'd go after Wrath and Lainule himself." Peyton cleared her throat, glancing at Wrath in the rearview mirror. But he just shrugged.

"The vampire would stand no chance. We have more powers than he can imagine." He glanced at me. "And *some of us* are letting our powers run wild."

I shivered under his watchful eye. I knew Wrath was pissed at me for disobeying him about the knife. And Lainule wouldn't be all that pleased by how casually I'd been using the fan, but too fucking bad. We didn't have a choice. And I'd proven one thing: We could scare Myst.

Peyton wound through the streets. It was unnaturally quiet in New Forest, hardly anybody on the sidewalks, even though it was now morning.

"Did something happen?" I glanced around sharply. There was a feeling in the air of foreboding. I could practically smell the fear.

She cleared her throat again. "There was another massacre last night. A theater. The Vampiric Fae got in and barred the other exits. It was . . . bad."

"How bad?" I didn't want to hear, but I had no choice. I had to know.

"Thirteen dead, before they could get the exits open. Another five killed in the streets. Four of them children. People are asking what happened to Geoffrey. Lannan's scheduled to give a speech tonight. He'd do it by television, but his image wouldn't show up on it, so he's going to give it via radio. A notice has gone out in the paper about it, and a news team will broadcast the audio simultaneously on television."

"Eighteen dead?"

"Yeah. There would have been more, but Lannan's guards busted up the scene. They took down seven Shadow

Hunters. Lannan said he's not going to pussyfoot around with the public. He's going to warn them about Myst and tell people to get the hell out if they can."

I stared at my nails, pretending to examine them. There he went again, doing something I was forced to give him credit for. I didn't want to give him kudos. I *wanted* to fault him for everything I possibly could, but the fact was that Geoffrey had tiptoed around this matter until people died. Lannan was taking direct action.

"That's going to be dangerous. You can bet Myst will try to stop him." The thought of Myst getting hold of Lannan set my stomach on edge. As much as I'd threatened to stake him, at the core Lannan wasn't the enemy.

"That's why Lainule must rise today. She can marshal the Summer Guardians. They take their orders from her. They would obey me, but they look to her for morale and inspiration and there is very little of that in the realm lately. If Lainule returns to health . . . they will willingly fight." Wrath leaned forward. "Can you drive any faster?"

Peyton nodded and stepped on the gas. The car roared and lurched forward. I leaned back in the seat, closing my eyes. I wanted to ask what Luna's sister had found but not in front of Grieve—there were too many risks for me to get his hopes up yet.

"Another thing," Peyton said as she rounded a curve, hugging the road with the car. She was an excellent driver.

"What now?"

"I called Ysandra at the Consortium. I told her that we need help tonight—that when Lannan gives the order to get out of town, we know Myst is going to try to stop him. She said she'd send one of their elite squads. I have no clue what she meant by that, but it sounds like the cavalry is coming." She sounded very pleased with herself and I gave a little cheer.

"Good going. We need all the help we can get." We were squashed into the car like bugs, but I didn't care. The promise of a hot shower and clean, warm clothes loomed large in my mind.

But first . . . first we would visit Lainule, and I would

take her the heartstone, and she would survive. For the rest of the drive we were silent, all deep in our thoughts. I leaned my head on Grieve's shoulder and he slipped his arm around my shoulders. At this point, any comfort was better than none.

❧

Wrath hurried us into the mansion, under the watchful eyes of Lannan's day-runners. He surprised me by instructing me to take a quick shower. "You need to revive yourself, to be at your best. And by now I know you enough to know that a shower will help. Your cousin must also come with us. And Chatter and Grieve. The rest—stay here."

Surprised that the others were coming, too, I acceded without question. I followed Peyton, who led me up the stairs of what had been Geoffrey's mansion and now belonged to my own master. *Master.* The word grated on my tongue, but I had to accept it—Lannan owned my contract. And we needed him too much right now for me to fight the fact.

The room he'd assigned to me was lush, with blatant sexual portraits lining the walls. Although they could all be called art, they were definitely erotica bordering on outright porn. Lannan was needling me but I ignored it. The bathroom beckoned, and I stripped on my way there, leaving clothes in a trail behind me. My skin was raw and chapped, and in the warehouse we'd had to use a sink to wash up. This bathroom was anything but utilitarian.

The spa tub lured me like a promise from a lover, but I knew that I didn't have time for that luxury. *But soon,* I whispered to it. Soon I'd be soaking in a bubble bath. Instead, I chose a vanilla-scented bodywash from the selection on the counter and entered the walk-in shower. The tiles were heated, radiant heat pouring through the floor, and I groaned as I sank to the bench in the stall. I turned on the rain showerhead full force and let the soothing, steaming water stream over my naked body.

My muscles hurt. My bones hurt. Everything ached. I closed my eyes, leaning back as the spray hit me full force from three directions. I pushed away the thought of where I was and just enjoyed the beading water on my skin. My hand drifted over my stomach, over my wolf, and I felt a warm growl come from it, and the flare of arousal.

Lightly stroking the tattoo, I closed my eyes and thought of Grieve, of his platinum hair streaming down his shoulders and his otherworldly features and those brilliant dark eyes, black as night, swirling with stars. I thought of his hands and how they played across my body, and his lean, muscled frame and how I felt when I ran my tongue across his chest and down toward the V leading to his cock.

My wolf let out a low rumble and I circled it with my hand. "My love," I whispered. "I am thinking of you. Wanting you."

The next moment, I felt someone watching me. My eyes flew open and I looked up to see Grieve, standing beside me, naked and aroused. I did not question him, said nothing, but opened my arms as he reached down to embrace me. He lifted me to stand in front of him, leaned me against his shoulder, danced with me under the water, slowly moving, kissing my hair, my face, my lips. I sought his mouth and pressed against it, my tongue sliding between the soft folds of his lips as he turned and sat on the bench, bringing me down on him, to slide down the length of his cock.

As he rigidly thrust inside me, I moaned, my pussy opening up like a flower blooming to spring. I leaned back, braced by his arms, the water pounding against my breasts and face, soaking in the heat of the steam and the heat of his body. Grieve let out a low groan and, holding me tightly, gently lowered me to the floor of the shower. As the water pulsed over us, he began to thrust, his cock rubbing against my clit, driving me higher. The steam grew thick around us, and the water streamed off his back, down his sides, to rain lightly against me.

I rested my head on the heated tiles, my back soapy and sliding as he drove into me, again and again. Seeking for something I couldn't even verbalize, I gazed into his face, drinking in his expression.

Grieve snarled, his teeth gleaming. And his snarl hit my

core like whisky, burning my throat, burning my stomach, making me ache for him to eat me up, drink me down, to possess me in a way no one ever had.

My breasts rubbed against his chest with every stroke he made, and I began to cry. The world was heartless and hopeless, but here, within this shower stall, within this tiny bubble where we were the only two alive, I felt the power that we could create between us.

"I love you. I love you with my heart and my soul, forever and ever." I whispered the words, not trusting the slipstream. If it caught them, it might carry them afar, to those waiting to destroy what happiness we'd managed to scrape together.

"Cicely, you are my own. You are my queen. You are the world for me. There is no life without you." He pressed his lips to mine again, driving the words out of my thoughts until only passion remained.

I wondered if we were going to meet Luna's sister before we left, but that was not to be. We were dressed and downstairs without too much delay, where Wrath simply looked at us and nodded to the crystal box sitting on the table. I slowly approached. Lainule's heartstone shimmered within, glowing, fading. Picking up the box, I felt it quicken.

Rhia and Chatter joined us, looking rosy-cheeked, and I had the feeling their shower had gone something along the lines of ours. But none of us spoke. There was nothing left to say until we found out if this was going to work.

Wrath led us out onto the grounds, where Peyton and Rex were waiting. They drove us to the rippling waters of Dovetail Lake—a large pond or small lake, depending on how you looked at it. We remained silent. So much rode on what would happen next. If Lainule failed to rally . . . I didn't want to even think about the consequences then.

Peyton and Rex waited in the car for us. Since it was daylight, the chance of being attacked by Shadow Hunters was almost nil. We headed out, to the portal leading to Summer.

A guard was on the lookout for us. I don't know how he

knew we were coming, but it was obvious he'd been expecting us. Wrath looked at him.

"My Lady?"

"Still lives, my Lord."

Wrath nodded, then led us through the shimmering veil into the realm of Summer. I reveled as the warm weather hit but was struck by the leaves on the trees. There was no mistaking it this time. They were turning color. Autumn had found its way into the Court of Rivers and Rushes, and the bloom was fading even as Lainule's powers waned.

We followed him through the grass, to the royal barrow. Once again, we were ushered into a hushed chamber, and from there, Wrath led us to Lainule's bedchamber. As I entered, I couldn't help but let out a prayer to whoever might be listening that this work.

"Approach the bed." Wrath motioned for the others to stand back as I slowly drew close to the four-poster bed and climbed the steps beside it. Lainule looked still as death, but her lips were parted and I could still see the rise and fall of her breast as she took shallow breaths.

"I have your heartstone." I leaned down and handed her the box, but she could not reach up for it. Biting my lip, I turned back, but Wrath would not speak to me, and I realized it was up to me to figure out what to do.

I opened the lid and the pulsing of the heartstone filled the room. I thought I heard panpipes, and drums echoing in the distance, and a sudden wash of the scents of apple and honey and sweet wine rushed past me. I closed my eyes as a ray of sun broke through the room, coming from the center of the heartstone as its brilliant green rays collided with the lights that sparkled in the air and on the walls.

Slowly, hoping I was not making a mistake, I lifted the heartstone out of the box and held it in my hands. It burned brightly against my skin, and I cried out, almost dropping it as my skin reddened. I turned quickly, on instinct.

"Rhia—come help me."

Rhiannon nimbly climbed the steps and sat beside me. She reached up, took the heartstone from my hands, and gasped, her head dropping back as a low growl of ecstasy rolled from her throat. I stared at her. Her hair sprang out of its braid, wild around her shoulders.

"On her chest—the stone must rest on her chest." I knew what to do, but it turned out I wasn't the one who could actually do it. However, I could pull down Lainule's comforter to expose her perfect, tanned breasts. They were lovely and I stared at her. Unearthly she was in her beauty, even though she was almost dead.

Rhia slowly lowered the stone to rest on Lainule's chest, between her breasts, and a rumble filled the chamber. The music grew louder, the drums grew stronger. I clasped my hands to my ears, but Rhia reached out and grabbed them, and we held hands, waiting and watching. The roar was deafening, and yet the music caught me up in its rhythm and I began to drift.

The stone began to glow so brightly that I thought it would blind me. And then it began to—*melt*? The gem began to liquefy against Lainule's skin, and the liquid emerald pooled between her breasts. I wanted to reach out, to touch the glowing gem's essence, but I knew better. I kept hold of Rhia's hands. We watched, wordless, speechless, as the gemstone liqueur began to soak into Lainule's body, leaving a red mark on her skin where it had been.

As the drumming grew louder and the panpipes more frenzied, Lainule's eyes began to flutter.

Wrath uttered a low moan and fell to his knees, hanging his head. He looked both overjoyed and bereft, the two emotions waging war in his eyes. Grieve and Chatter looked slightly confused, but then Grieve looked up at me and caught my gaze and I felt a stirring from my wolf, but this time it wasn't seductive so much as a recognition of something I felt I *should* understand but didn't.

Another moment and the heartstone had vanished into Lainule's skin. Her breathing grew stronger, and in the next beat she sprang to a sitting position, her eyes flying open. She turned to me, her face a whirl of expression, and then she looked at Rhiannon.

The next moment, tears began to trickle down her cheeks. "Thank you, my girls. Thank you. You are both my salvation and my doom." And with that, she rose from her bed, glowing like the sunrise, and I realized that I'd never truly seen her in her power. I'd only met her after Myst drove her from her center, from the core that made up her wellspring.

"What do you mean, your doom?" My words hung in the air as Lainule ducked her head, smiling.

She leaned down to give me a kiss on the forehead. "Worry not about it at this moment, child. What is to be is now in motion. What was is passing away. What is important is that we now have some control over this situation. Now I can fight back." She turned to Wrath, who sprang to her side. "My Lord, I am so sorry . . ."

"No more. Say no more. 'Tis all forgotten, my beloved." He wrapped her in his arms and kissed her, long and deep, and I felt their bond—an ancient one from times long past. "I will go with you, wherever you journey. You know that, my sweet." He rested his head on her shoulder.

"I can be a trial at times, and my whims are not always pleasant, but you have always been there, to walk by my side." She held the back of his head, a tender look on her face, and I felt like we should turn away, leave the room—this was a private moment, intimate in a way beyond even sex.

"And always, always shall I be."

They kissed again, and then Lainule turned to me. She held out her hand. "My stepdaughter, come. You and your cousin."

I stepped forward again, Rhia beside me. "Lainule, I am so glad to see you are well and healed." I gazed at her. Something was different, but I couldn't put my finger on what it was.

"Healed? I suppose you can call it that. Come now, I must be off to rally my warriors. There is to be havoc tonight—I can feel it rising in the air and Myst is behind it." She paused, looking at me again. "What did you do to yourself? Cicely . . . the fan . . ."

I hung my head. "I was facing Myst. I summoned up a hurricane. I became the storm." And that's when I realized that's exactly what had happened. I hadn't been caught up by the hurricane, I had *become* the hurricane. I had carried the winds with me as I moved. I turned to her. "That's why you warned me about the fan—why you had Ulean warn me?"

She smiled faintly, the aloof reserved nature creeping back. "Yes. Once the fan masters you, you will be forever ridden by the Element. You now belong to the air, my young one. It is good your Cambyra nature is Uwilahsidhe—the owl."

"What would happen if I'd had something where its primary element was earth?"

"You would be soil-bound, tied forever to the earth, unable to fly. You would be hobbled when in owl form. As it is, you have enhanced your natural abilities, but the price is a great one. However, you have paid a far greater price by restoring me. Do not think I will forget your deed."

I wanted to ask just what price I'd paid, but before I could, Lainule turned to Rhiannon. "By your births, you and Cicely are tied to each other's fate. Your life is about to shift, my dear, in ways you could never imagine. But there will be time enough for that later. I must be away, to round up my Summer Guardians. Quickly, tell me what is happening. I can feel the shift on the slipstream."

And so, a thousand questions whirling in the back of my mind, I forced myself to push them away as we told her about Lannan, Geoffrey, and the rumble we expected that evening.

⚜

Lainule dismissed us but bade us stay within the realm for a while longer. "I will have news for you. Go and rest for a moment."

Wrath stayed with her, while Rhiannon, Grieve, Chatter, and I left the barrow. The leaves on the trees were no longer fading—I could feel the shift, but they hadn't regained their color as I'd expected.

"I want to go flying while we're here." The feel of the sun on my skin made me long to shed my clothes and soar into the sky.

"Aren't you tired?" Rhia wrapped her arm around my waist as we sat on a stone bench outside the barrow. The cobblestone seat was engraved with runes and swirls, with delicate chips of peridot and garnet caught in the mortar holding together the smooth, rounded pebbles. I traced the stones with my fingers, listening to the *zing* of magic that raced up my hands.

I closed my eyes and leaned my head back, letting the sun stream on my face. "Exhausted of this battle? Yes. Tired? No. But I want to fly. I need to stretch my wings."

"Then do so." Grieve leaned over me, looking strangely out of place. "Fly free, my love. Take it on the wing."

I glanced around. "Would anybody mind?"

"Go ahead. It will be all right. And we are safe here."

I stood, shedding my clothes. I was beginning to feel less self-conscious about the process, and nakedness was starting to be commonplace with me. Rhia watched, a smile playing on her lips.

"I've never really seen you change. We've always been in battle, or you've shifted before I came on the scene, or something or other. Now I get to watch what happens. Does it hurt?" she asked.

I shrugged. "A little. More so when it's cold, but that's one of the downsides. It's like . . . shedding your skin. Putting on a new mask for the night. Or, rather, taking off a mask." I wasn't sure exactly whether the owl form was my natural form, or the two-legged Cambyra/magic-born, but right now I didn't care.

I stepped away from the bench and looked for a tree. The oak nearby would do. Nimbly, I swung up, caught the lowest branch, and climbed up the bark face, ignoring the abrasions it caused my knees and feet. After a few minutes, I was high enough to edge out on a thick limb—carefully, considering it was between my legs. I did not need a set of pussy slivers to deal with.

Cautiously, I held on to the trunk as I stood, balancing on the branch, bending slightly to keep several of the higher branches from knocking me off. The ground was a dizzying distance below, but it didn't bother me. Instead, I clutched my moonstone pendant and closed my eyes, feeling the power grow. Then, with one long deep breath, I spread my arms and toppled forward.

The rush of air whistled around me as I fell. The rush of plummeting to the ground sent me into a delighted giggle as I began to transform. Arms to wing, torso to body, nails to talons—and then I soared. The updraft carried me aloft, and I realized I could hear laughter in the wind around me.

Ulean? Is that you laughing?

No, but I am here.

Who did I hear?

The wind spirits. Sylphan ones. They are playing in the currents and they dance now around you. They want to play.

How do they play?

With their biting winds and whirling leaves.

And then I felt them. I could feel the swirl of their bodies, the tailwinds in their wake. I spun and flew, diving into the center of their circle and through to the other side. They wheeled around me, laughing. I rode the currents, soared upward, screeching loud as the freedom of being on the wing overtook me. All I wanted to do was fly, soar, hunt, ignore everything else. I rode the winds, feeling free again for the first time in a while.

As I swooped down to speed past Rhia and Grieve and Chatter, I heard their laughter as they watched me, Rhiannon pointing with wonder in her eyes. And then, as I circled, I saw the great horned owl—my father—waiting in the tree for me. I soared up, losing my playful spirit, intent. As I settled on the branch near him, I could feel his desire to hunt.

Come with me. We will hunt. You need the practice.

And so I followed him, wings outspread, into the wide field, as we went to catch our prey. Hunters, we were, and usually cloaked in shadows. Maybe there was a little bit of Myst in us both.

Chapter 14

We'd circled the meadow twice when I caught sight of a mouse and gave chase. I was winging in hard, fast, talons down and ready to snatch up my dinner when Wrath suddenly landed and turned back into himself. Worried, I gave the mouse a pass to freedom and made a sharp turn, gliding back to him. With a soft landing, I touched the ground and willed myself back to form.

It was becoming easier to change each time. My father had told me that eventually I wouldn't need the necklace. It really was just a booster and had triggered my latent abilities at first, but now that I was aware of that side of myself, the inner knowledge of what to do was coming to the surface.

Whenever I shifted back, I ended up in a crouching position, and this time was no exception. I fell forward, catching myself with my hands, then slowly rose, stretching into my full form. I stood naked, unabashed as various Fae walking by glanced at me. Grieve handed me my clothes and I quickly dressed.

"What's going on? Is Lainule all right?" I asked, worried that maybe she'd had a relapse. I pulled on my jeans and fastened my bra, then pulled my turtleneck over my head. It was too warm for the realm of Summer, but once we left we'd be right back in the middle of a snowstorm.

"She's fine now, thanks to you." My father gave me a long look, almost a sad one, but then shook his head. "You and Rhiannon saved her life. We've been summoned back to her chambers. She has rallied help for the meeting tonight with Altos."

I nodded, not wanting to think of the potential carnage that lay ahead. "I'm ready. Let's go." I reached for Grieve's hand as Chatter reached for Rhiannon's, and we followed Wrath back to the barrow.

Lainule was waiting for us, looking fresh and vibrant, like she'd never been sick. But when Wrath kissed her hand, a tear rolled down her cheek, dropping to his fingers. He pressed it to his lips, gently sucking it up. Something was definitely afoot, and I intended to find out what, but right now was not the time. Especially since she was surrounded by a dozen burly warriors.

The men were hardened—even I could tell that—and while they were full Cambyra Fae, they looked as deadly, if not more so, than any Were or yummanii. They were decked out in armor the color of the sun, and they carried dark blades—obsidian daggers like mine. The presence of so much of the stone sang to me, and I licked my lips as I eyed the serrated edges, wanting to reach out and touch one of them. Wrath looked at me, then at the blades, and slowly shook his head.

But Lainule ignored my reaction. "These men will fight for you. They will protect Lannan, and they will protect you. They will offer up their lives if need be, and should any of Myst's unholy Shadow Hunters arrive, they will battle to the death."

I focused my attention on them again, tearing my gaze away from their daggers. "We thank you. In this battle no one can stand alone against Myst and the Indigo Court. Have any of you encountered the Vampiric Fae before?"

Even as I said it, I wanted to sink into the ground. I was an *idiot*—a total fucking jerk. "I'm so sorry," I said, biting my tongue. "I did not mean to . . ." I stopped, just stopped. Anything I said would make it worse, I decided.

Their gazes did not flicker, but a ripple ran through the group. Lainule smiled at me softly when she saw my discomfort.

"Yes, you remember now. All of these men lost loved ones. They watched Myst's horde tear them to bits, eat their hearts out alive. The floors of my barrow ran red with blood the day the Indigo Court lay siege. They did not stop for children or women or the old and infirm. All who could not run were devoured or enslaved. Some—like Grieve—were turned to be their allies and servants. A few—like Chatter—were saved by the grace of those who could keep their sanity after the change. So, yes, Cicely, all of these men have met Myst in battle, and all would give their lives for revenge. However, they've been ordered to act only when you and your friends give orders. They will come to you later this day, at Lannan's mansion, and they will journey with you through the night. I will not be far from hand, either."

As Wrath led us back through the portal, Rhia turned to me.

"What do we do if Myst doesn't show?" She kept her voice low. But I could tell everyone else had heard her.

"She will be there—or her allies. There will be blood tonight."

We headed back to Lannan's mansion, grim. Along the way, I could only wonder what waited in store for us this evening—and just how bad the carnage would be.

❧

The first thing that happened when we walked through the door to what had been Geoffrey's manor was that Kaylin hurried toward us, looking haggard but relieved. He motioned for us to follow him into one of the side rooms, where we found a luxurious lunch set out.

Lannan's touch was obvious—exotic meats and cheeses lined the table, along with fresh bread hot from the oven and sliced fruit with whipped cream. And wine. Enough wine to drown an elephant.

I glanced at the woman who was acting as hostess. She was obviously from Lannan's stable—she had long dark hair to her butt and was curvy, buxom, and pale. A bandage covered her neck—discreet but placed right where I knew his fangs had been. She wore a low-cut vest held closed only by a thin leather lace, and a pair of skintight jeans. Another bandage covered a spot right above her left breast.

She seemed to notice my attention, because she gave me a sly smile and winked at me. "My Lord has bid me attend to any of your needs, Cicely. *Anything* you want, you just have to ask." Her words gave *May I help you?* a whole different meaning.

I swallowed back a retort and simply smiled in return. "Do you have any sparkling water? I don't want any alcohol."

"As you so wish." She dug around in the minibar under the counter and came up with a bottle of Paviina—one of the more expensive brands of sparkling water. As she poured it over ice and added a twist of lime, she caught my gaze again. "My name is Juliana. Should you need anything else, please ask. I would welcome the chance to attend your needs."

As I carried my glass of water to the table, where lunch was spread out buffet-style, I let out a long breath. Lannan was determined to entice me into his world, but he had the wrong number. I didn't swing that way, though Regina had set me off with a kiss once. But even if I wanted to play in the women's camp, I wouldn't pick one of his bloodwhores to experiment with.

At the table, I wearily fixed a plate for myself—bread, sliced ham, aged cheddar, a handful of cherry tomatoes, some fruit salad. I added a chocolate cookie to the mix and sat down beside Luna, who was sitting next to a tall, willowy blonde. The family resemblance was there, though—even though they were opposites, with Luna being short, dark, and curvy.

"Cicely! Meet my sister, Zoey." She waved for Grieve and Chatter to join us. "Zoey brought a bunch of references. I've been going through them since she got here

Monday. Grieve—I'm so glad you're here. We may have found something that can help you." Her eyes were glowing, and she looked so excited that it was almost hard to watch. Hope had become something I both clung to and feared. But it had let us down too many times.

Grieve, on the other hand, jerked his head up, his eyes wide. "Do you think it will work?"

Zoey shrugged. "Hard to tell. In a sense, what it looks like is a spell to separate the energy of the Indigo Court from the host energy—almost like peeling apart two merged layers. Myst's bite, her forcing you to drink from her, changed your nature, but if we can separate out her signature from yours, we might be able to help you at least control the condition."

"You think there might be a chance, then?" Grieve caught her gaze and held it.

Luna nodded slowly. "We do. But, Grieve, I don't think there's ever going to be any way to fully revert you back. Not to how you were before she got hold of you." She stopped eating her bread at that point, staring at the table as if she expected Grieve to throw a fit, but he just sat there, looking stunned.

"If there's *any* chance I can gain some control over this curse, I want to hear about it. I never expected there to be a cure, so I'm not disappointed about that." He looked up, over at her sister. "So, you have found records?"

She nodded. "Yes. And they have detailed rituals about ways to reverse certain aspects of the curse. But they aren't easy, and frankly, I think all of them have a chance of backfiring."

He held her gaze. "What's your guesstimate on percentage of backfiring?"

Zoey bit her lip. "Forty percent . . ."

"Pro or con?"

"Con. In my estimation, there's about a sixty to sixty-five percent chance this will work. The other thirty-five percent? Hard to tell. Either not work at all or backfire. And you can never tell which way it's going to swing."

I swallowed the last of my sandwich and wiped my

fingers on a napkin. "What kind of magic do we need in order to cast the spell?"

Luna and Zoey exchanged glances. Luna pushed her plate back.

"First, we need five witches—four for the elements and one for spirit." Luna hung her head. "I can hold spirit, but the responsibility . . . what happens if we fail?"

"Then we fail." Grieve looked at me. "Chatter and Rhiannon can both hold the fire, but Chatter can also command earth. You hold the wind. We need water."

"What about you, my love?" I gazed into his eyes, both frightened and hopeful. We could do this. The possibility that we could actually free him from some of the chains Myst had placed around his neck overwhelmed me. It was hard to even speak.

"Grieve cannot take that part. Not when he's the focus of the ritual." Luna shook her head. "I can call the water, too, but then we'd need someone for spirit."

Just then, Peyton walked over. "Let Kaylin hold spirit."

Luna clapped her hands. "Yes, that would be perfect. So we have our five Elemental watchtowers." She turned to Zoey. "What else do we need?"

"A drummer—I can do that. I've been trained on the doumbek. But I think we still need water. Luna, you'll have to be the singer of souls for this. The ritual demands that you and the person holding spirit—Kaylin—enter Grieve's mind to unwind Myst's energy from his." Zoey looked around. She pointed to Rex. "What about him? Can he hold water?"

Wrath stepped in, shaking his head. "I will do this. I am the King of Rivers and Rushes. Water is my element as well as the air."

I turned, startled. "You will help us?"

"If this can help Grieve, we should attempt it. Even if we destroy Myst, he'll always have the tendency to revert back to the energy of the Indigo Court." Wrath glanced at the clock. "We dare not attempt the ritual before the speech tonight, just in case something goes wrong. But that will give us time to gather the rest of the components needed. What else does the spell require?"

Zoey pulled out a book and showed us the title: *The Tide of the Indigo Court*. "This was written several hundred years ago, and I found it tucked away when I went searching through the archives."

"What will the Akazzani do to you if they find out that you've removed material from the catacombs?" Luna gazed up at her sister, and all I could see was gratitude in her smile. But her smile disappeared when Zoey spoke again.

"They would punish me. There are crypts deep in the fortress, and they contain the shades of the dead historians who have passed out of our realm. When someone does something egregious, they're locked down there for a time with only the shadows and ghosts for company. They seldom ever break another rule."

She sobered, then shook her head before Luna could say anything. "I chose to do this. You needed my help. I understand why. I told them I was taking family leave for an emergency. This qualifies."

"We can't ever let them find out. I can't bear that you might undergo that treatment." Luna paused. "You could stay with us. When it's over. I miss you."

Zoey frowned, staring at her feet. "You know I am Akazzani. I've lived my entire life thinking I will die in the fortress. I have broken the rules for you, but I don't know if I could willingly leave them. They are my family, Luna, in a way you and our parents can never again be." She pressed her lips together.

Luna let out a little cry, clutching the table. I could tell the comment had cut her to the quick and that she was trying not to burst into tears. I wasn't sure if I should say anything or let it go.

Kaylin, however, wasn't as reticent as I. "If Luna isn't your family, what the *hell* are you doing here? If she's family enough to break the rules for, then obviously she's more important than the rest of your colleagues." He leaned over Luna and placed a protective hand on her shoulder. She glanced up, a startled look on her face, but smiled at him.

Zoey's eyes narrowed, and she looked to be on the verge

of making some snide retort, but then she just shook her head. "You don't understand. I didn't mean I don't love her—or my parents. But there's a bond . . . It is created when we are brought into the Akazzani, and nothing short of expulsion can break it."

"Don't argue, please." Luna let out a short sigh. "If we are to work magic for Grieve, we have to be united. Let it go, Kaylin. If Zoey is happier with the Akazzani, she should remain with them." And that was the end of that.

Wrath intervened as well. "Cicely, you must be exhausted. Rhiannon, Grieve, Chatter, Kaylin, all of you as well. Go rest. You will need the reserves tonight." He stopped me as we filed out of the room, drawing me to the side.

"What is it?" I glanced up at him.

He lifted my chin, looking into my eyes. "Tonight be cautious, my daughter. There will be bloodlust flying. I have foreseen it. The power of the winds, they are now a part of you in a way that you do not yet realize. The fan—open it now."

I pulled out my fan, spreading it open. As I held it in my hand, I realized I couldn't feel any sparkle of magic from it, no tingle, no . . . nothing. "What happened?"

"You became the hurricane. You became the wind. The power of the fan transferred into your soul. You no longer need it to harness the winds. You can pass it on to another because now you are part of its Element. But it's a double-edged sword. Because you no longer need an anchor, it makes you dangerous. You haven't had a chance to train yet, to realize just all you can do."

I sighed, leaning against his shoulder. "First, I find out I'm not just magic-born but that I'm also half–Cambyra Fae. Then I find out I was Myst's daughter in a past life and that obsidian sets off the bloodlust still in my soul. And now you tell me that the winds have settled in my being? I feel like I'm losing myself."

"No, my daughter, you are actually in the process of finding out who you really are. In time, all of this will become second nature. You are evolving, Cicely, into a force like none I've ever seen. You are vulnerable, in danger, but the potential within you is frightening." He stroked my shoulder gently, placing a soft kiss on the top of my head. "When we go to protect Lannan this evening, you must be cautious when you call on the winds."

"Let's pray I don't have to do that." After a moment, I asked, "What of the Unseelie? If Myst was Unseelie and she is now Queen of the Indigo Court—what of the rest of the darker Fae? Did they all become part of the Indigo Court? And Lainule, is she the Queen of Seelie?"

Wrath looked surprised at my question but walked me toward the grand staircase leading upstairs. As we ascended, he tried to explain.

"There are the Grand Courts, and then the Lesser Courts. There are Fae Queens all over the world—each rules a different region. Lainule—and I—are Queen and King of about half of this continent. Myst wasn't the Unseelie Queen before she was turned, but she killed Tabera, who was, by destroying her heartstone and set herself up in her place. She may have taken the title of Winter, but she is not recognized as the Queen of Ice and Snow here, though. She is an upstart."

"So what happened to the Unseelie under Tabera's—is that her name—rule?"

"Myst terrified them. They scattered. The Wilding Fae are remnants of some of them, and others joined the Court of Rivers and Rushes even though they don't really fit in." Wrath frowned, looking very much like he was trying to decide whether to tell me something.

"What is it?" I pressed him. If the Fae were part of my heritage, it was important I know things like this. "I want to learn. It's my heritage."

"So it is." After a moment, he stopped and leaned on the curved railing. I sat down on the step next to him. "The balance has been disrupted in this region for so long that chaos became normal. As I said, when Myst reemerged, she took the place of the Unseelie Queen—the Queen of Winter, who rules over chaos."

"Myst doesn't strike me as someone who likes to share."

"No, she does not. Myst seeks to conquer. Here, it's easier to build her armies because the Grand Courts live far away on the other side of the world. Summer and Winter are the sun and the moon—day and night, and while they do not necessarily like each other, they accept the necessity for both powers to instill a natural balance."

I nodded, slowly beginning to understand. "But why haven't the Grand Courts stepped in?"

"There are many things that are too difficult to explain in one brief talk. They are old, Cicely, in a way that Lainule and I are not, and they often overlook the dangers that evolve outside of their area. The Grand Courts are so far removed from the world in which we live that they ignore things until it's too late."

"Almost like Crawl is for the vampires . . ."

"Yes, they live in a different realm, so far in the mists . . ."

"So Myst was able to sneak in and cause havoc."

Wrath clapped me on the shoulder. "You do understand. Very good. But we cannot allow her to succeed—her idea of normalcy is to fill the world with skulls and sinew, to rip and shred and destroy. She is destruction incarnate, without check. She is the untamed force of the storm, of death on a rampage."

"If she is a force and fury, then perhaps she cannot help herself," I said softly. "If Myst killed Tabera, and for a time there was nothing to check Lainule as Myst gained her power, why didn't Summer rage through, since she has had no opposition all of these long years?"

"My Lady rules with justice. It may not seem kind, at times, but the Queen of Rivers and Rushes understands the nature of checks and balances. She sees the universal scale of creation and destruction and understands the need for both, even if we haven't had our opposing force for so very long."

Cautiously, I said, "When we were in the woods, Rhiannon could see the door to Lainule's chamber. Only Cambyra Fae can see those magical doors." I looked at him, waiting.

But my father merely shushed me and I knew better than to press the matter for now. "No more questions now. Up and to bed. Sleep deep. We will all need our strength tonight, my daughter."

As he sent me on my way, I thought about what he'd said but the swirl of his words became a fog in my head, and I yawned again, barely able to drag myself into my room. Ignoring the leering pictures and tapestries around me, I stripped, then crawled into bed, sighing as I drew the soft covers up around my chin. The mattress was heaven. The blankets were soft against my skin. And even the thought of the evening to come couldn't intervene as sleep claimed me and carried me off to my dreams.

※

I was walking through the forest, with Rhiannon beside me, and we were holding hands. I turned to her. "Show me. Show me yourself."

"I don't know how," she said, looking over her shoulder. "I don't even know where to begin." She let go of my hand and walked over to one of the cedars that towered in the woodland. As she played with one of its boughs, fingering the needles, she said, "These are not the forests of my dreams. I dream of forests filled with oaks . . . with rowan and hawthorn. I dream of the smell of peat and the misty mornings overlooking the ocean."

Nodding, I glanced up at the tree. "These are my roots—this land is my anchor. Even when I was Myst's daughter, this was our homeland. But where were you?"

Rhia smiled faintly. "I'm only beginning to remember. But long ago and far away . . . it's in a fog, but I remember the forest. And I was there. I was on my belly . . ." Her voice dropped and she lowered herself to the ground, stretching out. "I remember, on my belly, through the grass and the trees. Through . . ."

Silence fell between us. Rhia looked up at me, her irises shifting, her pupils becoming slits. "On my belly . . . in the grass." She began to transform, and as I watched, her legs fused together and her arms to her sides.

I stepped back. No, she shouldn't be this . . . *Danger*, my owl self whispered to me. *There is danger here. Fly away.*

I shifted into owl form effortlessly, still wearing my clothing, and flew up into the branches of the tree. This was my homeland, this was my land, this was my rightful place. And below . . .

Below, Rhiannon's skin scaled over, and her hair flowed into the scales, creating a beautiful diamond pattern down her back. She wove back and forth, rising, sleek and muscled and mesmerizing. I watched as she coiled, staring up at me, her tail rattling. I could feel her hunger, and my own was stirred. I had carried off snakes before, my talons keeping them from striking me.

But something stopped me from sweeping down on her to snatch her up. Some recognition that we were both necessary, that we could not harm the other. And in her gaze, I saw the same feeling reflected back at me.

We are the new way. My thoughts reached out to her.

We are two of a kind. We are amber and jet—fire and ice. We are kin. Her voice whispered in my head.

And then the snake wavered back and forth, in a dance of sorts, and turned, slithering off into the undergrowth. I watched her go. There would be other meetings, other altercations, but she and I would remain linked. Forever, whatever shape our bodies might take.

✦

"Cicely, it's time to get up. Time to get ready." Peyton shook me awake. I wanted to brush her off, to say "Come back later," but then I remembered where we were going and I struggled from under the covers. At least the room was warm, unlike the warehouse.

"Do I have time for a shower?" I loved showers. Showers woke me up and made me feel ready for whatever was coming.

She nodded. "Yes. But a quick one. I'll see you downstairs." As she left the room, I pulled my hair back in a ponytail to keep it dry, and stepped under the glorious water,

rubbing bodywash over my body in a thick sweep, the lather
sudsing up to make me inexplicably happy. I rinsed and then
stepped out of the stall, wrapping the towel around me.

As I headed back into the bedroom, I heard a noise and
whirled around, ready to yell at Grieve for startling me.
But it wasn't Grieve standing there.

Lannan was leaning against the wall, looking golden
and brilliant and impeccably dressed. I glanced at the door
and saw that he'd turned the lock so no one could get in. He
laughed at my expression as he slowly crossed the room.

Frozen, I couldn't move, my thoughts slogging in slow
motion.

As he reached my side, he slid one arm around my waist
and drew me to him, his lips bare inches from mine. "Welcome back, Cicely." His voice was low and I could feel no
breath as he spoke, no pulse of heartbeat racing through
his fingers. His face crinkled into laughter. "Your expression is priceless. Aren't you going to greet your Master
after being gone for so long?"

Before I could speak, he pressed his lips to mine, and
suddenly he was kissing me as an explosion of desire
rushed through my body. I struggled against him, but he
squeezed my waist a little harder, and then—before I could
stop myself—I was kissing him back.

Chapter 15

"What the hell are you doing?" I fought him away as soon as I realized what I was doing.

He didn't let go of me but broke out of that delicious, decadent kiss. "Why, simply welcoming you to your new home." His voice dripped with sarcasm. He sat down on my bed, still holding on to my waist, and he pulled me down on his lap so that his knee thrust between my legs. I wasn't wearing underwear and the knowledge that my pussy was against the denim of his jeans both repulsed me and titillated me.

I wanted to crawl off and hide. Lannan had the perfect knack for making me feel two inches tall. "Thanks, but I need to get dressed now."

With a laugh, he let go, but as I stood up, he grabbed my towel and it fell away. I grimaced, scrambling to try to cover my boobs, but one look at the delighted expression on his face and I stopped. I stood straight, naked, facing him. Let him look if he liked.

After a moment, I turned to my closet but instantly realized my mistake. He was at my back in a blur of motion, pressing me against the dresser, spooning me. I could feel him rigid beneath the front of his jeans, hard and demanding. He slipped his hands around to run them over my nipples.

"You like this, don't you?" His voice was rough as he pinched my breasts, rubbing hard. "One word and I'll fuck you. One simple 'please' and my cock will be up in you so fast you won't be able to blink."

My wolf growled, low and threatening. "Take your hands off me now before Grieve shows up here with a stake. And he will."

"Perhaps I should have him put down. Rabid curs are dangerous." But the next moment, Lannan let go and stepped away. He gave me a narrow look. "Oh, sweet Cicely. I hear you are going to protect me tonight against Myst and her minions."

"I wouldn't laugh them off so easily if I were you." I grabbed a pair of bikinis out of my drawer and stepped into them before he could get a better look at my snatch. I fastened my bra, yanked on my jeans and zipped them up, and pulled a thick sweater over my head.

"Perhaps not, but would you have me turn tail and run from the Goddess of the Ice Sculpture?" His voice was still sarcastic, but he sobered somewhat and I could see beneath the veneer. Lannan wasn't quite as confident as he sounded.

"Where's Regina? Will she be there?" Maybe I could get his mind off my body by mentioning the one woman—well, vampire—he seemed to actually give a damn about. The fact that they were brother and sister squicked me out, but hey, it worked for them, and as long as I didn't have to join their reindeer games . . .

He shrugged. "She is preparing. She will be there, along with a veritable army of my guards. We should be able to put down any uprising by the Indigo Court."

"There's also a group coming in from the Consortium and twelve of Lainule's elite warriors. As well as the rest of us, for all the good we can do." I brushed my hair back, sleeking it into a ponytail. I didn't want to put on makeup, but at a look from Lannan—he pointedly nodded to my dresser, where I saw a palette of cosmetics set out—I sighed and sat down at the vanity, making quick work of painting my face.

"So, you really expect there to be trouble?" This time, his voice was sober, and I could feel his eyes on my back even though I couldn't see him in the mirror.

I nodded slowly. "Think about it. Not only did we rescue Grieve, but I stole something away from her grasp. Something she wanted so much that I guarantee you she's out to kill me. Furthermore, when you give the order for the town to evacuate, Myst isn't going to like the idea of relinquishing her feedlot without a fight."

"Yes, I know about Lainule's heartstone. I heard the story. Wrath told me." Lannan's hands were on my shoulders, but this time, he didn't seem out to grope me. He leaned down to whisper in my ear. "You are brave, Cicely, for one of the magic-born."

"I am also my father's daughter." I let out a long sigh and glanced over my shoulder. "Lannan, we can't let them win. Do you understand why I went to the Consortium?" I was hoping against hope that he wouldn't hold it against me. "I know Crawl would probably order you to kill me or something equally as bad because of what I did . . ."

Lannan dropped his hands away from me and strode over to a chair where he could look me in the face. He quietly crossed his right leg over his left, folding his hands on his crotch. Nervous, I waited for a moment, but he showed no sign that he was about to jack off in front of me, so I relaxed.

"Cicely, I am not my predecessor. Yes, I am a hedonist. Yes, I would love to fuck you in every hole you have, but trust me—I do not relish altercations. Though I could probably take them on, I have no desire to fight your father and Grieve. Not at this moment. But you must understand something about me."

He leaned forward, staring intently at me with those jet obsidian eyes. "I am not stupid. Never underestimate my intelligence. I don't crave the same type of power Geoffrey sought. I am Regent by default. I would not keep this position if given the choice. I am far happier being free of these responsibilities, but when the Crimson Queen gives a directive, I obey to the best of my abilities."

"Then you aren't going to punish me for talking to Ysandra?" Surprised, but relieved, I relaxed. I'd been expecting nothing short of a beating, although knowing Lannan, it wouldn't be a flogging but another humiliation scene.

"No. The Petros woman is nothing for me to worry about. The Consortium is as corrupt as the next institution, but if they offer help, I will accept it. Frankly, I could care less about fighting Myst. This is not my war. Geoffrey started this battle, and he wanted to soothe his bruised ego. So I welcome help. We may not need it, but I won't turn away those who might be useful to me in the future."

And with that, he stood and motioned to the door. As we passed through into the hallway, Lannan offered me his arm. Startled, and feeling unable to refuse—when Lannan showed a gallant side, it paid to acknowledge it—I took it and we quietly descended the staircase.

❧

I had deliberately avoided telling Lannan about our plans to help Grieve, and I hoped no one else would spill the beans. Right now, we needed to focus our efforts on emptying the town without interference from Myst. Luck was with me when we entered the room. The others looked over at us but said nothing.

Grieve's face was overcast with a dark shadow and I knew he'd felt Lannan's advances toward me. As he glanced from Lannan to me, I shook my head at him, mouthing *Let it be. Leave it alone . . .* into the slipstream. Grieve snarled. Still scowling, he did nothing. But he kept his gaze glued to the vampire.

"We'd better make plans now that you've had a chance to sleep for a while." Wrath spread out a blueprint on the table. "Here's the radio station—it's housed in the World-Com Building, midtown. The building is used for a number of businesses, including a local credit union and a series of offices on the upper floors, which house architects, a couple of lawyers, and a decorating firm."

We studied the plans. I flipped back to the first floor and tapped the paper. "The New Forest Radio Station looks to be recorded in a studio on the main floor. There are numerous entrances and exits, too many to assign guards to."

"I disagree." Lannan said. "I have enough willing guards here to cover every door into and out of that building." He looked up, daring anybody to challenge him.

I stepped up to the plate. "That's not the most productive use of your men. It will scatter them too widely. If you cover every stairwell, every door, the Shadow Hunters will be able to overpower them. That would mean a loss of manpower because while you are better matched to fight the Vampiric Fae than we are, your men can still be destroyed."

"Then what *do* you suggest, my lovely Cicely?" Lannan glared at me.

I shrugged. "I think it's better to cover the studio doors with numerous guards and set up several men on the roof with cell phones to keep watch. Then send out the rest of your men to the streets. Because you can bet that the moment word goes out that you want people to evacuate New Forest, the Shadow Hunters will be hunting anybody they can find. I believe the Regent is under legal obligation to guard the city in cases like this."

"Does Myst even *know* you're making this announcement? Why should she think anything amiss? Why are we expecting a fight tonight?" Peyton leaned back in her chair. "I agree, we should be prepared, but I am curious as to why you think she has inside information."

Lannan shrugged, turning to Peyton. "Geoffrey still has spies among my men. I know this, but haven't been able to ferret them out yet. I think he would not be above sabotaging my efforts by arranging for Myst to overhear the scuttlebutt. Also, an announcement that I'm making an emergency speech has gone out in the paper this afternoon."

"Myst has eyes and ears everywhere in this town." I shook my head. "She'll be ready. And when she arrives, she won't be alone."

"Myst had a personal vendetta against you before," Rhia said. "But after that little show in the chamber room, I don't think she'll stop at anything to avenge herself." She turned to Peyton. "Myst was there. She almost had the heartstone, but Cicely snagged it right out of her grasp. The look on Myst's face was terrifying."

Peyton sucked in a deep breath. "I've seen that look." And she had—Myst had captured Peyton, and Heather had given her life to save our friend.

Rhia shivered. "I thought she was going to swoop down and rip you apart right there . . . but then . . . when you went after the Shadow Hunter, something changed. You frightened her. And a vicious dog is bad enough, but one that's cornered—far worse."

"That's my thinking. She knows I'm a real adversary and I'm a little afraid she'll overestimate me and plan accordingly. She won't rest till I'm gone." I stared at the plans bleakly. "We're going to have to wing our way through this. There's no way to predict what's going to happen but—" I stopped as one of the butlers entered the room.

He bowed to Lannan. "Sir, a contingent from the Consortium to see Miss Cicely."

"Show them in, but keep a close eye on them." Lannan turned to me. "If they pull anything stupid in my home, all bets are off."

"Understood." My neck was on the line.

As we waited, the butler led the group in. I wasn't sure what to expect. Would they all be in robes? Would they all be carrying staves or wands? Would they be crackling with magic?

One out of three wasn't bad, considering the odds we were up against.

The group filed in, silently. I was shocked to see Ysandra leading them, wearing a catsuit, formfitting and pure white. But her belt was made of crystal—quartz spikes ringing her waist—and they were humming with energy. Her hair was pulled back in a sleek braid that hung down her back, and her glasses were gone. The prim librarian had turned into Lara Croft. She smiled at me, nodding.

Behind her, the range was as varied as one might expect in a costume party. Five more women, and six men, stood at attention.

Five were in robes—three of the men and two of the women—like I'd thought they might be—the material flowing and black as the night, and they carried wands ranging from silver to copper to wood.

The rest of them wore jeans and what looked like hoodies, which I soon realized were made of a very thin, slick material.

Ysandra noticed my gaze. "We're all dressed according to our abilities and what we intend to do. The material of their jackets will keep them warm in the snow but not impede movement." She turned to Lannan. "You are Regent?"

He nodded, as the door opened again and Regina came hurrying through, regal as always, but her heels marking a swift pace on the floor.

Regina Altos—Lannan's sister and his lover—was Emissary to the Crimson Queen, and she was also one of the scariest vampires I'd met. She was ruthless compared to Lannan, but she was also willing to listen to reason. And she adored her brother. In many unnatural ways.

"There are Fae at the door." She stopped, staring at Ysandra and her group. "Consortium . . ."

"Yes, we are from the Consortium and we're here at the request of Cicely and the Moon Spinners. They are members of our group and they have a right to call on us for help." Ysandra stared down Regina, an act I'd never found advisable, and to my surprise, Regina looked away first.

"I see." Regina turned to Lannan. "You knew of this?"

"I did. Let it drop. If Cicely is correct, and I happen to believe she is, we will need all the help we can get. Let the Fae in." He turned to Wrath. "Perhaps you should escort them?"

Wrath excused himself and headed out of the room. I turned to Regina. "I'm glad to see Geoffrey didn't harm you." And honestly, I was. Even though she scared the crap out of me, there was something about Regina that I respected. She was a hedonist like Lannan, but first and foremost, she was wedded to her job. She took her position as Emissary seriously and I admired her work ethic, even if I wasn't all that fond of the vampires.

She gave me a surprised look, but then an aloof smile stole across her lips and she inclined her head. "Cicely, you are looking well. I hear that Geoffrey tried to have you and your cousin kidnapped. We cannot allow that to happen, so I told Lannan to bring you here."

I blinked. "You told Lannan . . ." Then I stopped. Lannan had led us to believe it was all his idea but apparently not. Instead, I simply smiled back. "Thank you for your offer. I hope we aren't an imposition."

"The living are always an imposition of one sort or another but one we willingly accept into our home at this point." And with that backhanded compliment, she turned to Lannan. "I have orders from the Crown. You are to proceed with your plans to evacuate the town. We cannot allow Myst to take control of New Forest, nor can we allow her to destroy the population. It would damage our position and treaties with the yummanii and the magic-born."

Ysandra stepped forward. "That is precisely why *we* are here. The Consortium's treaties forbid us from turning a blind eye when one of our members' lives is threatened, whether personally or by a force intent on overthrowing local government. Since you are local government—"

"We do not rule," Lannan started to protest, but Ysandra waved away his arguments.

"Do not attempt to deceive me. I'm fully aware that the Vampire Nation truly rules a good share of the towns where you have established Regencies. The Consortium does the same, although we tend to keep a lower profile. While there are puppet governments in place, most of this world is now divided between your rule and ours." She glanced over at me. "Don't gape, it's not becoming. Surely the influence of the vampires and the magic-born has not escaped you?"

I pressed my lips together and shook my head. Then, finding my voice again, I said, "Influence, yes, but controlling government, not so much. But I spent most of my life in bigger cities, on the run with my mother. Remember—I had as little to do with authority as possible."

Lannan, Regina, and Ysandra stared at me, then shook their heads and went back to discussing politics. I sidled away, moving next to Luna and Zoëy.

Zoey had a strange look on her face. "This is why we keep our records," she said softly. "This petty bickering over who controls what. They'd all be surprised if they would read some of the records in the great halls of the Akazzani fortress. There are older powers than both the Vampire Nation and the Consortium at work in this world. And no, I'm not talking about the Fae."

I glanced at her, wanting to ask her more, but at that moment Wrath returned. At his side marched Lainule, and behind them, the contingent of Fae.

They were solemn, looking neither right nor left, as they spread out in two lines behind their King and Queen. As I gazed at them, my heart soared, a surge of pride racing through me. I realized I was beginning to identify with my Fae nature more and more.

Lannan looked at the Fae, then at the magic-born. "We might as well move to the bigger chamber and bring in my men as well. It's time to talk strategy so we don't all end up shooting each other by mistake." And with that, he and Regina led the way and we filed out of the rapidly filling room and into one of the ballrooms where we could spread out and discuss plans.

❧

The next hour was a flurry of consulting with Lannan, Regina, Lainule and Wrath, Ysandra, and my own group. The warriors—Fae, vampires, and magic-born—stood at attention, listening and keeping quiet so that everyone could hear us.

We argued, mostly about where to post the guards. Lannan still wanted to cover every door, but neither Wrath nor I thought it practical. Finally, we agreed on covering the main entrances, securing the side doors, and keeping lookouts armed with cell phones on the roof so they could call us with any developments.

I glanced over at the Fae warriors. Their obsidian blades still called to me. Wrath caught my look. "You dare not take your blade into battle—look at what happened with the fan."

Lainule frowned. "What are you talking about, my husband?"

Wrath stared at me and—reluctantly—I explained the hold the blade had over me. Lainule forced a cold smile to her face. "It gives her an edge. And any edge over Myst . . ."

"You cannot be serious, my wife. It puts her in danger." Wrath stared at Lainule, shaking his head. I held my breath, hoping they wouldn't have another falling out this close to battle.

"Danger? We are all in danger. She is your daughter, and she is as good as my adopted daughter, but whatever danger there is, we *all* share it."

"Would you be so quick to put your niece in as much danger?" Wrath's nostrils looked pinched.

Lainule narrowed her gaze. "Leave *that* subject alone, my husband. That discussion is for *another time*." Her voice was hard, cold, and she stared at Wrath until he finally inclined his head in agreement.

Ysandra broke in. "There is time for arguing later. We are agreed, then. We cover the main doors, the hallway leading to the studio, and the roof. Meanwhile, Lannan—Regent—you send out troops onto the street to guard against insurgents from Myst's court taking the city when the word goes out."

Lannan nodded, a look of amusement playing over his face. "As you so wish, Lady Ysandra." But his tone was lightly patronizing and his lip twitched when he said her name. I had the feeling Lannan would just as soon have retreated to his study for an evening of reading.

"We have gone as far as we can with these plans. Myst must make the next move." Regina pushed out of her chair and stood. She'd not bothered to change, still in the red leather bustier and black pencil skirt she'd worn earlier.

Her perfectly coiffed chignon and brilliant red lips never shifted, and I wondered if she ever got dirty or unkempt. A little part of me wondered what she looked like when she and Lannan were at it, but I quickly dismissed that thought. I didn't need to know and I sure didn't want to be invited to join in.

We headed toward the door, filing out in order. As we waited for the others to leave, I turned to Peyton.

"We haven't had a chance to talk and I guess now isn't the time, but how's it going with your father? And has Anadey shown her face?"

She shook her head. "I haven't heard a peep out of her, or about her. That's just as well for now. As for my father . . . Rex is a good man. I really resent the fact that my mother kept us apart all these years. He made mistakes, but he was willing to try and compensate for them. She wouldn't listen. I guess I understand—he hurt her—but sometimes . . . not often, but now and then a person can change."

I nodded. "We killed Heather while we were out in the woods," I said softly so that Rhiannon didn't hear me. "The snow hag warned us she was there. Rhia and I . . . we staked her together."

Peyton blinked, ducking her head. "Ouch."

"Ouch is right. But she's out of the picture now. She can rest, and Myst can never control her again." I hadn't mentioned Heather much since we got back. Rhia had been through a lot—more hell than she was used to—and I didn't want to compound it by ripping open the still-bleeding wound. "I just thought you should know."

"Thanks. I don't want to step on delicate territory." Peyton fell silent as we swung into line, filing out the ballroom door last. As we headed to the foyer, behind the others, there was a noise and a vampire—one of the guards— staggered in through the grand double doors. He was bleeding, with several stakes thrust into his body, but none had managed to reach his heart.

Lannan stopped short, motioning for his guards to close the door. "What happened?"

But before the guard could speak, before the men could

reach the door, all hell broke loose. A flurry of activity hit the foyer, as Myst's Shadow Hunters spilled into the hallway. Screams echoed around the large room, as they went into action, attacking whoever was closest.

I turned to the others. Myst had decided to take the offensive. She'd come to us and all our plans were so much spilled milk. Frantic, I waved at the others. "Spread out! Whatever you do, don't let them corner you."

Wrath whirled around. He held out his hand and there was my obsidian blade. "Take it," he said hoarsely. "We have no choice. This is going to be bloody."

I laid hands on the blade and felt the tingle stir within me. As I sought for the winds, whispering a prayer to Ulean that she might help me, the Shadow Hunters continued to pour through the door.

And with that, the battle was on.

Chapter 16

"Holy crap." Rex's voice echoed from somewhere to the side as the horde of Shadow Hunters pushed through the doors. There must have been twenty or more—it was hard to count in the milling throng. I heard a scream but couldn't see who had cried out in the sudden flurry of chaos.

The vampires were flying into battle—everywhere I heard their snarls, as they fell upon Myst's brigade. They were a vision in black, snapshots of carnage, and there in the front, Lannan and Regina led the way. At least the pair didn't lack for bravery. And then I saw them take on one of the Vampiric Fae; they closed in on the cerulean-skinned man, fangs down, hissing as they approached from both front and back.

They toyed with him, like cats with a mouse, Regina shoving him into Lannan's arms even as he shoved the man back into her embrace. She dipped her head and struck, fangs sinking deep into the flesh, as the creature screamed and flailed. He didn't have time to defend himself. They had taken the offense. Then Lannan fell on him. He sank his fangs deep into flesh at the base of the throat, ripping down through the skin, leaving two long gashes in his wake. The blood flowed freely and Lannan pulled away, laughing hoarsely before licking his way up the man's chest.

The Shadow Hunter was screaming, still alive, as Regina held him fast, sucking deeply. I could hear the gurgle of blood in her mouth as she drank him down, and the smell of copper filled the air. As the Shadow Hunter quit struggling, dropping limply in her arms, Lannan grabbed him and thrust him up, bench pressing him over his head.

"We do not take prisoners!" He turned and, with a mighty throw, sent the Shadow Hunter hurtling into the crowd at the door. The look on his face was triumphant, and he grabbed Regina, kissing her deeply as the turmoil raged on.

In the chaos, I stumbled back, turning to find myself facing one of Myst's guards. His eyes glittered and he began to unhinge his jaw. I screamed, first out of fear, then out of outrage. I brought the knife up, staring at it, feeling the tingle race through my hand. It would be so easy to give in . . . to let the rage overtake me.

The Shadow Hunter saw the blade and a streak of fear fled across his face. He started to back away, and I followed, arm still upraised, the blade urging me on. *Kill them, kill them, take their blood, take their bodies, feast on their souls, drink their spirits . . .*

And why not? They are intent on feasting on us. The thought sprang to mind, and I laughed, slow and easy, as I leaped on him. He rolled to the side, though, before I could reach him, and my blade shrieked, cheated out of its offering. I turned, altering my position to match his. As he once again dodged to the side, I anticipated his move and was there waiting.

"Surprise! I'm not so unobservant, after all." I swiped the knife at him, stabbing for his shoulder, and the tip of the dagger kissed cloth, ripping through his shirt. He howled, and once again his jaw stretched as he tried to transform. But I struck again, this time with the edge of the blade, and sliced a thin weal across his face. Blood began to drip down from the gash, and my blade sang to me.

Thirsty, thirsty, thirsty, take him now, take him for me.

I wanted to obey, but reason caught the little part of me that was actually listening, and whispered, *No, you must control the blade—you cannot let it to continue to control you.*

Fighting to retain mastery, I forced away the drive to wantonly strike back.

Clear thought, I must have clear thought. Winds of the world, clear my head. I hadn't expected an answer, but a clear light breeze rushed through my mind and the desire to indiscriminately kill and feast backpedaled. My glance darted quickly around us—there were people fighting on all sides, and I could hear the groans and sighs of those going down for the last count, on both sides.

A nearby section of the massive fight opened up and I caught sight of Grieve in wolf form, a bloody arm in his mouth. It looked like one of the Shadow Hunters'. At that moment, the gap closed and I couldn't see him anymore, but I had my own worries.

The Shadow Hunter had taken advantage of my momentary lapse of attention to scuttle closer. He was on me now, and I could feel his breath and see the needle-sharp teeth poised over my shoulder. His eyes—the same black with sparkling stars as Grieve's—glimmered with bloodlust.

"Mine," he whispered. "The heart, give me your heart."

Only he wasn't asking for my love. He lunged at me and I brought up the knife. The blade sang as I slashed forward, ripping into his throat, severing his jugular. The dagger gave me good aim, it guided my hand, seeking out the flow and pulse of blood, and now as the liquid spurted from the severed artery, the blade shrieked with delight. I knew better than to pull back—the dagger would be furious, and so I bathed it in the blood, and the sensuous feel of the slick, viscous liquid pouring down the blade and over my hand sent me reeling. I came right there, the orgasm ripping a shriek out of my throat.

"Cicely!" Chatter's voice echoed through the brawling mob, over the sound of groans and thuds and the whistling of blades landing in flesh. He broke through a fight between

two of the Fae and a Shadow Hunter, but he took one look
at my face, then at the blade and the Shadow Hunter who
was writhing on the floor, and stopped.

"Finish him off and get on to the next one," was the only
thing he said.

I caught his gaze, and whether it was repulsion or worry,
I couldn't discern, but the look on his face sent an icicle
through my heart. Snorting, I turned back to the Shadow
Hunter. Let Chatter fight his battles his own way. He didn't
understand the glory of the blood. I fell on the Vampiric
Fae and finished him off, leaning down to lick up a long
swath of the crimson life-force. As I did, two boots landed
in front of me, and I looked up to see Lannan staring down.
He gave me a slow, sensuous smile, full lipped, and then
blew me a kiss and was off again.

I dragged myself up in a haze brought on by the energy
of the fight, the taste of the blood, the urging of the blade.
In fact, blood was flying everywhere, and it was a wonder
the vampires were keeping themselves in check.

The fight was thick, and I pushed my way through a
group of Fae engaging a couple of the Shadow Hunters. As
I came out the other side, I saw Ysandra and the five Consortium members wearing robes. They were facing a group
of five Shadow Hunters. Ysandra was gritting her teeth, her
hands palms forward, as if she were pushing a great weight.

The ripple from her hands told me she was keeping back
the Shadow Hunters while the five robed witches prepared
a spell. Another moment and they joined hands, forming a
human pentagram with Ysandra in the center. The energy
began to flow, surging through their arms as the elements
entwined. Earth to air, air to fire, fire to water, water to
spirit, and finally, spirit combined them and focused them
through Ysandra. She opened her eyes abruptly, as if she'd
woken from a deep sleep, and then her palms quivered and
a blast of energy ricocheted from her palms, sending the
Shadow Hunters sprawling, howling as they tried to cover
their eyes.

The force, strong and brilliant, rippled through the room,
and every Shadow Hunter there screamed. The next moment,

four of the Fae warriors moved in and, before they could protect themselves, the five Vampiric Fae on the floor were lying dead, their throats slit neatly through.

Ysandra folded, caught up by the arms of her comrades, then within seconds, she stood again, looking ragged. I pushed my way up to her. "Can you do that again?"

"Not for a while, the force of the power racing through me tears me up inside. But I have other tricks up my sleeve." With that, she turned and vanished into the crowd, looking for the next enemy.

Another flash, though not nearly as intense, told me that more magic was being cast, and then I saw Rhiannon and Peyton. They were fending off one of the Shadow Hunters. Luna was singing something that seemed to be giving them extra strength, but the Vampiric Fae was a strong one, and he looked hungry. He was pressing in on them.

I rushed up behind him and plunged the dagger between his shoulders, again shuddering as the blade tasted blood. I was really beginning to take a dislike to the dagger as much as I welcomed the help it gave me.

The Shadow Hunter stumbled forward, tripping over one of the Cambyra Fae who looked very dead. I ripped the blade out of his back and struck again, but this time he turned to block me with his arm, and the dagger slipped from my fingers, they were so slick with blood.

He grinned and came at me. I turned to run, but he caught me by the legs and took me down, crawling up me as he turned me on my back. Looming over me, he tilted his head and licked his lips. "You are the one the Mother wants. I will reap a great reward because I have you." And he pulled my hands together and began to bind them.

"No!" My scream echoed through the hall and I felt something well up within me. The winds were pressing me. Ulean shrieked at me, and the next moment I tilted my head back and caught hold of the gusts.

"Gale force." My words came out in a whisper, but they echoed around me as a great force pushed me to my feet, ravaging my mind, chilling me through as it carried me forward. I cast aside the rope, arms opening wide. As I began to turn, my feet left the floor, and I felt myself rising up, caught aloft on the wind that began to rattle through the room.

As I whirled, hanging in midair, I began to catch up chairs and vases and lighter objects in my vortex. Slowly at first, I spun, head hanging back, arms spread wide, and from my fingertips the winds began to come, first lightly and then—as the spinning increased in speed—harder. A chair went crashing across the room, then another. A tapestry flew off the wall to cover a group of combatants. The fireplace tools sailed though the air, becoming lethal weapons as the poker sank itself deep into the chest of one of the Shadow Hunters.

Swept into the dance, I was unable to control what was happening. And then, as the fighting came to a halt, all eyes on me, I began to laugh, terrified, as the vortex began to spin in earnest.

※

Lainule pushed through the crowd, somehow withstanding the winds. I could hear Ulean at her side, though I could not hear what they were saying. The slipstream was as useful to me now as a piece of gum.

But as I tore the room to shreds with the fury of the wind, they joined forces and the rocketing gusts shot out from under me just as quickly as they'd come. I went crashing to the floor, along with everything else caught in my maelstrom. Landing hard, I felt something in my side strain, but I ignored it as I tried to scramble to my feet, only managing to send myself into a dizzying stagger. Lainule grabbed me by the shoulders and gazed deep into my eyes.

"Clear." She whispered so low only I could hear her, but within seconds my mind cleared and I found myself blinking, trying to make sense of what was happening. The sounds of shrieking, the sounds of dying, crowded in on me and my head began to pound. I whimpered, collapsing into her arms.

She pushed me back. "You have no time for this. We have work to do."

I forced back my tears and looked in the direction in which she pointed me. The remaining Shadow Hunters were fighting tooth and nail. The dead—from both their side and ours—lay scattered on the ground, blood painting the floor red.

Lainule forced a dagger into my hands. I glanced at it—not the obsidian blade, but a fine silver dagger with inlaid sapphires on the hilt. She pushed me forward and turned to join two of her knights who were battling it out with a particularly tough Shadow Hunter.

I stumbled over one of the dead Cambyra, but managed to catch myself before I fell. I looked up to see Luna screaming as one of the Shadow Hunters fastened on her shoulder with his teeth. Zoey was beating on the creature's back, and Peyton was racing over to her side. Kaylin was off somewhere else, embroiled in another battle.

I shook my thoughts clear and leaped over the body in front of me, racing in to plant the silver dagger deep in the Shadow Hunter's shoulder. This time no bloodlust overwhelmed me, but my own desire to see these freaks dead took over. I stabbed him several times, twisting the knife as I plunged it in up to the hilt.

The Shadow Hunter stumbled, falling to his knees, and without a single hesitation, Luna brought out a short dirk and planted it in his forehead. She yanked the blade out again and the Shadow Hunter gurgled and fell forward, hitting the floor with a slick thud. I shoved him out of the way with my foot and turned to find the next one.

And on we went, driving through. There had been at least twenty of them coming through the door, and who knew how many more behind them, and so we fought through the mob, one after another, losing count. Peyton, Luna, Zoey, and I formed a quartet, moving in from all sides, our daggers on overtime.

At one point, we dropped a Shadow Hunter just in time to see another attacking Rex. He was doing his best to fend off the creature and looked about to shift, except I knew that even in his cougar form he wouldn't be able to fight the Shadow Hunter. It transformed into the true monster it was and bit down on his leg, ripping a chunk of flesh from the bone. Rex screamed and toppled, and the four of us moved in. Peyton jumped in front of her father, trying to protect him, as I attacked from the side.

When they were in their natural form, the Shadow Hunters were far more deadly, albeit with less choice in weaponry. I landed the dagger in its shoulder, plunging deep into the muscle. Zoey swiped it down the hindquarters, leaving a nasty trail, and Luna began to sing a charm that made the blood flow much more quickly. The Shadow Hunter, bleeding out, turned on us, mouth gaping wide, wicked teeth razor sharp and serrated.

I glanced at Rex. He was near the sideboard, and there was room beneath it for him to hide. I motioned to the heavy furniture. "Get beneath it, bind up your wounds. I know it hurts, but get under there." He'd be safer out of the way, and his leg was bleeding like a stuck pig.

Peyton pushed him under, shoving her bandanna in his hand. "Use this. Please don't faint on us. You have to take care of yourself until we're done. Keep yourself alive."

She turned back and we whaled on the Shadow Hunter, stabbing the beast over and over until it broke away, looking for someplace to hide. But at that moment, a couple of shurikens came singing through the air, striking it in the forehead between the eyes. The creature collapsed before it could make it another foot. Kaylin dashed over, grabbed up the shurikens, stopped to give an astonished Luna a quick kiss, then raced off again.

Peyton made certain that Rex had bound up his wound and then the four of us pressed on. We swung back into the fray. I caught sight of Rhiannon and Chatter, working in tandem, creating fireballs to scorch and disrupt the Shadow Hunters. Grieve was still in wolf form, attacking as he could. Wrath and Lainule were working with the Fae. Lannan and Regina were yucking it up over another dead body, and the vampires were still scuffling. And Ysandra and her witches surrounded three of the Shadow Hunters, finishing them off with a well-placed lightning bolt.

The dizzying scent of blood was too much. I staggered

over to an urn and, using it to lean on, upchucked everything I'd eaten that day. The sour smell filled my nose, and my mouth felt like I'd eaten rotten eggs, but my stomach felt better. I wiped my lips on my sleeve and turned around. One last shriek echoed through the room, and then, without warning, we were standing alone, no one left to fight.

※

The sound of heavy breathing and an occasional moan filled the room as I stared over the carnage. It was hard to tell how many were dead.

I quickly scanned for my friends—everyone had made it, though Rex looked worse for the wear. It was hard to tell where our enemies' blood left off and our own took up. The vampires gathered around Lannan, and Lainule called for the Fae to line up. Ysandra snapped her fingers and the Consortium members still alive joined her. We added up our losses.

Twenty vampires were missing. No doubt they'd been staked. And five of the twelve Fae warriors were dead. Two more were severely wounded and I doubted they'd make it. Five members of the Consortium team were dead.

Grieve counted the bodies of the Shadow Hunters. He looked up, his face grim. "Thirty-five. We lost thirty . . . possibly thirty-two," he added, glancing at the wounded men. "It's bad but not as bad as it could have been."

Lannan motioned for his remaining men to begin separating the bodies. "Make certain the Shadow Hunters are truly dead. Then take the remaining Fae warriors and scour the grounds. Nobody goes unattended. Make certain our defenses are back in order."

As they began the gruesome work of cleaning up the dead, we wearily filed back into our planning room. We were all covered with blood and I noticed more than one vampire's nose twitching as we walked by. But to give them credit, they didn't make a move.

I was at the back of the line heading into the room when Lannan stopped me. I turned to him, still caught up in the adrenaline surge of the battle. He stared at me for a long moment, then pushed me against the wall, his tongue slamming into my mouth as he spread my legs with his knees.

My blood ran hot at his touch. I pushed against him, not wanting to feel aroused, but the adrenaline surging through my body was desperate for a release. "Lannan, stop. Grieve will kill you. Especially with emotions running so high. And frankly, though I wouldn't weep over your death, we need you right now."

"You need me right now," he said, his hand pressing against my breasts. "Admit it. You need me. You need to fuck and you need to fuck hard. You don't want love right now, you want pure carnality. Pure lust, to work off the strain of battle." His hand slid down to unzip my jeans.

"No, stop it—stop." My body responded, but my anger was just as real. "Don't touch me."

Lannan slid me along the wall, around the corner. His men went about their work, never once looking up at us. But I could see the Fae staring at me, and I motioned to them. They began to head our way.

"Keep it up and Grieve won't need to put a stop to this." I bit his lip, drawing blood, and without thinking, licked the drop that welled up off his mouth.

He snarled, jamming his hands down my pants. I could feel his fingers oh so near me, and my body wanted to squirm, to assist him, but before I could battle it out in my mind, one of the warriors shoved him away from me. I dropped to the floor, tears of desire and of humiliation spilling over.

The warrior helped me up and turned to Lannan, who was staring at him with pure fury. But he simply shook that gorgeous mane of golden hair back into place and, giving me a long look, whispered, "We aren't finished with this, Cicely. We aren't done by a long shot." And then, adjusting his bloody clothing, he turned and walked around the corner.

"Thank you." I looked up at the Fae guard who was staring at me with what looked like pity. "Thank you. I . . . I . . ."

"Go now. Your friends await, Mistress of the Owls. Go and be safe."

His niceness eating a hole in my heart, I smiled faintly and grabbed his hand, pressing it to my cheek. "You too. He will seek any way he can to punish you for helping me. And Lannan . . . as much as he can help, he can hurt."

"Remember, I came through the routing of the Summer barrow. I have fought darker demons than Altos, and I am still alive. Go now." And with that, he turned, and I walked into the boardroom. Everyone was milling around, and a servant had brought food, hot coffee, and a first-aid kit.

Rex was lying on the table, Peyton by his side, holding his hand. The chunk the Shadow Hunter had bitten out of his leg was long gone, and there would be a nasty scar, but hopefully it would heal without getting infected. A member of the Consortium was examining the wound and whispering healing charms over it while dousing it with antiseptic and preparing a bandage.

I looked over at Lannan. He caught my gaze and those dark eyes of his drew me in. Shivering, I turned away to see who all had been hurt.

We all were covered with bruises and scratches, and I had a nasty bite in my shoulder, but my enemy hadn't managed to rip flesh out of me. As I stripped off my shirt, sitting there in my bra, waiting for the healer to attend me, somebody pressed a cup of coffee in my hand, along with a couple of cookies. My mouth felt dry and fuzzy, and I wanted to go rinse it, but before I could, weariness hit me like a sledgehammer and I hung my head, staring at my feet.

We were managing to stay alive, and we'd taken out a sizable number of Myst's guards—but at a great cost. We'd lost almost as many of our own. I looked up, staring at the others with a bleak heart. It was time to pick up the pieces and decide our next move.

"What next? What the fuck do we do next?"

"We go down to the station and I make my announcement. We have to do it tonight or we'll never get another chance. Not after this fiasco." Lannan's voice was clear, showing none of the antagonism he'd aimed at me only a few minutes ago. I was beginning to think he was bipolar.

I let out a long sigh. "And then?" But I knew what came

after that. We would sleep, and tomorrow we would perform the ritual on Grieve. And maybe, with a little luck, the
tide would turn and something would go our way for once.

Lainule moved to my side. She rested her hand on my
good shoulder and leaned down to whisper in my ear. "You
must see that Grieve maintains control. I can only hope
this ritual works. Much depends on it."

Startled, I turned. "You know what we're planning?"

She nodded. "Wrath told me. Cicely, so much more
depends on you and Grieve than you realize. And on Chatter and Rhiannon, too. The four of you must stay alive, no
matter the cost. Before, there were other options, but
now . . . those are gone. You four are the hope for the
future. Remember that. Be safe. Do what you need to in
order to stay alive. *Anything you need to.*" With that
pointed bit of advice, she moved away again, leaving me to
wonder how much worse things could get.

Chapter 17

We had to clean up before we could head to the radio station, and so I took my third shower of the day. Grieve came in with me, for which I was both grateful and nervous. I didn't tell him about Lannan's kiss. We were under enough pressure as it was, and if he knew Lannan had been groping me again, well, that would just put the nail in the coffin. Or the stake in the vampire.

"Where did they put the cats? I can't stand to think of them in danger from Lannan's people." Cats didn't like vampires. They had good reason.

Grieve smiled softly as he washed my hair. "Worry not about the furry creatures. Luna has been given a large suite and they're all in there with her, safe and sound. I have to admit, for all of his folly, Altos seems to like Luna—he treats her with a respect that surprises me. I saw it while you were out of the room today."

"She has a way of inspiring that in both man and beast." I paused, my hands on the knobs of the shower. "I was worried she might be too easily hurt, too vulnerable, but I have the feeling she has a lot more power than I gave her credit for. It's a quiet energy but runs strong in her."

As I turned off the water and we dried off, I wanted nothing more than to take another nap. I was bone-weary, more tired than I'd ever been. The battle had been draining, even with allies, and the adrenaline that had been coursing through my body was now just as quickly departing.

I leaned against the wall, trying to focus. "I need more coffee or something."

Grieve pulled me over to the bed.

As much as I loved him, as turned on as I'd been a half hour before, now I couldn't muster up enough oomph to even *think* about sex. "I'm sorry, I just don't have the energy—"

"No, my love. That's not what I had in mind." He sat me down and took my hands. "I taught you many things when you were little. Now I will teach you again. You are half–Cambyra Fae. You have the blood of a king in your veins. You will have some of the powers of the Fae, but you have to learn how to call upon them, to activate them."

I waited, letting him hold my hands, drifting on his words. I was so sleepy, I just wanted to sail out to sea, to glide on the winds, to let the currents take me where they desired.

"Close your eyes. Listen to my voice. Follow me down, into the energy, into the slipstream."

I followed his instructions, slipping into a light trance, letting his voice lead me into a somnolent state. The energy swirled around us, light whisperings on the slipstream, and I listened as they fluttered past, the light pattering of butterfly wings on the current.

Grieve's voice echoed past. "Now enter the slipstream and follow me inward. Follow the trail I leave."

And so I dove into the slipstream, and there it was, the trail of lights that signaled his energy, the trail of bread crumbs leading me onward. I spiraled and looped, the wind racing through my hair, through my thoughts, clearing the cobwebs out, refreshing me. We were running, racing through the slipstream, letting it carry us along, and for one moment, everything felt perfect.

"Now jump . . . follow me. Keep your eyes closed."

I jumped. And the scent around me was of autumn and

bonfires, and I felt it lure me in because it was Grieve's energy. He was no longer the sweet freshly mown grass of summer, but the sound of crisp autumn leaves beneath my feet, and the scent of rain on cedars, and his lips tasted like sweet pumpkin and cinnamon sticks. I embraced his change, sank into it, realizing he was no longer of the Summer Court, but neither did Winter fully claim him. He was balanced between the two realms, walking a thin line.

And then his voice swirled around me like a flurry of leaves. "Cicely. Look deep inside. Find the part of yourself that connects to the owl. Find the Uwilahsidhe within you."

I sank deeper, following the path inward. The slipstream seemed very far away now as I lowered myself into my core, as I let his voice lead me into myself. Past the jaded exterior, past the fear, past the weariness, past the loss, deep into my center where I felt a warm glow. And there . . . there waited my owl. There waited my father's blood.

"Draw on that strength. Draw on that reserve. You have so much power there for the using. Feel your spirit rise, lifted on owl wings. Do not shift in body, but draw on your owl to carry you aloft, to free you from the weariness, to buoy you up. Can you do this?"

I inhaled deeply and connected with my owl. And then a rush of energy raced through me—of renewal, the rush of wind in my hair, of wind beneath my wings, the exaltation of being aloft, and yet I did not transform.

"Can you feel it?" His voice slid over the words, sultry and seductive.

"Yes," I whispered.

"Claim it. Coax it out. Let it be your source right now."

And so I claimed the Cambyra side of me, and my doubts slid away, my worry that I might not be worthy of the blood. And as it did, I began to rise, back into the slipstream.

"Come back now. Return to here, to now, reenergized, refreshed, aware of your inner power, and your connection to that power."

As his words drifted away, I slowly rose through the slipstream and out, and opened my eyes. The weariness was still there but much diminished, and my body didn't ache nearly as much as it had. Best, my mind felt clear, replenished, and I realized that I could think again.

"Thank you." I took Grieve's hand and pressed it to my lips. "I love you so much."

"You are my everything." He reached out and stroked my face. "I mean it, Cicely. You are why I have resisted Myst, why I have had the courage to still live, even as the monster I've become."

"You're not a monster. You're a Fae Prince. The sentinel in Lainule's secret chamber called you the Wounded King. And so you are. You are wounded, deeply, but even with all the dangers you've faced, the hell you've been through, you waited for me, and you've done your best to harness the wild blood that runs through your veins." I pressed my lips against his hand again. "We will perform the ritual and do whatever we can to free you from Myst's chains."

"If Myst should die . . . I think I could control this much easier."

"She will. We will find her weakness, and we will exploit it. I pledge to you with my life, I will do whatever it takes to destroy her." As I gazed into his eyes, my heart swelled, my love for him sweeping through me.

"Come, we'd best be off. Altos will need us. Even though the enemy came to us, I don't trust them allowing him to reach the station unharmed."

Grieve rose and, taking my hand, headed for the door. I followed, ready to face whatever it was that waited for us on the other side.

❧

The guards escorted us out to our cars. Lannan's crew followed us. We were in the big limousine. Lannan sat in front with the driver, while Grieve, Chatter, Rhiannon, Peyton, Kaylin, Wrath, and I sat in back. We'd left Luna, Zoey, and Rex behind. Rex was in no shape to fight, and Luna and Zoey were preparing for the ritual.

Lainule's warriors—the survivors—were to meet us at the building. They would not travel via car, but they assured us they would be okay. The surviving members of the Consortium, including Ysandra, rode in another limousine, under the protection of more of Lannan's guards.

The streets were a silent shroud of snow, sleeting down with bulletlike intensity. I wondered if Myst knew yet just how many men she'd lost. And if another contingent had been dispatched to the radio station. We'd find out soon enough, one way or another.

As the limo glided over the snow and ice, the tension built. Regina had stayed back at the mansion. The Emissary could not knowingly walk into battle without approval from the Queen of the Crimson Court. But she had promised to contact the vampire queen and ask for advice.

We approached the WorldCom Building, which was in downtown New Forest. The streets were empty, under a curfew that Lannan had ordered. My heart sank as I realized just what the beautiful little town had come to: a haven for terror, a horror-movie director's wet dream.

As the cars pulled to the curb, parking, we cautiously stepped out of them. A third, fourth, and fifth car arrived, filled with vampires who immediately formed a protective circle around us. We slowly began the walk to the building. I could feel creatures watching from the shadows of the alleyways and the hidden recesses, nooks, and crannies that we could not see, but that I knew were there.

"They're here. I can feel them." I glanced over at Lannan.

Grieve nodded. "I can, too. My blood is singing with recognition." He slipped an arm around my waist and pulled me close.

"Cowards." Lannan stared at the shadows. "Come out, come out, wherever you are, and show yourselves."

But nothing moved, not even a whisper. We approached the building, Lannan's guards going first. They were joined by a group of approaching Fae warriors. Ysandra and her witches stayed near us. The guards unceremoniously yanked open every door in the hallway, peering in to see if anybody was hiding, and we slowly made our way to the studio. The guards fanned out, covering every entrance to the building.

Lannan cautiously entered the radio station. He glanced around, but there seemed to be nothing amiss. As the workers in the booth fired up the mike, he motioned to me.

"I obviously cannot see myself in a mirror, so attend me. Make certain I look the part and do not fail me. While I may not be on camera, I want to feel as if I could be without embarrassing myself." His voice was cool, but I recognized a faint tremor in his voice. For once, he was nervous.

I managed to tidy him up and brush out that glorious golden hair—it was like silk in my hands. Peyton watched me, and at one point Lannan stared at her till she looked away. No words passed between them. None were necessary.

"Fifteen minutes, Lord Altos." The camera man motioned to the clock.

"No." Lannan shook his head. "We go on *now*. Trust me." He took his place in the booth. The announcer scrambled, the radio lights blinked, and the rest of us huddled outside the glass. The aide gave the *five four three two one* sign with his fingers, and Lannan turned to the microphone.

The announcer took a deep breath, then said, "Citizens of New Forest, we are interrupting our regularly scheduled programming for an important announcement from the Regent of the Vampire Nation, Lord Lannan Altos. His speech will be simultaneously broadcast on television and will be replayed throughout tonight and tomorrow. Please listen carefully. This concerns the safety of every person within this town. And now, Lord Lannan Altos."

Lannan leaned forward. "Citizens of New Forest, we are facing a grave danger. As you know, there have been a number of unexplained deaths over the past months, and we have identified the killers. But they are at large—and there are many of them."

As he launched into a simplified explanation of the Shadow Hunters, I began to notice an uneasy feeling creeping up on me. There were too many whisperings on the slipstream. I looked over at Grieve and Chatter, who both nodded at me, and we moved off to the side.

"Something's up. I can feel it."

"You're right—but I can't catch the words." Grieve closed his eyes. "I do sense the Shadow Hunters near, but they are not . . . in the building, I think."

Chatter paled. "It's a trap."

"You're sure?" I turned to him, horrified. Had we walked right into their plans?

Just then, Lannan's voice echoed through the intercom. "I urge you, tonight lock your doors and stay inside. Tomorrow pack up your necessities and get out of town. Take what you can and run. The danger is far too great. Be you yummanii, magic-born, Were, or Fae, leave this town—"

And then, at the precise moment when he'd originally been scheduled to deliver his speech, a low rumble began to shake the station, growing into a loud roar like a freight train. The building quaked as the roar grew into an explosion, and suddenly bricks and wood and stone were falling everywhere.

Rhiannon let out a short scream, but she looked unharmed as the lights flickered against the crumbling walls. And then we were plunged into darkness, and the destruction went on and on and on.

※

Chatter, Grieve, and I had been standing near the door. When the lights vanished, I felt a hand on my wrist and suddenly found myself being dragged out into what was left of the hallway. The lights were off, and it was impossible to see. I began to cough. Dust was swirling everywhere, and my throat felt like it had been burned dry. I was tempted to call on the winds, but if the underpinnings to the building were damaged, that might bring everything toppling down on us.

Grieve held on to my wrist, his hand never wavering, and Chatter held on to my other elbow as we stumbled through what had been the lobby. A flickering light began to shine. One of Lannan's guards was holding a flashlight and he motioned for us to follow him. He shone it down at the floor, so we could do our best to skirt the toppled plaster and beams. The building hadn't collapsed in toto but it had been severely damaged.

I tripped over a large chunk of something—whether it was stone or wood I couldn't tell—but Grieve and Chatter righted me. We reached the door, where one of the guards was waiting. He hurried us out to the limousine. I could hear fighting a few yards away, but when I turned to help, the vampire yanked my arm and shoved me into the back-seat, along with Grieve and Chatter. He slammed the door, locking it, and ran back to the building.

"What's going on? We have to go back for the others!" It was a relief to be in the comfort of the car, but all I could think about were the rest of our friends, trapped inside. I struggled toward the door, but Grieve and Chatter held me firmly, while the driver peeked into the backseat.

"Stay here." His voice was gruff, and the vampire looked big enough to enforce his command. "The guards are searching for the rest of your party."

"They *planned* it. They planned for the station to blow right before Lannan began his speech, but he started early." Grieve shook his head. "If he hadn't started fifteen minutes early, the word would never have gotten out. But it's going to be a bloody night. People are going to try to get out of town now, even though Lannan told them to wait until morning. Especially since they had to have heard the explosion over the air. The Shadow Hunters are going to have a field day."

I cringed. He was right and there was nothing we could do. Hanging my head, I couldn't stop thinking of the slaughter that was imminent.

A few moments later the door opened again and Rhiannon and Peyton climbed in, covered in dust. Neither looked seriously hurt, though Rhia was sporting a nasty bruise on her forehead. Chatter immediately opened his arms and she crept into his embrace. Another tense period passed—I don't know how long it was, it seemed to take hours but it could have been minutes—and Wrath, Kaylin, and Lannan stumbled into the car.

I glanced out the window. The building was burning, flames lighting up the sky, and I realized I'd been hearing sirens without noticing it. Firemen moved in, their hoses aiming toward the fire, as we pulled away from the curb.

"The mansion." Lannan's voice was muted and even he looked wiped out. He glanced over at me and for once, his gaze wasn't focused on my boobs or my body, but instead, was haunted. "I knew we had to go early. I wish I'd thought to make it even earlier, but at least the word got out."

"We were kind of embroiled in a little war earlier." Peyton gave him a quick shrug. "At least you warned them."

Lannan nodded at her. "Yes, but was it enough?"

"What about Ysandra? The Consortium members? Wrath, what about your warriors? Did they escape?" I pressed my lips together. Nothing was going right.

He nodded. "I think so, but I can't be sure. If they did, they'll go back to the mansion. But it's clear that the war has begun. And it's not just against the vampires. Myst is out to conquer. And she'll do whatever she has to in order to win."

As we drove through the streets, even now we could see families piling into cars, carrying a hodgepodge of suitcases and backpacks. At one point, we heard screams but by the time we found where they were coming from, there was only a grisly blood smear left on the ground and a few mangled limbs. I didn't want to know how many the Shadow Hunters had taken. I didn't want to know how many would die tonight at Myst's hands.

✳

We pulled through the gates and a shout startled us. As we emerged from the car, we could see the guards fighting off a handful of Shadow Hunters.

Furious, raw from all we had witnessed, I shook off Grieve's hand and ran forward, reaching deep inside to where I could feel the fury of the winds, waiting. I focused, mustering up all the energy that I could summon, and without a word, I was walking in the middle of a funnel cloud. Narrow and precarious, it was still a danger, and so I drove it forward, aching to sweep away the death and destruction that had laid siege to the town.

As I reached the fight, the vampires got out of the way quickly, leaving me a straight shot in mowing down the Shadow Hunters. I pulled on every ounce of energy I could, and sent the twister out of myself, giving it freedom, aiming it right down the center of their little group. As it raced toward them, they tried to run but they weren't fast enough and the vortex swept them up, spinning them round with the dust and debris that I'd managed to pick up on the way, and then, as my anger grew, the cloud grew more vicious, and the Shadow Hunters came flying out, hitting the ground with a dull thud as necks and backs snapped.

I couldn't hold on to the energy any longer, and I let out a long breath, the twister vanishing as quickly as I'd summoned it. The last of the Vampiric Fae came tumbling out of the sky to land at my feet. I bent over, and he opened his eyes, still alive. Without thought, without mercy, I drove my dagger down, slicing through his throat, pinning him to the ground. He jerked spasmodically and was silent.

As I turned around, the others were staring at me. I didn't care what they thought, didn't care if they approved. The only thing I could think about was destroying Myst and saving my love, my friends, and me.

But as I walked back to them, Kaylin clapped me on the back, and even my father smiled at me. Grimly, yes, but it was still a smile. Grieve slipped one arm around my waist, and Peyton took the other side. Leaning on them for support, I slowly climbed the grand steps as we headed inside, shutting the rest of the world out.

Regina was waiting. Despite her cool demeanor, I could tell she'd been worried. She raced over to Lannan and encircled his waist with her arms, drawing him to her. They looked a lot alike; I wasn't positive if they were twins but it sure looked that way. Her hair was as golden as his and they were both so gorgeous it hurt to look at them. As her lips sought his, he sank into her embrace and they kissed, deep, dark, and sensuous.

I turned away, heading toward the stairs. I just wanted some peace and quiet, even for a moment, to relax.

But Regina's voice rang out behind me. "Don't be so quick, Cicely. We have to discuss what happened."

I turned to find her staring at me, coyly giving me a sly smile. "I'm exhausted. I thought I'd take a quick shower to wash the dust and grime off of me first, before we talked." We were safe enough in the mansion, and whatever might be going on outside tonight, there wasn't much we could do about it.

She caught my gaze, and slowly licked her lips. Once. Then with a throaty laugh, she shrugged. "Perhaps that is best. You all look worn out. Go take your shower and I will tell the cook to prepare you food. But do not take long—tarrying is not advised at this point, and there is much to discuss."

And with that, she led Lannan away.

Relieved that she didn't offer to come with me, and that she didn't order me to go with them, I motioned to the others.

"Let's get cleaned up. She's right. We have a lot to discuss and not much time in which to do it. Let's go." But the stairs were more than my legs could muster. I was exhausted, bone-weary. Summoning up the twister had drained me and three steps up, I crumbled and sank down, leaning my head against the railing. Grieve was at my side instantly, sweeping me up and carrying me up to my room.

He set me down on the bed. "Undress. I will prepare a bath for you." He disappeared into the bathroom and I heard the sound of running water and smelled sweet vanilla and warm musk.

Even though I'd had at least three showers already, the thought of a bubble bath suddenly took over. I pulled off my clothes, realizing just how bruised I was from the shattered building, and how exhausted I was from calling up the winds. I was shivering because, although the mansion was warm enough, the cold outside had gotten to me, and I couldn't seem to shake the chill that had crept into my bones.

I glanced at the clock. It was well past midnight, and I wondered if the day would ever end. Or would we just keep going and going until finally, we faded into history?

My clothes in a pile on the floor, I pulled a throw from the foot of the bed around my shoulders and closed my eyes, leaning against one of the bedposts, taking stock. My ribs hurt, my muscles hurt, my joints ached, and my mind was so cloudy I could barely think. Not even Grieve's exercise on pulling on my Fae nature would help me this time. A moment later, I felt him near me.

"Cicely, your bath is ready." I dropped the blanket and let him lead me into the bathroom. He'd lit candles, and the dancing lights gently illuminated the spa tub that was filled with sweet-scented bubbles. I inhaled deeply, holding the warm scent in my lungs, as Grieve lowered me into the tub. The shock of the hot water was momentary, and then I sank back, leaning against the back of the tub as I rested my neck on the edge, and closed my eyes.

As the hot water began to work its magic, pulling the ache out of my body, Grieve's gentle hands were slowly caressing me. With a washcloth, yes, but also the pads of his fingertips. I gasped, slightly parting my legs. I was far too tired for sex but this . . . this sensation was marvelous and so I said nothing, just opened my mouth ever so slightly as his fingers dipped into the water.

He slid his fingers down my stomach, over my tattoo, and then down into the bubbles to reach between my thighs. I moaned gently as he began to stroke, light butterfly touches, flicking me to life, igniting the embers of a low fire that burned steadily, if not brightly.

I shifted, another moan escaping from my throat. "Grieve . . ."

"Shush. Be still. Let me play you. Let me release some of the tension."

And with that, I gave myself in to his hands as he worked me, flicking this way and that with his fingers, softly encircling me to stir my desire, to stir the embers to life. As the feel of his hands on me heightened, as my stomach tightened, I shifted in the water, squirming under his gentle but firm ministrations.

I couldn't keep quiet any longer. I began to pant, raggedly, as the pressure mounted, wanting him in me, wanting him to satiate the driving need that raged through my body.

Grieve was suddenly naked and climbing in the tub, and I pulled him to me, the hardened length of his cock sliding firmly inside my cunt as I pressed my breasts to his body. The loss and devastation of the night began to sink in and as he rocked against me, his hips pulsing as he drove himself deeper and deeper, I burst into tears and held him close, coming as hard as I was crying, in a burning mixture of relief and of loss. Grieve moaned into my ear as he gave one last, long thrust, and then he cried out, exploding within me.

As we lay entwined in the hot, frothy water, all I could think about was how even in the darkest times, the union of bodies, the connection of hearts, could wipe away all pain for at least a brief moment. I gazed into his eyes, the sparkling eyes of the Vampiric Fae, and whispered words to him I never thought I'd hear myself say.

"If we come through this . . . if we survive, I want your child within me. I want to create life with you. I'm tired of destruction."

Grieve nodded, holding me close. "When we win this war, you will be my queen, and I will be your king, and we will give rise to a kingdom. Cicely, you will be a queen. You know that, don't you?"

"What are you talking about?"

But he silenced me with a kiss, then with one final move, lightly leaped out of the water and pulled me to my feet. "We must get dressed and downstairs. They will be waiting for us."

I stared at him, wondering what he'd meant, but there was no time for debate because a low sound rang through the room—the chiming of bells. Lannan was summoning us to his side. And right now, the last thing I wanted was a punishment for disobeying the vampire who held my reins, who forced me to call him Master.

Chapter 18

Grieve handed me clothes from my dresser and I wearily drew them on. He had it easier—the full Fae were able to fashion their clothes from the air around them. Changing was easy. That was one attribute I would have given a lot to have—to never have to worry about shopping again. Decadence!

As we headed downstairs, the smell of roasting beef made me salivate and I realized just how hungry I was. I looked over at Grieve and smiled, feeling both sleepy but recharged. He knew what I needed, and I had needed to cry, to rage, to let go of tension, to fuck, to connect.

Lannan and Regina sat at the head and foot of the table. "I've had the chef prepare another meal. You must keep your strength up," he said.

Neither of them had plates, but the rest of us were served sizzling slices of roast beef with a peppercorn sauce and a fluffy mound of fork-whipped mashed potatoes. A row of string beans glistened with melted butter, and crusty bread rounded out the meal. Lannan started to say something, but as the rest of us fell to the food, starved after all the fighting, he shook his head.

"I'll wait until after you dine. Perhaps then you will be

too full to do anything but listen to me." But he said it with a faint whisper of a smile, and I had the feeling that, superior bastard or not, he wanted his guests to enjoy themselves.

I dug in, scooping up mashed potatoes. I was starving. As I sliced into the steak and dipped it in the peppercorn sauce, something rang an alarm, but I was too hungry to pay attention to it. But when I put the steak in my mouth, I knew something was wrong. The minute the sauce hit my tongue, my mouth began to tingle, along with the back of my throat.

I dropped my fork and shoved my chair back, spitting out the food as my throat began to swell. Frantic, I scrambled for the EpiPen I always carried in my pocket, but it wasn't there. Rhia saw what I was doing and raced around the table.

"Her EpiPen! Did someone take it out of her clothes? Goddamn it, hurry! She's having an allergy attack!"

Rhia patted me down as Lannan streaked out of the room. As the room began to spin, I couldn't think straight. My lungs begged for oxygen, but there simply wasn't any. I couldn't breathe, couldn't feel my fingers or toes. Regina was by my side the next moment, loosening my top, as Rhia cried out something to someone that I couldn't understand.

I am here. Calm, child, calm. Lannan is bringing your medication. Try to remain calm. Ulean's voice swept over me, and for a moment I relaxed, but then the gasping for air began again and I began to thrash about.

Then, a sudden rush seared through my body as someone stabbed me with the needle-sharp pen, and as I began to shake, the tension in my throat began to ease. I coughed, shivering as I broke out in a cold sweat. Dizzy, I buried my head in my knees as Rhiannon rubbed my back gently until the attack subsided. Lannan stood there, used EpiPen in hand, looking terrified.

By the time I was able to sit up, everyone was seated again, except for Lannan, Rhia, Grieve, and Lainule. I stared at the table. My poison came disguised as food.

I could hear Lannan tearing down whoever it was had cooked the meal.

"She's allergic to fish and shellfish. This, I told you. Who put fish in the sauce?"

"It has lobster in it, Master, not fish." The voice was high and breathless. I glanced over to see a young woman— probably in her early twenties—wincing as she glanced over at me.

"Imbecile! Lobster is a *crustacean*." At her blank look, he really let go, screaming in her face. "*Shellfish*. Are you brainless? Dolt! I want you out of my stable. I should punish you, but I don't want to waste the energy. Gather your things and be out of this house in fifteen minutes." He turned his back on her.

The girl fell to her knees, crying. "No, please, Master. Please don't turn me away!"

Lannan whirled back around. His voice was low this time, so controlled that I shivered. "I gave you an order. One more outburst and I'll rip out your throat. Go now, while you still live. And be glad for my mercy. You won't get a second chance."

The girl backed away, then scrambled to her feet and ran out of the room weeping. Lannan strode over to my side, pushing everyone away. He leaned down, took my hand in his.

"Do you need a physician? Shall I summon a doctor?" He sounded worried. Too worried for my comfort. I liked Lannan better when he was ignoring me.

But he was right, I needed to assess my health and whether I'd make it without a second injection. Sometimes one dose of epinephrine just wouldn't do it. But the itching in my mouth and throat were subsiding, and I could breathe, and it didn't feel like anything was starting back up.

"No . . . wait . . ." I squinted, trying to remember if I had another EpiPen in my dresser. I usually carried three. And yes, I'd replenished them the last time I'd inadvertently swallowed a piece of cod. And they were still good. "I'll be okay for now, though tomorrow I should replace this EpiPen."

Regina frowned lightly. "You know, if you would let us turn you, you would never again have to worry about dying from a bite of fish." Her offer sounded genuine, and she looked almost confused when I shook my head.

"Thanks but . . . um . . . no. That's not enough reason for me to give up life as I know it and take up feasting off blood. But I appreciate the offer." I tried to smile at her, to show her I wasn't being sarcastic. Hell, after a jolt of epinephrine, sarcasm was the last thing on my mind. But the adrenaline flowing through my body would sustain me until I crashed.

"Let me help you upstairs." Rhia turned to Lannan. "The rest of us can discuss matters afterward. Cicely's going to need to rest. These attacks are pretty harsh on the system and she's already drained her energy today."

He frowned but nodded and stood back as Grieve and Wrath edged him out of the way. My father picked me up, and as if I were no heavier than a stuffed animal, he carried me upstairs to my room. Rhia and Grieve followed. Rhia helped me get into a nightgown and she crawled into bed next to me.

"I don't want to leave her alone in case she has another reaction. You guys go down and talk to the others. You can tell us what went on later."

As Grieve and Wrath left the room, I leaned against Rhia's side—she was sitting up against the headboard—and closed my eyes. I was tired, very tired, but I was also jittery from the medication. But after a few minutes, the sound of her breathing began to calm me, and she stroked my head gently, smoothing my hair, until I closed my eyes and fell into a deep sleep.

※

I found myself in a frozen wasteland, wearing a pale blue gown that shimmered with silver embroidery. At first I wondered that I was not cold, but then I realized the snowflakes felt good against my skin, cooling me and soothing my thoughts. As I turned, a pale bird appeared—an owl. I raised one hand in greeting to it, and it dipped low, winging by, to land on my outstretched arm. I slowly brought it toward me, bending my elbow, keeping my arm straight, and the owl gazed into my eyes, and its eyes burned with frozen fire.

"Where have you been, my friend?" I whispered to it, and my voice was caught on the slipstream and went echoing out through the woodland, and as I spoke the ice on the stream shattered into a thousand pieces and the water began to flow again. The ice skittered together to form a figure, tall and glistening, and it knelt by my feet.

"What have you seen, my friend?" Again, I whispered to the owl, and the trees began to shake, the snow showering off their boughs to dust the forest with yet another layer of crystal rain.

The owl let out a soft hoot, as we locked gazes. And in its gaze, I saw the dance of Summer, bidding me to come and play, with golden roses growing wild on a warm dusky night, and the scent of fragrant jasmine and honeysuckle washed over me. The invitation was strong and I longed to join the warmth, but it was not yet time and in my heart, I knew that I could not enter that realm. Not yet.

"Send back this message," I said. "I will come and play when the Oak King and Holly King battle under the longest day of the year. Then we will play, and spend time, and dance and revel. And when the holly meets the oak, I will invite Summer to my home, and we will once again make merry as the battle renews. The longest night will be ours to enjoy. Go now, and take this message, send it along the slipstream, and take my love along with it."

And the owl took flight, rising from my arm, winging through eternal night. The trees were silver against the dark moon, and the snow reflected the chill in my soul. Nearby, a wolf howled, and with a smile, I turned to join my love.

⚜

I woke with a start, and my owl self was pushing me to go to the window and fly. Rhiannon was taking a shower—I could hear the water running. A glance at the clock told me I'd been out for several hours.

As I slipped out from under the covers, I was drawn to the window. Outside, the snow fell, relentless in its invasion. With a quick sweep, I opened the window and dropped my nightgown to the floor. Crouching on the sill, I stared out, wondering what it was that was pushing me so hard. But something was calling me, and I had to find out what it was.

My pendant around my neck, even though I suspected I no longer needed it, I dove off the sill, spreading my wings as I transformed into my owl shape. As the updraft caught me, I felt Ulean join me and let out a low hoot as she danced around me, giving me a good tailwind. I soared over the grounds of the Regent's estate, reveling in the feel of the wind under my wings, in the feel of the night shining down on me. I was too tired to think of hunting, but I knew there was something I needed to know—something I needed to see.

And then there it was—a group of figures moving in the snow below, just outside the fences and barriers. I swept down, wondering if it was a group of Myst's people, but as I neared the silent forms, I could feel the energy roiling off of them. Wilding Fae, not Shadow Hunters. And they were searching for someone.

They seek to talk to you.

Me? Why me?

Because, they have something to say.

It was a simple answer, and I felt like laughing, but since I couldn't, I let out a long shriek.

As I landed in a low tree near the figures, I saw there were five of them, all odd and misshapen and yet, they struck me as very powerful by their stance. The snow hag was among them. I realized that I wouldn't be clothed when I changed back, but if we were quick, I might not catch my death of cold.

As quickly as I had shifted into owl form, I let myself shift back. As I fell forward, almost lurching out of the tree, I managed to catch myself on one of the branches. I held on, while the snow hag looked up at me, her eyes aglow and her mouth crooked and smiling.

"She came, she came. Riddle me this, who was it that called the owl from her sleep?" Her cadence was familiar, and I found myself slipping into the riddle-talk almost naturally.

"One who has something to say—a guess that it was she who called the owl from her slumber." I narrowed my focus, trying to remember everything Chatter had taught me about the Wilding Fae. It was difficult—I was already starting to shiver, but I forced myself to concentrate. "But tell the world this, should there be something to say, it should be said fast, or the owl-daughter may have to return to her form—the cold, it bites the skin."

"The owl-daughter will be winging home soon, never to fear. But riddle me this, what does a body need in order to fight another body? Weapons are plentiful, but what might be a rare exchange?"

I thought for a moment. We had weapons, but what we didn't have was manpower. "It occurs that a rare exchange might involve an allegiance. Allies against a common enemy."

"One might be correct if one were to guess such an answer. And common enemies make for common targets. One might think that it would be better to join forces than to walk into battle alone." She smiled then, her snaggle-tooth grin fierce.

"A correct assumption, but at what price? One has to know the cost before one purchases the trinket." My teeth were chattering now, and I tried to shield myself from the wind. I gazed down at the other creatures standing beside the snow hag, but they were difficult to focus on. They seemed to be blurring in and out of reality, as if I were drunk.

The snow hag laughed. "One might be called a good businesswoman if she haggles the price. Perhaps this price will be to a good businesswoman's liking: a small section of woodland, once the Queen of Shadows is routed."

I stared at her. How was I supposed to promise them *that*? Those were Lainule's woodlands. I struggled to find the right words. "There are prices that even a good businesswoman might not be authorized to pay."

"Oh, surprise surprise, there are always surprises in store. A baker may become a tailor, and an owl-child may become a queen. Stranger things have happened. In theory then. If a good businesswoman *were* authorized to make such a deal, would she?"

What should I do, Ulean? I don't know how to answer that.

Answer the truth: If you had the authority to promise them a corner of the woods, would you?

Well, yes. Anything for the extra help, especially from powerful beings like the Wilding Fae. But—

But nothing. Answer. And do not fret.

"I think a good businesswoman, if she did have such authority, would happily promise up a corner of the woodland to her allies."

"Then the deal is struck. And allies will be sending a message to such a businesswoman tomorrow, so she should listen to the slipstream, and she should also remind her friend that he owes a certain ally fresh meat."

Kaylin had forgotten! "That deal will be closed, with interest." And then, before I could say another word, the figures vanished into the forest, and I was alone with my thoughts.

I was truly freezing by now, and before I gave any more thought to what had just transpired, I decided to hightail it back to the mansion. Who knew what else lived out in these woods?

I sucked in a deep breath and dove out of the tree, sweeping into my owl form without even thinking. On the way back to my room, I wondered what the others were like—the Wilding Fae were all different, all unique, and they were all powerful, ancient beings. They would fear no vampire, no Shadow Hunter unless someone managed to snare them—as Myst had snared the snow hag. But they had no need to fear the likes of me, or even my father.

I flew to the eaves of the roof, then once I was alight by my sill, I turned back and crawled through the window. As I looked up, I saw that Rhiannon, Chatter, Grieve, and Peyton were gathered in my room. Luna and Zoey opened the door as I looked for a blanket to cover myself. Kaylin walked in just as I huddled in the throw that Rhiannon handed to me.

"Okay, where were you?" Grieve's voice was less accusing than concerned and for once, I felt that they weren't angry, just frightened.

"I felt something calling me outside, and I knew that I needed to go." I quickly told them what had happened. I was halfway through when Wrath entered the room, so I had to start again. But when I finished they were staring at me, and I saw hope in Wrath's eyes.

"The Wilding Fae, when they take an interest in matters, can be devastatingly powerful. To have them on our side rather than Myst's is a great blessing." He pressed his lips together and stared at his feet. There was something he wasn't telling us—or me. I wasn't sure what it was but wanted to find out.

"What was all the talk about asking me to promise them a piece of Lainule's woodland? I can't do that and they should know it."

But if I expected my father to open up, I was mistaken. He shook his head. "Leave such matters for when they are to be discussed. Do not dwell on them. For now, we have to focus on destroying Myst. While you slept, Ysandra returned. She's lost two more of her Consortium members and fears leaving this night, so she'll stay till morning. And one more of the Summer Knights fell. We were unprepared. We knew they would attack but did not anticipate the level at which they chose to make their move. We have to think bigger now. We have to anticipate how far Myst is willing to go in order to destroy us."

"Are there any reports of what's going on out beyond the gates?" I didn't want to know, but felt that we better accept the reality of what we were facing.

"The police scanner is fraught with incidents. The police aren't venturing out and there are calls coming in all over the place. People trapped in their houses, people missing—men going out to walk the dog and not returning, people heading to their cars to leave and getting attacked.

It's mayhem out there. The Shadow Hunters are feeding well." Kaylin looked grim. He caught my gaze and held it. "That we have the Wilding Fae on our side is good news, but I fear what we need is a miracle."

"We need to know where Myst is hiding so we can go after her during the daylight. That's the only time we can strike without fear of her people. And I wouldn't put it past them to be searching for a cure, so we'd better move quickly." I paused. "Come morning, we do the ritual on Grieve. Then, we plan a preemptive strike. Meanwhile, we're all exhausted and need sleep. It's late, but we can sleep in a little and get in at least six or seven hours."

"Cicely is right. Back to sleep." Grieve stood and escorted everyone to the door. Chatter and Rhiannon turned off into her room, and I smiled softly. At least they were getting their chance at love. Who knew how long any of us would survive, so we might as well be as happy as we could be for now.

I turned to Grieve when he shut the door behind the last person, and moved to kiss him. He held me tight, grazing my lips, the feral look in his eye gleaming. But he restrained himself. He did not nip at my neck, he did not graze my wrist when he kissed it. He merely held me, for a long while, shushing me every time I would have said something, until we silently moved to the bed, climbed under the covers, and let sleep claim us.

※

Morning came and we allowed ourselves the luxury of sleeping till past nine o'clock. Zoey and Luna had ordered a simple breakfast for us all—high in protein and complex carbs for energy. I flipped on the television, dreading what I'd hear. And sure enough, most of the cable was out except for one local station. The announcer looked grave, shaking his head, as one of Lannan's most trusted day-runners stood there.

"Once again, we regret to inform you that the town of New Forest is under siege. During the night, forty-three people lost their lives to the Shadow Hunters. I am here to reiterate what Lord Lannan Altos said last night in his aborted speech—if you can possibly do it, gather your family and get out. The Vampiric Fae will rise again at sundown. Leave before then."

The announcer cleared his throat. "What is being done to counter this attack, and why weren't we warned before now?"

The day-runner looked a little uncomfortable. "The previous Regent was addressing the matter privately, but it became apparent he could not perform his job correctly. This morning, before dawn, Regent Altos and the Emissary from the Crimson Court received word that another contingent of magic-born from the Consortium will be arriving this afternoon. And the Crimson Court will be sending in trained combatants this evening, the moment the sun goes down."

"What can we do—what can the yummanii and the Weres do?" The newscaster looked positively horrified.

"Your best bet is to leave town or only go abroad during the daylight hours and lock down your homes after dark. Weres and yummanii are not all that effective against the Indigo Court. The Shadow Hunters are strong and cunning. In essence, they are sentient killing machines, a plague that seeks to spread throughout the country."

He paused and then continued. "The Vampire Nation and the Consortium have instructed the yummanii government to allow us to take care of this incident. We are now tracking down other pockets of the Vampiric Fae that might have made their homes around the nation. If you are not police, or medical personnel, we encourage you to stay off the streets once dusk hits."

I turned off the TV. "At least we know help is on the way, and the Wilding Fae will be contacting us today. By the way, Kaylin, you owe the snow hag meat—remember? You'd better pay the debt before she decides to come collecting."

He slapped his head. "I cannot believe I forgot. This afternoon, after the ritual, I will take out the chicken and steak I promised her for her help."

"We'd better get started then."

We asked Lannan's lackeys for space and privacy and they jumped to obey. I suppose we didn't seem ready to go staking the vamps, so they weren't interested in what we were about to do.

We cleared a side parlor that we'd been told we could use by Lannan's servants and began to set up for the ritual. It involved a great deal of space, apparently, and Grieve would be strapped down to a table while we took the Elemental points around him.

"Before we begin, we need to dress in robes the colors of our Elements. I asked Lannan's people to help us and they found us some costumes that should work." Luna smiled at us, and I suddenly realized she was firmly in her element. Her magic involved ritual and tradition and song and training, while mine was wild and untamed.

She handed out the robes, and they were indeed works of beauty. Whoever had sewn the velvet gowns had done an exquisite job. Mine was pale silver, Chatter wore a robe of forest green, Rhiannon was dressed in crimson, and Wrath in deep blue. Kaylin wore black, and Luna wore white. Zoey was wearing a brown robe. The vampires must have had one hell of a costume party because the gowns were all the same—unisex, flowing, and crushed velvet.

Zoey had scrounged up a copper doumbek with an elk-hide head. She knelt near the fireplace, letting the heat tune the drum. As she thumbed it, listening to the tone, she tightened the head.

I walked over to Luna, who had closed her eyes and was breathing deeply. "Am I interrupting?"

She smiled, then opened her eyes again. "No, I'm just grounding and centering. Preparing for ritual. We'll be ready to start soon. I hope this works." She glanced at Grieve, who lay naked on the table, his arms and legs tied down with long ropes that wrapped around the four legs.

"Is that really necessary?" I hated seeing him like that. It seemed so undignified.

"It's the only way to be sure we'll all be safe. If something goes wrong . . . he could do a lot of damage, Cicely.

He could kill us all before we could react, especially if we're in the middle of ritual. Remember, as much as you love him, he was turned by Myst. He is one of the Indigo Court, even though he defies her power."

She placed a hand on my arm. "It's always hard to see someone you love treated in such a fashion. Once, a demon tried to possess my mother and we had to tie her down in order to exorcise the creature. It had come in through a portal that was in a haunted mirror we'd inherited. But had she been free, we wouldn't have been able to concentrate on doing what we needed to."

"I understand." And I did. I just hated seeing him like that. "So, in your private opinion, do you think this is going to work? Do you think we'll be able to save him from his nature?"

She frowned. "I don't know, to be honest. I wish I could give you a better answer than that, but I can't. That he wants to be free of Myst's power bodes well. But the ritual is ancient, and who knows if it's been performed since it was first written down? With any rite this old, there is danger. There is also the danger that his blood will reject the attempt, regardless of his will. I think we should just hope for the best, and do whatever it takes in order to try to free him."

At that point, Zoey stood. "We're ready. Come, gather. Peyton, you may stay, but Rex should leave. We must not be interrupted."

As Peyton helped Rex limp out of the room, then returned to take up a post by the door in order to keep unwelcome visitors out, the rest of us gathered around the table. It was time. And I prayed that we'd succeed and that Grieve would be set free of the bonds of ice that held on to his core.

Chapter 19

The room was dark because all of the windows were covered during the day in the Regent's mansion. Heavy velvet drapes made it feel like night, even though it wasn't. The scent of sage and cedar burned through the room, followed by an undertone of musk and heather.

Zoey rang a bell and we gathered around the table in our respective positions—I was in the east, Rhiannon in the south, Wrath in the west, and Chatter in the north. Luna stood at Grieve's feet and Kaylin at his head. Zoey began by circling everyone with a ring of sea salt, swiped from the kitchen. We had salt in our components stash, but why use ours when we could plunder Lannan's pantry? He didn't eat, so he wouldn't notice it was gone.

"Spirits of protection, come to this place and ring it with a circle of salt that nothing unwelcome may enter within." She closed the ring of salt and put down the bowl with which she'd been pouring out the white grains, then picked up a bowl of crushed sulfur. This was from our stash—or rather, it had originally been Marta's stash and was now mine.

"With a ring of sulfur, I do encircle this ritual, that nothing unwelcome may enter within. Let all negative spirits be

kept at bay, and let nothing disrupt our rites and rituals."
She trickled the sulfur out in a fine line, atop the ring of
salt, and the energy began to increase. The pressure of the
air weighed down on my shoulders. Whatever else she
might be capable of, Zoey could summon energy, that
much was apparent.

The third bowl held a fine dust with a silvery sheen.
Zoey trickled this out carefully, a few grains at a time, and
when she spoke, I understood why she was being so frugal.
"With this ring of silver shavings, I do encircle this ritual,
that nothing unwelcome may enter within, and nothing
within may escape outward."

Shit. *Silver.* We'd better clean up thoroughly after we
were done or Lannan would have our blood for sure. I made
a mental note: Sweep and mop. Several times. Vampires
hated silver. But for me, the energy of the metal made me
feel jazzed, almost like I'd had a shot or two of caffeine or
sugar. Speaking of food, after the fish incident, I'd been
very cautious about accepting food and drink from the staff.
Kaylin had made sure that the cooks preparing our breakfast had been careful, to avoid another nasty surprise.

Zoey put the dish down and then drew out a dagger. It
was not silver—Lannan's guards would have never allowed
a stranger to bring silver weapons into the mansion—but
hand-carved bone and antler, and it had what looked to be
a wickedly sharp blade on it.

She held it outstretched in her left hand, and moving
clockwise around the ring, she began to cast the circle. "Circle of art, circle of might, I call on the spirits to gather round,
I cast this circle with salt and sulfur and silver and sound."

Here, Luna began to intone a low note. Her voice sounded
almost harmonic, as if a second person were singing with
her. As Zoey encircled the room, Luna's voice followed her,
raising and lowering at odd intervals. After a moment, I
realized that where the energy felt weakest, Luna's voice
would lower, creating a bridge. And where it was strong
along the ring, her voice would flow upward, smoothing over
the top. It was as if she were filling in the gaps with her song.

As I looked at her again, I could see what she was doing.

Her eyes were closed and her arms raised, and she was weaving back and forth, swaying in time to the flow of magic. She was weaving a spell with her song, as sure as if she were using words instead of notes.

I closed my eyes and let myself flow into the melody. A *blink*, and I found myself on a high cliff, with the air rushing through my hair and the moon overhead. Below, I could see a forest stretching out, so far that I could not see the end of it, and the forest was covered with frost and snow, but it didn't frighten me like Myst's snow. It felt crystal clear, natural—winter that would come and go as it should. I stared up at the moon as the clouds boiled across it, but the moon was full and haunting and called to my owl self.

The wind whistled past, and I could sense Ulean dancing along the slipstream. I wanted to call up a gust, to transform and go winging into the forest because that was where I belonged, but instead I knew—instinctively—that I was to catch hold of the air, to slide into its nature and listen to the song it was singing.

As I sank into the energy of the wind, I felt the essence of clarity, of keen insight. I realized that my mind felt clearer than it had in weeks—perhaps years. By riding the wind, I could see far beyond my own little world, and a strange peace descended on me.

Slowly, the song began to die away and, my eyes fluttering, I found myself back in the room, as Zoey finished weaving the circle around us. Luna's song faded away, vanishing with a soft hush.

A wave of sadness rushed over me. I wanted to go back to that place, to stay there, to embrace the energy that had flowed surely but steadily. As I glanced at Rhiannon and Chatter, I could see the same feeling written across their faces. Wrath's expression remained impenetrable. Kaylin was just as unreadable. I let out a long breath, releasing the sense of loss, realizing that we had to be focused and clear for the ritual to work.

Zoey lit a green taper candle that was sitting on a small table near her, then turned to Chatter. "You may call upon the Element of Earth."

Chatter cleared his throat and ducked his head. With arms outstretched and palms toward the floor, he let out a low vibration—not a song woven in sound like Luna had charmed but a guttural roar from the depths of his core. It was the moving of earth, the rumbling of mountains. It embodied the depths of caverns.

"You who are bone and stone and crystal. You who are branch and leaf and twig. You who are the Elemental forces of Earth, I call to you. You who are the bones of the world, I summon you. You who are foundation, and manifestation incarnate, I bid you come forth. You who are our body and bones, O Elemental force of Earth, I beseech you to walk this circle, to embody your essence into our rites."

The timbers creaked, the bones of the mansion echoed a long, dark cry, as bone and root and leaf took hold. The energy worked its way into the room, encircling us, hovering over Grieve, a thick vapor of brown and green that enveloped the room, weighing us down. I felt like I'd gained twenty pounds as the forces of gravity rooted me firmly to the floor, and in another moment, a flash of energy—gnarled and strong as oak—worked its way into my feet, spreading through my body. The vapor settled into the ring of salt and sulfur and silver. And then—everything seemed back to normal. Chatter lowered his arms, a faint smile on his face.

Lighting a white candle, Zoey pointed to me. "Summon the winds. And do *not* become them."

I would have glared at her, but I realized that she was serious, not being snide. She was right. This was no place to let loose the powers of the fan—apparently now *my* powers. I gave her a short nod and sucked in a deep breath. I'd never done this formally before, though I'd been playing with the winds since my childhood.

I focused, recalling the mountaintop to which Luna's song had taken me. That was the feeling of the wind I wanted to invoke. I wasn't a singer, couldn't keep on key if you tried me, but I sought for the pitch that represented that feeling. When I thought I found it, I let out one long, clear note and held it for a moment, then let it fade.

"Spirits of the Wind, spirits of Air, I summon you. You who are the fresh breezes of spring, come to me. You who are the warm winds of summer's evening, hear me. You who are the chill gusts of autumn and the boreal winds of winter, come to this place. You who are the breath of our body, the air that keeps us alive, be with us." I wasn't sure of the wording, but I let the words flow on their own, as they would. "You who are communication and thought, you who are clear sight and intuition, come to this circle and join our rites. You who are the Elemental forces of Air, I summon you to be with us in this circle, to infuse our rites with your powers."

I stopped as a rush of wind raced around the circle. Where the earth had brought vapors weighing us down, the wind threatened to carry us aloft, to sweep us into the fray. I found myself laughing and realized the others were, too, in the whirl and swirl of this crazy dance we were on. But then as quickly as they had come, the winds departed, leaving everything with a crystal clarity that made me want to weep. Nothing seemed muddy now, nothing seemed static or stagnant.

Zoey smiled then and gave me a long nod. I wondered what Ysandra would make of this woman from the Akaz-zani, but before my thoughts could run musing in that direction, she lit the red candle and pointed to Rhiannon.

Rhia invoked the Elemental forces of Fire, and the room warmed considerably, as sparkling light danced around the circle, and then my father summoned the Elemental forces of Water, and a wash of autumn melancholy swept through me, as the sorrows and joys of the past weeks tumbled in on my shoulders, then were washed clean.

When all the Elemental forces had been summoned, Kaylin stepped forward and held up his hands. He dropped his head back and for a moment, I saw the shadow of a bat-like creature raise up to tower above him. He let out one pure note that felt like it was shooting directly through the top of my head.

"Spirit of Spirit, I summon you. Elemental forces of magic, Elemental forces of the will and of purest energy, come forth. We seek your realm, seek to harness your

strength, to bend our will against your power. Come, O
Spirit of Magic, be with us, crackle through us, wield us
even as we wield you. We are your instruments, we are
your bodies, we are your manifestations within this world."

As he spoke, a crackle ran around the room and everything began to spin. The force of magic, the force of the
fifth Element—Spirit—took over and my hands became
charged, energy flowing from them—intensifying the Elemental force of Air. I glanced at the others—I could see
sparks flying from Rhiannon, one look at Wrath and I
could see a wave rising up behind him, and Chatter had
ghostly vines emanating from his palms. I looked down at
my own hands and could see a wavering breeze waft forth.

I stretched out my arms, palms facing sideways, and the
others did the same. Earth met Air and blended, growing
stronger. And Air merged with Fire and the force grew
even more. Fire kissed the Water and the circle felt like it
was becoming a sphere. And then, when Water connected
with Earth, we were solid and impenetrable—the Elemental guardians holding us strong in their embrace.

We held the energy while Luna and Kaylin moved to the
center, standing on either end of Grieve. From just outside
the circle, Zoey drummed a rhythmic, hypnotic beat. Kaylin took hold of Grieve's head in his hands, leaning over
him so close it almost looked like they were kissing.

Luna placed her hands on Grieve's feet and began to
sing in a language I didn't understand, that I'd never before
heard. I didn't even know if it *was* a language—the sounds
were floating against the rhythm of the drum, long, sinuous, and haunting as they echoed through the room.

Luna looked taller in the candlelight, and it was obvious
she was in a trance, her eyes were glazed as she held tight
to Grieve's feet. The music snaked and crawled, coiled
around us, an ancient melody, dripping with power as it
flowed effortlessly from her lips.

Kaylin cried out, stiffening. He leaned back as far as he
could, his back arching, but still he held Grieve's head in his
hands. My beloved Grieve looked in pain, and yet—and
yet—my wolf did not whimper, nor was he afraid. Instead,

as I let myself connect with him, I felt a wonder, and a sudden field of stars flashed in front of my eyes. I could see them—the stars—they were filling my vision, filling my sight, and their beauty was far-reaching and cold, aloof.

The drum continued its slow, steady cadence, forcing our attention. Luna's voice interwove with it, rising and dipping, swirling like an ancient instrument, so smoothly that never once did I hear her catch her breath. I focused on her singing, followed the note, trying to find my sweet wolf again, but the way was blocked, and I realized, in a sudden whisper from Ulean, that I was not allowed to take part in what Kaylin and Luna were doing.

If you are with him, it will disrupt the ritual. He must walk through this darkness alone. Kaylin and Luna are the only ones here who can guide him.

As much as I didn't want to hear this, I accepted it and went back to holding the Element of Air—keeping it steady as the four of us kept the circle intact.

A sudden crack of thunder filled the room, startling us, but not once did we waver. As we looked up, a field of stars spread across the ceiling overhead. But some were caught in a maelstrom of mist—a swirling cerulean storm. I realized we were seeing the links that connected Myst and Grieve, her energy field imposed over his through her turning him.

As Kaylin sucked in a deep breath, the mist began to disperse, unweaving and retreating. Grieve began to thrash, but Kaylin and Luna held tightly to him, and the restraints kept him on the table.

Some of the fog surrounding the stars seemed impenetrable; it would not budge, though I could see the rocking energy trying to dislodge it. But most of the outer edges whispered away, vanishing. As Kaylin strained, trying to unweave the thickest part of Myst's energy, Grieve let out a scream and Luna's voice stumbled as he ripped the cords binding him to the table and broke free from the table.

Kaylin leaped toward him as Grieve, holding his head and moaning, staggered toward the edge of the circle near my father. Wrath dropped his hands and lunged forward, catching Grieve as he sank to the floor, thrashing in a horrible convulsion. I let go of the air, racing across the room, not giving a damn about the broken circle.

As I fell to my knees near my love, my wolf began to howl in pain, and I began to shake and quiver, unable to control myself. Grieve and I had somehow become bound, in such a way that his pain became my pain—we'd experienced it before, but I'd thought that we might have broken those cords.

Anadey—Peyton's mother—had turned on us, casting a spell to break the cords between Grieve and me, knowing very well that it might kill us. The spell had worked to some degree—the venom of the Vampiric Fae no longer held me in thrall when I was bitten by them, but we had not known just how far she'd managed to disrupt things.

Wrath reached out to Grieve, did something—I couldn't see what—and Grieve slumped to the floor. The convulsions wracking my body stopped immediately, and I slumped, aching and frightened but free from the seizure.

I scrambled to my hands and knees, crawling over to Grieve. "My love, my love . . . is he . . . he isn't . . ." I couldn't think of him being dead.

But Wrath eased my fear. "He sleeps. I put him into a deep slumber for now, until we figure out what's going on."

"I know what happened." Kaylin paled, looking nervously at the prone form of my lover. "I went too far in trying to unravel Myst's energy from his. I didn't realize I was at the core—the part that cannot be undone. And I tried to push beyond that boundary line—"

"I saw you do that. I could see what you were doing." I took hold of one of Grieve's hands, rocking gently as I brought it to my chest. "I thought the rest of you could, too."

"No." Chatter shook his head. "I could see something— but it was a blur and I had no idea what it was." Rhia and Wrath nodded in agreement.

"You could, because of your link to him. If I had pushed too far"—Kaylin grimaced—"you could have died with him."

"When Grieve dies, I die. We thought that before, when Myst punished him and I took the punishment on my own body. Now I think we know it's true." Oddly enough, I wasn't afraid—not terribly.

I wasn't the type of person to live my life for another, although it seemed like I'd done that for my mother, but Grieve—he and I were two parts of a whole. We'd created a bond that would outlast death, and I knew that if something happened in this lifetime, we would return together again and again until we finally managed to get it right. But, having said that, I wasn't ready to die yet. I wasn't ready to let Myst win. I wanted to grow old with Grieve.

Wrath leaned down and lifted Grieve in his arms. "I think he should go into the realm of Summer. He'll be protected there and maybe the healers can do more for him now. At least some of Myst's curse is lifted—some of the threads undone."

"Will Lainule allow that?" I had thought that she'd proscribed him from entering her realm, but then again, she had bid him come with us on the journey to find her heartstone. I had a feeling the Queen of Rivers and Rushes knew more about what was unfolding than she was letting on.

"Oh, she will. It is daylight—the vampires sleep and so does the Indigo Court. I will take him, along with my guards. Do nothing until I return. Today we hunt down Myst in her lair. Today we go to war and I will bring reinforcements." He caught my gaze.

I nodded, swallowing a lump in my throat. "We will prepare. I am taking my obsidian blade into battle."

Wrath frowned. "I do not like it, but then that usually doesn't stop you, daughter. Do what you will. But neither you nor Rhiannon nor Chatter can fall. Grieve . . . we have to make sure he survives this. So if you find yourself in danger, pull back. Let another take your place."

"Why is this so important? What are you not telling me?" I wanted answers. I was tired of being a pawn in this convoluted game. Something big was going down and if I was going to be a part of it, I wanted to know what.

"Don't question me, girl—"

"Don't you think you owe her the truth, Wrath?" A voice from the door cut him off. It was Ysandra Petros, standing there with the three remaining members of the Consortium. Peyton looked at me apologetically and shrugged.

They were dressed for battle, looking a bit worse for the wear considering what had happened. She strode in, all business—whether she was wearing a prim dress or a weatherproof jumpsuit, Ysandra Petros remained fully in charge.

"I think this matter is no concern of yours." My father stared at her, his eyes narrowing.

"I think it's *every* concern of ours . . . the Vampiric Fae are a plague on us all, a danger to everyone. And what has happened so far will change the future playing field. Cicely and Rhiannon deserve to know more than you've told them, if only to reinforce the necessity of them staying alive during this battle."

Ysandra's lips were pursed and she looked pissed. I'd never seen someone stand up to Wrath—except for Lannan, and even he cowered when push came to shove.

My father grumbled, shaking his head. "It's too soon—"

"When *will* be the time? When she goes charging in, trying to help save the day, and finds herself in the jaws of one of the Shadow Hunters? She has no more clue as to what's happening than the mass of yummanii and Weres out there who are counting their dead from the night's feast. You cannot protect her forever." Ysandra pointed at me, shouting now. "The die has been cast, the bargain made. The girls have sealed their fate. They deserve to know what's going on. I warned you of this, years back, before you refused our help. I knew this was coming from the beginning."

"From the beginning? What do you mean, from the beginning?" I turned to her, blinking. "How long have you known about this? Why isn't anybody being straight with me? Did you know what was happening when you came to the house the first time? I'm getting fucking tired of being left out of the loop!"

Rhiannon joined me, slipping her arm around my waist. "I want to know, too. If I'm involved, I need to know. I helped kill my mother the other day because of what Myst did to her. I demand to know what's going on. And I want to know why I was able to see that door that only those with Cambyra blood are supposed to be able to see."

We stood, a frozen tableau. Wrath glanced at Ysandra, then to Rhia and me, uncertainty filling his face. I almost felt sorry for him—it was obvious he was struggling with a decision.

Kneeling beside Grieve, I turned to Chatter, who was sitting on the floor beside my Fae Prince, lifting him so that Grieve's head was resting on his lap.

"How is he?"

"Sleeping deeply. It's hard to tell what's going to happen when he wakes up. He should be monitored. I thought we were taking him to the realm of Summer?" Chatter glanced at Wrath, and it seemed like the frightened Fae I'd met upon my return to New Forest had vanished. He was strong, almost regal.

Wrath let out a long breath. "I suppose it is time to tell you the truth. I'm not sure what Lainule will say, though."

"I say we should tell them." Lainule's voice echoed through the room. "We must sort things out in order to rout Myst this afternoon, and to do that you must know the past as well as your future." She pushed Ysandra out of the doorway as she entered the room, followed by eight strapping Fae warriors. "I have brought an army—they are outside, awaiting our orders. I also brought healers. We march to reclaim our land today."

I twisted around, still holding Grieve's hand. "Please, can you help Grieve?"

"Attend him." Lainule moved to the side as a woman stepped from behind her and entered the room.

She was Cambyra Fae and a healer—the energy rolled off of her from across the room. She silently glided across the floor like some ethereal spirit to kneel beside Grieve. Motioning for Chatter and me to move, she felt Grieve's pulse, then brushed his hair back and placed a hand on his forehead.

A moment later, she began to hum, and Luna moved forward, as if called by the song. The healer looked up at her, nodded, and Luna knelt beside her and began to match harmonies, blending her voice with the voice of the healer. As they worked in unison, the healer gestured to Zoey, who began to match their cadence with a slow beat. As the soft fall of her hand swept the head of the drum, Luna and the healer began to sing.

I am calling your soul back from the depths,
I am calling your soul back from the darkness.
I am calling your soul back from the crypts,
I am calling you back to yourself.
You are lost and alone, out in the starlight,
You are lost and alone, so far from home,
Come back to me, Princeling, cease to wander the
*   byways,*
Come back to me, Princeling, no more to roam.

As their voices fell to a whisper, Grieve's eyes began to flutter, and he moaned, but this time there was no pain and my wolf began to stir. I pressed my hand to my stomach as he sat up, but again—I felt no pain, only the joy of consciousness, and a freedom that I'd never before experienced.

The healer and Luna lifted him to a sitting position, holding him steady as he struggled for a moment, then sucked in a deep breath.

"Grieve?" I moved forward, slowly, not wanting to startle him.

He looked up at me, and the stars were still in his eyes, but they were changed somehow—they weren't frightening, only beautiful and vivid against the black backdrop. The feral edge I'd sensed when I first returned had fled. He might be Indigo Court, but he was my Grieve once more, and he smiled when he saw me and held up his arms.

"Cicely, my beautiful Cicely." His voice cracked then, and he slowly sat up, shaking his head. "I've come back to you, as far as I ever can return. Myst . . . she holds no power over me anymore."

"Grieve, my Grieve." I gathered him in my arms, kissing

his cheeks, his forehead, his lips. "My beloved. You are free."

"I will always be Indigo Court, but now I am free of the compulsion to hunt. I will always have the dangerous edge in my nature to cope with, but I can control it." He struggled to his feet. "I feel both stronger, and weaker."

"The violent nature of their blood gave you extra strength, young Prince. But you will regain the strength without the fury behind it as you get used to this new state of being." Lainule motioned to Wrath and he moved to her side. She turned to Rhiannon and me. "And now we will tell you what you wish to know. But understand: You may not be prepared for what you hear."

I nodded. Whatever it was, as long as Grieve was by my side, I'd weather the news. Rhiannon moved to my side and we held hands, waiting.

"We're ready," she said. "I want to know who my father is. And do I bear Wrath's blood in my veins, like Cicely? Am I part Fae?"

Lainule looked at Wrath, who let out a long sigh.

"No, you are not *my* daughter," he said.

"Then who was my father?" Rhia looked like she might cry. She'd waited all her life to know who her father had been, and when Heather died, it looked like there was no chance of finding out.

Lainule looked at her. "You are my niece," she said. "My brother sired you—you are his child. He was killed during the battle with Myst. You are part Cambyra like your cousin. And as my closest female heir, you, my dear, will be the next Queen of Summer, even as Cicely becomes the new mistress of Winter."

And with that, our world shifted forever.

Chapter 20

The silence was deafening. Rhiannon and I stared at her, as if she'd suddenly said we were turning into Martians. Ulean swirled around me.

I'm so glad you finally know. I have had such a hard time not telling you over the years. You will be my Queen, even as Lainule was until she gave me to you. I could feel the swish of her tailwind as she danced.

Rhia stammered, seeking words, unable to speak.

But I found my tongue. "I will not become Myst!"

"I did not say you were to become Myst, my child. You are Cambyra Fae, not Indigo Court. You will become the next Queen of the Snow and Ice, even as Rhiannon will be Queen of Rivers and Rushes. There has been no true Queen of Winter here since Myst killed her long ago and took her place."

"Tabera. The Unseelie Queen."

"Yes, I see your father has been giving you history lessons." She smiled at Wrath, then looked back at the two of us. "Myst knows nothing of balance, of give-and-take. She must be destroyed and the proper equilibrium returned. This will also negate your contract with Lannan, though he might still enforce it as an allegiance, but that is acceptable." Lai-nule smiled softly at me. "You were born to the waning year, as Rhiannon was born to the waxing. You are two of a kind, born on the cusp. Cousins, who mirror one another."

Rhiannon stammered. "Your *brother* was my father? Did our mothers know all of this?"

Wrath shook his head. "They knew some of it. They were chosen from the beginning. Your family has long held the Veil House and land—they have an interwoven history with the Golden Wood."

"Then what is my animal form, or like Chatter, do I carry Fire as my Elemental form?" She licked her lips, and the eagerness in her voice was tinged with fear.

I turned to her. "Snake. I dreamed it."

Wrath shook his head. "You and your dreams. But Cicely is correct. You are of the snake people. But for now, leave that be. You do not have time to master the form and it would be too cold for you outside."

He sighed. "We chose your mothers to bear the two of you when we realized that Myst was rising again. Before she ever made a move, we knew we had to ensure that there would be a summer and winter queen to come, should the unthinkable happen."

"Why didn't you stop Myst back then? Before she destroyed your Court?" I shook my head. "Why not prevent a problem before it started?"

"We could not. We only knew she was here, not where she was hiding. Geoffrey thought it was the vampire court she was after, but that was only a part of her plan. He was shortsighted and arrogant. And the prophecy of the Blood Oracle is partially true—she is out to diminish their control."

Ysandra moved forward. "We knew all of this, but the Court of Rivers and Rushes turned their back on our help. But we've been working on our own, in other towns where the Indigo Court has been making inroads. There have been battles waged that no one will ever hear of—behind the scenes, bloody and costly to the Consortium but also costly to Myst's domain. You have no clue of how powerful she is and how vast an empire the Vampiric Fae have bred over the years."

"We chose not to ask for your help because we believed this to be a matter for the Seelie and Unseelie Courts. We were mistaken." Wrath looked pained, as if he'd swallowed something bitter.

"All well and good, but look at the cost your isolationism has caused. And it's not just here, it's in other small towns like this, around the world. But it is not just you . . . the vampires were of no help, either, believing the war was theirs alone." Ysandra shrugged. "Arguing is useless now. There is no blame any longer. We must work together. Join forces against our common enemy."

Lainule nodded. "She speaks the truth. And this is why you must take reign as the Queen of Snow and Ice, with Grieve as your consort. Once Myst is routed, the Indigo Court will seek another queen. You will have to hold the winter against them, until our combined forces have managed to destroy them all." She smiled softly. "I can hold my position only awhile longer. Through the coming war. Then Wrath and I must leave the Golden Wood. Rhiannon and Chatter will take our places as Lord and Lady of Summer."

"But why? What happened?" I didn't understand. Losing them seemed a huge blow and I still hadn't managed to grasp the significance of what they were saying. It was too overwhelming.

"When Myst neared my heartstone, you saved my life. Do you remember when I told you that by doing so, you would set into motion something that would forever change the future for you and Rhiannon?"

I nodded, still not understanding the exact nature of how things had shifted. "Yes."

"When a Fae Queen reabsorbs her heartstone, when the energy returns to her body, she forfeits her crown. The heartstone, once hidden and separate from the Queen, will forever hold her realm until it is either destroyed or returned to her. By saving my life, you destroyed my reign. But it was my choice to make. I could have died a queen, but I chose to live, to battle Myst and fade into history."

Tears clogged my throat and I wasn't sure why I was crying. "I don't understand . . ."

Chatter stepped up to Wrath. "You will go with your Lady, then?"

Wrath nodded. "It is the way. Once we have routed Myst and reclaimed the Golden Wood, Lainule and I will turn over the reign to the four of you. The Golden Wood will be divided between you. Summer will reign over it during the waxing year, then retreat to her realm for the winter. And Winter will guard it during the waning year."

I gasped. "My dream . . . we met on the solstices . . . but then that means . . ."

"Yes . . . you will be divided, at odds and yet in alliance. Summer and Winter can only mingle on the days they make the exchange. You and your cousin will forever live separate. This is your sacrifice. This is the way it's always been."

Rhiannon burst into tears. "I'm not ready for that."

"This is your destiny. There is no turning away." Lainule stepped forward and embraced her. "Long have I wished to welcome you into the family, to tell you who you were, but like Wrath and Cicely, I could not do so until the right time. I wish we could have prepared you both for this, but there was no way. War does not give us an easy route, nor does it make allowance for fear."

A knock at the door startled all of us. I stepped forward, my mind reeling. The changes over the past few weeks had been intense and confusing. Now to find out that Rhia and I had been born to a destiny neither of us had dared even dream of sent me reeling. I had so many questions, but as I opened the door, I knew they'd have to wait.

A group of magic-born from the Consortium waited. Ysandra stepped forward. "Reinforcements are here." She turned to Rhiannon, Grieve, Chatter, and me. "Do you see now why you cannot chance being killed in this battle? Why you must lead the battle and yet, let others take on the brunt of the fighting? You are the heirs to the thrones. You cannot let yourselves be hurt."

I bit my lip. Once again, we were pawns of destiny, but

I had the feeling that would shift once we took the reins of power. Then we would be forming the future rather than reacting to it. We weren't ready for this, but then . . . would we ever be? We were being tested, and fate had a way of shoving people into situations in order to strengthen them.

"We're being tempered. Fire and Ice." I turned to Lainule. "When do we march against Myst? Your warriors are here. The witches and mages are here." And then—a whisper caught my attention.

We are here, outside the gates. It is time for two witches to lead their people into battle.

I turned to Wrath. "I just received a message from the snow hag. The Wilding Fae are ready. We cannot wait for the vampires to wake—when they rise, so will the Indigo Court."

"Then we will go to battle. We will do what Myst did to us, and once again, the barrows will run red with blood, but not from the Cambyra Fae this time." He stood, then added, "Do you understand why you cannot carry the obsidian blade?"

I licked my lips. As much as I wanted it in my hand—it gave me comfort—I nodded. "I'm too impulsive when in the grips of its energy. It forces me to act rashly. I have the dagger you gave me, I will content myself with that and with the force of the wind."

And so we instructed Lannan's servants to sweep up the ring of salt and sulfur and silver—no use having him pissed at us because of the mess and the metal barrier—and prepared for battle. Lainule and Ysandra instructed their brigades to meet us in front of the Veil House—four dozen Fae warriors, and two dozen magic-born, including three healers.

As for the Wilding Fae, I sent a message through the slipstream for them to meet us at the Veil House. I received a riddle in return that told me they would.

We drove through the streets, taking Lannan's limousine. Along the way, we saw scattered remnants of the bloody battle from the night before. The streets were filled with cars making their way out of town, frightened faces pressed against the windows. I felt a sense of loss, gazing over the exodus. With hope, we could make it safe for them to return—but would they? Would they brave coming back to a town that was so full of blood and bones?

As we pulled into the driveway, the warriors were there, along with the members of the Consortium. The Wilding Fae appeared as we spilled out of the car and cast our gazes over the assembled army.

"Be cautious." Wrath's voice echoed over the yard as we gathered in front of the burned shell of the Veil House. "While Myst and the Vampiric Fae will be asleep, you can rest assured they will wake when we attack, and the light-rage will make them strong and deadly. We go in with the element of surprise, but do not be complacent. We will not retain that edge for long. Kill all of the Vampiric Fae you see—but do not mistake and harm Prince Grieve, whatever you do. Are you ready?"

The warriors let out a loud cry and turned to the Golden Wood.

Grieve, Rhiannon, Chatter, and I stood apart, surrounded by Kaylin, Luna, Peyton, as well as Zoey, who had opted to join us. We stared at the woodland. While the others were focused on finding all the Shadow Hunters they could, it was our goal to find Myst's personal nest. And Grieve knew where she was.

"There will likely be creatures guarding the woods," he warned everyone. "Goblin dogs and other ill-fortuned Fae. Do not be deceived by the seeming weakness of some—they are all dangerous."

The Wilding Fae nodded. They weren't speaking much, but I could see the glimmer in their eyes. They seemed to anticipate the battle and I wondered just what I'd gotten myself into, aligning with them. Kaylin had thought to bring the snow hag's meat with us, and he set it on the ground in front of her, neatly wrapped. She gave him a snaggletooth smile and motioned to the car.

"One might store this, if one had a thought, until after a skirmish is complete. Otherwise, beasties might snag the meat and be off with it and then both parties would be out meat and money."

Kaylin let out a chuckle. "One might be wise to listen to such advice." He put the meat back in the car until we were done.

And then, with nothing to hold us any longer, and the afternoon upon us, we marched across the backyard toward the Golden Wood. Toward our destiny.

❧

The warriors went first, stretching through the undergrowth. Following them were the members of the Consortium, as the Wilding Fae spread out to the sides. We followed, taking the path with a group of eight guards to the front, and I was surprised to see Lainule waiting at the trail mouth. She answered my questioning look with a gentle smile.

"This was my home. This was my kingdom. I will fight to regain it for you and your cousin. I will not go easily into the fading mists." She stepped into the formation beside Wrath, and leading the rest of us, they swept into the woods, and we followed.

The woodland seemed hushed. Neither bird nor beast made a noise, and I began to think that the Shadow Hunters had killed them all. We silently moved through the bushes, doing our best to keep from setting off any traps. Webs glistened between the trees, huge and filled with the giant fat snow spiders that were Myst's pets and sentinels. Gold and white, they were as beautiful as they were deadly, and I kept my eyes overhead, making sure we weren't being trapped from above.

As we approached a web stretching across the path, the warriors went first, shooting them with gleaming arrows. The spiders chattered, scuttling away, but one dropped, and soon a second and third. One of the guards stepped up to tear down the web that crossed the trail, but another spider that had been hiding in the trees lashed out, catching him in its mandibles. He let out a shout that was cut short as the creature injected him with its venom and he went limp. Three others who were at the front of the trail sent arrows into the spider, and it tried to run but then stumbled and fell, jerking spasmodically.

Two men brought the fallen guard back, but it was too late. The poison had worked quickly and he was stone dead. Laying him gently to the side, we moved on, cautious as the snow thickened and the woodland grew darker.

Everything seemed to glisten and glow in the dim light of afternoon. The silent hush of snow falling illuminated our backdrop as we followed the path to the ravine and set off down the hill. We'd fought a skirmish with Myst and her Hunters here, not all that long ago. It was slow going, but this time, the Shadow Hunters weren't on the other side, and we could focus on making it down the hill in one piece.

My thoughts drifted ahead.

I was to be the Winter Queen. That seemed so preposterous on one hand, and yet . . . and yet . . . it felt like the snow and ice had become my unending home. And from now on, it would be. Winter would be my realm, and I would guard and caretake it like Lainule had been guarding the realm of Summer. I glanced over at Rhiannon and Chatter. So many times we'd joked about being amber and jet, fire and ice. And now it was true.

She looked so much stronger than just a few weeks back. Adversity often brought out the best in people. It formed character. And she was looking strong and confident and determined.

So deep was I in my thoughts that I did not see a stone in my path, and as I tripped over it, I went rolling down the ravine for a good ten feet before one of the guards managed to put a stop to my impromptu tumble.

"Are you hurt, Lady?" He offered his arm.

I took it, righting myself. After a brief check, I shook my head. "I'm fine. But you don't have to call me Lady . . . I'm simply Cicely."

He smiled softly. "Not for much longer, Lady. You are the Winter Queen–elect." And with that reminder, which also felt like a gentle rebuke, he let go of my elbow and returned to breaking the path through the snow.

I looked over at Grieve. He'd asked me to be his queen, when all of this was over. I'd never quite thought about what that would mean. Now, I began to get a true glimpse into what the future would be like.

Summoning up a deep breath, I forced away thoughts of the years to come. We had to get through this mission first. We had to destroy Myst before any plans could come to fruition. And so I focused on putting one foot in front of another, in the silent march down the ravine to the stream below.

We reached the frozen stream but it would not be able to hold up those of us not of full Fae blood, who could simply glide over the ice. But the warriors picked the rest of us up and, with the blurring speed with which they could run, we found ourselves on the other side of the creek, dry and ready to press on.

Up the other side of the ravine we went, the silent snows so deep around us that should we break through, we could sink to our chests. Grieve took my hand as we walked, and the warmth of his palm in mine shored me up. Whatever happened, we had each other, and Myst no longer owned him, though he would never be the Cambyra Fae he once had. He was a new breed and would rule as king over a new kingdom.

I watched as Lainule and Wrath glided over the snow, dreading the knowledge that they would be fading away into whatever lands they were headed to. She turned, as if she could read my thoughts, and whispered something into the slipstream. I stopped and closed my eyes, listening.

Cicely Waters, it was foretold that you would be my savior and you would be my doom. Do not despair—it is the way of the world, it is my destiny. I am content and will be even more so after we rout the Mistress of Mayhem from my barrow. Wrath and I will live out our lives in the obscurity and safety of the Golden Isle. A smile crossed her face before she turned back to the path.

A good two hours longer, and we were at the barrow. Between twin oak trees, a portal stretched. We would have to pass through it in order to be fully within the realm of the Indigo Court. Only this time, I would not be going in with Kaylin, dreamwalking in the shadow realm.

We approached the towering trees, bare of leaves. The crackle of energy raced between them and I sucked in a deep breath. This was it. We were here.

We waited for the rest of the warriors, the Consortium, and the Wilding Fae to catch up with us. They converged from various parts of the woods, reporting only two Shadow Hunters out and about, and now dead.

"Then we pass through. Remember: once wakened, they are deadly. We will have a short time in which to catch as many by surprise as we possibly can. We don't know if they've had spies out there watching us. However, the light-rage will still affect them, even if they've been warned." Wrath stared at the portal.

"My husband, let us enter and reclaim our home." Lainule's voice was light, even as her eyes shimmered and flashed. "Today, we retake what is ours."

He motioned to the warriors. All but twelve took up their place in front of us. Next came Ysandra and her crew, then us. The rest of the guards moved in back of us to watch the rear. Without further ado, the front line plunged into the portal, and we all followed. This was it. We were going in.

※

As we entered the portal, two things became apparent. Some of the Shadow Hunters were waiting for us. And they were in a frenzy. The light-rage held them in thrall, so they were in terrible pain, which made them only that much more angry. They fell on the guards with horrific screams, but the warriors were ready and the fray was on. While the Fae guard took care of them, the rest of us slid out from behind and moved over to the barrow.

Grieve motioned for us to follow him, and so Kaylin, Peyton, Rhia, Chatter, Wrath, Lainule, and I plunged into the barrow. I motioned to Ysandra to bring several of her witches and she nodded, trailing behind us, along with a handful of the Fae warriors.

The barrow was familiar—we'd rescued Peyton from

here not that long ago—but it was a confusing labyrinth of tunnels, and there was no way I could remember where we'd been. Grieve, however, seemed to know directly where we were going. And so did Lainule and Wrath. As we passed chambers, several of the guards split off and we heard muffled screams as they slit the throats of the sleeping Shadow Hunters.

And then we were in front of a large chamber door, and Lainule let out a low laugh. "The halls of my barrow ran red, and so shall they again this day." She slammed open the door.

There, a hive of Shadow Hunters awaited, and I could see on the other side of them, Myst, a pained look on her face as she barked out orders. I could not hear what she said, though. The slipstream was running wild here, and the screams of pain from the light-rage were ricocheting like bullets through the room.

The room became a blur of blades and blood. I found myself facing one of the Vampiric Fae and had no more than dodged one blow when one of the guards shoved me out of the way and took my place. As I stumbled back, I caught a glimpse across the room of Myst. She was heading toward a door behind her. I dodged through the battle, through the clashing blades and gnashing of teeth and spraying blood, managing to skirt the room until I came to the door.

As I peered down the hall, I could see her at a distance, with two of her guards. And then Grieve and Kaylin were with me, and we were racing after her. I couldn't let her get away—couldn't let Lainule down.

At the sound of footsteps on our heels, I glanced over my shoulder. Luna, Rhia, and Chatter had noticed where we were headed and they were behind us. We raced through the passage, the glowing tiles shimmering as we passed, for what seemed like hours. As we began to make headway on Myst and her Shadow Hunters, she broke through another door and we could see the glimmer of the outdoors shining in.

We slammed through the door after her and spread out, trying to circle her. The Shadow Hunters began to transform and I did the only thing I could think of doing—I summoned the wind.

Ulean was with me. *Call the hurricane . . . it will knock them off their feet.*

And so I raised my hands to the sky and summoned the winds to sweep through me. As the raging gusts began to swirl around me, I dropped my head back, laughing.

"Do not run. You will not survive my storm." I turned toward Myst. "Surrender now, and we will make it easy on you."

She cocked her head, her face a mask of pain as the light hit her eyes. "Do you really think I'd surrender to you? I have no intention of letting you capture and kill me." And as she spoke, she began to grow, stretching up and over the woods, shimmering in a cerulean shadow.

I cast out, grabbing hold of the winds and sending them swirling out in front of me as I began to move forward. Trees began to shiver and, in a fury, I uprooted a small one and sent it hurtling toward one of the Shadow Hunters, hitting him square on with it. His partner began to howl and moved back, eyeing me cautiously.

Myst hissed, reaching out with one long, thin arm. "*I* am the Queen of Winter, not *you*, my girl. You will not usurp me, long-lost daughter of mine. We are not done yet." The snow began to pour so thick and fast we could barely see. The flakes caught in the vortex of wind I was spinning, blinding the world, clouding it with a fury of white.

Cicely, let go of the storm. Myst can traverse a blizzard and while you will soon become the Queen of Winter, right now she has the power to command the weather in a way that you don't.

I didn't want to listen to Ulean, but I knew I had to. I pushed one final gust toward the last place Myst had been standing and then released the winds. As they died down, I glanced around anxiously. The blizzard was raging now and it was impossible to see beyond my outstretched hand.

Is she here? Where is she?

She is gone. Ulean let out a long sigh. *She has vanished for now. The other Shadow Hunter went with her.*

The snow began to die down, and we were standing there alone but for one crushed Shadow Hunter. And Myst was nowhere to be seen.

Chapter 21

"We lost her." I stared at the woods. "She's gone."

"There's nothing we could have done. But we can help back in the barrow." Kaylin shook his head. "We will find her again. Or . . . she will find us."

"He's right." Grieve put his arm around my waist and turned me toward the barrow. "Myst will not forget that she has you to thank for this. And she will wish to return the favor. We are in far more danger now than before. But come, let us return to the others and see if they need our help."

As we reentered the passage, I tried to put the sting of defeat out of my mind and hoped that the others had had better luck than we had. We hurried back to the main chamber, shutting the door to the outside behind us and locking it. Myst might've been able to break through, but Luna sang a charm to trigger an alarm should the door be opened from the outside. It was the best we could do until someone with stronger powers could get to it.

When we reached the main chamber again, I feared what I would see but took the lead anyway and marched into the room. There was plenty of carnage, but it looked like our warriors were on the winning side this time. The room was slick with blood and dead Shadow Hunters. And a handful of our own, as well.

Lainule and Wrath looked up from where they knelt over one of the warriors. He was dying, and as Lainule murmured something in his ear he closed his eyes and let go.

We stood, waiting. A group of guardsmen came in from the passage leading into the main chamber. They were covered with blood—and some were hurt—but they knelt before Lainule.

"Your Majesty, we have routed the enemy. The barrow is clear. There are still more outside, but we've sent word to the realm of Summer for more volunteers to come scour the woodland and find the rest. We killed over three hundred Shadow Hunters this day, and more."

Lainule smiled softly. "You have done well. Have my guard comb the forests. Be cautious, Myst is still on the run." She looked over at me.

"We could not catch her. She is still out there, but she had only one Shadow Hunter with her. She'll likely gather the remnants of her people to her before she makes another attempt. Is there a way to guard the woodland so she can't summon new recruits?"

Ysandra, who looked weary beyond belief, nodded. "We can set a ring of wards around the Golden Wood, but it will be a great task. We need a treaty with the Queen of Rivers and Rushes before we can set to such an undertaking."

Lainule let out a small laugh. "I will make such a treaty as one of my last acts here." She turned to Rhiannon and me. "You must undergo your initiations as soon as possible, so that Wrath and I may take our places with the others who have reigned and passed out of this realm."

I stared at her. "It's all happening so quickly."

"And so it must. There is no time to process the journey, owl-daughter. If we had time, I would willingly give you more. But so it must be . . . and so it will be." And with that, she dropped to one of the divans that had escaped being splattered with blood. "I already feel my power beginning to wane. Night is coming for me, at least here in this world."

Lainule and Wrath sent us back to the mansion for the night while their people cleaned the barrow. Myst had vanished, and no one knew where she was. Ysandra and her squad from the Consortium returned to Lannan's estate with us. We reached the gates late—and apparently every vampire on the premises was out looking for us.

As we wandered through the doors, blood-soaked, cold, and exhausted, Lannan was standing there, waiting. He stared at me, his gaze holding me fast. After a moment, he scanned the rest of the crowd.

"Get them clean clothing, showers, and food. Cicely, you will attend me in my office when you are warm and clean and dressed." And with that, he turned and exited the room.

I didn't have the energy to argue. So much had gone on that I almost welcomed the chance to sit and talk about it with someone who wasn't entirely involved. Grieve glowered, but I just shook my head as we trudged up to my room.

"Don't even go there. Just don't. All I want to think about right now is a hot bath and clean clothes, and to feel like maybe, for just an hour, we can breathe without something else happening." I kissed him on the nose, then stripped off my clothes.

Grieve let out a snort. "You know as well as I do that he'll try anything to get in your pants. But my love, you will do as you must. As you always do." He seemed at ease with himself, no longer struggling with his inner demons since the ritual, as if a constant edge were gone. "Shower, and I will lay out an outfit for you."

The water sang against my skin, and I embraced the heat, drawing it in, letting the stream pound on my sore muscles. It began to ease the knots in my back and my legs. Soaping up with a lavender-scented bath gel, I lingered under the shower as long as I could, until the water began to cool.

As I stepped out and wrapped a towel around myself, I wiped the fog off the mirror and stared at myself. So much had happened. So much was happening still, and I wasn't quite sure how to take it all in. Staring at my reflection, I finally shook my head and stepped out of the bathroom.

Grieve was waiting for me, and before I could say a word, he drew me to him and silently, slowly, kissed me. But instead of moving to make love to me, he stood back and handed me my bra and a clean pair of jeans and comfortable turtleneck.

"You will not be wearing these much longer, my love. The Queen of Snow and Ice will not wear jeans." His voice was wistful, and I realized he'd been hoping we'd return to the land of Summer. That we'd live in the perpetual warmth and light of his homeland.

"I don't even pretend to grasp the significance of what this all means. But all my life I knew I'd return to New Forest, and that I'd return to you. And I have, and I am with you. As long as Myst lives, we're still in danger, but now . . . I feel we have a fighting chance. We have the possibility of life beyond her reign." I sat down on the bed as I dressed. "But I'm bone-weary and have no clue where we go from here."

"Lainule was correct. The rituals must be done quickly. She will fade, and she must be out of this world before that happens. If she returns to the land in which she was born, then she and Wrath will live and grow old together. If she stays here now, she will fade into a spirit, into vapor and mist and a ghost." He hung his head. "I have never known any other mother except for her—my own mother died when I was young. Lainule is my aunt. Her sister was my mother. And before you ask, yes, Rhiannon is my cousin as well, by Fae blood."

"How long have you known?" I finally dared ask him the question that I'd been putting off. Somehow the answer didn't seem to mean as much now.

"Since before you were born. Remember, there are

many levels of fate working here—the one we brought upon ourselves when you were Myst's daughter. The one brought about by Lainule and Wrath when they realized Myst was encroaching. The one by your mothers, who both agreed to bear daughters of the Seelie realm. Don't for one minute think that Heather and Krystal didn't realize what was going on. They knew."

I motioned to the floor. "Hand me my shoes, will you? So . . . they knew? Then why did my mother run?"

He handed me my sneakers and I welcomed them after wearing boots in the recent battle. "She changed her mind. She couldn't handle the powers she had, let alone think of a daughter who might one day be destined to rule over the Fae. Things are changing. The Courts here—they have long been insular, and inbreeding has been a problem. You are not fully of Fae blood, you bring a new life to the realm. It is time we opened up, spread out in the world."

"What about the purity of the line? If we have children, they will not be fully Fae." I couldn't believe we were even talking about a family. And while I knew we had to hunt down Myst and destroy her for good, I realized, too, that I wanted Grieve's children. I wanted to create the family I never really had.

"Trust me, the Grand Courts will always remain Fae alone, but we are of the Lesser Courts, and there has been too much isolation for too long. Lainule saw this, and while she and Wrath could not break the cycle themselves, they could ensure that our people grow and thrive into the future. We must join the world that moves around us."

A knock on the door interrupted us. It was one of Lannan's servants. "The Master bids you to attend him." But the look on her face told me he hadn't put it quite like that.

"In other words, get my ass in gear. Right?" I smiled at her, and she smiled back. For some reason, the thought of dropping the bomb on Lannan that I was to become the Queen of Snow and Ice seemed like icing on the cake. I knew he'd be pissed.

With another kiss from Grieve, I headed out the door and down to Lannan's study. The mansion was bustling now that the vampires had woken up, and I saw several groups of them arming themselves. Regina was organizing them. She waved me over.

"You had quite a little adventure out in the woods, I hear." She was walking down the line of vampires, adjusting a strap here, a weapon there. They stood at attention and I realized these were the guards that the Crimson Court had sent out to replace those who'd died. "We were hoping for a bigger piece of the action, but there are still Shadow Hunters to be found and so I send my men out to battle them. Lainule's warriors are tired and weary. These men will take their place."

I waited. Regina didn't make small talk. She had to have some reason for calling me over, and until I knew what it was, I didn't want to chance saying the wrong thing. After a moment, she turned to me and with those glassy obsidian eyes, she held my gaze.

"I have heard what is in store for you and your cousin. Don't ask how—I have my ways of finding out what I need to know. I think it a good thing. The Cambyra have cordoned themselves off from society too long. You will bring a much-needed infusion of reality to the Courts. I'm not sure if you can handle the job. You and your cousin are young by many standards, though if we're speaking in yummanii years, many a woman has become queen far younger than you. Whatever the case, the Crimson Court will wish an audience with you both, to forge new treaties, to discuss alliances."

I stared at her. For once, she was treating me with respect, instead of like a toy or a plaything.

"Cats have your tongue?" She flashed a crooked smile at me, with those perfect pearly fangs showing.

I found myself opening up to her. Not a good thing, perhaps, but vampire or not, Regina was an astute and savvy diplomat. "I have no idea what to say, though I suppose you're right about the allegiances. But as far as handling the job—we have no choice. I should have realized— Lainule dropped hints when we went to retrieve her heartstone. But without it, she would have died."

"Sometimes you simply work with what you're given." Regina drummed her fingers on a console table. "My brother is waiting for you. I wanted to warn you: He is not in a good mood. Do not provoke him. He's not stupid, but sometimes he's impulsive, and right now the last thing we need is another complication." She gave me a long look.

I sucked in a deep breath. "Yeah, that's the truth of the matter."

"You'd best attend him. If you need me, I will be right here outside the door . . . listening." And that little offer scared the hell out of me.

I gave her a curt nod, then turned and entered Lannan's study. He was behind his desk—the desk that had been Geoffrey's—brooding. As I entered the room, he looked up at me, a scowl on his face.

"You took your own sweet time answering my summons."

Oh yeah, this was going to be a barrel of laughs. "I'm exhausted. I was covered in blood and dirt."

He pushed himself up from behind his desk and wandered around to stare at me. "So, I hear you are to become the new Queen of Snow and Ice. I suppose you expect this to negate my contract with you."

I wasn't sure what to say. He was up to something, that much I could see, and he was angry, very angry.

"Nothing to say to me, lovely Cicely? Not even a thank-you for offering my house to you and your friends, for doing my best to keep the people of New Forest safe? Not even a kiss of gratitude?"

"Thank you, if I haven't said it." And I realized I hadn't. Lannan was a prick, but he had been of invaluable help to us.

"A begrudging lip service, if ever I've heard one." He swung around behind me and leaned in close, whispering in my ear. "A little bird whispered that you are to marry the Fae Prince. You'll truly be the ice princess you pretend to be. But I know you better."

I let out a long breath. I had no clue of how to answer him. I doubted that anything would calm him down.

"And don't think that I don't know about the ritual you did here—in *my* house. Bringing *silver* into my home? Not a good choice, Cicely. But I know you would do anything to save him, wouldn't you?" He rested a hand on my shoulder and the lust emanating from him soaked through my body.

I shivered. It seemed to be a real question. "What are you getting at, Lannan?"

He brushed my ear with his lips. "Just that should it become necessary, I want you to think about what you would pay in order to save your lover's life. What would you be willing to do?"

I steeled myself. I'd had enough, and though I took Regina's words to heart, I didn't want to deal with any more of this crap. I shook him off and turned around. "I don't know what you're playing at, but right now, there is no need to save his life. Grieve is fine, and since the Crimson Court is interested in forging new alliances with the coming realms of Summer and Winter, there'd better not be anything disrupting his health from your quarter."

He let out a low growl and grabbed me, pulling me to him. "I will do as I see fit and I need no upstart bloodwhore telling me what to do."

"But I'm not your bloodwhore, and I've never been one." I grimaced as he shoved me against the wall and forced his knee between my legs. "Think before you act. I know you're angry, and I don't understand why. You have Regina, you have the Regency and this mansion. You will soon be freed from having us under your roof. We do thank you—*seriously*. As much as I hate to admit it, I have to give you credit. You've helped us survive, and I'll never forget that." Nor would I ever forget him manhandling me, but that I left unsaid.

Lannan pressed against me. I could feel him harden, and for a moment, I thought he might lose control. Once again, I'd put my foot in my mouth. He slipped his hands under my sweater, squeezing my breasts, and I gasped despite myself.

"You don't understand at all, do you, little girl? *I always get what I want, and I want you*. You've thwarted me, you've been oh so polite and oh so obedient. You've begrudged me every touch, every kiss, every offer I've made. You almost let me fuck you, you call me your angel of darkness . . . and then you run just out of reach the moment it might become real between us. You're using him as much as you're using me, you little cock tease."

He had me pinned. I struggled, trying to break free, when a knock on the door took us both by surprise.

His face a mask of anger, he barked out, "Who is it?"

"Regina. We have to discuss several edicts from the Crimson Court."

She was lying. I could feel it in her voice, which flowed along the slipstream, as sure as I knew that she was also saving my butt. But why would she? She was devoted to Lannan and wanted him to be happy, even if it came to using me as a piece of meat.

Lannan gave me a long look, his eyes narrowing. "You are free from your contract. Go to your throne. Take your crown."

By the look in his eyes, it was obvious that he knew he couldn't enforce a contract over the Winter Queen. He had to let me go, like it or not, but he wouldn't give up that easily. And by his next words, I knew I was right.

"But know this, Cicely: I will never rest until I have you in my bed. I don't care how long it takes, you will be mine. Queen or not, you'll never be free from my presence." He let me go then.

I quickly straightened my sweater. I stared at him for a moment. "Why do you want me so much? Is it just because I've said no to you?"

He turned away. "Get out of my office. Go do whatever it is you have to do, *Your Highness.*"

As I exited the room, I passed Regina. One glance at her and I knew she'd overheard everything. As I silently passed her, she leaned down and whispered, "You little fool. You really don't *see,* do you?"

I stopped. "See what? All I know is that Lannan is determined to humiliate me, to use me, and then toss me aside."

"Lannan humiliates *everyone*. But that is not his goal. He's right. You have no clue, do you?" She paused, and her voice shifted from irritated to bemused. "My brother has taken a fancy to you. Love would be too strong a word but . . . call it infatuation. You've bewitched him, Cicely. He's obsessed with you and you refuse to give him what he wants. I've known my brother for thousands of years. He always gets what he wants in the end. Trust me, he'll stalk you till the day either you give in, or he dies. Now go, while I can still calm him down."

And then, without waiting for an answer, she swept into the study and shut the door behind her.

I ate dinner in my room, and then, locking the door, Grieve and I slept through the night. Lannan did not bother me, nor speak to me again, and by the time morning came, I'd pushed aside what Regina told me. I had enough to deal with now, I didn't have time to focus on a lust-obsessed vampire. I'd cross that bridge when—and if—it became an issue.

The morning moved swiftly. After breakfast, our little group gathered in the drawing room that Lannan had assigned for our use. Ysandra joined us. She looked tired. We all did.

I did not tell them what had happened the night before, other than that Lannan had vacated my contract and that Regina wanted to make new treaties with the realms of Summer and Winter.

Wrath let out a long sigh. "I suppose you will have to do so. The time when the Fae could remain in peace, retired from the world, is ending. We must take an active part now—or you must. Lainule and I will be slipping away into the shadows, where we can rest without all of this turmoil."

"How are we going to know what to do and what not to do? We don't even know anything about the Grand and Lesser Courts—in fact, yesterday was the first time I'd heard mention of them."

Lainule pressed her hand on my shoulder. "Be at peace. We will leave you with advisors. And Chatter and Grieve have full knowledge of the hierarchy. It will be difficult, but you will find your way. And our people will accept you."

"That's another question. You are Queen of the realm of Summer. Rhiannon will take over there. But if there are no Unseelie left here, just who will Grieve and I rule over?" I was truly confused.

Wrath laughed. "If that is the worst of your concerns, never fear. There are Unseelie around, they've just kept to the shadows. Now they will come out, unite, and learn a new way of life from you. The Wilding Fae have taken a liking to you and will hearken to your reign. And as I said, some of the Summer Court feel more comfortable with the night and the snow. They will join the Winter."

There was so much I didn't understand, but I held my tongue. We had a while yet to figure things out. And hopefully our initiations would help us to understand our new roles.

Wrath stood. "The barrows are clear—our warriors have cleaned out the last of the Shadow Hunters they could find, but we know there are more in the woods. Lannan and Regina sent fifty armed vampires out there last night and they destroyed another forty-five Shadow Hunters. They combed the woods, so any left are in deep hiding. Myst and the rest of her people have gone into hiding."

He stretched, then motioned for us to follow him. "Come now. Both you and Rhiannon must become familiar with your new home. Midwinter is almost upon us, and so are your intiations. And the double wedding."

A million questions still in my heart, I stood and followed them out to the foyer, where we readied ourselves for another trip into the woods.

Chapter 22

One week had passed since we'd routed Myst out of the barrows, and now the Cambyra Fae lived there once more.

At the end of Vyne Street, the Veil House stood empty, but rebuilding was already taking place. The Consortium had floated a quick loan for Rhiannon and me, and we were having the house rebuilt even though we weren't going to be living here. Peyton and Luna would take over ownership, and Kaylin would join them. The Moon Spinners would continue, with their high priestess—namely me— also being a Fae Queen. We'd decided on twice-monthly meetings, thus skirting the old tradition of the Summer and Winter queens only meeting twice a year. I had a feeling we'd be changing a number of other rules as we went along.

Our initiation was set for three nights hence, on midwinter's eve. The day after that, on the solstice, we would be married in a double ceremony to Chatter and Grieve.

Although my heart was singing, fear still kept the woodland and town in its grasp. Myst was still out there, and we could feel her, brooding and watching. Geoffrey, too—and Leo—were in hiding and we fully expected them to make trouble.

As for Lannan . . . he hadn't spoken to me since I'd left his office. I wasn't particularly unhappy over the fact, but it didn't bode well for future entanglements. Regina warned me to keep out of his way for a while, and this time I followed her advice. He'd been too close to the edge, and I didn't want him toppling over, taking me with him. Stalkers of any sort were scary. Vampire stalkers—much worse.

Grieve and I were sorting through the kitchenware, deciding what was salvageable and what wasn't. I found another one of Aunt Heather's dishes that had escaped the fire and looting. As I ran my hands around the soot-stained china, a slow tear eased out of my eye.

"What's the matter, love?" Over the past few days, I'd watched Grieve go from haunted to whole. He'd never again be the Prince of Summer, but now he was poised to be the King of Winter and he'd grown, no longer bound by Myst's shadow. He even seemed taller, and his beautiful platinum hair was gleaming in the ray of light that shone through the window. The sun was a welcome sight, and the snow—while it wasn't melting—was taking more breaks between storms.

"I was just thinking about my aunt. About how much she loved this house, and Rhiannon, and how much she loved me. I miss her." And I did—Aunt Heather had been my touchstone to childhood.

Grieve took the plate and stacked it with the others for washing later. He let out a long sigh, leaning back against the sink. The kitchen had taken a lot of damage and would have to be totally renovated. The rest of the house, while gutted in areas, had held up better and would take less work to restore. He held out his arm and I slipped into his embrace, leaning my head on his shoulder.

"She was a good woman. She resisted Myst as much as she could." He paused as if wanting to say something. After a moment, he continued. "The morning we met her on the trail? She could have easily killed us. She held back. She let us win and then she asked us for release. But she could have killed us."

I hung my head. Somehow I'd known that. Heather had

been strong enough. She'd chosen to let us win. "Grieve . . . how long have you known that we were to take over the Winter Court?"

He shrugged, not letting go of me. "I knew that you would someday be my Queen. I knew it from the beginning. But I couldn't say anything. I always thought we'd rule the Summer, though." He smiled, resigned—but it was still a smile—and turned me to face him. "We've a long history together. Longer than even we know."

"Ulean told me the same thing."

"I promise you, I don't know anything more than what I've told you so far, but I imagine someday we'll find out together." He picked up a creamer and handed it to me and I tucked it to my chest. "We'll have a family, Cicely. We'll have children, and we'll rule a kingdom together."

"First we have to find Myst and kill her for good. But I'm beginning to believe. I'm beginning to truly think . . . that the future exists for us." And slowly I raised the creamer—another of Aunt Heather's treasures—and kissed it softly before setting it on the counter.

"Oh, we have a future. Our battles aren't over, but we have the upper hand. And soon we'll be married and even Lannan Altos can't touch you then."

And with that, we went back to sorting out the kitchen. The Veil House would rise again. Grieve was free from Myst's rule. And I . . . I was about to become a queen.

✤

On our last morning at the Veil House, Rhia and I sat on the back steps, eating our lunch. Only now, three guards stood at attention near us. We could barely go to the bathroom without an escort.

"So much has happened." Rhia finished her sandwich, then dusted her hands on her skirt and put her gloves back on.

The Shadow Hunters were still around, a few had been caught, but Grieve estimated that at least sixty to a hundred had escaped, and we had no doubt they'd found their way to Myst. The barrow was ready, though, in case she made another attempt. It wasn't there that we would have to take the greatest care.

"New Forest feels so empty." I stared at the silent road. A few people had moved back, but a number of HOUSE FOR SALE signs had cropped up lately, and things for our little town were changing.

"People will return. Whether they are old or new inhabitants, well, that remains to be seen. Anadey is still running the diner. Peyton said she left a voice message last night, wanting to see her."

I cringed. Anadey had betrayed us. "What is Peyton going to do?"

"I don't know, but she seems in no hurry to visit her. Rex is healing up. The infection from the Shadow Hunter's bite has died down, but it will take him some time to fully recover, and he'll always have a chunk of muscle gouged out of that leg." Rhia crossed her arms. She stared around the backyard. "I'll miss living here."

"Me too, but I guess we can't stay here now. At least Peyton and Luna and Kaylin will be near us." In the short month or so that I'd been home, these people had become my family as well as my friends. "Did Zoey make it off all right?"

"Yeah, she went back to the Akazzani." Rhia stood, staring at the sky. The snow had finally begun to slack off, but it hadn't fully stopped. Myst still held the town in her wintery grasp, though it wasn't nearly as tight as it had been. "We'd better get down to the barrows. They're waiting for us."

She held out her hand and I took it. As we began to walk across the yard, toward the Golden Wood, followed by our guards, I felt a shadow cross my path. I whirled quickly, but there was nothing there.

As we came to the trail mouth, I glanced up at the sky. A woman's face peered down at me from the silvery clouds. Myst . . . it was Myst. I could feel her in the snows and on the slipstream, waiting, biding her time, longing for revenge. She was out there, waiting for us to slip up, and it was only a matter of time until she returned. But this time we'd be stronger, and perhaps we could end her terror for good.

Character List

CICELY AND THE COURT OF THE MAGIC-BORN

Anadey: Traitor; was a friend of Heather's and mentor to Rhiannon. One of the magic-born, Anadey can work with all elements. She owns Anadey's Diner and is Peyton's mother.

Cicely Waters: A witch who can control the wind. One of the magic-born and half-Uwilahsidhe (the Owl people of the Cambyra Fae). Born on the summer solstice at midnight, a daughter of the moon/waning year. Destined to become the Queen of Snow and Ice.

Heather Roland: Rhiannon's mother and Cicely's aunt. One of the magic-born, an herbalist, now turned into a vampire by the Indigo Court.

Kaylin Chen: Martial-arts sensei, a dreamwalker, has a night-veil demon merged into his soul.

Peyton Moon Runner: Half-werepuma, half-magic-born, she's Anadey's daughter.

Rex Moon Runner: Werepuma. Peyton's father.

Rhiannon Roland: Cicely's cousin, born on the same day as Cicely, only at daybreak, a daughter of the sun/waxing year. Rhiannon is also half–Cambyra Fae and half-magic-born, and she controls the power of fire. Destined to become the Queen of Rivers and Rushes.

Ysandra Petros: Member of the Consortium. A powerful witch who can control sound, energy, and force.

THE COURT OF RIVERS AND RUSHES

Chatter: One of the Summer Court. Grieve's best friend. Is Rhiannon's fiancé.

Grieve: Prince of the Court of Rivers and Rushes, one of the Cambyra Fae (shapeshifting Fae) turned Vampiric Fae. Cicely's fiancé.

Lainule: The Fae Queen of Rivers and Rushes, Grieve's aunt, the Queen of Summer. Destined to fade back to the Golden Isle.

Wrath: Cicely's father—one of the Uwilahsidhe (the Owl people of the Cambyra Fae).

THE INDIGO COURT

Myst: Queen of the Indigo Court, mother of the Vampiric Fae, the Mistress of Mayhem. Queen of Winter.

Grieve (*see* **The Court of Rivers and Rushes**)

Heather (*see* **Cicely and the Court of the Magic-Born**)

THE VEIN LORDS/TRUE VAMPIRES

Crawl: The Blood Oracle. One of the oldest Vein Lords, made by the Crimson Queen herself. Sire to Regina and Lannan.

Geoffrey: Former NW Regent of the Vampire Nation and one of the Elder Vein Lords. Two thousand years old, from Xiongnu.

Lannan Altos: Professor at the New Forest Conservatory, Elder vampire, brother and lover to his sister, Regina Altos.

Hedonistic golden boy. New NW Regent of the Vampire Nation. Obsessed with Cicely Waters.

Leo Bryne: Was Rhiannon's fiancé, a healer and one of the magic-born. Leo was a day-runner for Geoffrey and now is a vampire.

Regina Altos: Emissary for the Crimson Court/Queen. Originally from Summer with her brother and lover, Lannan. Was a priestess of Inanna. Turned by Crawl.

Playlist for *Night Seeker*

I write to music a good share of the time and have been sharing my playlists on my website. I finally decided to add them to the backs of the books for my readers who aren't online.

—Yasmine Galenorn

Adam Lambert:
  "Mad World"
Air:
  "Napalm Love"
  "Surfing on a Rocket"
  "Playground Love"
  "Another Day"
  "Cemetary Party"
Android Lust:
  "Dragonfly"
  "Stained"
  "Sex and Mutilation"
Avalon Rising:
  "The Great Selkie"

"Dark Moon Circle"
Awolnation:
    "Sail"
Black Rebel Motorcycle Club:
    "Shuffle Your Feet"
    "Fault Line"
Bobbie Gentry:
    "Ode to Billie Joe"
Buffalo Springfield:
    "For What It's Worth"
Cat Power:
    "I Don't Blame You"
    "Werewolf"
Cat Stevens:
    "Katmandu"
Chester Bennington:
    "System"
Chris Isaak:
    "Wicked Game"
Cobra Verde:
    "Play with Fire"
Corvus Corax:
    "Filii Neidhardi"
    "Mille Anni Passi Sunt"
    "Ballade de Mercy"
Cul de Sac:
    "I Remember Nothing More"
    "Into the Cone of Cold"
    "The Moon Scolds the Morning Star"
    "The Invisible Worm"
    "Song to the Siren"
    "Cul de Sade"
David Bowie:
    "Sister Midnight"
David Draiman:
    "Forsaken"
Death Cab for Cutie:
    "I Will Possess Your Heart"
Depeche Mode:

"Dream On"
"Personal Jesus"
Disturbed:
    "Stupify"
Faun:
    "Sieben"
    "Punagra"
    "Deva"
Foster the People:
    "Pumped Up Kicks"
Gary Numan:
    "Walking with Shadows"
    "Prophecy"
    "The Angel Wars"
    "Melt"
    "A Child with the Ghost"
Gypsy:
    "Spirit Nation"
    "Morgaine"
Heart:
    "Magic Man"
Hedningarna:
    "Gorrlaus"
    "Juopolle Joutunut"
    "Tuuli"
    "Räven (Fox Woman)"
    "Grodan/Widergrenen"
    "Täss' on Nainen"
Hugo:
    "99 Problems"
In Strict Confidence:
    "Promised Land"
    "Forbidden Fruit"
    "Silver Bullets"
Jace Everett:
    "Bad Things"
Jay Gordon:
    "Slept So Long"
Jorge Rico:

"Theme from *Picnic at Hanging Rock*"
Julian Cope:
    "Charlotte Anne"
King Black Acid:
    "Rolling Under"
Lady Gaga:
    "Paparazzi"
    "I Like It Rough"
Lacuna Coil:
    "Our Truth"
    "Swamped"
    "Fragile"
Little Big Town:
    "Bones"
Low:
    "Half Light"
Marilyn Manson:
    "Arma-Goddamn-Motherfuckin-Geddon"
    "Tainted Love"
    "Godeatgod"
Nine Inch Nails:
    "Sin"
    "Get Down, Make Love"
    "Deep"
Nirvana:
    "You Know You're Right"
    "Heart-Shaped Box"
Notwist:
    "Hands on Us"
Orgy:
    "Blue Monday"
    "Social Enemies"
A Pale Horse Named Death:
    "Meet the Wolf"
    "Cracks in the Walls"
PJ Harvey:
    "Let England Shake"
    "The Words That Maketh Murder"
    "In the Dark Places"

Puddle of Mudd:
   "Psycho"
Red Hot Chili Peppers:
   "Californication"
R.E.M.:
   "Drive"
Ringo Starr:
   "It Don't Come Easy"
Rob Zombie:
   "Mars Needs Women"
Róisín Murphy:
   "Ramalama (Bang Bang)"
Sarah McLachlan:
   "Possession"
Saliva:
   "Ladies and Gentlemen"
Seether:
   "Remedy"
Sully Erna:
   "Avalon"
   "The Rise"
Susan Enan:
   "Bring on the Wonder"
Tamaryn:
   "The Waves"
   "Mild Confusion"
Tina Turner:
   "One of the Living"
Toadies:
   "Possum Kingdom"
Warchild:
   "Ash"
Woodland:
   "Morgana Moon"
   "The Dragon"
   "Blood of the Moon"
   "Winds of Ostara"
   "Gates of Twilight"
   "First Melt"

"Into the Twilight"
Wumpscut:
    "The March of the Dead"
Yoko Kanno:
    "Lithium Flower"

Dear Reader:

I hope that you enjoyed *Night Seeker*, the third book in the Indigo Court series. There will be two more books in this series. I love writing these books and think of them as a dark Faerie tale. For me, it's an opportunity to explore a world steeped in mysticism. Cicely's world is one in which everything—from rock to tree to the weather itself—is inherently magical. The fourth book—*Night Vision*—will be out next year.

Until then, I hope you'll enjoy the upcoming releases in my Otherworld series. Book twelve, *Shadow Rising*, Menolly's next book, will be available in October 2012. And book thirteen, *Haunted Moon*, will be available in February 2013.

For those of you new to my books, I wanted to take this opportunity to welcome you into my worlds and I hope you enjoyed the journey enough to come back for more. And to those of you who've been reading my books for a while, I wanted to thank you for revisiting Cicely and Grieve's world once again and for being so supportive of my work.

Turn the page for a preview of *Shadow Rising*!

Bright Blessings,
The Painted Panther
Yasmine Galenorn

Following is a special excerpt from

SHADOW RISING

the next book in the Otherworld series
by Yasmine Galenorn

Coming October 2012!

I hadn't been home to Otherworld in a while—not for any length of time. As we stepped through the portal into the barrows near Elqaneve, the Elfin City, the brilliance of the night sky hit me, untainted by the light pollution running rampant in the Earthside cities. Over there, even in the country, the stars sparkled more faintly, muted and dim. But here . . . I stared up at the heavens, stunned.

Had I really been away long enough for me to forget how beautiful my home world was? And yet . . . and yet . . . the city lights that sparkled over the Earthside landscape called to me. The hustle and bustle of Seattle had worked its way under my skin, and I wasn't so sure I wanted to return home for good, even should we be offered the chance.

We arrived in Otherworld just shy of seven P.M., and the darkness of the spring evening was spiraling over the sky. My sisters were relieved to see the chill weather begin to break, but I preferred the winter, when the sun set earlier, and rose later. During summer, the long sleep of daylight claimed too much of my time. But the wheel must turn, and now the spring held sway. The vernal equinox

was due in a week, and along with it, my promise ceremony with Nerissa.

We still hadn't settled on details for the ceremony and
time was running short. As was my girlfriend's temper. It
irked her that I couldn't come up with ideas for a concrete
plan. My continual stream of "Whatever you wants" was
wearing thin, but the truth was, I had no clue what I wanted.
When Dredge had turned me into a vampire, I'd let go all
hope and plans for love and weddings, and now I couldn't
remember what I had thought I wanted before I'd lost my
life.

But thoughts of Nerissa and home and rituals drifted to
the back of my mind as Trenyth approached. The advisor
to Queen Asteria, he was meeting us to escort us back to
the palace in the center of the Elfin City.

"About time he got here. I'm freezing," Delilah mum-
bled as she blew on her fingers.

Camille jabbed her in the ribs with an elbow. "I'm cold,
too, but be nice. He probably got held up by something
important."

"He can't hear me from over there." Delilah glared at
her, then shrugged and jammed her hands in the pockets of
her jeans.

"Don't bet on it. Elves have extremely sensitive hearing."

"Shut up, both of you. Whining about the cold won't do
anything to warm you up." I felt a little guilty barking at
them. After all, I was immune to the chill. Vampires didn't
feel much in the way of weather changes unless it was
extreme, one way or the other. I knew my sisters and our
escorts were freezing, but I didn't want Trenyth's feelings
hurt.

We'd divided up the manpower, making some of the
guys stay home. Accompanying us were Trillian, one of
Camille's husbands; Shade, Delilah's half-dragon fiancé;
Chase, the human detective with a touch of elf in his background; Rozurial, an incubus; and Vanzir, a demon who
worked with us. That left us with a fighting contingent, but
still enough manpower over Earthside to protect the house.
And protecting our home there was an absolute necessity,

especially now that Iris and Bruce were back from their honeymoon, and Iris was pregnant.

Trenyth looked tired, and for the first time, I noticed a few tiny age lines around his eyes. Elves seldom showed their age. Time passed for them differently, leaving them untouched and unperturbed. And most exhibited a patience that defied understanding. Unlike some of the more volatile denizens of Otherworld, that Elfin quality seemed to grow with the centuries.

Standing medium height, Trenyth was thin but not gaunt, elegant to a fault, and carried himself with a regal air. He was decorum incarnate, and his manner wasn't a façade, as it was with some members of the royal courts.

"Welcome back to Elqaneve, girls." He sounded rushed, and kept glancing back at the carriages behind him.

"Trenyth!" Delilah apparently had forgiven him for letting us stand out in the cold. She stepped forward to give him a hug.

Trenyth blushed lightly, awkwardly returning the embrace. "Delilah, blessings to you and your house." He turned to Camille, and held out his hands. "And you, my lady. How are you doing?" A look of concern washed over his face as she took them and pressed them to her heart for a moment before letting go.

"Are you . . ." His words slipped away.

Camille ducked her head. "It's going to take a while, but I'm making progress. I don't think I'll ever be the same. You can't be, not after something like that. But it helps that Hyto is dead and that I saw him die." Her smile turned to ice. Camille had become harsher since her ordeal, darker in nature, but it seemed to suit the transitions through which she was going.

"Camille's right," I said quietly. "What she went through with Hyto . . . what *I* went through with Dredge, traumas like that change you forever. But it doesn't mean you can't find happiness, or grow stronger than before." Life had a way of forcing you to either take charge or knuckle under, and neither my sisters nor I were the knuckling kind.

Trenyth nodded. "And the two of you have gone above

and beyond what I'd expect of anybody, under the circumstances. Now, come, please. We have much to discuss—events are transpiring that you must know about. And although spring is on the way, the night is still cold and the carriages are waiting for us."

And quick as a cat, we were tucked into the carriages with blankets spread over our laps and heading once again toward the castle of Queen Asteria.

❧

Elqaneve was a city of cobblestoned streets that wound through beautiful gardens surrounding low-rising houses. Windows glimmered, gently illuminated by the soft glow of lanterns. The town was simultaneously elegant and cozy, and while I appreciated its beauty, it felt too gentle for me. Though perhaps *gentle* wasn't the right word. Elves weren't gentle. They could be dangerous and terrifying when roused. No, perhaps the word I was looking for was *subtle*.

The Elfin race wasn't known for being in-your-face, and that's exactly the type of person I was. I hadn't always been like this—*take no prisoners, my way or the highway.* I'd been a loner when I was younger, and only in the past twelve or thirteen Earthside years had I turned into the fury that I could become.

When I became a vampire, I came out of my shell . . . once I managed to climb back *into* my mind. Sanity had been sporadic for the first year, and it had taken the Otherworld Intelligence Agency a lot of patience and training to teach me how to function and how *not* to turn into the monster Dredge had planned for me to become.

I glanced over at Camille. She seemed lost in thought, gazing out the window, leaning against the side of the carriage. Trillian sat next to her, holding her hand, stroking it lightly with one finger. The jet black of his skin glowed against her pale cream, and for a moment I thought I saw a swirl of silver race from his fingers to hers, but that couldn't have been right.

Chase was sitting next to me, and he, too, stared quietly

out the window. Delilah, Shade, Rozurial, and Vanzir were with Trenyth, in the carriage behind us.

"Hey, you get lost somewhere in there?" I spoke softly, but Camille's eyes flickered and she shook her head.

"No, not really. I'm just wondering what Queen Asteria wants to see us about."

She was lying. I knew it. Most likely, she was thinking about our father. It was hard not to, now that we were back in Otherworld. He'd disowned her, and as a result we'd disowned him. Everything was convoluted into a horrible mess, compounded by his lack of sensitivity. At this point, we could probably qualify for an Otherworld episode of the *Jerry Springer Show*. No doubt *that* would thrill Delilah to pieces, as long as the ringmaster himself hosted it.

With another look at her face, I let the subject drop. We'd hashed and rehashed the family drama to the point of no return. It was moot. Father didn't approve of Camille's choice in husbands—Trillian in particular—nor her pledging herself as a priestess to Aeval's Court. But she'd had no choice. Love doesn't always give you a choice, and neither do the gods.

As a result, we had said "buh-bye" to both dear Daddy and the Otherworld Intelligence Agency, and now we worked for Queen Asteria.

"Why do you think Queen Asteria summoned us? And why ask me to come along? I almost never interact with her—that's more your and Delilah's department." Being able to come out only after dusk had its drawbacks.

"I was wondering why she asked me to come along, too." Chase frowned.

"You *are* a distant relative of hers, you know." I gave him a poke in the ribs, careful not to shove too hard. Sometimes I forgot how freakishly strong I'd become. It was easy to hurt my friends and family if I wasn't careful.

"Doesn't track. She made it a point to invite me, and I doubt familial bliss has anything to do with it." He played with the buttons on his new blazer, fastening and unfastening the bottom one until I thought he was going to rip it off. "You really like my new jacket?"

Camille and I exchanged looks. This had to be the twentieth time that he'd asked since we started out for the portal at home.

"Yeah, it's nice." I wasn't good with diplomacy, but Chase was nervous and I didn't want to hurt his feelings. Unfortunately, the pseudo-military look didn't suit him at all. However, since Sharah—his elfin girlfriend and the future mother of his child—had given him the blazer, he was better off pretending he liked it. Humans had *nothing* on the elves or the Fae when it came to pregnancy-induced hormonal mood swings. It was in his interest of self-preservation to lie to her.

But that didn't mean I couldn't needle him. "So tell us, in the privacy of the carriage, you really think you can rock that look?" I grinned at him. His expression when he was under fire was priceless. By now, he knew when I was serious and when I was just blowing smoke. Though it *had* been more fun when I could scare the crap out of him just by tickling his neck.

He squirmed. "Do *not* do this to me, Menolly. Don't put me on the spot." But even with the pleading in his voice, his eyes twinkled and he laughed. "Only you would force me into a corner."

"I only torture the people I love." With a snort, I folded my arms and leaned back in my seat. "Don't answer. I can tell you don't feel comfortable in it. But we promise we won't tell Sharah. Or her aunt. *The Queen.*"

That sparked another ripple of fear in his expression. Queen Asteria happened to be the aunt of his girlfriend. And therefore, the great-aunt of his child. I had to admit, I wouldn't want to be caught up in the web of politics Chase was facing.

Another thought struck me. "Does Asteria even *know* Sharah's pregnant?"

Camille swiveled her head, glancing at Chase. "She *doesn't*, does she? You'd better come clean, because you don't want us saying something stupid to her."

Chase shifted uncomfortably. "Um, well . . . the truth is . . . *no*. She doesn't know. Sharah wanted to wait. We haven't decided what we're going to do yet. I've asked her to marry me but she won't. She said we aren't ready."

"You *aren't* ready." I stared at him. "You know that. She knows that. Why rush it?"

"She's carrying my child—" He paused, then let out a long sigh. "I guess I'm thinking about it from Earthside morality. I'd be a scumbag if she wanted to get married and I said *no*."

"She isn't cutting you out of the baby's life, though." I cocked my head. "Wait. She hasn't cut you out, *has* she?"

"No, it's not that. Sharah said I'll be part of the baby's life as much as I want." He looked so uncomfortable that I couldn't help but wonder what the root of the problem was.

"So tell me again, what's the problem? You in love with her?"

He blushed this time and Camille broke in softly. "Perhaps the issue is that Sharah offended him by insinuating he might not want to participate."

Chase shifted in his seat, and glowered. "Exactly! *I'm not my father. I'm no deadbeat and I'm not going to vanish on my kid.* And since she's choosing to have the baby, I will be there to make sure the child knows his—or her—heritage."

The words poured out so fiercely that at first I thought he might be pissed, but the hurt that flashed across his face spoke volumes. Chase was afraid someone would even *think* he might consider abandoning his child. He couldn't take being seen as a carbon copy of his missing father—the father he'd never known. His childhood had left him with some deep emotional scars. The situation with Sharah must be triggering fears and resentments from his own past.

I sheathed my fangs. "We know you'd never abandon your child, Chase. And Sharah knows that, too. Nobody who knows you would ever think you'd bail."

I was about to reach out, pat his hand, but stopped. I simply wasn't the comforting type, and he knew it. I opted for catching his gaze and holding it. I silently focused on him, willing him to relax. It wasn't polite to use our half-Fae glamour on our friends, but sometimes we opted for what was needed over what was ethically correct.

After a moment he relaxed, breathing softly, and leaned his head back against the rocking carriage.

"Don't think I'm unaware of what you just did," he said softly. "But thank you. I needed to relax. Delilah knows that Sharah hasn't told anyone yet, so she won't say anything, either. We talked about it last night on the phone."

Chase and our sister Delilah had been involved in what was a downward spiral of a relationship. Now they were both with other people, a lot happier, *and* they'd saved their friendship.

At that moment the carriage shifted and Camille peered out into the evening street. "We're nearing the palace." She smoothed her skirts and pulled out a compact, peeking into the mirror to make sure her makeup was set.

"Me too?" Not for the first time, I wished I could check my own damned makeup, but that wasn't ever going to be a reality, so I sucked it up and asked for help. She leaned close, brushing my face with a quick sweep of powder.

"You're good to go. You look great." She winked. "Not that the Queen's going to care but . . ."

"But it isn't politic to visit royalty looking like a slob." The carriage lurched to a stop and the door opened, the driver reaching in to help us down. "I guess we'd better see what bad news is in store for us now."

"I don't even want to know." Camille flashed me a wry grin as the driver put his hands on her waist and swung her down from the carriage step to the rain-slicked path below. "But I guess we don't have a choice."

Once Delilah and the others stood next to us, Trenyth led us into the palace to meet the Elfin Queen.

Overhead, the stars glimmered. They were beautiful but all I ever saw were the stars and the moon and dark clouds against the night sky. Sometimes it seemed like sunlight had become a myth—a dream I'd once had that was beautiful but fleeting. For me, only the starlight existed.

❊

The palace of the Elfin Queen rose in gleaming alabaster. Simple, elegant lines mirrored the symmetry of the city in general. Amid a flurry of gardens, the royal courts were clean, quiet, and decorous. They were nothing like the Court and Crown of Y'Elestrial—our home city-state, which was a hotbed of lush opulence and debauchery.

The cul-de-sac ended in front of the entrance to the palace and, as we quick-stepped up the path behind Trenyth, Camille sighed happily.

"What is it?"

She clasped her hands under her chin and whirled around, staring up at a tall tree. The faintest of green leaves were beginning to show among tiny starlike white flowers that covered the branches.

"The scent of the *untahstar* tree . . . we're really home." A catch echoed in her throat as she stared up at the vine-laden tree that grew only in the northern reaches of Otherworld. I could sense the war waging within her. She loved being Earthside, but this was her home. She was more wistful now than ever, since Father had exiled her from Y'Elestrial.

Delilah followed her gaze and smiled softly. "It smells like childhood, doesn't it?"

Our father's home—the house of our youth—had two untahstar trees growing in the front yard. Their branches had wound together and Mother used to joke that the trees reminded her of their marriage. Two trees, on opposite sides of the path, reaching together across a void.

I allowed myself a quick breath. I didn't have to breathe and by now was out of the habit, but when I wanted to smell something, I could force my lungs to take in air, to hold and catch the scents riding the wind.

The spicy floral fragrance swept me back through the years, to days long gone and dreams that had belonged to my former life—the one I would never, ever be able to reclaim. Disconcerted, I shook them off, not wanting to be caught up in memories. Memories were dangerous for me, even now.

Trenyth motioned for us to get a move on. We followed him into the alabaster palace, leaving old dreams and lives behind.

✦

Asteria, ancient queen of the Elfin race, wore the tire tracks of age on her face—which meant she was probably older than anyone we would ever meet with the exception of the dragons or the Hags of Fate.

She had been queen before the Great Divide, before the Great Fae Lords split the worlds apart, when Otherworld was forcibly shifted away from Earthside. She had been old when Titania and Aeval were young and new to their thrones. As she swept into the throne room, she ignored the throne hewn of oak and holly—and crossed to a marble table standing to one side. As we waited, she gave us an impatient look and motioned for us to join her.

Trenyth's mood had gone somber. It was clear we weren't here for a potluck or a game of monopoly. Something bad had gone down and whatever it was, the fallout filled the throne room.

Camille gave me a cautious look. She shook her head and mouthed, "Bad." Delilah edged her hand into Shade's as they glanced around the room. Trillian, Vanzir, and Rozurial moved closer. Even Chase seemed ill at ease. As for me, the tension set me on edge to the point where my fangs came down in auto-defense mode, breaking the skin of my lip.

Camille curtsied while the rest of us bowed. "Your Highness, we came as soon as we received your summons. Something is wrong, isn't it? What happened?"

Asteria looked at us, one after another. Tension rode her face. Even in the darkest circumstances, I'd never seen this much stress on the Queen's face before.

"Sit. There is much to discuss and we have little time."

As we slid into the chairs around the table, Trenyth motioned to one of the Elfin guards who'd been standing nearby with a long scroll. He brought it over and rolled it out on the table. A map of Otherworld, it filled the table, and we held it flat as Trenyth picked up a long pointer. Serving maids quietly offered us food and drink—they'd even filled a goblet with blood for me, though the girl's nose wrinkled as she handed it to me.

Head down, Queen Asteria closed her eyes, her arms crossed across her chest. She looked like she was gathering courage.

After a moment, she looked up and said, "We have dire news."

Delilah let out a little gasp. "The spirit seals are missing, aren't they? We feared—"

But before she could get out any more, Camille silenced her. "This is worse, isn't it? This is far worse."

Inclining her head slightly, with a pained voice, Asteria answered. "Yes, far worse. Although, yes, it does have something to do with the spirit seals. At least, the two that Shadow Wing has managed to steal away from you."

Silence followed, as we waited for the bad news. For more death and bloodshed and panicked plans to descend. We'd been embroiled in war for months now, going on a year and a half, and there was no easy way out.

"Telazhar has returned to Otherworld, for the first time since we exiled him. And he's brought the war with him."

Her words hung like a crystal in the air, then shattered into a thousand shards, raining down on us. Everybody started talking at once, but after a moment, I jumped up on the table and, putting my fingers in my mouth, let out a loud whistle.

"Shut up. It's not going to do any good if we all talk at once." In the lull that followed, it occurred to me that my spiked heels might not be the best for the marble table but the Queen gave me a soft smile as I leaped down and took my seat again. "You know this for a fact?"

"Thank you, my dear. I'm too weary to whistle and shout. And yes, it's true. Shadow Wing is behind it. Telazhar, wearing one of the spirit seals, has been spotted in the Southern Wastes. From what our informants say, he's inciting the sorcerers to align with him. He's rallying them to war."

"The Scorching Wars." I stared at her, unable to comprehend what this meant for Otherworld, beyond one hell of a bad party.

"Yes. He seems to be planning to create another series of wars as bad—or worse—as the Scorching Wars. Only this time, the sorcerers have a Demon Lord at their back. While Shadow Wing can't gate over here—*yet*—Telazhar can raze half the world if he has a mind to. I'm afraid that, very quickly, Otherworld will be embroiled in such turmoil to make the recent battle in Y'Elestrial look like chicken scratch."

We sat in silence, digesting the news. This was far worse than what any of us had been imagining.

Camille shifted, and after a moment whispered, "Will the sorcerers follow him? Do we know the extent of his influence?"

Queen Asteria moved back to let Trenyth take over. He pointed to the city of Rhellah, the last city before a long stretch of desert in the Southern Wastes, where rogue magic played free and easy on the winds, bonded with the grains of shifting sand.

"We're readying a trio of spies. They'll head to the south, first to Rhellah, to discover what's actually going on. From there, they will infiltrate the desert communities. The cities farther south—down in the heart of the Southern Wastes—are dangerous and wild and filled with slavers and sorcerers. We don't dare just barge in. Our spies must proceed carefully. They can adapt to the climate in Rhellah while planning out the next step."

"How long have you known about this?" If this had been going on for a while, then we had wasted valuable time.

Trenyth looked straight at me. "Lady Menolly, we first learned about this development four days ago. We dispatched a runner to check out the rumors at their source—over in Dahnsburg. The rumors *are* true. And our runner was caught. He managed to escape, and made it home. Missing an arm, his tongue, and one eye."

I shut my mouth, suddenly pissed at myself for questioning him. Although we couldn't accept things blindly and we had to question, I also needed to remember the elves were on our side. We were all in this together. Queen Asteria wouldn't have stirred this in her cup for weeks before summoning us. No, if anyone was to blame for anything, this was *our* fault. We'd let Telazhar—and another spirit seal—slip mostly through our grasp.

Delilah must have picked up on what I was thinking, because she leaned her elbows on the table and rested her chin on her hands. "We're to blame. We didn't take him out when we had the chance at the Energy Exchange. We failed."

"Bullshit. We were overwhelmed, and if you'll remember, Gulakah, the Lord of Ghosts, just happened to be there. Along with Newkirk *and* all of their cronies." Vanzir slammed his chair back against the wall and rested one ankle across the other knee. He slapped the table. "We did what we could. Nobody's to blame except Shadow Wing and his fucking delusions. He's fucking insane."

"Vanzir is right." Camille cleared her throat. "We simply didn't have the manpower to take them all on. And we aren't going to do anyone any good by moaning over what we did—or didn't—manage to accomplish. We have to focus on *now*. On what's going on this instant."

"Well said, my wife." Trillian slid his arm around her waist and kissed her brow. They made a striking couple and, when her other two husbands were in the picture, a formidable quartet.

"Then the question becomes, what do we do next?" Rozurial said, playing with the belt on his duster. He had an armory stashed in his coat and was forever delighting in finding new toys to replace ones he grew tired of. He made Neo from *The Matrix* look like an amateur.

Queen Asteria crossed to the throne. "That's where our spies come in. I want you to meet them, because you will be working together from now on. You must exchange every scrap of information that you have about Telazhar. They will remain in contact with you while on their mission."

As she settled into the chair, the Queen arranged her

skirts and let out a sigh that I heard halfway across the room.

"You're tired, aren't you?" I didn't mean to speak aloud, but my words cut through the room and I cringed, realizing what I'd done.

But Asteria merely crossed her hands in front of her. "Yes, young vampire. I am weary. But that does not negate my power, nor my determination. It merely means that I wear my crown a little heavier now, and lean on my staff a little harder." She motioned to the serving woman for a glass of wine. "War is thirsty work."

"Have you any allies here? Besides us?" Trillian let go of Camille to take a closer look at the map. "Have you talked to King Vodox?"

"As asked, so answered. As I prepare my armies for war, so do my allies. King Uppala-Dahns of the Dahns unicorns and Tanaquar have pledged to arm their soldiers in my service. I have sent messages to King Vodox, and to the kingdom of Nebulvuori. We wait for their response. And . . . another ally has pledged her service. Derisa, the High Priestess, from the Grove of the Moon Mother."

Camille nodded. "Truly, my order would be obligated to join you. The sorcerers and the sun god are our nemeses. I wonder . . . will Telazhar approach the temple of Chimaras? The sun brothers are still seeking any reason to wage war against the Moon Mother's grove, from what Shamas tells us."

Queen Asteria clutched the gnarled arms of her throne. "Shamas? What does he know of this?"

We had protected our cousin's secret since he told us the truth a few weeks ago, but now, any information he had might come in handy. "Shamas was studying with a sorcerer in the Southern Wastes. A Tregart named Feris, who was bent on waging war on the Moon Mother's Grove. Shamas spilled the beans on him at risk of his own life."

"Tregarts? The Tregarts were over here a year ago?" Queen Asteria leaned back against her throne and cast a long look to Trenyth. I had a feeling there was a discussion going on to which we were not privy.

Trenyth sprang into action. "We have no time to spare. We must send our spies out in the morning via the portals. They can travel as far as Ceredream and from there, walk afoot to Rhellah." He moved to the side door and opened it.

Three figures stepped in. I didn't recognize any of them, but Trillian and Camille both gasped as one of the figures let out a low chuckle. He was a Svartan, ruggedly handsome with the same blue eyes and silverish hair as Trillian. But rather than mirroring my brother-in-law's smooth metropolitan look, this man's eyes were wild and he felt slightly uncivilized. He was also far more muscled than Trillian, who was no slouch in the buff department.

"Darynal!" Trillian was around the table before they'd cleared the door, hugging the man, who clapped him on the back. Camille joined them, giving him a kiss on the cheek.

"*Lavoyda* . . . it's been too long. Bound by oath, bound by blood." The Svartan held out his hand and he and Trillian performed some sort of intricate handshake.

"Bound by oath, bound by blood, my brother." As Trillian broke away, Darynal turned to Camille and gave her a low bow.

"Your woman, she is looking good. Camille, lovely to see you again."

She offered her hand and he took it, kissing it gently. She reached out and stroked his face, brushing a stray curl out of his eyes.

"My husband's brother, it's so good to see you again."

And then I remembered who he was. Darynal was Trillian's blood-oath brother. Pledged to back each other to the death, they weren't lovers but brothers on a level that was almost soul-bound.

"Lavoyda. I'm glad to see you here and healthy. But what are you doing with the elves?" Trillian suddenly stopped, as if aware all eyes were on them.

Camille brushed him on the shoulder. "We should let Queen Asteria tell us," she whispered, and they positioned themselves near Darynal as the three newcomers took their seats.

Queen Asteria favored them with a brief smile. "I knew

that you would be surprised, Master Zanzera, but I chose to let Darynal's appearance speak for itself."

Trillian cocked his head, and winked at the Queen. Shaking my head, I repressed a snicker. He was incorrigible, but he'd come a long way from the arrogant bastard to whom Delilah and I'd taken an instant dislike. We'd been wrong about his character, for the most part. Our prejudices had been showing.

Asteria gave no sign whether she noticed the wink, but instead she motioned to Trenyth, who introduced the others in the trio.

"Darynal is our lead scout in this mission. You know his background, you know he's a skilled mercenary, so allow me introduce the others. This is Quall, an undercover agent for Elqaneve for many years. He's an assassin."

The tall, lithe Fae stood. With pale blond hair barely cresting his shoulders, he was almost albino except for his eyes, which were a startling green that shimmered against the pale cream of his skin. He looked almost anorexic, but upon closer look, I saw the tightly wrapped muscle molded beneath his skin.

Assassins were an odd breed, especially those employed by governments. They danced to their own tune, made their own rules, and usually ran outside the law in almost every way. As I looked into his eyes, I knew right then how much Quall enjoyed his job. He enjoyed the hunt, and ten to one, he enjoyed the kill. He caught my gaze and held it, an insolent sneer lurking behind the brief nod.

The third member of the team was of average height, cloaked so heavily that I couldn't tell exactly what race he belonged to. Only his eyes gleamed from within the fiery red robe. He said nothing as Trenyth introduced him.

"This is Taath. He's one of our sorcerers."

"*Your* sorcerers? But . . ." Camille looked confused.

"Yes, my dear. We have our own sorcerers. After the Scorching Wars, we vowed Elqaneve would never be caught unprepared again." The Queen leaned forward. "Sometimes the only way to fight fire is with fire. Sometimes the only way to fight hatred is with violence. Often people think the Elfin race a passive one. We are not. We think first, but when we act, we do not hold back."

"I'm starting to realize that," Camille said.

"Perhaps now is the time to tell you. Your beloved Moon Mother trains her own sorcerers, although she will not call them that. They wield dark moon magic . . . *death magic*. Why do you think Morio's magic comes so easily to you?"

Camille gasped, staring at her, but she said nothing. None of us did. That was a revelation we'd address later.

After a moment, Asteria turned to me. "I asked you here because we will need all of your talents soon. Your father requested that all of you come to Otherworld." She held up her hand, stopping any outburst. Delilah and Camille looked like they wanted to say something but kept their mouths shut. As for me, I could be very petty when I chose, and I refused to ask about him.

Queen Asteria looked my way. "He asked for all *three* of you. Do not ask me why. When you finish here, you will travel to Y'Elestrial, and there you will meet with your father."

"But—" Camille sputtered, but the Queen stopped her in her tracks.

"Camille, give me no mouth. We align our powers. War has come to Otherworld, on the wings of demonic forces. The same war you are fighting over Earthside. There can be no more borders. No more division."

The room fell silent. We were facing Shadow Wing on two fronts now. I'd been waiting for the shoe to drop, and now that it had, I realized that I'd never expected us to wrap this up easily.

From the first time Shadow Wing claimed a spirit seal, I knew—*absolutely knew in my gut*—that we wouldn't make it out unscathed. We would have to face a long, bloody battle. We'd had collateral damage so far, but this . . . this was a full-scale attack. The war had only just begun.

Asteria and Tanaquar might be able to stem the tide of sorcerers. But those who would join the sun brothers, the goblins and ogres and other malcontents, would ensure that a bloody swath would mar the landscape. Otherworld had existed in relative peace for centuries with only minor skirmishes. But that peace had been a fragile veneer. And now it was crumbling. Once again the sounds of battle would fill the air.

I stood, the ivory beads in my hair breaking the silence. "Tell us what we need to do and we'll do it." And just like that, we jumped from the frying pan into the flames that were brewing down south.